Praise for Lydia Dare's
Regency Werewolf series

"Deliciously witty and sensationally sensuous... delightful historical romance that readers will find hard to put down."

—*Romance Junkies*

"Engrossing... combines paranormal abilities, mortal angst, and great storytelling."

—*Fresh Fiction*

"Truly captivating... an enticing and addictive read."

—*Book Junkie*

"A fun romp of a book, Lydia Dare continues to amuse and intrigue."

—*Fresh Fiction*

"Wonderfully contrived works... Ms. Dare has been added to my must-read authors."

—*Night Owl Romance* Top Pick

"A great series... romantic, fun, and filled with magic."

—*Fangtastic Books*

"Ms. Dare has created a sizzling hot romance that is impossible to put down."

—*Star-Crossed Romance*

Wolfishly Yours

Lydia Dare

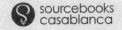

sourcebooks
casablanca

Published by Sourcebooks Casablanca, an imprint of Sourcebooks, Inc.
P.O. Box 4410, Naperville, Illinois 60567-4410
(630) 961-3900
FAX: (630) 961-2168
www.sourcebooks.com

Printed and bound in Canada
WC 10 9 8 7 6 5 4 3 2 1

*Jodie: For Brandt ~ Thank you for your smile,
your sense of humor, and your adventurous
spirit. I don't know what I would do without
you. I love you more than anything.*

*Tammy: For the many, many people at Sourcebooks
who make this process so seamless. From the
publicists to the editors to the artists and everyone
who has their hands in the production, distribution,
or handling of our books in any way, shape, or form,
you have our utmost appreciation. We probably
have no idea how many things you take care of, but
we know that without you we could have wontons
all over the place! So, thanks for all that you do!*

One

MISS LIVIANA MAYEUX SHIVERED, AND SHE CURSED HER father anew. Blast him for sending her to such a horrid place. She could very likely freeze to death before her feet touched solid land. The frosty English air swirled about her ankles and stung her lungs as she took a deep breath. She would never survive this ordeal. Never. She wasn't meant to live in a climate such as this. Papa, of all people, should have known that.

When a shove to her back moved her forward, Livi stepped off the gangplank onto British soil and pulled her pelisse tighter around her shoulders, rubbing her hands along her arms and hoping against hope that warmth would finally seep into her bones. How in the world had her mother lived in this godforsaken frozen wasteland? Livi was certain her blood was much too thin, not to mention too hot, to survive here. Why had Papa done this to her?

She glanced back at *Vespucci's Marauder*, one of her father's many vessels and her floating home since she'd set sail from New Orleans, and contemplated stowing away for the frigate's return trip across the Atlantic. Wouldn't Papa be surprised if she returned to Louisiana all on her own? What would he do with her then? He'd have to come up with a different plan to turn her into a lady, wouldn't he? Unless she could convince him otherwise. Not that she'd had much luck with that the last time.

"Mademoiselle Mayeux!" Captain Broussard called, breaking her reverie. The swarthy Frenchman waved his tricorn hat in the air to catch her attention as seamen bustled in front of him along the docks.

She certainly couldn't sneak back on the frigate with Captain Broussard watching her. Livi suppressed a scowl as her maid touched her shoulder. "Over there, Miss Livi. The captain is waiting for us."

"Marie, I don't suppose you'd distract him so I could escape back onto the ship?" she asked hopefully. "I've got all of *Maman*'s jewelry with me. You can have whatever you'd like."

Her maid glowered at her. "There are many men I wouldn't be afraid of crossing, miss, but Philippe Mayeux isn't one of them."

"Papa's not all *that* fearsome," Livi protested. Only on the night of the full moon, but the rest of the time Papa was as gentle as a lapdog. Or mostly, anyway. However, he had been adamant when he'd announced that Livi would sail the Atlantic to live with the grandfather she'd never met. Papa had been quite unreasonable about the entire affair, which was very unlike him, all things considered. He usually couldn't care less if she ran around in trousers or rode her gelding astride or caught crawfish with her brothers. Not until that blasted, busybody Father Antonio had insisted Livi was too wild for polite society.

Marie gave Livi a gentle push from behind, urging her forward. "Go on, miss. The captain is waiting for us."

There was nothing for it. With Broussard before her and Marie behind her, Livi had no hope for escape. Well, at least not at the moment. She'd think of something. She had to. She couldn't live in England, of all places. And she certainly was not about to be turned into an English lady. The idea made her stomach roil more than the choppy ocean ever had along her voyage.

The icy wind whipped about her skirts as Livi pushed her way through a crowd of sailors and dockworkers to where the captain awaited her. *Bon Dieu!* How did anyone live here? Wretched, freezing place. What she wouldn't give to be exploring warm swamps back home with Armand and Etienne right now. Livi clasped a hand to her head to keep her bonnet from blowing away in the wind and she scowled. Papa had never threatened to send her brothers across the Atlantic to become gentlemen. It was wholly unfair to send her away to turn her into a lady.

Captain Broussard stepped through the throng of men and offered his hand to Livi. "Mademoiselle Mayeux." He gestured to a dour-looking young man adorned in a drab black coat. "This is Monsieur Turner. He works for Lord Holmesfield. He'll see you the rest of the way."

Mr. Turner looked Livi up and down as though he disbelieved she could possibly be the granddaughter of an earl. "Miss Mayeux?"

Livi stood her tallest. She'd known pirates and trappers and soldiers in her day, and she was not about to be cowed by some English servant, no matter if he did work for her grandfather. "You'll be retrieving my trunks, Mr. Turner?"

The man tried, unsuccessfully, to smother an arrogant smile. "Just Turner will suffice, madam." Then he gestured to a crested carriage a short distance away. "Let's get you settled and then I'll retrieve your things."

Settled. Just as soon as he turned his back, Livi could make her escape. But then Marie linked her arm with Livi's and huddled close to her. "This wind will do terrible things to your hair," her maid whispered.

Livi sighed. How did she keep forgetting about Marie? Probably because at home, Marie never played the role of chaperone. At home Marie never cared what she did or didn't do. But ever since Marie had given her word to Papa to keep Livi safe, her maid had become a blasted nuisance. She couldn't possibly escape with Marie holding on to her. "I can't walk with you so close," she complained.

Marie snorted. "*Non.* You mean you can't run off with me so close. Do you think I just met you, miss? I made a promise to Mr. Mayeux, and I'll see you delivered to Lord Holmesfield if it's the last thing I do."

Livi frowned as she followed Turner to the carriage he'd pointed out. "I don't know what you're talking about, Marie. Where would I go if I ran off?"

Her maid harrumphed and muttered something, though it was drowned out by the whipping, briny-scented wind.

Where would she go, indeed?

⤬

Hadley Hall, Derbyshire

Grayson Hadley looked at the cup of tea before him. Certainly Lady Sophia had lost her mind. He *did* know how to drink tea, for God's sake. He'd learned to drink from a teacup around the same time he'd learned to walk. And it wasn't a skill one typically forgot.

"Well, Mr. Hadley, I *am* waiting," his infernal tutor urged.

"Oh, yes," his brother Archer, Viscount Radbourne, chortled from the threshold of the breakfast room. "Do show us how gracefully you can sip your tea, Gray."

"If you don't shut up, you'll see how good my aim is, Arch, and you'll be *wearing* my bloody tea."

"Language, Mr. Hadley." A beleaguered sigh escaped Lady Sophia and she rose from her spot at the table. "And please don't think yourself superior to your brother, my lord. I have a cup of tea waiting for you as well."

Archer snorted. "Hell will freeze over first, my lady."

"Language, Lord Radbourne," she admonished. "I'm certain you don't want me to inform Lord Eynsford that you are being difficult again, do you?"

Gray picked up his cup and very slowly brought it to his lips. He took a small sip and then returned the cup to its saucer. He dabbed his lips with a napkin and said as smoothly as possible, "Might I be excused, Lady Sophia?"

This earned him a scowl from his brother and a winning smile from their tutor. "Yes, you may," the lady agreed with a nod.

"Doing it up a bit brown, aren't you?" Archer grumbled as Gray rose from his seat.

Making certain Lady Sophia's attention was on Archer, Gray winked at his older brother. "Do enjoy your tea, Archer. It's delicious." Then he brushed past his sibling and strode into the corridor.

Freedom at last. Or at least until Lady Sophia thought up some new inane task for him to participate in. But with Archer's flippant attitude, Gray was certain their tutor would be busy most of the day trying to break his brother's spirit. She'd never accomplish that goal, which would allow Gray a little time to himself. And he needed time to himself to look over the financial papers the Hadleys' solicitor had sent over in regards to their gambling endeavor. In fact, he needed to make a trip to London to see the man in person, but his training had kept him in Derbyshire the last month. Training and his oldest half brother's edict that they learn to comport themselves in public or else. Nonsense, all of it.

"Grayson!" his mother squealed as he nearly knocked her to the ground.

"Oh!" Gray caught his mother's arm and steadied her. "I am sorry. I didn't see you there."

Lady Radbourne shooed his hand away. "I am fine. Just watch where you're going."

"I'd better," he agreed conspiratorially, "or Lady Sophia will have me walking corridors back and forth to prove I can do so without tripping or causing others to scramble from my path in fear."

His mother giggled. "She's only trying to help you."

Gray's brow rose indignantly. "By proving that I can sit through a concert without ripping someone's head off or that I can drink tea without splashing it all down my cravat?"

"The three of you could use a little culture. It's good Lord Eynsford has your best interests at heart."

Gray scowled at his mother. His half brother could go hang for putting him through this ordeal in the first place. "The three of us? Somehow Wes has escaped this nonsense entirely."

Lady Radbourne shrugged. "Well, Weston has a wife to manage him. You don't." She patted his shoulder as though in consolation. He shivered at the very thought of being saddled with a wife.

His twin had a wife he'd abducted and then eloped with. If any of the three of them needed gentleman training it was Weston Hadley, but Gray held his tongue as it was pointless to voice his thoughts on the matter. What's done was done.

"Are you finished for the day?" his mother asked.

"As far as I know. Why?"

She grinned at him. "Lord Holmesfield asked me to call on him today. Would you like to accompany me?"

Holmesfield was an ancient prig and not a particularly healthy one at that. Gray could go the rest of his days without seeing their closest neighbor, but who knew what inanity Lady Sophia would come up with if he stayed. Gray inclined his head. "It would be my honor to escort you, Mother."

She tucked her hand in the crook of his arm. "You can say Lady Sophia makes you do foolish things, Grayson, but I have seen you blossom under her tutelage."

Gray somehow kept from growling. "I am going to pretend you didn't say that."

❧

A prisoner, that's what Livi was. Oh, the prison was an opulent one, to be sure, covered in silks and damask and adorned in gold trim. But a prison was still a prison. It would have been nice to have at least one ally in this foreign land, but Marie had assimilated into the British household much faster than Livi could have ever imagined. One would think her maid had completely forgotten the attempted English invasion only six years ago in New Orleans. Which was mildly infuriating. It wasn't really that long ago, after all. Livi hadn't forgotten those days, and she never would.

Men ranging from the notorious privateer Jean Lafitte to the courageous and ruthless General Andrew Jackson had sat in her father's study back in those days, and Livi along with her brothers had waited in the corridor, their ears pressed against the door to listen to the plots and plans. Having heard all of Papa's impassioned speeches against the British, she felt his turnabout in sending her to England like a dagger to her heart. Blasted traitor! She would never have thought him capable of such a betrayal to either his country or his daughter.

She'd dearly love to get her hands around Father Antonio's collared neck for putting the idea in Papa's mind to begin with. Blasted priest should mind his own business and keep his interfering nose out of…

A scratch came at her door.

Livi frowned. What was it with all the scratching? Sounded like a battalion of mice had taken up residence in Holmesfield Court. "Yes?" she grumbled.

Her door opened quickly and Marie stepped over the threshold. "His lordship would like you to join him in the blue parlor, Miss Livi."

So he could tell her again that she would never amount to anything? Livi was perfectly happy sitting in her prison of a bedchamber. Well, not perfectly happy. She'd much rather be home. But she was happier in her bedchamber than she would be in her grandfather's presence. When she arrived, the earl had taken one look at her and declared she didn't resemble her mother in the least, and he hadn't smiled at her since. Well, she *was* half French. What did he expect?

"I'm not feeling at all well. I believe I'll just stay here, Marie."

Her maid heaved a sigh. "Don't make this more difficult than it has to be, miss. Lord Holmesfield is expecting Lady Radbourne any minute, and he would like for you to be there when the lady calls."

Livi scoffed. "What do I care about some lady I've never met?" She shook her head. "*Non.* I'll just stay here, Marie. And stop scratching at my door, will you? All my life you've knocked, and I don't see why that should change now."

Marie narrowed her dark eyes at Livi. "Because

things *have* changed, miss. And once you accept that, you'll be much happier."

Livi suppressed a snort. "Happier? Hardly. If you'd like to help me secure passage to New Orleans, I'll be as happy as you've ever known me."

"Blue parlor." Somehow, Marie had acquired an edge to her voice, like the strictest of taskmasters. "Now." Where had Marie found that tone? She'd never used anything slightly like it in the past.

Livi started for the corridor. "I do like the old Marie much better, in case you were wondering."

Her maid muttered, "I wasn't."

Well, Marie could stay in this wretched place forever if she liked it so much. But Livi needed an escape. And the faster, the better. Livi kept her head held high and navigated Holmesfield Court's corridor and cantilevered staircase. Then she meandered around the first floor, in no hurry to see her grandfather until the inevitable couldn't be put off any further. Livi took a steadying breath and then stepped into the earl's blue parlor.

At once, her grandfather looked up from the ornate high-backed chair he was sitting in and let his dismissive eye sweep across her form. "I suppose that will do."

What would do? Livi or her choice of day dress? Not that she cared one whit about her grandfather's opinion on either matter. She curtsied and forced a smile to her face. "Good afternoon, my lord."

"Sit." He gestured to the sapphire damask settee not far from him and returned his eyes to the papers in his lap.

Her grandfather spoke to her as though she were a dog. That particular thought did bring a genuine smile to her lips. If he only knew how close to the truth that was. "I understand you wished for my company." She strode across the room and slid onto the settee he'd pointed out.

Lord Holmesfield grumbled something that didn't quite meet her ears, even with her excellent hearing. "I've asked Viscountess Radbourne to call on me today."

"How nice."

"It's not nice at all," the old man replied. "It was necessity. She's our closest neighbor, and though she raised sons, she might have a better idea about what to do with you than I do."

"You do me such an honor." Livi frowned at her grandfather. Why did he have to make it seem as though she was a hopeless case? Not that she wanted his help in being turned into a proper lady, but did he have to be so insulting with his tone or choice of words every time he opened his mouth?

"Violet Radbourne was a friend of Grace's, and she might be willing to help smooth your way into society. She married poorly and her sons aren't well thought of, but we don't have a plethora of choices where you're concerned."

The air in Livi's lungs rushed out all at once. "She knew *Maman*?" Her question came out as little more than a whisper.

But her words were loud enough that her grandfather heard her and he scowled. "How many times have I asked you to speak English?"

She ignored his censure, choosing to focus on the

information he'd given her instead. Lady Radbourne had been a friend of her mother's? Livi barely remembered *Maman*. She'd been such a small child when consumption had taken her mother from her, from all of them. What Livi did remember was a delicate woman who was beautiful, kind, and generous. She remembered the fairy tales *Maman* would tell her at night, the kisses she'd dropped on Livi's brow, the way she smelled of magnolia flowers and summer rolled into one.

"I'll never forgive Radbourne for introducing Grace to Philippe Mayeux, but if Violet can be persuaded into helping you, it would be a start to paying off that debt."

Radbourne. Livi did know that name. Papa had mentioned it once or twice. Why hadn't she recognized it when Marie muttered the name in her bedchamber? Probably because Livi wasn't thinking about her mother at that time; escape had been the only thought on her mind. But now...

From the doorway, Holmesfield's stoic butler cleared his throat. "Lady Radbourne and Mr. Hadley, my lord."

The earl's frown deepened. "I didn't invite any of her disreputable sons," he grumbled. Then he heaved a sigh and sent Livi a look that made her feel like the worst sort of burden. "Do show them in, Browne."

Two

GRAY WINCED. WHY HAD HE AGREED TO ACCOMPANY his mother on this little excursion? Oh, yes, to avoid Lady Sophia and Archer back at the Hall. Still, how was he supposed to smile and make polite conversation with Lord Holmesfield after the man had just called him disreputable? With his Lycan ears, he had most definitely heard the insult. His human ears twitched and the hair on the back of his neck stood up, just like the dog that he was. He forced himself to lower his upper lip, releasing the snarl that twisted it.

A moment later, Browne, Holmesfield's butler, appeared in the threshold of the small salon where Gray and his mother had been led upon their arrival at Holmesfield Court. "His lordship will see you now." Then the old man guided them to a good-sized parlor swathed in shades of blue.

Gray's eyes swept across the room until they landed on a stunning girl sitting on one of the parlor's settees. She was like no one he'd ever seen before, almost exotic with her dark hair and skin that looked as though it was often kissed by the sun. He might have gaped at her forever, but his mother elbowed him in the back.

"Grayson," she whispered, bringing him back to the present. If he stared at the girl much longer, he'd have to wipe the drool from his chin.

Gray cleared his throat. "Apologies," he muttered softly. Then he inclined his head to the Earl of Holmesfield. "I am glad to find you looking well, my lord."

"I'm not glad you found me at all," Holmesfield muttered. But then he turned to Gray's mother, inhaled deeply, and said, "I don't know what to do with her." His eyes slowly crossed the room until they landed on the very lady Gray had just been staring at.

The lady in question jumped to her feet with a startling show of dexterity. "My grandfather isn't certain if he's more mortified by my looks, my breeding, or my country of origin," she said. Then she cocked her head to the side and continued. "Perhaps you can help him decide which part of me he should hold in the highest contempt."

"Liviana," the earl scolded.

Gray's mother covered her lips with the tips of her fingers, just as a muffled sob erupted from her throat. "Are you all right, Mother?" he asked as he laid a hand on her shoulder.

"She looks just like her," his mother whispered beneath her fingertips, the words muffled to the point where Gray, with his wolfish ears, was probably the only one in the room who could hear them. He was about to ask who the girl looked like, but his mother didn't look like she would be capable of speech for quite some time. So, Gray just rocked on his heels and waited for an introduction.

The lady looked more than startled when his mother crossed the room and wrapped her in her arms and hugged her tightly. "When did you arrive?" his mother asked. But then more questions exploded from her mouth. "How was your trip? Was the weather nice?"

"Pray allow her to answer, Mother, before you bombard her with more questions," Gray teased. The girl looked up at him, and Gray got caught in the heat of her gaze and was nearly taken aback. He cleared his throat. But she continued to appraise him. Her gaze dropped from his hair to across his face, to his shoulders and downward.

"Close your mouth, dear," he heard his mother whisper to her like a conspirator. The lady's mouth snapped shut quickly, and a rosy blush settled on her cheeks. "Hadley men are handsome, aren't they? And though they're friendly enough, they're like pups who haven't been shaken by the scruff of the neck quite often enough." His mother raised one brow at the lady. "This is my son, Grayson Hadley." She motioned him forward with a frantic wiggle of her fingers.

He bowed his head, and the visitor held out her hand. Gray took it in his, and the heat of her skin seeped through his gloves. "Does the lady have a name?" he asked.

The blush on the exotic beauty's cheeks grew even more vivid, and she dipped into a hasty curtsy. "Liviana Mayeux, my lady," she said to his mother. "And sir," she amended quickly to the end.

Gray lingered a little longer over her hand than was proper, he was sure. But she smelled like a spring meadow. Fresh and inviting.

"You can release her now, Hadley," the earl spat in his direction.

Gray did so reluctantly, letting her fingers slide through his grasp slowly. "What brings you to the area, Miss Mayeux?" he asked. He wanted to hear her talk. She didn't have the same cadence to her voice that the British did. He could probably listen to her all day.

"My father's fear that I'll disgrace him, I believe," the chit said without even cracking a smile. Then she shot a caustic look toward the earl. "And now that my grandfather has met me, he fears the same. Must be the French in me." She shrugged her delicate shoulders, then speared Gray with a glance. "I've been sent here to learn how to be a lady."

"Which is not something you should go announcing to any ruffian who stumbles over my threshold," the earl barked.

So now Gray was a disgraceful ruffian, was he? Normally, he would be quite annoyed by the earl's assessment of his character, but as he stared into Miss Mayeux's cerulean eyes, Gray turned a deaf ear to her grandfather's criticism.

Gray's mother crossed the room and whispered something quietly to the earl, and Gray allowed his gaze to roam as freely down the American chit's body as her gaze had slid down his. "It doesn't appear to me that you need any help being a lady," he said slowly.

"It's the social graces that I don't fully understand."

She looked decidedly uncomfortable, and Gray felt a little uncomfortable for her. "But it appears as though you don't either, so I'm in good company, aren't I?"

She couldn't have surprised Gray more if she'd offered him a bone to gnaw on under the dinner table. "My manners are in fine form," he retorted. Weren't they? Had he committed some egregious error already? He'd only just walked into the blasted room. He glanced back toward the earl and his mother, and discovered their heads close together as they whispered. Gray couldn't hear a damn thing when they whispered, and his mother was well aware of that. Miss Mayeux was not.

"Don't worry, they're discussing how to manage me, not you," she said, one corner of her mouth turned up in disgust.

"I'm curious to find out what you've done to deserve such a careful management stratagem," he said with a low laugh. She looked harmless enough. Well, harmless in an "I'd sell my soul to the devil for a taste of her" sort of way. He shifted his stance, aiming for a much more careless air.

"You name it, and she has done it," the earl barked from across the room. Then he leaned closer to Gray's mother and the pair resumed their whispering.

"Pray tell?" Gray prompted the tempting American.

She looked him straight in the eye, as though she considered answering his question. But then she slightly shook her head and muttered, "They plan to feed me bread and water until I succumb to their social restrictions. I'm certain of it."

He couldn't help but smile at her. "Oh? And how

long do you suppose one might last on bread and water alone?"

"Hopefully, long enough to find a way back to New Orleans," she groused.

"I take it you're not happy to find yourself in Derbyshire, then."

"Well, you're quick witted, aren't you?" Her dark blue eyes flashed at him. "I figured it would take you at least a fortnight to figure out how much I loathe the very idea of being here."

"On the contrary, I think I understood that when I first walked into the room." Audacious little thing, wasn't she?

"Bully for you," she murmured.

Gray hid a smile behind a closed fist as he coughed into it.

"Do you think you could help me escape England?" She looked up at him, pierced him with her pretty eyes, and batted her lashes.

"Not ready to surrender to your fate, Miss Mayeux?" he asked.

"I surrender to no one," she retorted hotly. "I do not want to be here. And I will return home at the first opportunity." She sniffed. She regarded his mother and her grandfather through narrowed eyes. "What are they saying?" she asked, looking up at him with a curious regard.

"I've no idea," he remarked.

"Do I look like I was born yesterday, Mr. Hadley?" She tapped the toe of her slipper against the oak floor.

Liviana Mayeux looked to be twenty or so, but in his estimation women rarely wanted an answer to a question involving age. So, he decided the wiser course of action was a noncommittal shrug.

She pointed to the area beneath her left ear. "That little mark you have there, Mr. Hadley, I know full well what that is."

She did? Gray almost swallowed his tongue. Most people assumed his birthmark, the only physical evidence of his being a Lycan, was a love bite. But what did Miss Mayeux know of such a thing? "Beg your pardon?" he asked.

She reached out as though to touch his neck, to touch the very thing that marked him as a beast, but he stepped back before she could do so. "Who'd have thought you boys from this side of the Atlantic could be so timid?" she mused. The little minx was thoroughly enjoying his discomfort.

Gray raised his brows at her. "I don't believe any Hadley man has ever been called timid before."

"Are there more of you?" she asked.

"There are three of us," he said with pride. Not to mention Dashiel, but he wasn't a Hadley, at least not in name.

"Three Lycan men," she said, appearing to savor what must have been a look of shock he couldn't keep off his face. "Certainly one of you might be willing to help me get back home." She smiled broadly at him and patted his chest. He couldn't have been more surprised if she'd bashed him over the head with an anvil. No one knew of his heritage aside from his own family. Gray began to speak but couldn't croak out a single word.

She clucked her tongue at him. "It's your turn to

close your mouth, Mr. Hadley," she whispered playfully. Then she dropped her voice to a silky purr that made the hair on the back of his neck stand up. "Are you certain you don't want to help me get back to New Orleans, sir?"

On the contrary, helping the little minx back across the Atlantic would be in his best interest. He couldn't have some chit who knew exactly what he was lying in wait for the perfect moment to reveal his secret to her grandfather or anyone else who would listen.

"Lycan?" he asked, hoping for nonchalance.

"Don't play me for a fool." She did laugh then, a warm sound that caressed his skin and settled in his heart. "I'd show you my mark, Mr. Hadley, but it's on my thigh and I don't think his lordship would approve of me lifting my skirts, do you?"

Damn it to hell, now all Gray could think about was lifting Miss Mayeux's skirts. She had a mark on her thigh? If he somehow was able to get under her dress, he didn't think that he'd pay the slightest attention to what was on her leg.

"Cat got your tongue?" she teased. "Or should I say 'wolf'?"

Gray grasped her arm and dragged her to the far corner of the room, hoping her grandfather wouldn't notice. "You can't go around saying things like that," he hissed.

"You sound like the earl," she replied with a pout.

"Miss Mayeux," Gray frowned at her, "I don't know how things are in America, but here we don't go around talking about Lycans or mentioning... parts of one's body."

"*Non*?" she asked with more innocence than Gray thought she possessed. "Did I fluster you?"

More than he'd like to admit. "I'd rather not be shuffled off to Newgate Prison, if you don't mind. So don't mention Lycans unless you'd like to end up there yourself."

Her blue eyes sparkled with mischief. "Prison? Do you think they'd deport me back to America?"

"I think they'd stretch your pretty neck on the gallows."

She touched her neck and heaved a sigh. "Well, that wouldn't do."

"Well," Gray's mother declared from her spot across the room, "I do believe that will be perfect."

Gray's eyes shot to his mother and Lord Holmesfield. "What will be perfect?"

"Bath," his mother answered. "His lordship would like to go and partake of the waters. And as there is so much going on there this time of year, we'll be able to escort and entertain Miss Mayeux in the evenings."

Who exactly was "we"? Before Gray could ask, the earl added, "It will give my granddaughter an opportunity to navigate society before being thrust among the *ton* next season."

The idea of the odiferous medicinal waters in the Pump Room almost made Gray gag, as did the idea of having to participate in Bath's social scene. However his mother would enjoy the activities. Hopefully, she could impress upon Miss Mayeux the importance of keeping her pretty mouth closed on the subject of Lycans. And while they were away, he could finally travel to London to visit with his solicitor.

After all, it wouldn't do for either Gray or Archer

to stay behind at Hadley Hall with Lady Sophia alone, would it? Now that he thought about it, his mother traveling to Bath with Miss Mayeux and Lord Holmesfield was a brilliant plan.

"Well, I hope you have a wonderful time, Mother. How long do you expect to be gone?"

His mother's eyes narrowed a bit. "I know that tone, Grayson Hadley. You're plotting something."

Gray scoffed. "I'm hardly plotting anything, Mother. While you're away, I'll head into Town with Archer as we have some business to attend to. Nothing nefarious at all."

"But we'll need escorts, Gray. So you and Radbourne and Lady Sophia," she glanced at the earl, "my companion, you know," she returned her gaze to Gray, "will all be headed to Bath with Lord Holmesfield."

A sickness settled in the pit of Gray's stomach, and he was certain a similar malady would befall Archer as soon as his brother learned their presence would be required on this little excursion. "We truly do have business matters, Mother," he protested.

But his mother simply shook her head. "I'm certain Weston can manage whatever it is." Then she turned her attention to the earl. "You did hear that Weston recently married the Duke of Hythe's daughter, did you not?"

"I heard something to that effect," the old earl grumbled.

"Such a dear girl Lady Madeline is. We are so happy to have her in the family. So graceful and proper, she has completely transformed my son. I'm certain you wouldn't even recognize him."

"Let's hope *you* can completely transform my

granddaughter." Lord Holmesfield's critical eye landed on Miss Mayeux, and Gray had the overwhelming urge to jump in front of her to shield her from her old man's glare. What a fanciful notion. Lord Holmesfield and Miss Mayeux meant nothing to him, and as long as the latter kept her pretty mouth closed on the subject of Lycans, he'd prefer to keep it that way.

Three

EVIDENTLY, THE HADLEY BROTHERS HAD A SECRET TO keep, and Livi could fully use that little tidbit of knowledge to her advantage. It gave her something to bargain with. Knowing that she had the upper hand made her feel marginally better about her situation. When Lady Radbourne and Mr. Hadley were gone, she sat down in a high-backed chair in her grand-father's study and rested her chin on the heel of her hand. She regarded her grandfather with a critical eye. One he didn't appear to notice.

At least not until he barked at her. "It's ill-mannered to stare," he clipped out.

"It's ill-mannered to ignore people who are attending you in your domain. Particularly when the person is a guest." She could almost taste the disdain in her words. And they weren't sweet. But they were very true.

He sat back and templed his hands in front him. His glare might have felled a lesser person. But Livi simply crossed her hands in her lap and glared back at him. When he didn't back down, she arched a brow at him.

He tossed his quill with a rough slam onto his desk. The quill clattered to the floor. So, he had a temper too. Nice to know.

"Did your father teach you to be so brash?"

No, actually, it had been her brothers. She shrugged instead of saying so.

"He never did have the sense God gave a mountain goat," the earl muttered, but she heard him none the less.

"What did he ever do to you?" she asked. Her father and brothers were a constant in her life, and even if her father had sent her to this horrid place, to this horrid man who obviously didn't want her, she would take up for him until the day she died. Particularly against someone like her grandfather. Someone much more concerned with propriety than actually caring for a loved one. Her mother was a perfect example.

"He passed himself off as an example of good breeding. And then he stole your mother away." He balled up a piece of parchment and tossed it into the rubbish bin with much more force than was necessary. Would her head be next? Or would he continue to take his anger out on his personal possessions?

"You can't steal someone who goes willingly," Livi said softly. Much more softly than she felt like saying.

His eyes shot up to meet hers. His glare darkened. After a moment, he bent and retrieved his quill from the floor. Then he tossed it onto his desk with a heavy sigh.

"She loved him," Livi continued. If there was one thing that wasn't in question, it was the abiding love between her parents. She had been young when *Maman* had passed, but her brothers had been older.

And they and their father told her stories of her mother that were steeped in affection.

Maman's journals were full of pages that chronicled how her parents had met and how *Maman* felt about Papa. The pages spoke of the abiding love she'd felt when each of her sons was born. And the joy she had felt at finally having a daughter. It was a tragedy Grace Mayeux hadn't lived longer, for Livi to have had her throughout all these years. But Livi still had her father. Until he'd sent her away.

"Are you happy at all that I'm here?" she asked, hating the hesitation she heard in her own voice.

His gaze rose, and for a mere moment, she thought she could see something there. Some spark of affection. Something that said he cared about her in some miniscule way. In this cold, cold house, on this cold, cold continent, she needed something warm. Something that could warm her from the inside.

"I am happy to see you well," he said.

That was it? That was all she got? *Happy to see you well?* He'd have known she was well when she was on the other side of the Atlantic, if he'd taken the time to ask. He never had, not in twenty years, at least not to her knowledge.

"Thank you for your devotion," she said with more force than necessary. "Were you this cold with my mother? If so, I understand why she never spoke to you again after she left."

He sucked in a surprised breath but held it, apparently not willing to respond to her goading.

Livi jumped to her feet, as impatient as her father

had ever accused her of being. "Why don't you just send me home? That's where I want to be."

Her grandfather released his breath. "I didn't ask for the responsibility of your care."

Then send me home! Please!

"But I accept it as my duty. To your mother. You're obviously too much for your father to handle properly."

"Too much what?" For some reason, she was finding it difficult to draw in a deep breath.

"Too much of a challenge." He shook his head absently. "Your mother was a paragon of virtue until she met your father. His influence on you cannot have been in your best interest. I probably should have sent for you years ago."

So she could be reared by a cold governess, just as her mother had been? *No, thank you.* "He wouldn't have let you have me."

"Yet he has sent you to me now," he said, his voice cold and flat. "I'll do my best to secure a good match for you."

"Good match? You mean a title and wealth?" A marriage with no feeling. No love. No passion. No trust. Just what her mother had run from.

"To begin with," he agreed.

Lovely. Just lovely.

"And the Hadley brothers," he began.

"What of them?" she said, realizing by the look on his face that her tone was a tad too sharp. But she was beyond caring.

"They're not of our ilk."

Thank goodness for that. "The eldest is a viscount, I understand."

"A viscount without two shillings to rub together, until a recent turn of fortune. They're involved in some business dealings that are less than respectable. While we will be traveling with Lady Radbourne, you will not become attached to either of those ruffians." He pursed his lips as though he smelled something foul. "Lady Radbourne has a companion that you can learn a great deal from. Lady Sophia Cole is the only reason I'm allowing this trip to Bath. The lady will be a good influence on you." He shook his finger at her. "But you will stay away from the Hadley men."

"Is that an order?" she asked sweetly.

He smacked his hand onto the surface of his desk with enough force that Livi flinched. "Yes!" he barked. "It's an order."

"Let me go home," she pleaded one last time.

"I finally have some say about your life. And it's my duty to turn you into something your mother would be proud of."

Not someone. Something. "My mother would be proud of me as I am."

"Your days of climbing trees and trudging through swamps are over," he spat out. "Your days as a lady of quality are beginning, as of today. Consider yourself in training to be a lady."

"Like a dog that's being trained to hunt?"

His gaze narrowed. "And heel and sit and do as she's told."

She would never, ever heel. Never. He was in for a rude awakening if he thought she would.

❧

During the entire trip back to Hadley Hall, Gray had tried unsuccessfully to get his mother to change her mind about Bath. All he could hope for was that Archer would have better luck with the viscountess than he'd had thus far. As soon as the coach reached the estate, Gray left his mother in her private parlor and went in search of his brother, in hope that reinforcements would aid their situation.

He heard an exclamation of frustration escape from Archer's study. Gray had grown accustomed to that particular sound ever since Lady Sophia had taken up residence in Hadley Hall. The lady must be in the study as well. Archer didn't make that sound if she wasn't within earshot.

Despite his own frustration with their mother and one very specific American chit, Gray couldn't help but smile. There was something vastly amusing about the way Lady Sophia always left Archer tongue-tied and blustering like a dolt. Gray cleared his throat before knocking on the door of his brother's study.

"Devil take it!" Archer growled from inside the room.

Gray almost chuckled, but doing so would only serve to annoy Archer, and in this unfortunate situation, they needed to be united. He pushed the door open and stepped inside. "Quite an interesting way of inviting one's brother into one's study."

"I didn't invite you." Archer grimaced. "What do you want?"

Gray leaned against the doorjamb and nodded to Lady Sophia, sitting across from his brother. "I gather your hands have been full while I was away."

She smiled as she rose from her seat. "My hands are always full with the two of you."

"All you have to do is leave," Archer grumbled from his large leather chair. "And we'll all be happier."

"Not until you're a proper gentleman," Lady Sophia remarked as she started for the door. "At this rate, I'll be here until you die of old age." She brushed past Gray, into the corridor. "Do continue your practice, my lord," she tossed over her shoulder as she made her exit.

Looking at the outraged expression of his brother, Gray did finally laugh. "I take it things didn't go well with Lady Sophia?"

"Do things ever go well with that woman?" Archer raked a hand through his dark hair. "If I didn't know better, I'd think she stays up late every night thinking up new ways to vex me."

"And me," Gray agreed, thinking about the tea-sipping from that afternoon. Utter rubbish.

Archer scoffed. "You get off easy. She barely pays you any mind at all. Yet she takes special delight in tormenting me."

Well, Archer *had* won Lady Sophia's family's fortune, leaving her late father penniless, despondent, and perhaps even suicidal. But voicing those words aloud would be a surefire way of getting himself a broken nose. And though Gray would heal from the injury within moments, he wasn't in the mood to spar with Archer, not when they needed to band together. Besides, Archer wasn't aware Gray knew the particulars behind his new fortune, and more pressing matters needed to be dealt with at the moment.

"You won't believe the afternoon I've endured."

"Did you have a harridan insist you work on your penmanship for hours upon hours?" Archer sat back in his large leather seat with a huff, folding his arms across his chest. "I'd sooner have my valet shave my manly parts than I would answer all the correspondence she put before me."

Gray bit back the acrid taste that filled his mouth at the very thought of Archer's valet getting anywhere near his manly parts, particularly with a sharp instrument, and then pushed himself from the doorjamb and stepped farther into the study, closing the door behind him. After all, it wouldn't do for any household staff to overhear his next words. "Holmesfield's granddaughter is in residence at the Court."

Finally a ghost of a smile lit Archer's lips. "Oh? Was Mother matchmaking?"

That thought hadn't even occurred to Gray. "I don't think so." Though she had been awfully eager for him to accompany her that afternoon, hadn't she?

"Ever since Wes married, Mother's been hinting that she'd like to see each of us follow in his footsteps."

"Without the abduction part, of course."

"Well, that goes without saying." Archer kicked his Hessians up on the edge of his desk. "She'd probably feel fortunate if we avoid the scandal part too."

Gray raised his brow and nodded toward his brother's feet. "If Lady Sophia saw you do that…"

"I do not answer to Sophia Cole."

No, but he did answer to Dashiel Thorpe, the Marquess of Eynsford, their half brother and pack alpha. And Dash *had* hired Lady Sophia. Gray shrugged.

"If you want to risk your own tail, it doesn't matter to me." He dropped into a seat across from his brother. "Holmesfield's granddaughter knows I'm a Lycan. She knows there are three of us."

Archer's feet fell back to the floor with a thud, and his mouth dropped open. "How does she know that?"

"I told her."

"You did what?" Archer roared.

"I told her there were three of us," Gray amended. Then he touched the mark beneath his left ear. "She has the mark of the beast on her thigh, Arch."

"On her *thigh*?" His brother's golden eyes widened with either horror or surprise, Gray wasn't certain which. "Am I to take it you are freshly betrothed to the lady then?"

Gray scoffed. "I didn't see the mark, you arse. She told me where it was."

"She told you? What sort of lady is this chit?"

"She's not one." Gray frowned. At his brother's quizzical expression, he hastened to explain. "I wouldn't exactly call her a lady, that is."

"What would you call her?"

Temptation incarnate. "Our worst nightmare." Gray sighed. "She told me she knew what I was, with Holmesfield just a few feet away. She has no sense of decorum, Arch. Can you imagine what would have happened if the earl had heard her? We're just fortunate the old prick is half deaf."

Archer's brow furrowed as though he was trying to make sense of the situation. "How long will she be in residence?"

"Until she escapes, but that might be too late for us."

"Escapes?"

"She'd like to catch the next frigate back to New Orleans, but she's been sent here to learn to become a lady."

"Sounds like she could use the training. Wait!" Archer's eyes lit up. "Perhaps we could convince Holmesfield to employ Lady Sophia, and then we'd be rid of her. Kill two birds with one stone, so to speak."

"Oh, Lady Sophia will get the chance to meet Miss Mayeux. We're all going to Bath, you and me included."

"Bath?"

"Mother has apparently promised Holmesfield that she'll help smooth Miss Mayeux's entrée into society. They think to start with Bath now, so she'll have a taste of what's to come in Town next season."

Archer looked as grim as Gray felt. "Why would Mother do such a thing?"

Gray shook his head. "You should have heard her all the way home from Holmesfield Court, gushing about Miss Mayeux. Apparently Mother grew up with the chit's mother. They were dear friends, and Father actually introduced Lady Grace to a French Lycan of his acquaintance. The rest is history. But now Mother is determined to help her old friend's daughter. And you and I have been recruited into this nonsense."

"It is nonsense. I won't do it." Archer shook his head.

Gray sighed with relief. "I was hoping you'd say that. If we band together..."

A knock came at the door, and Archer mouthed the word "Mother" to Gray. "Yes? Come in."

A moment later, their mother stood in the threshold, glowing with more joy than Gray remembered seeing in a very long time. "Oh, perfect. You're both here. Archer, did Grayson tell you the wonderful news?"

"He told me you expect us to head to Bath, but—"

"Oh, she looks just like Grace did, darker though. More French, like her father. But with her eyes and cheeks and lips, I would recognize her anywhere as Grace's daughter. Such a pretty little thing, isn't she, Grayson?"

"Pretty?" Archer's brow rose. "I think you neglected to mention that part, Brother."

"She could expose us all," Gray hissed.

"Oh, yes, pretty," their mother continued as though Gray hadn't spoken. "Stunning, really. Wouldn't you agree, Grayson?"

Liviana Mayeux *was* stunning. But that was neither here nor there. "Mother, both Archer and I are too busy at the moment to head to Bath. We've discussed it and—"

"We cannot wait to accompany you, despite our other duties," Archer chimed in. "When do we leave?"

Four

GRAY SHOULD HAVE RUN ALL THE WAY FROM Derbyshire to Somerset, if for no other reason than to avoid the caustic glares and constant bickering between his brother and Lady Sophia along the journey. His head throbbed as he stepped from the Radbourne carriage onto the cobblestones before the Earl of Holmesfield's elegant Bath home. What he wouldn't give to be almost anywhere else.

"So where is your pretty little French poodle?" Archer whispered in Gray's ear as he clapped a hand to his back.

Gray glanced over his shoulder and scowled at his brother. "I wouldn't call her *mine*, and I wouldn't compare her to any breed of dog where she can hear you unless you'd like to get her on a subject we should all avoid. She may have Lycan blood in her veins, but she needn't bandy that fact about."

Archer grinned unrepentantly. "Indeed. Maybe she'll show me the mark on her thigh."

"*You* planning on marrying the chit?" Gray returned. "It would probably serve you right. I'd dearly love to see the knots she'd leave you in. Probably exactly what you deserve after the life you've led."

"It would be so nice," came Lady Sophia's disembodied voice from inside the carriage, "if one of the gentlemen outside would offer a hand of assistance to Lady Radbourne and myself."

Archer frowned. "She can't be worse," he nodded his head toward the coach, "than that one."

Except that Lady Sophia had never heard the word "Lycan," and if she did, she'd never utter it. Gray nodded toward the coach. "Shall you do the honors? Or shall I?"

"I'll do it," Archer grumbled, then turned around and helped their mother alight from the conveyance.

Once Lady Radbourne was safely on her feet, Archer shut the coach door with a slam and offered his arm to their mother. "Shall we?" he asked, ignoring the huff of indignation from inside the carriage.

"Archer!" their mother admonished. "You shut the door on Lady Sophia."

"Did I?" he asked, sarcasm dripping from his voice. "Perhaps Gray can assist the lady. Come along, Mother. Lord Holmesfield awaits us with his supposedly stunning granddaughter."

Gray itched to send his brother sprawling across the cobblestones, but that would hardly do in broad daylight in front of the earl's home. So he opened the coach door and offered his hand to Lady Sophia instead. "Sorry, my lady," he said. "Awful gust of wind."

"Windbag, you mean," the lady retorted as she stepped from the coach, smoothing her dark locks back in place. "Your brother is insufferable."

Gray agreed with a nod. "Indeed. And I've been suffering him all my life."

"You have my condolences."

"And I appreciate them," Gray returned, offering her his arm. "We should follow to make sure he doesn't make any blunders upon greeting the earl."

"I'll be happy if he makes but one blunder, Mr. Hadley."

As long as it was only a small one, Gray was in agreement. The two hurried along the short walk to the front door and joined Archer and Lady Radbourne on the stoop as an aged butler gestured them all over the threshold.

"His lordship and Miss Mayeux are in the parlor. This way." The old man led them down the corridor and through the first open doorway. "Lord and Lady Radbourne, Lady Sophia and Mr. Hadley, my lord."

"Yes, yes," the earl grumbled from a high-back chair near a wide window. "I saw them arrive. Have their things brought in, Flemming. And some refreshments."

"Of course, my lord."

Gray's eyes immediately landed on Liviana Mayeux on the opposite side of the room, pacing as though she were a wild animal trapped in a cage. If it was possible, she seemed even lovelier than she had when he'd first met her. Her dark locks were piled high on her head, and the scooped bodice of her gown drew his eyes to territory he fully wanted to explore.

"Archer," their mother gushed as she stepped into the parlor, "allow me to introduce you to Miss Liviana Mayeux."

"Livi," the chit corrected.

Her grandfather harrumphed. "You'll excuse me if I don't rise," the feeble Lord Holmesfield said.

Lady Radbourne nodded. "Sophia and I understand completely, my lord." Then the viscountess returned her attention to Miss Mayeux and smiled. "Livi, this is my oldest son, Archer, Viscount Radbourne, and my companion, Lady Sophia Cole, and you know Grayson already."

Livi Mayeux's blue eyes flashed to meet Gray's gaze, and the breath rushed from his lungs. If she looked at any other man that way, the mark on her thigh would be discovered in a heartbeat. Not that anyone other than himself or his brothers would know what it was.

"Miss Mayeux." Archer bowed in greeting. "My brother sang your praises, but I must say you are even more beautiful than he led me to believe."

"There's no reason to flatter her," Lord Holmesfield barked. "And there's no reason to flirt or pay court to her, either. The two of you scoundrels are here to serve as escorts *only*."

"Like trained dogs?" Archer asked, which was rewarded with a husky laugh from Livi Mayeux.

"Dogs indeed," the earl grumbled. "Now sit, so we can discuss our plan of attack."

"Attack?" Lady Sophia asked as she dropped Gray's arm and started for the closest settee. "You make it sound like a battle, my lord."

Holmesfield gestured toward his granddaughter with his head. "'Battle' would be a euphemism, Lady Sophia. I do hope you and Lady Radbourne can do something with her. *I* am at a total loss."

"I assure you," Lady Sophia replied, "I have handled worse cases."

Meaning Gray and Archer, but Gray wasn't so certain Lady Sophia's estimation was correct. Not if the rebellious flash in Miss Mayeux's cornflower eyes was any indication. "We are happy to help," he heard himself say, and couldn't imagine what imp had forced the words from his mouth.

"You can help," the earl said as he glanced in Gray's direction, "by escorting the ladies to the Longboroughs' musicale tomorrow evening."

Musicale? Gray would rather listen to the mating of cats. At least the cats managed to stay on tune, at least in comparison to Lady Longborough's daughters.

"You may be excused until then," Holmesfield said. "But stay out of trouble. Liviana doesn't need any unnecessary scandal attached to her name."

Miss Mayeux could well provide the scandal herself.

"Come on," Archer said, smacking Gray on the shoulder. "We've been given a reprieve so let's not waste it."

❧

Livi watched the two Lycans escape her grandfather's parlor and her spirits sank. She'd do just about anything to leave with the two men. Wherever they were headed had to be more fun than enduring the earl's icy treatment and having to pretend to possess social graces for Lady Radbourne and Lady Sophia's benefit.

"Liviana," her grandfather barked, "take a seat. Pacing is for fellows who face the gallows."

"How fitting," she muttered. Though she did leave

her corner of the room and sat in a chair near the earl's. She forced a smile to her face when she met Lady Sophia's gaze. The lady seemed too haughty by half. Livi didn't have a prayer of enjoying even a moment's worth of fun with Lady Sophia, so she turned her attention to Lady Radbourne. "So nice to see you again, my lady."

"And you." The older woman smiled warmly, the first bit of warmth Livi had felt since arriving in Bath the previous day.

"So I understand," Lady Sophia said to the earl, "you are in need of my services."

The old man glanced over at Livi and scowled before returning his glance to Lady Sophia. "Lady Radbourne says you can work wonders. I sincerely hope that is the case."

Lady Sophia smiled. "What are you most concerned about, my lord?"

"It would be hard to pinpoint one thing. She is too brash. She is too sharp tongued. She is too common. She is too French. She is—"

"*I* am in the room." Livi heaved an indignant sigh.

Lady Sophia turned her attention on Livi and seemed to assess her as one might a gown that was two seasons too old while deciding whether or not to keep it. "You are slouching, dear," the lady said softly. "Sit straighter and square your shoulders. I should think a bit of aloofness would go a long way where you're concerned."

"Lord Holmesfield," Lady Radbourne said, stepping forward, "have you partaken of the waters at the Pump Room yet?"

"Not yet," he replied.

"Well, why don't we do so together and allow Sophia and Liviana to get to know one another."

"A wonderful idea." The earl slid to the edge of his seat and struggled to his feet with the help of his cane.

"Would you like some assistance, my lord?" Lady Radbourne asked.

"I can do it myself," he grumbled sourly. Then he leaned heavily on his walking stick and started for the door. He glanced back over his shoulder at Lady Sophia. "Do not let her out of your sight."

"I'm certain we'll get along well, my lord."

He harrumphed. "We'll see about that."

Lady Radbourne smiled at Livi. "You are in wonderful hands, my dear." Then she followed the earl from the parlor, leaving Livi with the very formal English lady.

"So you are to work wonders with me, are you?" Livi asked.

The lady shrugged. "That remains to be seen. I get the feeling you don't want to improve, which would make my task an impossible one."

Improve. Livi scowled. "I'm perfectly fine the way I am."

"And yet your father sent you to England to become a lady, did he not?"

"He's a traitor," Livi grumbled.

"Ladies do not mutter under their breath, Miss Mayeux. It's considered ill-mannered. If you have something to say, you should make certain your companions can hear you clearly. And if it is something you shouldn't be saying, well, then you shouldn't say it aloud at all."

Livi cleared her throat. "I said," she was careful to enunciate, "my father is a traitor, and I don't care who knows it."

Lady Sophia frowned, but even with a frown she seemed the picture of propriety. "I am certain he has your best interests at heart. *Most* fathers do."

The way she spoke made Livi think the lady had left something unsaid. "Does yours?"

"I beg your pardon."

Livi shrugged. "You seem poised and confident. What would make a lady such as you take a position as a lady's companion?"

A bit of color stained Lady Sophia's cheeks. "I don't believe we were discussing *my* father."

"*Non?* Well, you mentioned mine. I didn't realize yours wasn't a topic for discussion."

Lady Sophia sat a little straighter and leveled Livi with a haughty stare. "Very well, Miss Mayeux. *My* father has passed away, as has my mother. But if he were still living, I am certain he would have my best interests at heart. Papa's title, as well as his holdings, have passed on to my cousin, but I do not wish to reside under his roof. Therefore I needed to find a way to take care of myself, and providing companionship to Lady Radbourne is as much a pleasure as it is a position. Now if you are done delving into my past, we truly should return our attention to you and your situation."

Now the lady was more a mystery than she had been before divulging all that information. "Certainly you could have married." After all wasn't that what was expected of proper English ladies? The merging of families and empires?

"English gentlemen prefer wives with dowries, Miss Mayeux, which Lady Radbourne assures me *you* are in possession of. So why don't we focus our efforts on you?"

"Because I do not have any desire to marry an English gentleman."

"What do you want, then?" Lady Sophia asked.

And it was the first time since she'd arrived in England that anyone had asked her that question. "I want to go home," Livi replied quietly. "I want to secure passage to New Orleans. I want to sail the Atlantic. I want to step off the ship and have the warmth of Louisiana wash over me and seep into my bones. I want to watch Etienne wrestle alligators and catch crawfish with Armand in the swamps. I want…" *my old life back.* But Livi couldn't say those words aloud.

"But you're here now." Lady Sophia replied, not unkindly. "As you find yourself in this situation, I will do my best to help you navigate your way through these waters."

Livi shook her head. She didn't want help navigating these waters. She just wanted her father to love her enough to let her come home.

"I wish for things too, Miss Mayeux. But I have to know which dreams are possible and which are not."

Livi sighed. It wasn't a matter of possible or impossible dreams; it was a matter of right and wrong. She should never have been shipped off to England. She should never have been sent to her grandfather. "Where do you suppose Mr. Hadley and Lord Radbourne have gone?"

Lady Sophia closed her eyes as though the thought

of the men gave her a headache. "The Lord only knows." Then she sat forward in her chair and speared Livi with a look of determination. "Those men are hardly your concern. We need to spend the time we do have preparing you for the Longboroughs' musicale tomorrow. Do you sing?"

Livi nearly swallowed her tongue. "Sing?" she croaked. "Will they ask me to sing?"

Lady Sophia shook her head. "One must always be prepared. Can you sing?"

Not in front of people. She sang in the bayous at home with her brothers, but she would never sing in front of a group of rigid Englishmen. "Can you?" she countered.

"I'm not on the market, Miss Mayeux. You are."

But Lady Sophia *should* be on the market. She would make some stuffy gentleman a much better wife than Livi ever would.

Five

Livi settled deeper into the feather ticking of the most uncomfortable bed she'd ever had the misfortune of sleeping in. They simply did not make beds on this side of the Atlantic the way they did in America. They were harder and lumpier, and they smelled as old as the villages did. She balled her pillow up under the side of her face and tried to will herself to sleep. But sleep was elusive. All she could think about was her conversation with Lady Sophia and the blasted musicale that she would be forced to attend the following night. One night to acclimate herself to Bath, and then her grandfather planned to thrust her into this world he lived in without any thought of her wishes on the matter.

Livi rolled to her side, adjusting her pillow with a fierce growl. That was something her grandfather would highly object to, as well. Evidently, ladies were not supposed to grunt or growl, even when they were annoyed. She supposed she would have to stop making Lycan noises if she wanted to fit in with society. But it was really difficult to drop a lifetime of learning. She'd grown up with Lycans, for goodness sake. It was impossible *not* to pick up some of their mannerisms, even if she didn't grow a tail and howl at the moon when it was at its fullest.

There was so much she didn't know. So much she couldn't possibly hope to understand. She sighed heavily and sat up, rubbing her eyes. Perhaps some warm milk would help. They did have warm milk in Bath, didn't they? She was certain she could find some. Livi slid her feet into her slippers and turned toward the door. She had no idea where the kitchens were, but certainly someone would be about who could direct her.

The servants in England never seemed to sleep. They prowled the corridors, waiting for a command. The complete opposite of what Marie did at home. They'd probably try to force her to allow them to get the milk for her. But she could get her own milk. Back home, she and her father met often in the dead of night to have a glass of warm milk and to steal the treats Cook left out just for them. Longing for home pierced her heart, but she stiffened her shoulders and left the room, sliding quietly into the dark corridor as she closed her door behind her.

Lady Sophia would hear her if she wasn't quiet, so she tiptoed past her door and didn't dare breathe until she was at the top of the stairs, far from the lady's realm. Lady Sophia would probably turn her nose up as though she smelled something foul just before she gave Livi a lesson about comportment. Livi searched the quiet of the night for sounds, but no one was about, aside from the aged servant who slept by the front door. So some of them did sleep, after all. At their posts, of course. The Hadley men must not have returned for the night yet, if the poor butler was still up this late. Blast those brothers and their late-night carousing.

Why did it bother her that they were out in the wee hours of the morning? Probably because they were allowed the freedom she would never see again, not if her grandfather had his way about things.

She stepped softly past the servant until she was out of his line of sight and smiled when he mumbled to himself. She stopped hesitantly, trying to make out his words. But they were unintelligible. She turned and headed toward where she assumed the kitchens must be.

❧

Gray cursed as he dropped his coins on the cobblestone walk. It was much too dark to find them, and the lights from the hack he'd hired simply created more shadow. He dug into his pocket for more coins and tossed the fare to the driver. The man snagged the coins in the air and looked at them appreciatively when he realized the sum was more than he'd expected. "Do you need some help getting to the door, sir?" he asked.

Did he look like he'd had that much enjoyment this evening? Gray shook his head, the action causing his world to unbalance, and he reached out for the corner of the coach to steady himself. "I believe I can make it," he grunted.

"Are you certain?" the driver asked, a grin lurking about the corners of his mouth. Damn his hide. He was enjoying this.

"Quite," Gray grumbled. Typically, he and Archer would lean on one another until they reached the safety of their quarters. But Archer was otherwise occupied, damn his eyes.

Gray tugged at the lapels of his jacket and smoothed his hair. "Do I look respectable?" he asked absently, as though he was talking to one of his brothers.

When the driver chuckled, he knew he'd made a mistake. "You look beautiful, sir. Shall I right your bonnet before you go into the house?"

Bonnet? The sun wasn't even out. Oh, dear God, he must have had more to drink than he'd thought. The earl would kill him if he found him in such shape on his doorstep. Gray scrubbed at his face. The driver chuckled again. Then he climbed back up into his seat and put his pair in motion.

Gray swayed in the wind produced by the departure. A stiff wind would most likely blow him over. He steeled himself and took a hesitant step forward. He could do this. He could get inside, fall into bed, and wake up on the morrow with no one the wiser. Couldn't he? Well, he'd done so before. Of course, he'd never spent one night under Holmesfield's roof before.

The doorway looked like it was fathoms away. But he trudged forward once he willed his feet to move. When he reached the door, he settled his palms against it, and then his forehead, leaning heavily into it for support. If it wasn't so late, the door would be formally attended. It was his own damn fault that he had to make noise at all. He was an idiot. But that was neither here nor there, not at this point.

He gently rapped upon the door. Within moments, he heard the light clip of footsteps and the door was flung open. Unfortunately, it did so while Gray was still using it for support. Within seconds, he found himself stumbling forward with all the finesse of a charging bull. And the butler, rather than waiting to be bowled over, stepped to the side to avoid being flattened instead of reaching out to stop Gray's fall. Back home, they had burly servants who could handle a crisis. Evidently, the Earl of Holmesfield employed skinny servants who couldn't handle a gentleman in his prime. Particularly not one of Lycan nature—tall and broad.

The butler did scurry forward as soon as Gray hit the floor. Gray landed on his elbow and rolled to cradle it. "Are you all right, sir?" the man whispered harshly.

Gray raised his head from the floor and glanced up at the butler, then lowered it back to land with a thud on the rug. It really was difficult to judge how hard a rug would be when one was foxed. "Do I look all right?" he grunted in response.

"Indeed, you look as though you have thoroughly enjoyed your evening, sir," the man said. "Can I help you to your feet?" He held out a hand.

Gray raised his head again and groaned. "You and who else?" he muttered. The butler could not possibly help raise him.

"I'm stronger than I look, sir," the butler said as his chest puffed up.

If that was the case, Gray wouldn't be lying on the floor. He rolled to his side and climbed up on his hands and knees, then toddled to his feet. The room spun around him, and Gray reached for the butler. Wiry little thing, he was.

Suddenly, the scent of summer hit his nose, assaulting him almost as harshly as the floor had a moment ago. "Was Miss Mayeux recently here?" he asked.

"The earl's granddaughter? Not that I'm aware of, sir." He avoided Gray's gaze.

"Ah, sleeping at your post, huh?" That made perfect sense. "If you'll keep my little secret, I'll keep yours."

The man smiled broadly. "Bargain accepted," he said.

Gray gestured down the hallway. "What's down that corridor?" he asked.

"His lordship's study."

Gray couldn't see Liviana Mayeux cavorting about her grandfather's study at this time of night. "What else?" He made an impatient move with his hand.

"The yellow parlor." The butler shrugged. "The kitchens."

Gray nodded. "You may go," he said. He had most definitely caught her scent. And despite his state of inebriation, he had a desire to find out why on earth Miss Mayeux would be wandering the corridors at such a late hour.

The butler looked somewhat relieved at being dismissed. "Shall I wait for Lord Radbourne?" he asked.

Gray highly doubted that Archer would find his way home that night. When he'd left Archer, he'd been heavily engaged in a game of cards. He was winning. Gray, on the other hand, was not. Once the liquor had begun to flow, he'd lost hand after hand. Archer, however, was quite the opposite sort. So, his older brother had taken a break long enough to put

Gray in a hack before returning to the tables—at least Gray assumed he'd returned to the tables. There were a few pretty bundles to be had, as well. Either way, it didn't matter. Gray was here and Archer was not.

"No need," Gray replied.

After the butler bowed and backed out of the entryway, Gray looked down the looming corridor and took a step. It couldn't quite be as long as it looked, could it? Certainly not. He picked up a candle from a table by the door and headed down the corridor. He followed Miss Mayeux's summery scent all the way to the end but stopped when he heard soft humming from the kitchen. It had to be her. He pushed the door open slowly and poked his head inside.

The vision that met his eyes nearly took his breath. Liviana Mayeux stood by the cookstove in nothing more than her nightrail, a flimsy one at that. If Gray hadn't been able to smell her scent, he would have assumed he was dreaming. Her virginal gown billowed around her shoulders and dragged along the floor. A lamp was lit behind her, casting her in shadows that outlined her body. A sudden and intense longing spread throughout his body. "What the devil are you doing in the kitchen?" he barked.

Miss Mayeux's hand trembled with surprise, and she nearly jumped from her skin as the spoon in her hand clattered to the floor. In the silence of the night, the sound was nearly deafening. She sighed heavily and looked down at the utensil, then back up at him. "What the devil does it look like I'm doing?" she asked.

It looked like she was trying to get herself mauled

by a foxed, overly amorous Lycan. But Gray certainly couldn't say that. "Attempting to catch your nightrail on fire? Surely there must be easier ways to escape the social scene in Bath."

"I wanted some warm milk, if you must know," she said tartly.

"Trouble sleeping?" He could probably be more eloquent if his tongue didn't feel like it had grown hairy and unwieldy.

Her gaze drifted up and down his body as he stepped fully into the kitchen. "Trouble holding yourself upright?" she returned.

Not really. He was doing well there propped against the wall. Wasn't he?

"I have brothers, Mr. Hadley," she said with a laugh. Then she pointed a spoon at him. "Don't think that I don't know where you've been."

A sudden chagrin seeped into his mind. "And where might that be?" he asked.

Miss Mayeux stepped closer to him. The fabric of her nightrail rustled with each step. He couldn't help but wonder if she wore anything beneath it. Such thoughts would only bring him trouble. But her hair hung in heavy, unbound waves over her shoulders, falling all the way to her waist. He wanted to bury his face in it and let her scent wash over him. He'd never smelled anything quite so decadent as her mix of flowery scents. She leaned close to him and inhaled deeply.

"You smell like a brewery," she said, scrunching up her pert little nose. Then she leaned even closer. Her nose touched his jacket, and she leaned back with a harsh noise.

"Visited a lot of breweries, have you?" he asked.

She didn't even look at him when she replied, "Visited a lot of whores, have you?" Then she stalked past him, back toward the cookstove.

"Wait," he said. She didn't stop, so he reached out to catch her elbow. If she were a wolf, she'd have snapped his hand off, if the look on her face was any indication. "I haven't been with a whore." He didn't know why he wanted to tell her that. Truly it was none of her concern. He couldn't even believe he was engaging in such a conversation with an innocent girl.

"I can smell her all over you," Miss Mayeux said. Again she avoided his gaze as she spoke. Was she bothered by the fact that he smelled like a whore? How interesting.

Well, a whore, more than one actually, had perched herself in Gray's lap that night. One had even lingered there for much longer than necessary. But he hadn't taken her up on her offers. He'd been much too deep in his cups by then to do so. "I wasn't with a whore," he said again.

"Perhaps you're too foxed to remember." She shook her head and tugged her arm, but he didn't release it. "Let me go, Mr. Hadley."

Gray heard soft footsteps in the corridor and winced. "Lady Sophia," he whispered as he released his grasp on Miss Mayeux's arm.

"Oh, dear God," Miss Mayeux groaned, tossing her head back in frustration. "All I wanted was a cup of warm milk."

The door opened slowly, and Lady Sophia's head popped around the corner. She took in the scene before her with a critical and appraising eye. "Miss Mayeux," she said with a nod. Then she speared Gray with a glance that would have dropped a lesser man to his knees. "Am I interrupting something?"

"Warm milk," Miss Mayeux said, retrieving a cup from beside the cookstove. She didn't even attempt to explain.

Lady Sophia kept her gaze leveled on Gray. "Long night, Mr. Hadley?" she asked.

"Quite." He refused to go into any detail. Who knew what lessons she'd dream up for him and Archer after this little conversation.

"Mr. Hadley might need someone to help him upstairs," Miss Mayeux said softly.

"Volunteering for the job?" he asked. If he wasn't quite so foxed, he would never have let that slip in front of Lady Sophia. Damn it to hell.

"Mr. Hadley," his tutor scolded.

But Miss Mayeux cut her off. "Not with the way you smell," she said as she turned on her heel and started for the door. She may as well have skewered him with a blade as with her sudden lack of interest.

If Lady Sophia wasn't there, Gray never would have let the chit walk away. He would have chased after her and ensured that her interest was piqued. But he didn't have that luxury tonight, so he just let her leave.

As soon as Liviana Mayeux was gone, Lady Sophia glared at him. "Don't even think about it, Grayson," she said.

Not think about it? That was like not being able to breathe when one's lungs were empty. Not think about it? He'd endeavor to do that. And to stop breathing too.

"I'm serious," she warned.

"You're always serious, my lady. You might be happier if you were less so."

She narrowed her eyes at him. "I do believe you are the last person I would take such advice from. Am I to assume that your degenerate brother has finally returned as well?"

Gray scoffed. "If you're looking for Archer, I wouldn't expect to see him step over this threshold until the very last second before he has to get ready for the musicale."

"Typical," she complained. "Stealing someone else's fortune, is he?"

"Can it be stolen if it is lost fairly over a gaming table?" As soon as the words left Gray's mouth, he wished he could call them back. A wounded look flashed in her eyes, but it was gone as quickly as it had appeared.

"Do find your bed, Mr. Hadley. And unless you'd like me to send an unfavorable report to Lord Eynsford, you'll keep your distance from Miss Mayeux. Do you understand?"

Gray gaped at her. "I beg your pardon?"

"I'm going to have a hard enough time helping the poor girl fit in with the *ton* as it is. Any time spent around you or Lord Radbourne will be a disservice to her. Keep that in mind."

"Can't have her associating with impoverished fellows, is that it?"

"Your wealth, or lack of, has nothing to do with the situation. I'm much more concerned about your blackened reputation. Hers is spotless. At least for now, and I plan to keep it that way." She folded her arms across her chest. "Besides, rumor has it that Lord Radbourne has come into a sudden windfall, which would take you out of the impoverished class, Mr. Hadley," she added coldly.

He gazed absently at his fingernails. It was much easier than looking into her face. "Archer's windfall doesn't line *my* pockets," he said. Then he chanced a glance at her, watching her face closely as he said the next. "I bet he would give it back to you if you asked nicely."

Her gaze jerked toward his. "My father's money?" She snorted, a very unladylike sound that Gray hadn't realized she was even capable of making. "I highly doubt it."

He stepped closer to her so that he could murmur the words: "The cottage, Lady Sophia. I bet he would give you Bindweed Cottage if you but asked nicely."

A flash of pain crossed her face. "How do you know about that?"

Because his new sister-in-law had confided as much to him, in hopes Gray could convince Archer to return the lady's property. But Archer never welcomed conversation about his newly won fortune, and Gray hadn't wanted to broach the subject. "I just do." He shrugged.

"Madeline should mind her own affairs."

Perfect. Now he'd gotten Wes' bride into trouble, and he hadn't even divulged her name. Perhaps he could smooth over his lapse. "Poor girl *is* married to my brother. Worrying about others keeps her mind off her own troubles. You can't blame her for that, can you?"

So much for smoothing over his lapse. Her anguished expression almost made Gray feel guilty for bringing up the subject in the first place. But then he remembered that he was in Bath at her command. Well, hers and his mother's. He should be at home, taking care of business dealings with Wes.

Gray watched her face as her mouth opened and closed. She obviously wanted to say something. But her lips clamped shut and she regally lifted her nose in the air.

"It must be hard keeping all that righteous indignation in check, my lady," he said. "Do you ever just want to explode with it? To scream to the heavens?"

"I've never wanted to do any such thing," she huffed, looking affronted at the very thought of behaving in such an outrageous fashion.

"Why did you come in here tonight, Lady Sophia?" he asked softly. He wanted to like the lady. He really did. Madeline thought highly of her. And he thought highly of Madeline.

"I heard Miss Mayeux leave her room, and I wanted to make certain she was safe."

"She was." He heard the bark in his own voice and tried to soften his tone. "She was safe," he confirmed.

"But how much of that is because of your honor and how much of it is because I walked into the kitchen?" She shook her head as though disgusted with the sight of him. "The girl was in her nightrail, for heaven's sake."

"Good God, you say that like she was naked," Gray grumbled.

"She may as well have been for all the scandal it

would cause for her," she said sharply. "Had someone else discovered the two of you…" She let her voice trail off. "You'd be married to the girl before you knew what hit you." She laid a hand on Gray's arm and looked up at him with enough seriousness in her eyes that he was slightly taken aback.

"Neither of you wants that. Don't ruin the girl's prospects, Grayson," she whispered. "You wouldn't want her to end up in a predicament like mine. Forced into a life she never would have picked for herself in order to survive."

Then before he could reply, she quit the room, her dressing gown billowing around her legs in her haste to escape.

He almost followed her, but his feet were still slightly unwieldy, and he wasn't sure what he'd say if he caught her. Gray swiped a hand down his face. He'd had way too much to drink. It would be the last time he ever let Archer bully him into drinking gin, god-awful stuff that it was.

Livi listened intently outside the door until it was suddenly flung open and Lady Sophia cannoned down the corridor. Livi backed into shadows and waited until her tutor had passed. She tried to digest what she'd heard. Of course, Lady Sophia had warned Mr. Hadley away from her. That much she'd expected. But she hadn't expected to hear so much about Lady Sophia's circumstances. Circumstances beyond her control.

It obviously had something to do with money. Lady Sophia's father's money, if she'd heard correctly.

Why did Radbourne have her father's money? And a cottage?

Livi tapped her chin as she stood there in the shadows. She'd have to give this a lot of thought so she could find a...

A cough broke her from her musings.

"It's quite impolite to listen to people's private conversations."

"It's equally impolite to stalk people in the corridors." She tried to make herself sound as haughty as Lady Sophia did. However, she merely sounded distraught, at least to her own ears. "And I wasn't listening."

He snorted. "Yes, you were. You're already plotting to use Lady Sophia's circumstances to your advantage somehow. Did you think you could coerce her into helping you escape to a port and then onto an American-bound ship?"

She hadn't even considered such a thing. If he wasn't standing so close to her, she'd have stomped her foot. But he might consider that to be childish. Did she care about his opinion? She sighed heavily as the truth hit her. Yes, she did care about his opinion, which was both mildly disconcerting and inconvenient. "I merely wanted to understand how the lady thinks," she murmured. "I can't figure her out."

"And you must 'figure her out' before you can befriend her?" he asked.

"It helps," she mumbled.

He chuckled lightly.

"I'm happy you find it amusing." She itched to hit him. Much as she did with her brothers, but in a completely different way.

"Lady Sophia could use a friend," he said softly. "Though I think that's the last thing you'd ever consider."

Livi's face warmed, all the way to her ears. "No, it's not," she said quietly. Then she sniffed.

"But her circumstances are almost as dire as yours. Even more so."

"Truly?" she couldn't help but ask. The lady was a conundrum.

He nodded once. "You might find an ally in her if you gave her half a chance."

"Have *you* found an ally in her?"

"Good God, no."

His response made Livi want to laugh. It was so genuine. Or at least she thought it was. How much of him was real? And how much was him playing the part of the gentleman everyone expected him to be? Was he feral at heart? She'd love to find out.

He jerked a thumb toward the stairs. "To bed, Miss Mayeux?" he asked.

Her heart skipped a beat. "I should think not," she blurted out, without even thinking.

He laughed again. "I was referring to you going to your bed. And me going to mine."

Livi stepped toward him and slowly stroked her hand down the front of his jacket. She let her voice drop down to a sultry purr. "Somehow, that doesn't sound nearly as entertaining," she said.

He stiffened beneath her hand.

She turned to go upstairs, but quick as lightning, his hand shot out and wrapped around her waist, drawing her flush against him. "Don't play with me, Miss Mayeux," he growled. His warm breath blew across the shell of her ear. His head bent, and his whiskers rubbed her temple as he spoke, he was that close. His voice rumbled across her skin like warm water, every bit as fluid, but not nearly as soothing. The hairs on her arms stood up. She stiffened her spine and pushed back from his embrace. It was like trying to press against stone. So she decided to try a different tack.

Livi stepped up onto her tiptoes and whispered in his ear. "What makes you think I'm playing, Mr. Hadley?" Then she gave him a little shove, which must have startled him, because he released her and reached for the wall to steady himself. She couldn't keep from giggling as she ran toward the stairs. He didn't follow. And she wasn't certain whether she was happy about that or really, really sad.

Six

WITH BOTH OF HIS ELBOWS RESTING ON THE BREAKFAST table, Gray held his head in his hands. If only he could get the throbbing in his brain and the ringing in his ears to stop. No more gin. Ever. What the devil had he been thinking? Perhaps he hadn't been thinking at all. That was a definite possibility in hindsight.

"Good morning," came Miss Mayeux's overly cheerful voice.

For lack of anything intelligent to say, Gray grunted in way of greeting.

"Ah, head aching from a wild night of debauchery and imbibing, is it?"

Gray opened his fingers wide enough to see her. "Shh."

An impish grin lit her face. "You need to eat sausage and drink a raw egg yolk."

The very idea turned his stomach. "Stop talking. You're making my head hurt worse."

She plopped down in a seat across from him. "I would have thought a man of your… heritage could hold his liquor better, Mr. Hadley. You English boys are a rather tame lot, aren't you?"

Gray lifted his head and glared at her. "No one has ever called me tame."

Her brow rose in disbelief. "Indeed? That is surprising."

"Elbows off the table, Mr. Hadley." Lady Sophia strode into the breakfast room and smiled at Miss Mayeux. "I thought we might head into town this morning. It is quite fashionable to be seen in the Pump Room during the morning hours."

"Take her, please. Then perhaps I'll be allowed some quiet," Gray complained.

Miss Mayeux shrugged. "I told him to eat sausage and drink a raw egg yolk, but he'd rather suffer in pain."

Lady Sophia's nose scrunched up. "Why would you tell him such a thing?"

"The poor man is suffering the aftereffects of too much imbibing."

Lady Sophia scoffed. "Well, that is exactly what he deserves then."

"You are too kind, my lady," Gray grumbled.

Lady Sophia smiled at him. "*I* did not pour drink down your throat, Mr. Hadley. Pray do not blame me if you do not enjoy the aftereffects." Then she turned her attention to Miss Mayeux. "There may be some fashionable gentlemen in the Pump Room this morning. If anyone catches your eye, point him out to me and I'll tell you what I know about the fellow."

"Marrying her off before she's even had a season?" Gray asked.

Lady Sophia shook her head. "We are here to practice for the season, Mr. Hadley." Then her face lit up. "Actually, if you are suffering so badly, the healing waters might do you some good."

The healing water was vile stuff, and given the choice, Gray would rather suffer all this day and the next than be forced to partake of "the cure." "I'd rather drink the raw egg yolk."

"Don't forget the sausage. The greasier the food, the better, Mr. Hadley."

Gray turned his attention back to the exotic American beauty. "Just how do you know so much about this, Miss Mayeux?"

"Well, I've known more than a few pirates and sailors and trappers in my day, Mr. Hadley. And one hears all sorts of interesting things."

Lady Sophia gasped and covered her heart with one hand. "Liviana, you shouldn't say such a thing."

"But it's true." She blinked innocently.

"Be that as it may, I'd rather not have anyone else learn the particulars. Pirates, for heaven's sake!"

"If I called them privateers, would that be better?"

Lady Sophia shook her head vehemently. "Absolutely not! On second thought I don't know that an excursion into town is wise. Perhaps we should spend the afternoon determining the best topics of conversation for the musicale this evening."

Gray groaned, his head pounding even harder. "Can't you determine that *in* the Pump Room?" With his ears, he'd hear them no matter where they were in the house.

"Ready to be rid of us, Mr. Hadley?" Miss Mayeux smirked.

"I would dearly love a little peace and quiet."

"Whether you're deserving of it is another matter." Lady Sophia sighed as she turned her attention to Miss

Mayeux. "I suppose we can go into town, but only if you promise to stay at my side."

"I would like to see a different set of walls. I haven't left my grandfather's house since we arrived in Bath."

◦◦◦

The half columns and honey-colored stone of the Pump Room gave the exterior a very grandiose feel. It did seem exactly the sort of architecture Livi would expect to see if she found herself in Rome. "It's very pretty," she muttered under her breath.

"Remember what we talked about yesterday, Miss Mayeux," Lady Sophia directed. "Don't mumble. Speak clearly enough for others to hear you, unless, of course, you shouldn't be saying something. In that case, close your mouth completely."

Livi shook her head. "I'm sorry. It took me by surprise."

"Much as you'll take Bath by surprise, if I have anything to say about it." The lady smiled kindly.

No matter what Livi had to say about it, she was sure. Lady Sophia obviously had plans for her. As soon as they entered the Pump Room, Livi wished she had remained back at her grandfather's house. Indeed, the morning hours did seem as though they were the fashionable times to see and be seen.

As soon as she stepped over the threshold, every eye in the room turned in her direction. Livi had never considered herself particularly shy, but she'd never been faced by a room full of people who didn't know her at all and who already looked at her with harsh judgment in their eyes. With the exception of Father Antonio, of course, judgmental man that he was.

"Breathe," Lady Sophia whispered.

Livi did take a deep breath and then wished she hadn't. There was a slight odor of eggs that had gone bad in the air. She coughed into her fist.

"You'll get used to it," Lady Sophia said quietly, which almost made Livi laugh. What happened to speak clearly or don't speak at all? Perhaps the same rules didn't apply to tutors. Lady Sophia linked her arm with Livi's. "We'll stroll about the room, shall we?"

There didn't seem to be a place to sit in the over-crowded room, so Livi nodded. What was wrong with the English? Could none of them smell the air? Or was her nose overly sensitive since her father's Lycan blood flowed through her veins.

"Many members of the *ton* holiday in Bath. They partake of the healing waters. Attend balls at the Assembly Room." Lady Sophia slowly led Livi toward a grand clock on one side of the room.

"Dancing?" Livi squeaked. And despite the warmth of the air in the Pump Room, she felt a chill wash over her.

"You do dance, don't you?" her tutor asked.

Livi shook her head. "Papa never saw the point."

Lady Sophia huffed indignantly as though such an idea was an affront to her personally. "Employing an instructor will be difficult here this time of year." She frowned. "I suppose I shall have to recruit Lord Radbourne and Mr. Hadley to help us in that regard."

Livi glanced up at the lady and frowned herself. "Do you not like the Hadley brothers?"

Lady Sophia laughed. "That obvious, is it?"

"Well, you did berate Mr. Hadley last evening for coming upon me in the kitchen, did you not?"

Lady Sophia stopped walking and turned her stare on Livi. "I thought you'd gone to bed."

Perfect. She clearly shouldn't have given herself away. But what's done was done. "At home, sometimes the only way to know what is truly going on is to eavesdrop. I suppose you'll tell me that isn't ladylike."

A smiled tugged at her companion's lips. "On the contrary, Miss Mayeux, many a lady has need to resort to that very thing. I've done so myself more times than I can count. I just don't enjoy being the one spied upon."

Nearby, a fellow cleared his throat and Livi looked up to find a tall man with blondish hair. His gaze raked from Lady Sophia's head all the way down to her toes, stopping at certain parts in between. It made Livi think of the way an alligator appraised its prey.

"My dear." The man smiled, and if it wasn't for the predatory gleam in his eye, Livi might have thought him handsome. "I never dreamed I would see you in Bath, of all places."

Lady Sophia must have seen the lascivious sparkle in the man's gaze because the muscles in her jaw tightened and she clipped out a greeting: "Lord Robert, always a pleasure."

It could hardly be a pleasure, however; the lady looked as tense as the bow of a fiddle. Apparently, prevarication was all right under certain circumstances, Livi noted.

"Indeed," Lord Robert replied smoothly. "Have you come to town with Lady Radbourne?"

"I *am* her companion."

The man heaved a sigh. "Taking such a position is beneath you, Sophie."

"On the contrary, it was by far the most complimentary offer I received, my lord. Do send my well wishes to your grandmother." Then she started to tow Livi around the man, but he stopped them when he placed his hand on Lady Sophia's arm.

"I had hoped you'd change your mind about that."

"Alas, I never shall, my lord. Please do let us pass. You are making a scene."

He released his hold on her arm and finally turned his attention to Livi, as though he had just realized she was there. It must have been the "us" that had clued him in. "We have not had the pleasure." He tipped his head in greeting.

"If you would like the pleasure," Lady Sophia began, "then I suggest you present yourself to the Earl of Holmesfield. If he deems you worthy, I'm certain he'll make a proper introduction between you and his granddaughter." Then she lowered her voice to a hiss, "Let us pass, Robert."

He did step aside, though a wounded look flashed across his face. "Always so wonderful to see you, my lady."

"Who was that?" Livi asked as soon as they were far enough away that she didn't think the gentleman could hear them.

"Lord Robert Hayburn."

That was all she intended to say? "He called you Sophie."

Lady Sophia closed her eyes for a moment as

though to compose herself. "He's known me a very long time. His sister is one of my dearest friends." Then she looked over at Livi. "Lady Madeline is now married to one of the Hadley brothers."

Ah, the brother her grandfather had sneered about and referred to as a kidnapper. "Oh."

"Whatever you've heard, Madeline is very happy and very much in love."

"How lucky she is then." Livi smiled at the thought. "Any hope I had for happiness or for finding love ended the day Papa put me on one of his frigates and shipped me away from my home." And if there had been any doubt about her future, her grandfather had made it perfectly clear that he would secure her an advantageous match. Happiness and love be damned.

"Mine ended the day my father died," Lady Sophia said quietly. Then she seemed to shake the unpleasant thought from her mind. "But, please don't think that your future is so bleak. You may be on a different continent than you'd like, but that doesn't mean you can't find love here."

"But my grandfather—"

"Is not in complete control," Lady Sophia interrupted. "We are just starting the process. You don't know who you'll happen to meet. Just keep an open mind, Miss Mayeux. That's all I ask."

For the first time since she stepped off that frigate in Bristol, Livi felt a ray of hope. Perhaps Mr. Hadley was correct. Perhaps Lady Sophia could use a friend, and honestly so could Livi. "Please," she looked at her companion and smiled, "call me Livi and I'd like to call you Sophie if that is what your friends do."

Lady Sophia smiled in return and squeezed Livi's arm. "I think I would like that, Livi."

"Lord Robert would be handsome if he didn't have a predatory look about him."

Sophie scoffed. "Lord Robert is not the sort I have in mind for you."

"What sort do you have in mind?"

"The sort who can make you happy."

"Lady Sophia!" barked an old woman a few feet away, seated at a table.

Sophie groaned. "I didn't realize *all* the Hayburns were on holiday here. Robert should have given me fair warning." She cast a sidelong glance at Livi and whispered, "The Duchess of Hythe is a bit of a dragon. Take my word for it, don't open your mouth unless absolutely necessary and unless you'd like her to jump down your throat." Then she turned a dazzling smile on the old woman. "Your Grace!" she gushed. "I had no idea you were here in Bath."

The old woman, who looked kindly despite Sophie's warning, gestured them forward. "Come and sit with me."

Sophie groaned again but made no attempt to take as much as a step toward the duchess.

"And be sprightly about it, Sophia Cole! I'm not as young as I used to be."

Finally Sophie crossed the floor toward the old woman, with Livi in tow. "I didn't want to intrude, Your Grace."

"Bah! You haven't changed a bit." The duchess snorted, and then she turned her gaze to a nearby table. "Herondale!" she barked. "Be a gentleman.

Give your chair to Lady Sophia and find one for her friend."

A middle-aged fellow bolted from his seat in his apparent haste to do the woman's bidding. Livi might normally have found the situation amusing if it wasn't for the pained expression on Sophie's face. The tutor had warned Livi the duchess was a dragon.

In no time, Herondale, whoever he was, had swiftly brought two chairs to the duchess' table and then made a hasty retreat as though afraid the old woman would ask him to do something else.

"Thank you, sir," Sophie called out to his retreating back.

"Pay the man no mind," the duchess directed. "Now sit, Sophia. I want to hear how you're getting along in your new position."

With no possible escape in sight, Sophie and Livi both sat. Sophie gestured to Livi as she feigned a smile. "Your Grace, I'd like you to meet Miss Mayeux. She's—"

The duchess waved a breezy and dismissive hand in the air. "Yes, yes, I know who she is. Holmesfield's recalcitrant granddaughter. When did you arrive, gel?" She turned her icy eyes on Livi.

But before Livi could answer, the duchess motioned, well... barked was more like it... for a footman to bring her another biscuit. While she did so, Sophia leaned close to Livi's ear and murmured, "The Duchess of Hythe gets away with more than most. Don't let her scare you. And don't let her outspoken nature worry you."

On the contrary, Livi found the duchess to be a refreshing change.

The duchess wore an eyeglass that hung around her neck and, at the moment, it was tucked directly between her breasts. With a mighty heave, she retrieved it and held it up to her left eye. The eye grew about ten times in size as her light blue orb blinked at Livi. "Pretty little thing," she said. Then she lowered her eyepiece slowly and cocked her head at Sophie. "Doesn't look like a banshee. She looks like her mother but a bit darker. Must be the French in her."

Livi did wish people would stop saying that as though it was an insult.

"I'm certain Lady Grace was just as delightful as Miss Mayeux is," Sophie replied and kicked Livi under the table. Blast, she must have been scowling.

Livi sat up straighter. "Lovely to meet you, Your Grace."

"Lovely?" the woman crowed. "It's never lovely to meet old ladies." Then she turned her eyes back to Sophie. "Madeline is worried about you."

Sophie shook her head. "She is sweet to do so, but there is no reason."

"So Violet Radbourne is treating you well?"

"Of course."

"And what of her scurrilous sons?"

"I see very little of them to be honest, Your Grace."

The old woman harrumphed. "Did you know they are opening a gambling establishment?" She lowered her voice to an annoyed hiss. "*My* granddaughter married to the proprietor of a gambling establishment."

An expression of sympathy settled on Sophie's face. "You know she loves him."

Finally a smile cracked the duchess' lips. "And that

is why he continues to breathe." Then she winked at Sophie before turning her attention to Livi. "How are you enjoying the Pump Room, Miss Mayeux?"

"To be quite honest," Livi said, leaning closer to the duchess, "I'd rather be anywhere than here, smelling these foul waters."

Sophie stiffened in her seat. "But we're happy to be here taking advantage of the healing waters," her tutor added.

The duchess interrupted her with a harsh snort. "Healing waters. It's more like social hour. Seeing and being seen." She narrowed an eye at Livi again. "Wouldn't you agree, Miss Mayeux?"

"There must be some benefit to smelling that rotten odor. It's worse than the docks in June," Livi said. "The fish wash ashore and the ships come into port. The men smell like they've been at sea for months and didn't have a pot of water to wash themselves in." She inhaled slightly, which made her cough. "I think this is worse." She winced.

Sophie dropped her head into her hands beside her. Livi was probably making a mess of things. "Do you remember we discussed appropriate topics of discussion?" Sophie hissed at her. "Unwashed men do not fall into that category."

"Did I hear something about unwashed men?" a voice asked from behind them.

Seven

THE SMELL OF UNWASHED MEN? *BON DIEU*. SHE'D made a mess of it, hadn't she? Livi glanced over her shoulder at the man. He was tall, with broad shoulders, and his handsome face was completed with a nose strong enough to match his jaw. "Lady Sophia." He bowed in the tutor's direction.

For the first time since Livi had met her, Sophie wore what appeared to be a genuine smile. "Henry Siddington, what brings you to Bath?" she asked pleasantly.

"Robert Hayburn invited me to accompany his family," the man said. He adjusted his jacket and looked a bit awkward for a moment. "I couldn't find a good reason to decline."

The duchess snorted and the man grinned at the old woman.

"The fact that he's a reprobate, a ne'er-do-well, and a drunkard were not enough for you?" Sophie asked, without even breaking the serene look on her face. Sophie shook her head at the tall fellow. "Certainly, you can find better company."

"One would think so," the duchess agreed.

The man arched a brow at the tutor. "Certainly, you can still skewer a man without even holding a sword." He clutched a hand to his chest as though her words had wounded him. "Pray introduce me to the lady, Sophie," he said.

Another gentleman who called her Sophie. Interesting.

"Oh, where are my manners? Miss Liviana Mayeux, this is my cousin Henry Siddington. I've known him since he was in short pants. We have played together most of our lives. Until we grew too old to play, that is."

Mr. Siddington looked offended. "One is never too old to play, my dear cousin." He turned his full gaze toward Livi. "Enchanting to meet you, Miss Mayeux," he said.

"Henry." Sophie tapped the man's hand. "I've need of you for a few moments this evening," she said. "You do plan to attend the Longboroughs' musicale, do you not?"

"I'd hoped to avoid it. I'd rather listen to Robert blather about his latest conquest than listen to young misses struggle to stay on tune." He shuddered, which brought a smile to Livi's face.

"And his conquests are many and varied," Sophie tossed in.

Talk about improper discussions.

"Yet you seem to have avoided falling into his trap," Mr. Siddington said. "Bravo for you." He clapped lightly and dramatically. Then his face softened. "Truly, how are you finding your position with Lady Radbourne?"

"Heavens." Sophie sighed heavily. "Everyone wants to know the same thing. Is there a wager on the book at White's that Lady Radbourne would throw me to wolves or something?"

Wolves? A sputtering sound escaped Livi at hearing that particular turn of phrase. Did the man know of Lycans? Mr. Hadley had made it seem as though no one knew of such things.

Mr. Siddington cast Livi a confused expression before turning his attention back to his cousin. "I suppose none of us are accustomed to seeing you in a subservient role. You can't blame us for that. You know you always have a place with me, Soph," he said gently. "And I won't even force you to wash chamber pots or bring tea."

Livi tried to hold in a giggle, but to no avail. She couldn't imagine Sophie bringing tea or washing chamber pots. Mr. Siddington was quite amusing. And handsome. And he seemed to be friendly enough. Her laughter drew his attention back to her once more.

"That sound is the most melodious tinkle I've heard all day." His brown eyes twinkled with happiness. "Miss Mayeux, you should do it more often."

Sophie shot him a stern glance and then looked at Livi. "Well-placed laughter is fine. But try to contain your mirth when you're able."

"Still spouting rules and regulations, Soph?" He made a noise in his throat. "At some point, you'll have to stop being quite so proper and have some fun."

"I'll have fun when I have my cottage back," Lady Sophia said in a soft voice.

Mr. Siddington's face fell into a sympathetic smile.

There was a story there. And Livi was determined to find out what was so special about this blasted cottage. She fanned her face. "I find it very stuffy in here," she said.

"Indeed," the duchess agreed.

"So, tonight, at the musicale—"

"That is a very nice try, Sophie," Mr. Siddington cut her off. "Only the loss of an unfortunate wager would make me attend that musicale. I'd like to still have my ears in working order this time tomorrow."

Sophie sighed. "You were always so difficult."

"One of my better qualities."

"Henry," Sophie pleaded. "Miss Mayeux is new to England and hardly knows a soul. If you won't attend the Longboroughs' musicale tonight, then I'll expect you to show your face at the Assembly Room tomorrow. And I'll expect you to partner Miss Mayeux for at least one dance."

Mr. Siddington gazed at Sophie critically and said in a teasing voice, "So I can tread upon her toes? You know dancing is not my forte."

"Then the two of you shall suit perfectly," Sophie said. She gave him a pleading look that reminded Livi of her brothers' hounds.

"Oh, good God. I'll do it." He bowed toward Livi. "Until tomorrow, Miss Mayeux?" he asked.

Dancing? Livi nodded reluctantly. He seemed like a nice enough man, especially if Sophie liked him. But dancing?

Sophie cleared her throat as though urging Livi to accept the offer.

"Until tomorrow," Livi muttered.

Mr. Siddington nodded to someone across the room, then smiled back at the women at the table.

"Do excuse me." Then he turned on his heel and made his way through the crowd to Lord Robert's side. Indeed, *that* man made the hair on the back of Livi's neck stand up. How was it possible that the two men were friends?

"If only Mr. Siddington could be a good influence on Robert," the duchess grumbled, "I'd leave the man half my fortune."

Anxiety gnawed at Livi's stomach. She looked at Sophie, who appeared to be engrossed in thought. "I believe you forgot one thing," Livi said.

"What is that?" Sophie asked, her brow knitting.

"I do not know how to dance."

The duchess gasped and Sophie rushed to soothe the old woman by placing her hand on one of the duchess'. "She is jesting, Your Grace. Miss Mayeux is a beautiful dancer."

And Lady Sophia was a fantastic liar, but Livi held her tongue. She and her tutor would have to have a long talk as soon as they left the odiferous Pump Room. How in the world could Livi possibly become a beautiful dancer in only one day?

❧

Gray slumped into a high-back chair in the front parlor, a copy of *The Times* in his hand. Thankfully his head pounded less, though that probably had more to do with the fact that no one but himself, the mostly silent servants, and the still sleeping Earl of Holmesfield were in residence than with the damned raw egg he'd swallowed. He couldn't imagine what had possessed him to try such a thing. Positively disgusting.

He heard the front door creak open just as Holmesfield's butler said, "My lord, welcome back."

"Thank you." Archer's voice filtered into the parlor. "Be a good man and tell me the best path to take to avoid Lady Sophia."

Gray sat a little straighter. "No one is here but me, Arch!" he called loudly.

A second later, his brother stood on the threshold, wearing the same clothes he'd donned the day before and with hair so rumpled that only a whore's fingers could have done the job. "You look like hell."

"So do you."

Archer scoffed as he leaned against the doorjamb. "What you see before you is a gentleman who is both relaxed and in high spirits."

His brother must have done even better at the tables after Gray returned to the house last night. "Hmm. What I see before me is a viscount who was just begging a butler to tell him how to escape a little slip of a lady."

Archer's golden eyes darkened. "A harpy, you mean. Where is she, by the way?"

Gray gestured toward the front window. "Out."

"A man of few words today, are you?"

"If your head ached like mine, you'd say very little yourself."

At that Archer chuckled, then pushed himself from the doorjamb and sauntered into the parlor, dropping onto the settee across from Gray. "Did the gin not set well, little brother?"

Gray growled low in his throat. Lycans had a high tolerance for spirits; however, even Lycans had their limits. "I had a little more than I should have," he agreed, "and then Miss Mayeux coerced me into drinking a raw egg."

Archer's face scrunched at the very thought. "A raw egg? Does that double for an aphrodisiac in America?"

An aphrodisiac? Gray narrowed his eyes on his brother. "It was to help with my headache."

"And did it?"

His head did feel a little better, or it had until his brother returned home. "I'm not sure."

Archer smirked. "And where is your little poodle?"

Gray didn't even bother to correct his brother. Doing so would only inspire Archer to needle him more. "With Lady Sophia. They headed into town for a morning in the Pump Room."

"Then we should be safe for the time being." Archer seemed to relax as he leaned back in his seat. "After you left last night, Lavendon took me to a very nice establishment."

"Filled with pretty doxies?"

Archer chuckled. "How did you know?"

"Your hair looks as though you spent all evening standing in the middle of a tempest."

Archer touched a hand to his hair. "They were a bit of a whirlwind. But that's not where I was going with this. Well, not really. With the spot we're using off the Thames for our establishment, what do you think about transporting a barge full of wenches to see to our customers' needs and perhaps provide distraction from the play on the tables?"

Gray scoffed. "I think Wes would put a bullet in your skull. He dreamed up this idea as a source of income for each of us, not so we could make ourselves glorified flash men. He has a very proper wife, you might remember."

"His connection to the Hayburns is a thorn in my side."

"I cannot even imagine what the duchess would do to us if we connected her granddaughter to a place filled with whores. She'd turn us all into eunuchs before slowly murdering us."

Archer scowled. "Her Grace is here in town, by the way. Lavendon told me as much last night. Why don't we abandon all this nonsense in Bath and head for London?"

That was exactly what Gray had wanted to begin with. But before he could say as much, someone cleared her throat in the doorway. At the same moment the scent of violets drifted into the room. Lady Sophia. Gray's and Archer's eyes both shot to the doorway to find their tutor frowning at them with her arms folded across her chest. They both leapt to their feet like chastened schoolboys.

"London?" she asked. "Did I overhear you correctly, Lord Radbourne?"

Archer looked supremely satisfied. "Afraid you'll miss me, sweetheart?"

"I have asked you not to call me that."

"And I have asked you to go away." Archer grinned unrepentantly. "Apparently, neither of us is to get our wish where the other is concerned."

Lady Sophia heaved a sigh. "Neither of you are escaping to London. I need your assistance here."

"You need us?" Archer quipped.

She narrowed her eyes on him. "You are to help me with Miss Mayeux, both of you."

"She's just one slight girl," Archer protested. "Surely you can handle her all on your own, sweetheart."

Lady Sophia straightened her spine. "I have yet to send my weekly report to Lord Eynsford. Please do not make me have to inform him that you are being difficult, my lord."

A muscle twitched near Archer's eye.

Gray cleared his throat. "I don't see why you need us. Holmesfield doesn't want us anywhere near the girl, and serving as escorts is really unnecessary, all things considered."

A frown marred Lady Sophia's pretty face. "I'm not certain what all I'll need you for, Grayson. But today… Well, today I need your help in teaching Miss Mayeux to dance. I'm afraid she doesn't know how, and tomorrow we'll be at the Assembly Room."

Teaching Liviana Mayeux to dance? Gray's heart sped up at the thought of holding the chit in his arms. Honestly, staying in Bath couldn't be that taxing, could it? He could stay a day or two more. London wasn't going anywhere.

"If we do this," Archer began, "may we be excused from the musicale this evening?"

She glared at him. "Why, my lord? So you may find your own entertainments as you obviously did last night?"

"One must be entertained," Archer returned.

"But must one wear the same clothes two days in a row?" She sighed heavily and turned her attention back to Gray. "Please meet us in the music room in half an hour for her first lesson. And please make sure your brother is actually presentable." Then she turned on her heel and disappeared down the corridor.

"Who knew," Archer said quietly, "that she paid attention to my attire?"

Gray couldn't help the laugh that escaped him. "You look a mess, Arch. Have you even peeked in a mirror? I'm not certain you can be ready in half an hour."

"Then won't that little harridan be disappointed," his brother grumbled.

Eight

LIVI BIT THE INSIDE OF HER CHEEK AS SHE STOOD ALONE in her grandfather's music room. Aside from a small piano in the corner, the rest of the room was empty. Settees and chairs had all been removed from the space so that nothing would hinder her first dancing lesson. First and last. *Bon Dieu*! She would never be ready in time for tomorrow night. Perhaps she could plead a headache and stay abed instead of heading to the Assembly Room. At least it would gain her a little time to learn what she was doing before being thrust into a ballroom.

"You look like a lady who has been sentenced to the gallows." Mr. Hadley's voice startled her from the threshold.

Shaken from her musings, Livi glanced up to find the handsome Lycan leaning his broad frame against the doorjamb. She laid a hand upon her chest to quiet her rapidly beating heart. "Mr. Hadley, you frightened me."

A small smile quirked the corner of his mouth. "You seem a much more stalwart creature than that. I didn't think you frightened so easily, Miss Mayeux."

She returned his smile with one of her own. "All these English formalities. 'Miss Mayeux' makes me feel like someone's governess. Please call me Livi."

Surprise flashed in his dark eyes and he pushed himself off from the wall. "Livi, then," he said as he took a step toward her. "You may call me Gray, if you'd like. Just don't let Lady Sophia hear you. You'll get us both in trouble."

Livi couldn't help but laugh. How could such a thing get him in trouble? "I had no idea your mother's companion held such sway over your life, Gray."

A frown marred his brow, but it vanished as quickly as it had appeared. He studied her face for a moment before saying, "She's not really my mother's companion."

If a big green alligator had rushed into the room, Livi wouldn't have been more surprised. Her mouth dropped open. Was there something between Gray and Sophie? Was that why her tutor had berated him the night before?

"She's not?" Her voice came out in little more than a whisper. "What is she to you?" And why did Livi care? That was a much better question.

He shook his head. "Actually, you're the only one I can tell the truth to, if you can be trusted. And I think you can. You're in much the same situation that I'm in myself, after all." He shrugged. "You know what I am. What Archer is. Our older half brother, our pack alpha, has hired Lady Sophia to turn us into gentlemen, as he found our behavior in polite society to be a bit lacking. But such a situation would ruin the lady in question, so to the rest of the world she is simply our mother's companion."

Livi's mouth fell open even farther. "He finds you too wild?" she asked, not quite believing Gray. After all, he was the tamest Lycan of her acquaintance.

"Among other things."

"But you seem so tame," she replied, and then wished the words back when he looked wounded. "I mean you look so average."

One brow arched at her.

"Oh, you know what I mean," she finally said.

He stared at her for a moment with such a serious face that Livi was afraid to speak. Then that slow grin she was getting so used to spread across his face. He took one large step toward her, his head tilting as he appraised her face. Appraised much too closely for comfort. "I'm not certain I do," he drawled. "Pray tell."

Livi stumbled momentarily over her own tongue. It suddenly seemed unwieldy and much too clumsy for her mouth. Gray chuckled, and heat crept up Livi's face.

"You were saying that you think I look average." His quirky grin made her want to smile along with him. And fan herself. Fan herself profusely, because it was suddenly growing unbearably hot in the room. Leave it to this man to break the chill she'd felt in her bones since she'd arrived in his country.

"'Tame' was my original choice of words."

"Tame? No one but you has ever referred to me as tame." He rubbed his chin between his thumb and forefinger as though he was thinking it over. "I feel a little disempowered by your estimation of me."

"Wounded your pride, did I?" She leaned her

elbows on the pianoforte and tried her best to appear unconcerned. "You probably work very hard to seem disreputable."

"On the contrary, trouble just seems to find us."

Livi wondered absently who "us" was.

"The Hadley brothers," he clarified, without her even having to ask.

She snorted. Sophie would probably scold her properly for making that noise. But Gray just grinned even broader.

"Never done anything to provoke the heaps of trouble that have fallen upon your head?" she asked.

He lowered his voice to a whisper. "Never," he said softly. "I am a paragon of virtue."

Just then, his older brother strolled into the room. "First, you discuss the birthmark on her thigh. Now you're discussing her virtue." Radbourne made a clicking sound with his tongue. "A wretched idea if her virtue is important to her."

Gray colored profusely.

"You discussed my birthmark?" she hissed at him.

"You, Miss Mayeux, are the one who brought up the subject of your birthmark." Gray avoided her censure.

"And you repeated it." She shook her head at him, feeling quite a bit like Sophie must feel on a daily basis. "I cannot believe you discussed my personal comment to you with your brother."

He tugged at the lapels of his jacket, as though it was suddenly too tight. "I couldn't believe you brought it up in the first place." Gray turned to his brother, who leaned casually in the doorway, a bored expression gracing his handsome face. "And you talk too much," he grumbled at Radbourne. "You're such an arse."

"Sweet nothings in my ear will get you nowhere, Grayson," he said as he crossed the floor and dropped onto the piano bench. "You probably owe the lady an apology," he added as he began to pluck out a tune. "For mentioning her unmentionables."

"I beg your pardon," Grayson grumbled.

"You talked about my unmentionables too?" Livi raised an octave. She would have to do him bodily harm.

"I most certainly did not." His eyes roamed down her body. "I can't discuss things I haven't seen," he drawled slowly. Then he arched an amused brow at her again. "I can discuss it whenever you'd like, however."

"Good Lord," Radbourne muttered. "The two of you will be leg-shackled before the fortnight is over if you keep that up." He scowled at them both. "Matter of fact, if you're going to continue making calf eyes at her, I'll take my leave," he quipped.

Livi jumped to deny his assumption. But Gray held up a hand to stop her. "I'll make calf eyes at her if I want to."

He would? Livi's heart skipped a beat. She'd assumed the heated glances were nothing of importance. Just a bit of flirtation. Was she wrong?

"I was just explaining to Miss Mayeux the odd circumstances regarding Lady Sophia's employment with Mother. Or lack of employment with Mother."

Lord Radbourne stopped playing and spun on the bench to face them both. "You told her that the harridan is here to teach us our manners?" He shook his head with what she assumed was disgust. "Have you taken leave of your senses? I'd never admit that to a lady I had a romantic interest in."

"He doesn't have any romantic interest in me," Livi blurted.

But Gray didn't deny his brother's accusations. He just looked at her. His eyes were so serious that he could probably see all the way to her soul with his piercing gaze.

"I didn't say marital interest, Miss Mayeux," Radbourne said over a laugh.

"You two think you're so scandalous with your improper discussions." Livi stepped away from them, hoping to calm her pounding heart, since she knew full well they could both hear it. "But you forget that I have brothers just like you. Worse, even. I've heard every bawdy joke ever told. And I've seen more in my years than the ladies you're used to dealing with."

Gray looked skeptical about her comment.

"I grew up on the docks," she rushed to inform him.

"And just what does growing up on the docks entail?" Radbourne challenged.

Livi suddenly felt discomfited by the tone of this conversation. Jesting about her birthmark was one thing. But asking her to admit to things a proper lady would never do couldn't possibly be to her advantage. Her grandfather would have an apoplexy at just the idea of mentioning such things. So perhaps…

A rustle of skirts in the doorway brought Livi out of her musings. "When in doubt, Miss Mayeux, take the high road." Sophie shot both men a scolding glance. Gray actually flushed beneath her censure. Radbourne, however, tried to pretend she wasn't in the room. He failed. But he did try. "Do not let men like Lord Radbourne drag you down to their depths."

"But it would be your job to lift me up from the depths of disrespectability, Lady Sophia," Radbourne said with an unrepentant grin. He laid his fingers on the keys again and began to pluck out a Vivaldi tune. "Shall we get to work teaching Miss Mayeux to dance? Something tells me Grayson is anxious to hold her in his arms."

And she was anxious to be held. What did that say for her?

Sophie scoffed. "My lord, if you would be so kind as to let me direct these lessons, I would greatly appreciate it."

"Enough to let me leave them all together?" Radbourne suggested as his brow rose expectantly.

"Would that I could," she grumbled. "Up, Lord Radbourne. Your mother will play as soon as she joins us here."

"I'm perfectly capable of playing, my lady," he insisted.

Sophie heaved a sigh as though dealing with the viscount would be the death of her. "And I'm sure you perform beautifully, my lord—"

"No one has complained thus far, sweet—"

"However," Sophie cut him off, her voice suddenly much louder than his, "it will be important for Livi to see each dance demonstrated as well as trying them herself. Therefore I'll need the talents of both of you gentlemen for this endeavor."

"Mother's back?" Gray asked.

"Where was she anyway?" Radbourne reluctantly rose from the piano bench.

Sophie ignored the men and smiled instead at Livi. "We are in luck. Lady Radbourne was successful in her mission this morning with Lady Cowper."

Mission? What in the devil was Sophie talking about? Livi had never heard of the woman. "Lady Cowper?" Livi asked.

Sophie nodded with glee. "Emily Cowper is one of the patronesses of Almack's. She is quite an important woman in society, with more than a little power and sway. We are fortunate Lady Cowper has always been fond of Madeline Hadley. Everything in life is who you know, Livi."

"Or who you were born to be," Lord Radbourne chimed in.

"Not necessarily," Sophie shot back more forcefully than necessary. "You aren't welcomed into prestigious homes, my lord, despite your title and newfound wealth."

"And who says I want to be?" the viscount returned.

"This isn't about you, Archer Hadley. This is about Livi. And your mother and her grandfather do want her to enjoy a warm welcome in society."

Bon Dieu. Livi's stomach roiled at the thought. "This was for me?" she squeaked. "Lady Radbourne's visit to this Lady Cowper?"

"Livi, you look a little green." Sophie stepped closer to her, as though to examine her color. She clutched Livi's hand in hers and squeezed her fingers reassuringly. "Take a deep breath. It's nothing to fret over. Lady Radbourne simply secured Lady Cowper's permission for you to waltz tomorrow night."

Which did not help Livi's roiling stomach in the least. She gulped. "Do I have to?"

A frown marred Sophie's face. "Well, you should be prepared. There will only be two waltzes at the very most. But you should be able to do so, in case you're asked. You're such a beautiful girl, so exotic. I'm certain gentlemen will want to waltz with you, Livi."

"I know Gray does," Radbourne tossed in for good measure.

Did he? Livi's eyes shot to Gray who was glaring at his older brother. "Will you mind your own affairs?" he growled.

"Well, Grayson is out of luck," Sophie continued. "Lord Radbourne, you'll partner Miss Mayeux, and Mr. Hadley will assist me in showing her the steps."

Lord Radbourne rose from the piano bench and grinned rakishly as he bowed before Livi. "My dear, I have always been the luckiest Hadley brother."

"That is the damned truth of it," Gray grumbled, but Livi heard him just the same.

"Language, Mr. Hadley," Sophie admonished. Apparently their tutor had heard him as well.

Gray glared at Lady Sophia. She was damned lucky he hadn't said something much worse. Handing Livi over to Archer, for God's sake. Gray sighed. He shouldn't have been surprised. Lady Sophia would never want Archer to partner with her for the sake of demonstration. Insufferable prick that he was, Archer would most likely stomp on her toes out of spite and make a complete nuisance out of himself just to torture her. None of that would help Livi at all.

But even knowing why Lady Sophia had made

the decision she did, Gray still didn't like it. He wanted nothing more than to take Livi in his own arms and hold her tight. The very thought of Archer being in such close proximity to the enchanting chit was maddening.

When else would he get the opportunity to hold Livi Mayeux close? It wasn't as though he could ask her to dance tomorrow evening at the Assembly Room. She was in Bath as a precursor to her first season of husband hunting. And Gray would never make her grandfather's long list of potential husbands, let alone his short one. The memory of her delicate hand on his chest the evening before had played across his mind more than once during the day. His heart actually constricted at the thought of watching a stream of London dandies whisk her out on the dance floor in their attempts to woo her. "If we attend the musicale tonight, can we be excused from the dancing tomorrow?" he asked.

Lady Sophia turned her attention on him, staring at him as though he'd grown a second nose. "No, you may not. We are not bartering, Mr. Hadley. Both you and your brother would be wise to accept your situation. You'll attend the functions I tell you to, and you'll behave like gentlemen the entire time you're there."

So she was going to force him to watch others pay court to Livi. Bloody wonderful. She'd probably do more than scold him if he were to remove said dandies' hands for touching Livi. Behave like a gentleman. To what end?

"Ah, here's your mother now!" Lady Sophia

clapped her hands together. "Lady Radbourne, I think we should start with a waltz. What do you think?"

Gray's mother stepped into the music room and nodded with the enthusiasm of a child about to get a sweet. "Wonderful idea, my dear. I think Holmesfield would agree."

Holmesfield could go hang. Gray shook his head. What the devil was wrong with him? He didn't have any reason to be jealous or sullen. Livi was nothing to him… Except that there was something about her he truly enjoyed. Something about her irreverence. There was something freeing in that she was aware of his Lycan heritage and what it meant. Perhaps her Lycan blood just called to him. After all, he didn't know any other girls with Lycan fathers.

"Are you all right, Grayson?" Lady Sophia asked, an urgent tone to her voice, shaking him out of his reverie.

"Why wouldn't I be?" Gray stood a little straighter.

"She's been calling your name for the last two minutes," Archer replied with a frown. "Now I'm concerned. Are you all right?"

"Perfectly," he clipped out. What else could he say? "Let's get this over with, shall we?"

Lady Sophia's blue eyes darkened with annoyance, but she nodded. "Brilliant idea." Then she turned to Livi. "This is actually a very simple dance, though it's still considered scandalous in some circles due to the proximity of the dancers to each other. There are three beats and you should follow the lead of your partner." She glanced back at Gray and gestured him forward. "Do you mind, Mr. Hadley?"

Would it matter either way? Gray heaved a sigh.

Things would go easier if he just got on with it. So he stepped toward his tutor, bowed, then placed his right hand on the small of her back. At the moment his mother began to play Weber's "Invitation to the Dance," Lady Sophia placed her hand on his upper arm. "You'll stand like so, Livi. Now Mr. Hadley will take his first step toward me with his left foot and I'll step back at the same time."

On the beat, Gray did exactly that, stepping forward once and then to his right. Excellent partner that she was, Lady Sophia followed effortlessly.

"You'll make a quarter turn for each of the three beats, and you'll essentially move around as though you were in a square, stopping in each corner. So, think of the steps as 'right foot back, left foot side, right foot stop. Then, left foot back, right foot side, and left foot stop.'"

"I count to three on the beats," Archer added. "Count it with the music. One, two, three. One, two, three."

Gray grumbled, "I had no idea he could count that high."

"Mr. Hadley," Lady Sophia admonished. "Do behave yourself."

She had no idea how well-behaved he was being at the moment. Gray scowled at her. As pretty as Lady Sophia was, he'd rather be in Archer's shoes. And he wasn't at all pleased with the fact that his brother was about to sweep Livi into his arms.

Silently, they continued the steps a few more beats, and then Lady Sophia stepped out of Gray's reach and turned back to Livi and Archer. "Now it's your turn. Step into the middle of the room."

Gray backed up and leaned against the wall, hoping he gave off an air of nonchalance as Archer placed his hand on Livi's back. Gray watched her nervously smile up at his brother.

"I don't think I have any rhythm," Livi said.

But Lady Sophia paid her no attention. "Listen for the beat and follow Lord Radbourne's lead."

Archer stepped forward and Livi stumbled backward, her arms flailing wildly before she fell on her very shapely derriere.

"What the devil is wrong with you?" Gray boomed before he bounded off the wall at the exact moment his mother rose from the piano bench with a gasp. Gray was hovering over Livi in the blink of an eye, offering his hand to her. "Are you all right, my dear?"

Her face flushed the color of a tomato, but she took his hand anyway. "Thank you, Gr—Mr. Hadley."

Gray glared at his brother. "You're supposed to be helping her, not sending her crashing to the ground."

"How was I to know one step would send her flailing? I've never taught anyone to dance before," Archer returned hotly.

"Maybe by using your brain," Gray growled.

Archer threw up his hands. "I don't have to put up with this nonsense." Then he turned his glare on Lady Sophia. "Not from him. Not from you. You want to write a nice little dossier for Eynsford? Be my guest. But I am through with dancing and musicales and soirees and everything else you come up with to torture me." He started for the corridor in a huff.

"You are a beast, Lord Radbourne!" Lady Sophia called to his retreating back.

"Something on which we can finally agree," he retorted before vanishing from view.

Nine

Livi's mouth fell open in surprise when both Sophie and Lady Radbourne bustled from the room after the viscount. *Bon Dieu!* What in the world had just happened? "I warned him I didn't have any rhythm," she muttered.

Gray squeezed her hand, the one he was still holding after helping her back to her feet. "It's not your fault Archer is an arse."

Blasted dancing. No wonder Papa had never thought it was worth her learning. If she never danced again, she'd be happy. "It's not his fault I'm dreadful at this."

Gray chuckled, and the warm sound fluttered across her heart. "You've taken one step, Livi. I hardly think you can say you're dreadful."

"I wouldn't even call it a step. I fell flat on my arse, Gray." She looked up at him, finding his dark eyes twinkling at her.

"So you did," he agreed. Then he pulled her into his arms, much closer than Lord Radbourne had done. "You shouldn't ever let anyone else ever hold you like this." He took a step forward, making her take a step back. Then he directed her one step to the left, and then he paused a beat before leading her into another step backward. "See," he said with a grin, "you're doing beautifully now."

She followed his lead, stepping to the right. "I'm dancing?"

"Who needs music?" He turned her toward the left.

Apparently no one. Livi stared up at him, and he took her around the music room as though she'd been dancing all her life.

"I'm holding you closer than I should, but doing so, I can lead more easily. Tomorrow, whichever lucky fellow finds you in his arms will be much farther away than I am. So close your eyes, get a sense of the rhythm of the steps, and you'll be fine."

Obediently, Livi did close her eyes, following his lead with each step. "Lord Radbourne said you wanted to dance with me."

"Any man would."

"Will you dance with me tomorrow?"

"I don't think that will be possible."

Livi opened her eyes to look at him. Why not? "Are you not going to the Assembly Room?"

"Lady Sophia has made it quite clear that I am."

He didn't want to be seen with her in public? Was that it? No matter that it felt as though she was improving in her steps; perhaps she was truly abysmal. "Am I that bad?"

He chuckled. "Why would you think such a thing?"

"You don't want to be seen with me?" she suggested.

Gray shook his head. "That is hardly it, Livi. It will

be better for you, for your chances on the marriage mart if you're not seen with me."

She did stumble then. He caught her with a hand at the small of her back. Her breath hitched at the contact as he pulled her flush against himself. "Are you all right?" he asked, his voice soft and silky, raising gooseflesh on her arms. She shook off the feeling.

"I'm clumsy as a newborn colt," she said as she blew at a lock of hair that had fallen across her forehead. Evidently, her hair had taken a tumble when she'd landed on her backside.

Gray reached up to brush her hair back, loosening his arms from their hold around her as he did so. The heat of him was suddenly replaced by the chill of the room. She shivered lightly as he tucked her hair back with a loose pin. "Cold?" he asked.

Not very likely. Not with him standing so close. Not with him holding her in his arms. "No," she said with a heavy sigh.

"Frustrated?" he asked casually.

"Quite." She inhaled deeply, taking in the sandalwood scent of him. She impulsively wanted to bury her nose against his cravat and take him in.

"I would give my right arm to know what you're thinking right now," he said softly as he tipped her chin up. His dark eyes twinkled.

"I would give my right arm for you not to know what I'm thinking right now," she breathed.

His eyes darkened perceptibly as he regarded her from below lowered lids.

It was a good time for a change of subject. "Will Sophie come back with your brother?" she asked as she stepped back from him. He let her go, looking at her with a half smile, as though he knew what he did to her. He probably did.

"I highly doubt that Archer will be back. He's having way too much fun vexing poor Lady Sophia, not to mention Mother."

"This is all sport for him, is it not?"

Gray thought about it for a moment. "I'm sure he didn't mean to knock you to the floor. He'll most likely find you to apologize later, but his pride is probably as bruised as your bottom at the moment."

"I feel certain you're not supposed to be talking about my bottom," Livi replied as she rubbed at it absently. She hadn't really landed that hard. But it smarted, none the less.

"I would volunteer to kiss it and make it better." He appraised her face much too closely. "But that would be even more inappropriate."

Bon Dieu! She could see now why he was known for his scandalous behavior. If he did this with every lady of his acquaintance, he probably had them swooning into a dead faint and landing directly in his arms. Heat crept up her cheeks. She was probably as red as a ripe strawberry. She put her hands on her hips. "If you think me some common tavern wench, Mr. Hadley," she said, taking great care to use his formal name, "you are sadly mistaken. Do take care with your offensive comments."

He grinned unrepentantly at her. "Offensive?" His gaze slid slowly down her body, doing odd things she didn't understand to her belly. "I highly doubt you found my comment offensive."

"Because I'm a hoyden?"

"Because you enjoyed it." He stepped closer to her and pulled her back into his arms, his hand on the small of her back. She clutched at the lapels of his jacket. "Hardly tame now, am I?" He untangled her hands from their frantic clutch of his lapels and placed one on his arm.

Was that what this was about? Her remark about him being tame? "Did I bruise your pride, Gray?"

His brow shot upward in surprise.

"It's just you're not quite like the other Lycans of my acquaintance."

"Shh. Just dance with me, Livi," he said softly.

Then he began to move. His leg went forward, his body so close to hers that they moved as one. Her leg went back along with his.

"Now look at me," he quietly encouraged. She did. And immediately wished she hadn't. Something hovered in the depths of his gaze, something hot and unsettling. Something that made a most delicious shiver creep up her spine. His pace quickened as he led her around the floor. He counted silently for her, his lips barely moving as he whispered, "One, two, three. One, two, three. One, two, three…" She couldn't look away from him. If she did, she would break the spell. She should break the spell, but drat it all, she was dancing. And she was enjoying it. Just a few minutes more couldn't do any harm, could it?

He moved so effortlessly, like he'd been spinning ladies about the dance floor since he was in short pants. "When did you learn to dance, Gray?" She was growing a bit breathless at the exertion.

He cleared his throat before he spoke. "I feel like I've never danced before, Livi Mayeux." One corner of his mouth quirked, his grin a bit self-deprecating. "In fact, I feel as unwieldy as a newborn colt myself."

"Clumsy," she corrected.

"I most certainly am not clumsy." He chuckled loudly, the sound warm and rich as it hung in the air between them.

"No, I'm the clumsy one." He wasn't counting for her anymore. He was talking. "Will I be expected to dance and carry on a conversation tomorrow night? All at the very same time?"

"That depends on the dance, your partner, and how much he's enthralled by your beauty."

She snorted. And immediately regretted it. "Apologies," she murmured. "Sophie would flay me for that." She tried to get past it. But it was damn hard with him looking down at her with that quirky grin. The one that made her heart skip. "Can you hear it?" she whispered without censoring her words.

"Your delicate little snuffle?" he said with a laugh. "Yes, I heard it. I'm not deaf, you know."

She hadn't been referring to that social blunder. She was referring to the frantic beat of her heart.

He continued smoothly, "I think it's adorable. And hope you never, ever become too cultured to do it."

If he were one of her brothers, she would slap him. But he wasn't. There were so many different social restrictions at play here. And she didn't know which way was the right way to continue. "May I speak my mind with you, Gray?" she asked, her voice full of more emotion than she'd intended to share.

"That is my most fervent wish," he said.

And she believed him.

"I'm scared to death." The words just rushed from her mouth. They came out harsh and without any care.

His hand spread on the center of her back, his fingers widening as he pulled her slightly closer to him. He held her against him as he continued to waltz. He hadn't counted for quite some time. And she was dancing as though she had been doing it her whole life.

"You're not scared of *me*, are you?" He looked slightly taken aback.

"Terrified," she whispered back. She may as well be honest. "Admit it. I know you can hear it." She squeezed his bicep. "My heart, you dolt. You can hear the beat of my heart."

He stopped dancing, which momentarily unsettled her. She fell against him. A moment before, she wouldn't have thought she could get any closer to him. But now she was. Much closer. "I assumed the rhythm of your heart was because of your excitement to find out you're such a beautiful dancer after all."

"You know that's not the case, but thank you for trying to preserve my feelings."

He swiped a hand down his mouth, an act of frustration if she'd ever seen one. And she'd seen plenty with her brothers. "I think we should stop our lesson now."

"Stop?" She sounded like an addled parrot, even to her own ears.

"Yes, stop," he said firmly. He stepped several paces back from her and spun to look out the window.

"Are you vexed at me, Grayson Hadley?" she asked, punching her fists into her hips. She'd opened up, told him what she was feeling. He'd said it was his most fervent wish. How dare he dismiss her so easily?

"I'm not vexed," he said to the window. "I'm…" He stopped and shook his head fiercely.

"You're…" she prompted him to continue.

"I'm intrigued, Livi."

Livi's heart kicked up again.

He spun back to face her, his look harsh and direct. "I'm so intrigued that all I can think about is the beat of your heart, and I want to search your body to find all the places where you're ticklish. All the ways to make you giggle and, yes, even snort." He stalked past her toward the door.

Where the devil was he going? "I never took you for a coward," Livi taunted, hoping to say something that would make him stay.

"And I never took you for a whore. So, don't entice me to treat you like one." And with that last comment, he turned on his heel. But then he turned back at the last moment. "Know this well, Livi. If you give me even the slightest bit of encouragement, I'll act upon it. And I am the last thing your grandfather, and probably your father, wants for you."

"What about what I want?" she whispered.

"How far have your wants gotten you? You're stuck in England, far from your home, searching for a life your grandfather wants you to have." He tilted his head and said slowly, enunciating each word, "So much for your wants."

❦

Gray stared into his tankard, wondering where his ale had gone. Damn it all, he needed another just to take his mind off Livi. Just as he lifted his head to catch the tavern wench's attention, a hand clapped him on the back with more force than was necessary. It was a good thing his tankard was empty.

"Have you even had a chance to sober up after last night's indulgences?" Nathaniel Hayburn, the Marquess of Lavendon, dropped into the seat across from Gray's.

"Bugger off, Lavendon."

The marquess chuckled. "Charming as ever, Hadley."

"Well if you don't like my company, you don't have to stay. I don't recall having invited you to join me."

"I didn't say that I don't like your company. Besides, we are relations of a sort these days, aren't we?"

Not really. Lavendon was Wes' brother-in-law, not Gray's. No matter how similar they looked. Gray gestured to the taproom at large. "This place is well beneath your usual fare. What brings you to lower yourself to this point?"

Lavendon shivered dramatically. "Hiding from my grandmother. What else?" Then he grinned and leaned forward in his seat. "Radbourne said Sophie Cole is in Bath with the rest of you."

"She *is* Mother's companion. Where one is, the other can usually be found."

"And you sound so happy about it." Lavendon laughed again. "I would gladly take her off your hands, you know."

"You mean Mother's hands," Gray corrected. "And I'd be glad to see her go. Perhaps you could make her a *proper* offer this time around."

Lavendon shook his head. "And give the little minx that satisfaction? Hardly. She had her chance to be my marchioness well before her fall from grace. Besides, I'm patient. She'll come begging soon enough."

Lady Sophia beg? Gray doubted she'd ever done such a thing in her life. She could be living on the streets without two farthings to rub together, and she'd still possess a refined air of superiority. "Do let me know when that happens."

Lavendon sat back in his chair and gestured for the barmaid. "As long as it's not blue ruin, I'll have whatever Mr. Hadley is drinking."

Gray nodded at the woman. "I'll have another as well." And he'd need it. If not to keep his mind off Livi, then to block out Lavendon's ramblings. The marquess could bluster with the best of them, and he looked as though he was prepared to stay the rest of the evening. Just Gray's blasted luck.

"Your turn. Why are you hiding here, Hadley?"

Because it was that or sit in his room and think about all the ways he could take Livi's virtue. "I'm not hiding. It's just better than being at Holmesfield's."

Lavendon nodded. "Almost word for word what Radbourne said last evening when we left the card tables."

"Well, we are brothers."

"True. Though Robert and I have never been accused of being remotely similar."

With the exception that both men had apparently proposed to Lady Sophia before her father lost his fortune, and both gentlemen had offered her a different kind of position all together once they learned of her penniless state.

After the barmaid deposited two tankards on the table, Lavendon eyed Gray as though he was sizing him up. "So," the marquess began, "this gambling establishment you're pursuing. Are you looking for investors?"

Gray shrugged. "We haven't been. Archer seems to have more than enough funds at his disposal."

"Easily obtained, easily lost," Lavendon replied. "Especially as recklessly as he plays."

Except that Archer seemed to have acquired some sort of Midas touch as though it was impossible for him to lose any game, match, or wager, no matter how ridiculous the odds.

"My sister is wrapped up in all of this now. I'd feel more comfortable if you'd let me in on this deal. To ensure her future, mind you."

Gray heaved a sigh. "Then you should probably be having this conversation with Weston."

"Ah, but Weston listens to you."

That explained the marquess' sudden chumminess. "Turned you down flat, did he?" Gray asked.

Lavendon's smirk reappeared. "Said it was an endeavor for the brothers Hadley."

"Well, there you have it then."

The marquess shook his head stubbornly. "You don't have a sister, Gray. You can't possibly understand my worry for Madeline."

What could he say to that? Gray didn't have a sister, well, other than by marriage. It couldn't possibly be the same thing. He had no idea the worries one might have if one did possess a sister by blood. Still... "She does have a husband to worry about her now."

"You can't blame me for questioning his judgment. He did abscond with Maddie, after all."

"Something she is quite happy about, as I'm sure you know."

"Love is blind."

"But lust is not," Gray muttered to himself as an image of Liviana Mayeux flashed once again in his mind. Had he ever lusted after a woman the way he did her? Not that he could remember. Damn it all.

"I beg your pardon?" Lavendon looked more than mildly affronted.

Gray shook his head and forced a smile to his face. "Sorry, something Archer used to say. I wasn't impugning Maddie, just finishing the line. 'Love is blind, but lust is not.'"

The marquess relaxed back in his seat and lifted the tankard to his lips. "Something I imagine you know a thing or two about."

"Lust?" Gray couldn't help the laugh that escaped him. "I'm sure I have just as much experience with lust as you do." Despite Lavendon's good name, he was a notorious rake, after all.

"I imagine so, living in the same home with Sophie Cole. I'd have to take icy baths on a daily basis, were I you."

At that Gray snorted. What an absurd thing to say. "I can assure you, Lavendon. Never once have I had a lascivious thought about Lady Sophia." She wasn't the sort that appealed to Gray. Not in the least. She was pretty, of course, but she was too delicate. She was too prim. She was too... tame. There was the word again. Tame. Liviana Mayeux wasn't tame in the least. He had a feeling Liviana Mayeux would be more spirited as a bed partner than any woman he'd ever known.

Gray downed his ale in one gulp.

"Getting foxed so early in the evening, are you?" Lavendon chortled. "And here I thought you had a musicale to attend or some other such nonsense."

The musicale. What a torturous affair. Listening to pedigreed ladies warbling out tunes or pounding on piano keys. Gray groaned and signaled the barmaid for another round. "I'm certainly not foxed enough to attend a bloody musicale."

"Well, in that case," Lavendon lifted his own tankard in a mock toast, "do drink up, Hadley. I'm not certain I've ever been foxed enough to attend a musicale."

Ten

LIVI ACCEPTED LORD RADBOURNE'S HAND AS HE helped her alight from the carriage. "I am sorry," the viscount winced a bit, "about this afternoon."

But she hadn't given the dancing incident with Lord Radbourne any further thought. Not since Gray had rushed from the room earlier, anyway. Livi shook her head. "Are you sure you don't know where Mr. Hadley is?"

Lord Radbourne looked at once apologetic. "I wish I did."

"Archer!" Lady Radbourne called from inside the conveyance. "You mustn't forget Lady Sophia or myself."

The viscount rolled his eyes. "As though either of them would ever allow that," he whispered. Then he released Livi's hand and reached back in the coach.

A moment later, the four of them climbed the front steps to the Longboroughs' fashionable Georgian home. From outside, Livi could already hear someone playing Schubert's "Ave Maria" and her heart started pounding in her chest. *Bon Dieu*! What if someone asked her to play something or sing? She couldn't do so, certainly not with an audience.

A cold chill raced up her spine, and she glanced at Sophie just as the Longboroughs' door opened before them. She caught her tutor's eyes and shook her head slightly. "I can't sing," she whispered.

Sophie grasped Livi's hand and smiled. "I won't throw you to the wolves, Livi. Just stay beside me and you'll be fine."

But Livi couldn't help wishing that Gray was there as well. Where had he gone after he'd fled her that afternoon? And why hadn't he come back? Was it because she'd called him a coward? She probably shouldn't have done that, but it's what she would have said to either Armand or Etienne. Then she would have shoved them and they'd have shoved her back, and they'd have ended up sparring with each other and rolling around on the floor...

Good heavens. Now all she could think about was rolling around on the floor with Grayson Hadley, but not in the same way she used to play with her brothers. Not in the same way at all.

"Are you overly warm, dear?" Lady Radbourne asked, her brows drawing together ever so slightly. "You look a bit flushed."

As cold as it was in England? The likelihood of that was somewhere between slim and none. But she couldn't admit that her pallor was due to the fact she was thinking about Lady Radbourne's son, could she? Certainly not. "Perhaps a bit," she said instead.

The viscount arched a brow at her, as though he knew she was lying. He couldn't, could he? Certainly not.

He muttered quietly to her, "I'll see if I can introduce you to a few upstanding fellows tonight so you can get him off your mind."

Livi tripped over her own toe. He did know she was lying. How was that possible?

The viscount reached out to catch her, but another pair of hands secured her, grabbing her tightly by the shoulders. Livi sucked in a breath as she glanced behind her to find Grayson Hadley's dark eyes boring into hers.

"Speak of the devil," Lord Radbourne said quietly. He regarded his brother with a scathing glance. "You're late."

Gray shrugged his shoulders and adjusted his waistcoat. "Couldn't be helped." He tilted his head at Livi and let his gaze rake down her dress. She thought she heard him murmur "lovely," but she couldn't be completely sure.

The viscount leaned closer to his brother and sniffed quietly. "You smell like you've had a busy afternoon. Perhaps you should go back to Holmesfield's and sleep it off."

Gray avoided his brother's comment and held out an arm to Livi. "May I escort you inside?" he asked pleasantly. But Livi had a brief flash of remembrance. Of his caustic comments that afternoon. Of his abrupt abandonment. So she reached for Lord Radbourne's arm instead.

"You get the harpy," the viscount said with a grin as he tucked Livi's hand into the crook of his arm and smiled down at her. "And I get the lovely Miss Mayeux."

He really didn't have to compliment her to get back into her good graces. He could do so simply by thwarting his brother. Besides, he obviously enjoyed doing so, and it was mildly entertaining to see the look on Gray's face when she chose Lord Radbourne's arm over his.

Sophie stepped closer to them and whispered harshly, "When the three of you are done with whatever it is you're doing, we should probably move forward. A line is forming behind us."

Radbourne took a step toward the door. Livi drifted along beside him. "Nervous?" he asked with a conspirator's grin.

A little. But not as much as she'd expected. That was, until she stepped into the Longboroughs' home. She was so startled by the crush of people that the floor could have tilted a little beneath her.

"Something wrong?" Lord Radbourne murmured, leaning closer to her ear.

"I had no idea this musicale would be so well attended," she admitted.

"Consider it practice for tomorrow night."

Goodness, would there be dancing tonight? "They simply play music, correct?" she hissed at him. "No dancing?" Heavens, she wasn't nearly ready to dance in public.

He sighed heavily. "Alas, tonight will be all about a room full of screeching cats, and we're expected to at least make a good show of enjoying it."

"Screeching cats?"

"If we're lucky."

It couldn't be that bad, could it? Radbourne

introduced her to their hosts, the Longboroughs. Lord
Longborough looked down his beak-like nose at her
and scowled. "You're Holmesfield's granddaughter."

Livi curtsied politely. "Thank you for inviting
me, sir," she said quietly. Wasn't that what she was
supposed to say?

"Radbourne," he grunted. Evidently, their host
was a man of few words.

"Longborough," the viscount grunted back.

The Longboroughs' footmen ushered them through
the receiving line and into their home.

"Care for something to drink?" the viscount asked.

"I would," Gray declared as he stepped up beside them.

"It appears as though you've had enough," Lord
Radbourne said caustically. He leaned toward his
brother. "If you cause any grief for me with Lady
Sophia or Mother, I'll make your life hell."

"How would that be different from any other day?"
Gray shot back.

"Perhaps you should make a polite exit, return to
Holmesfield's, and sleep it off," the viscount recom-
mended softly.

Sleep what off? Livi glanced between the two of
them. Gray did have a sheen to his eyes that wasn't
typically there. And a slight flush to his cheeks. Had he
been drinking? She'd never seen either of her brothers
quite so foxed and they imbibed quite regularly.

"Nothing to sleep off," Gray growled at his brother.
"I'll get some punch for you, Livi," he said quietly and
then turned on his heel and left. He wavered a bit as he
spun. But he righted himself well enough. Anyone who
didn't know him would think he was just a bit clumsy.

Lord Radbourne sighed heavily. "I had no idea you'd affect him the way you do. If I'd known, I wouldn't have agreed to come on this trip. Nor would I have allowed him to do so."

Affected him? Livi laid a hand on her chest in surprise. "I have no idea what you mean."

"I should have noticed it this afternoon when he nearly took my head off. You falling to the ground affected him much more than it should have." He scanned the room the whole time he talked. He was obviously able to perform more than one task at a time. Now she just wished she could rein him in so she could find out what on earth he was talking about. He chuckled. "Don't look at me like you don't know." He grinned broadly, a smile that was nearly contagious.

But she didn't know. "Enlighten me?" she prompted.

"My brother likes you."

Livi bit back a smile. "That's better than loathing me," she retorted.

"On the contrary, it would be much better if he did loathe you, I'm afraid," Radbourne said stoically.

Just then, the sound of instruments being tuned reached her ears. The piercing shriek of a violin and the rhythm of a poorly played cello filled the air. She winced. How could the viscount keep from howling at the sound? "That's dreadful," she mouthed at him.

"Just wait until they actually start to play," he warned.

Livi wanted nothing more than to prompt Lord Radbourne to continue his discussion about Gray liking her. But Sophie stepped forward and said, "We should find our seats. Somewhere near the middle."

"Why the middle?" Livi asked.

"The sycophants and family members sit in the front."

"And we are neither," Archer intoned.

Sophie glared at him. Then she continued as though he'd never spoken, "And the people who sit in the back dearly want to escape early."

"That would be me," Radbourne whispered, his lips exaggerating his words.

Livi absently thought that she could like him if he gave her half an opportunity, but that was not to be. At least at the moment, because Sophie took Livi's hand and pulled her toward a row of seats in the middle of the room.

"Should we save a space for Gray?" Livi glanced over her shoulder at the viscount.

Radbourne looked at her askance. "Gray now, is it?"

Heat crept up Livi's cheeks. She hadn't meant to say that. Drat it all. She was one walking blunder after another. "Mr. Hadley, I meant to say," she amended as she took her seat.

"Too late to take it back now, my dear," he said with a clicking sound of his tongue and sat beside her. "Just be certain you don't do it in front of anyone important." He glanced in his mother's direction. "They might have you leg-shackled to him before you can blink twice."

Married to Grayson Hadley? Livi couldn't even fathom the idea, and neither could Grayson Hadley. The image of him bolting from her grandfather's music room that afternoon flashed once again in her mind.

Livi's reverie broke when the crowd quieted and what she assumed was supposed to be music began at the front of the room. Livi crossed her hands in her lap and sat up straight. But out of the corner of her eye, she saw Gray approaching with a glass of punch. That must be her glass. It was sweet of him to retrieve it for her. He seemed as though he was trying to apologize for his boorish comment from that afternoon. Livi smiled at him, a genuine smile of thanks.

But something went dreadfully wrong when she smiled at him. He blinked twice at her, looked down at her lips, licked his own in a most lascivious manner, and tripped.

The expression on his face was that of sheer desperation as he fell forward. Livi looked down to see his foot hooked behind some ancient lady's cane, which seemed most odd. Had the matron tripped Gray on purpose? Livi spent a mere second looking down and didn't even see the glass of punch hurtling in her direction until it was too late. It wasn't until a sticky orange liquid splashed across her face and down the front of her dress that pure mortification washed over her as well.

"*Nique ta mère!*" she muttered.

All at once the music stopped, a large gasp echoed, and every eye in the room focused on her.

The vilest French curse Gray had ever heard escaped Livi's mouth, and censure hung heavy in the air. Dear God, this was entirely his fault. If he hadn't doused her with that damned punch, she would have never muttered such a foul thing. At least he didn't think she would have.

"Oh, God, Livi," he said, trying to scramble to his feet. "I'm so sorry." For what he'd done and for what she'd just done to herself. He wasn't the only French speaker in the room, and the words she'd used couldn't quite be mistaken for anything else.

Another gasp rang out in the air.

What had happened now? Archer kicked Gray in the shin just as he rose to his full height. "Cork-brained fool!" Archer hissed.

"I said I was sorry," Gray muttered, though no one seemed to pay him any attention. He bent and rubbed his bruised shin absently. That is, until Lady Sophia glowered at him.

"Lord Radbourne," Lady Sophia began, a martinet if Gray had ever heard one. "Please have your coach brought around. I believe Miss Mayeux would like to return home early this evening."

Archer was gone in a flash, or at least it seemed like a flash. In truth, if Gray had been completely sober, Archer's speed would not have surprised him in the least. But apparently he was more foxed than he'd realized.

Gray reached for Livi as Lady Sophia ushered her toward the corridor, but all he got was a fistful of air. "Livi," he called.

Someone elbowed him in his side. "You have done quite enough, Grayson." He winced at the shrillness of his mother's voice. "Pray close your mouth."

Mother was never shrill. Never. Not once that Gray could remember. He blinked as he gazed down at his mother, feeling the room spin just a bit with his movement. "I think I should sit down."

She glowered at him, which was very unlike her. "And ruin everyone else's evening? Stumble home. When you are sober, I want a word with you." Then she brushed past him, following in Livi's and Lady Sophia's wake.

Gray felt a roomful of eyes on him and he slowly glanced around the drawing room. What the devil was he doing here? And with these stuffy people? He dropped into the chair Livi had vacated and held his head in his hands.

After a moment, someone clapped a hand to Gray's back. "Mr. Hadley," Lord Longborough's voice invaded his thoughts, "I'm afraid I'm going to have to ask you to leave."

Gray snorted. He was being asked to leave? He never wanted to attend this bloody affair in the first place. He staggered to his feet and glared at the stuffy lord. "It will be my greatest honor to leave your home."

Another gasp sounded in the room. For God's sake! Were these people only capable of gasping? They must lead rather mundane lives and be rather light-headed most of the time. He turned on his heel and stalked from the room and down the corridor, weaving only the tiniest bit. He brushed past the Longboroughs' butler and out into the cool night air, just in time to see Lord Holmesfield's coach round the corner. Devil take it all!

"If," Archer stepped out of the shadows, "there's a bigger fool in all of England, I've never met him."

Gray closed his eyes and inhaled deeply. Perhaps if he couldn't see his brother, Archer might disappear entirely, just like the coach had done.

Archer snorted. "Don't ignore me, Grayson." So much for imagining his brother away. "Perhaps you don't mind having your arse handed to you by Dash, but I don't enjoy it. And particularly not when I've done nothing to deserve it."

Who knew Archer was such a whimpering pup? "Dash isn't even here," Gray protested.

"Not yet. But if you don't think he'll show up after the blistering letter Sophia Cole is sure to send him, you're a bigger idiot than I ever imagined."

"Don't you think you're making too much out of this? It was an accident, Arch. I didn't mean to trip. I didn't mean to dump that drink on Livi. I didn't mean—"

"Did you mean to use her Christian name?" Archer growled. "Two times, Gray! You called her 'Livi' two times in there. How long do you think that will take to get back to her grandfather?"

Had he? Gray's mouth fell open. He wouldn't have done that. He'd counseled her against doing so herself. He... He *had*. Gray thought he might be sick.

"Having an association with you is the last thing that will help her, you know."

"I know!" Gray roared, louder than was necessary, but it felt good to roar.

Archer stomped forward and grabbed Gray by the lapels of his coat. "And now you'll bring Dash's wrath down on both of us. And Cait's."

And truly their sister-in-law's wrath was worse. Cait would furrow her pretty brow and tell Gray how disappointed she was in him. Disappointing her was worse than disappointing their mother, because for some reason, Cait actually believed they could be welcomed by society if they just learned to behave. Hiring Lady Sophia had even been her idea. It was all a bunch of nonsense.

Gray shoved his brother away. "Get off me." Then he started toward Brock Street, staggering more than he'd like.

Before he knew it, Archer grabbed him by the scruff of his neck and hurried him in the other direction. "I may not be the alpha, but I won't have you ignore me, Grayson." He pushed him down Marlborough Lane, past Upper Bristol Road, and all the way to the River Avon.

Gray squirmed in his older brother's grasp. "What do you think you're doing?" he demanded.

"Sobering you up. Quickest way I know how."

With a hard shove to the back, Gray stumbled forward down the riverbank and splashed into the Avon. The chilly waters nearly turned his blood to ice, and he shot back out of the river like a cannonball, spitting out water and sputtering. "What the devil is wrong with you?"

Archer, in his nice and dry clothes, stood on the riverbank glowering at Gray. "You, for one thing," he sneered.

Gray sloshed onto dry land, shaking the river water from his hair like a wet dog as he went. "I can't believe you did that. If Lady Sophia had seen that—"

Archer rolled his eyes. "After your performance tonight, I'm sure she would have applauded me." He heaved a sigh. "Sober enough to talk to me? Or are you still going to act like an indignant pup who needs to be dunked again?"

Gray folded his sopping arms across his chest. "Say whatever it is, so I can get out of these wet clothes."

Archer nodded once. "Very well. You'll pack your things and head to London first thing in the morning."

Gray had never wanted to come to Bath in the first place. But now that he was here, now that he'd spent time with Livi, held her in his arms... "I promised Miss Mayeux that we'd work on the minuet and a country dance tomorrow." That wasn't true at all, but Archer wouldn't have any way of knowing that.

"Then I'll teach her."

Gray scoffed. "Send her landing on her arse again? I've seen how capable you are of helping her."

"You've hurt her much worse this evening than I ever could have."

And in the pit of Gray's stomach he knew Archer was right. Poor Livi. Had he hurt her chances beyond repair? He hadn't meant to, not at all.

"The chit has you all tied up in knots."

"No, she doesn't."

But Archer paid him no attention and continued, "Who knows what you'll do next? It'll be best for everyone, particularly Miss Mayeux and you, if you head to London tomorrow."

Male laughter from the road caught Gray's attention and he stared into the darkness toward the street.

"Grayson Hadley?" came Henry Siddington's voice. "Have you decided to swim the Avon? Or did you decide it was simply time to bathe?"

"Bugger off," Archer snarled, which only made Siddington and his companions laugh harder.

Eleven

"THERE YOU ARE, MISS." MARIE POURED ONE LAST bucket of hot water into a copper tub. Then she helped peel Livi's damp gown from her body. "You'll feel better after your bath."

Livi doubted she'd feel better, but it would be nice to wash the stickiness from her skin and the tears from her cheeks. *Bon Dieu*! She never cried... Well, she rarely cried. Life with Papa and her brothers didn't leave room for tears, but ever since landing in England, Livi had become something of a watering pot who'd lost control of her life. Though honestly, she had lost that control somewhere on the Atlantic, hadn't she?

"Thank you, Marie. I can take it from here," she said as she stepped into the tub.

Her maid nodded and then stepped around the changing screen. "Lady Sophia would like an audience with you."

Livi sank into the warm water and heaved a sigh. "I suppose you can send her in."

Marie glanced over her shoulder at Livi. "Listen to

her ladyship. I believe she truly has your best interests at heart."

And though Livi was certain of the same thing, she just wanted to be alone. That, however, was not to be. "I said you can send her in."

Without another word, her maid escaped into the corridor and Lady Sophia stepped into Livi's room. Though she couldn't see the lady with the changing screen placed in front of the tub, Livi could sense her tutor's unhappy presence. "Well," she said more brightly than she felt, "I suppose that's one way to get out of a musicale."

A large sigh echoed around the room and then Livi heard her bed creak just a bit as Sophie must have sat down. "Heavens, Livi, where did you hear such an expression?"

Livi winced. Her exclamation when she'd been doused with punch had been fairly vulgar. The mere suggestion of one having relations with one's mother was one for the scandal sheets. She would never live it down. Ever. "What expression?" she asked innocently, hoping against hope Sophie meant something else entirely.

She didn't. "That has to be the most vile thing I've ever heard."

Livi gulped. "Do you think anyone else heard it?"

Sophie scoffed. "I think everyone heard it, and those who weren't present tonight will have heard about it on the morrow. I don't even know how to advise you. How could you say such a terrible thing?"

Livi wasn't sure. "It just flew out," she tried to explain. "I don't know, Sophie. I didn't mean to.

I must have heard one of the sailors on *Vespucci's Marauder* say it, and it just slipped out." In truth, she'd heard her brother and cousins yell that very curse at each other most of her life, but she didn't really want to admit that.

"Well, however you came by that unfortunate phrase, you can count on your grandfather finding out about it in the morning. You may have ruined yourself beyond repair this evening."

Livi sat up straight in her bath, sloshing warm water over the rim of the tub. "Perhaps Grandfather will send me back to New Orleans, then."

Sophie gasped. "Liviana Mayeux, did you do this on purpose? Are you trying to get yourself sent away?"

She hadn't been. But it wasn't a terrible idea, was it? What if her grandfather and Sophie couldn't tame her? Would they send her back to Papa?

"Livi?" Sophie demanded.

"*Non*," she answered quietly. "I didn't do it on purpose."

The bed creaked again and Livi heard Sophie's footsteps as she crossed the floor. Her tutor walked around the changing screen and frowned at her. "I sincerely hope not. Because he won't send you home, Livi."

"Then what…?" she began.

"He mentioned a convent in Ireland to Lady Radbourne. I assure you, you don't want to end up there."

What bit of hope Livi had at seeing home again died a quick but sad death. "A convent?" So she could spend her days around other pious busybodies like Father Antonio? Livi would sooner run away in the dead of night and land a job as a tavern wench. Or perhaps she'd join a band of Barbary pirates. Or maybe she'd swim all the way to Louisiana on her own and confront Papa. How could he do this to her?

"Livi." Sophie's frown deepened. "I don't like that expression. Tell me you're not thinking of doing something rash."

Livi forced a smile to her face and shook her head. "Of course not. Rashness would only land me in a convent."

Sophie took what seemed like sigh of relief. "Good. We'll sort all of this out in the morning, then. I promise."

But Sophie's promise meant very little. Livi believed that her friend would try to help her, of course. But if her grandfather was set on sending Livi off to a convent, she doubted there was anything Sophie could really do to prevent such a fate.

"Sleep well, Livi, because I fear that tomorrow will be a difficult day for you."

Difficult, indeed. Insufferable. Positively dreadful. She sank lower in the bath until her head disappeared below the water. She stayed there until her lungs were ready to burst. And only then did she come up gasping for air. Why was it that her real life so resembled her bath? Constantly gasping for air.

❧

Gray paced back and forth down the corridor, careful to keep his footsteps light since Lady Sophia slept in the chamber just next door to Livi's. He rubbed absently at his forehead. The ache that was building between his eyes was one of epic proportions. And he deserved every last twinge and pain. What he'd done to Livi was terrible. Awful. He'd never, ever be forgiven. And he didn't deserve to be.

He stopped in front of her door again and raised his knuckles to knock. Then he halted at the last moment. Was she sniffling inside her room? Certainly she wasn't crying? He pressed one ear to the door, but the sound stopped. All he could hear was his own rapid heartbeat. He paced back down the length of the corridor. When he turned, he stumbled against a hard body.

"Bloody hell, Grayson. Either go tumble the chit and get it over with, or go to bed," Archer snarled at him.

Not that the thought hadn't crossed Gray's mind, but Liviana Mayeux was not a woman who could be tumbled and then discarded. "What are you doing up here?" he grumbled back. They both had rooms in the opposite wing. There was no reason for Archer to be on this side of the house unless he was visiting someone. "You weren't paying a visit to Livi, were you?" he asked, trying to keep from ripping his brother's head from his shoulders at the very thought.

"I came to save your hide, you bloody idiot. I could hear your pacing all the way in my chambers. If you're caught pacing this corridor, there will be hell to pay." He growled the words at Gray.

If Gray wasn't feeling quite so remorseful, he'd take a swing at his brother for good measure. But doing so would only cause a scene, a scene he'd do well to avoid. "I think she's crying in there," he blurted.

Archer raised a brow at him. "What makes you think that?"

"Because I'm the idiot who ruined her chance at making a good match," Gray hissed back at him.

"You didn't put those crude words in her mouth," Archer reminded him.

That much was true. But still… "She would never have said such a thing if I hadn't poured a vat of punch over her head," Gray said, massaging his forehead again. There was a dull thump just behind his temples that was growing louder and louder.

"It was hardly a vat," Archer chided. "And you splashed her with it. You didn't pour it on her."

"Same thing," Gray grunted.

Just then, Archer cocked his head to the side and stepped closer to Livi's door. "Did you hear that?" he asked softly.

Gray moved closer to him and listened intently. He didn't hear anything. But then a muffled sob reached his ears. "Oh, dear God," he groaned. "She *is* crying." He reached for the door handle but Archer's hand covered his.

"Don't do it," his brother ordered.

Archer could go to the devil. Gray wasn't going to leave Livi behind a closed door where she was sobbing her eyes out. Not a chance in hell. Instead, he opened the door a crack and listened. Then he heard it again. One mournful sob. A piece of his heart must have broken in that moment, because that sob shook him to the core. He shoved Archer to the side with all his might and entered her chambers. Then he closed the door and shut his brother out of the room entirely. And shut himself inside with Livi.

"You're going to live to regret this," Archer hissed through the door.

He was probably right. Gray would live to regret this. He already did regret it. But he regretted being the cause of her scandal much more. He couldn't stand on the other side of the door and listen to her sobbing. Not without going to her. He needed to drop to his knees and beg for her forgiveness.

He stood completely still for a moment with his forehead against the door, taking deep breaths in and out through his nose, waiting for the moment to alert her to his presence. He finally turned slowly and came face to face with her bedchamber. Her room was nice and tidy, with a huge bed taking up much of the space. A wardrobe stood open in the corner of the room, her personal items there for him to see. Green garters. She wore green garters. Who the devil wore green garters? Evidently Liviana Mayeux did. And now, every time he looked at her, all he would be able to think about would be green garters hugging the sensitive skin of her upper thighs. He drew in a deep breath. Then he heard that gasping cry he'd heard earlier. A light shone on the other side of a silk screen in the corner of the room. She must be behind it.

"Livi," he said softly. But there was no sound in return. Dear God, what if she had done herself harm in her delicate state? What if he found something he wasn't expecting behind the screen? "Livi," he repeated. He took a few tentative steps closer to the screen. "Miss Mayeux," he said. Then he heard that gasp again. And a sputter and a splash of water along with it. She was in her bath? "Livi," he barked.

"Who's there?" came a watery response.

"Livi, it's me, Gray," he said. He stepped closer to the screen when she didn't reply. "Are you all right?" He peered around the corner of the screen. He would just take a quick peek to be sure she was well.

"Don't come any closer," she screeched. He took a step back. Then another.

She jumped from the tub, and Gray could hear water sloshing from the copper bath as she did so. The beeswax candle behind her limned her body in shadow. Bloody hell. She was naked behind that screen. And he could see every dip and curve of her body in the silhouette created by the light and the screen. The light, the screen, and her natural beauty. And there was a lot of it. In minute detail.

She stood there frozen, and he couldn't draw his gaze away. Her round bottom. Her pert little breasts. Her narrow waist. It was all outlined for him. Gray couldn't have drawn a breath or spoken if he'd tried. All the blood in his body shot straight down to his manhood. He couldn't have formed a cognizant thought if his life depended on it. All he could think was *Livi, naked. Livi, beautiful. Livi, curvy where he hadn't expected it. Livi. Dear God, he wanted Livi.*

"Why are you here, Gray?" she asked, crossing her arms across her breasts.

He could do nothing more than grunt. He couldn't put together an intelligent sound. Not on his life.

"I beg your pardon?" she prodded. Then she sighed

heavily. "I hope it's you and not some prowler in the night," she said.

One slim arm sneaked out from behind the screen. It was naked all the way up to her shoulder. He followed the line of it, licking his lips as he went. If he moved one inch in her direction, he might even see the side of her breast. Suddenly, her fingers snapped, drawing him from his utmost desire.

"Could you please pass me my wrapper?" she asked. When he didn't move, she snapped those slim fingers again. He moved as though a gunshot had directed his actions.

"Where?" he finally asked. Evidently, she'd reduced him to monosyllables.

"On the bed?" she questioned. The bed. *Oh, dear God, the bed. The bed was right there and Livi was naked.*

"Grayson?" she said.

He picked up the wrapper and very nearly threw it at her. But that could be even more of a mess. Instead, he placed it in her hand. When she had it securely within her grasp, she jerked it behind the screen and shrugged into it. Her doing so made him physically ache, even more than he already was, to see her cover that beautiful body with a robe.

Then she stepped from behind the screen as she pulled one edge of her wrapper to cover the other. She tied it around her waist with a sash. The silky material clung to her damp curves in all the right places.

Gray wanted to grab her tightly and kiss her senseless. So she'd be half as senseless as he was. But with his manhood raging, there was no way he could touch her. "Bloody hell," he breathed instead.

The door cracked only slightly. "Miss Mayeux," his brother called. "Are you decent?"

Hell, no, she wasn't decent. She was decadent. She was naked beneath that wrapper.

"Decent as I can be, considering the situation," she called back.

The door opened wider and Archer stepped inside. He tried to bite back his grin, but it was nearly impossible. "It appears as though you've struck him dumb and speechless, Miss Mayeux," Archer said. He smothered a chuckle inside a cough in his open fist. Damn him to hell. "It would be best if you called on Miss Mayeux at a more appropriate time, wouldn't it, Grayson?" he asked. "And a more appropriate place."

Gray swallowed so hard he could hear it. "Better. Yes, better," he agreed with a nod.

Archer took him by the shoulders and directed him toward the threshold. "Pardon the interruption, Miss Mayeux. Gray needs a moment to put himself back together." His brother's gaze dropped pointedly toward Gray's trousers, where it must be quite obvious how Livi had affected him. Archer mumbled to him, "You had better put that thing away."

"I loathe you," Gray muttered as he let Archer lead him from the room. He didn't look back at Livi. He couldn't. He couldn't look at her at all.

Archer closed the door softly behind him. "Will you ever learn to listen to me?"

Probably not. But Gray wished he had.

Lady Sophia's door squeaked as it opened, and the lady poked her head into the corridor. "Lord Radbourne, Mr. Hadley." She sighed. "I can't imagine what would bring the two of you to my bedchamber at this hour."

Archer snorted. "We got lost."

She rolled her eyes. "Just find your way back to your own chambers." Then she turned her glare on Gray. "And, you… Lady Radbourne would like an audience with you first thing in the morning."

Gray seemed to remember his mother saying something similar when they were at the Longboroughs'. He nodded once.

"Now, sweetheart," Archer slid closer to their tutor, "Gray got a little foxed. He's terribly sorry about the entire affair. Lord Eynsford doesn't really need to hear about this little incident, does he?"

Lady Sophia shook her head. "Certainly you know better than to try to coerce me with your silver tongue, Archer Hadley."

"What will it take, then?" Archer growled.

"Well, if I was less scrupulous, I might ask for the deed to Bindweed Cottage." She stepped into the corridor, wrapping her robe tighter about herself. "But I genuinely care for Miss Mayeux and I wouldn't put my own interests over hers. Besides, you're wasting your breath." She smiled like the cat that ate the cream. "I have no intention of writing to Lord Eynsford about this evening's events."

Gray breathed a sigh of relief. At least he wouldn't have to deal with Dash too.

"Why not?" Archer narrowed his eyes on the lady. "Certainly it's not out of the goodness of your heart."

Gray shoved his brother's shoulder. Damned dolt. Was he trying to get Lady Sophia to change her mind?

"Because there's no reason to do so. The Eynsfords have arrived in Bath this very evening." She looked supremely pleased with herself. "In fact, Lady Radbourne has already paid them a visit. She went as soon as she learned of their arrival, after we returned from the Longboroughs'."

Archer huffed in indignation. "You told them to come," he accused.

"Because I knew the two of you would create some scandal? Do you attribute me with a soothsayer's ability now?" Lady Sophia shook her head. "On the contrary, Lady Eynsford simply wanted to partake of the waters in her delicate state. I had nothing to do with their western sojourn."

"Blast it to hell," Archer grumbled, echoing Gray's thoughts exactly.

Twelve

LIVI STARED UP AT THE CANOPY OVER HER HEAD AS THE first rays of morning filtered into her chamber. She'd lain awake most of the night. First, wondering what had possessed Gray to enter her room like that. And then worrying over her future.

What was she going to do? As soon as Grandfather broke his fast, he'd learn about what had happened at the Longboroughs' the night before, what she'd said... And then what? Would she find herself in some Irish convent?

She couldn't end up in a convent. She just couldn't. So she was left with a choice—successfully flee England or become the lady her grandfather wanted, assuming it wasn't already too late for that. Neither option was particularly to her liking. But her choice would have to be made soon because she couldn't imagine life behind a convent's walls.

A knock came at her door, and Livi blinked toward the sound. Wasn't it too early for visitors? Then her mind flashed back to the strange visit Gray had paid her the night before. Had he come back?

She pulled the counterpane up to her neck and called, "Come in."

Sophie stepped over the threshold and frowned. "I didn't wake you, did I?"

Relieved that it was her friend and not a hulking Lycan, Livi sat up in bed. "Come in, Sophie. I'm awake."

Sophie sighed warily and then closed the door behind her. "It's the earl." The tutor crossed the floor silently, but each step she took increased Livi's anxiety tenfold.

Bon Dieu! It was too late. "He wants to send me to Ireland?"

Sophie shook her head. "No, no, not yet," she said soothingly. Then she took Livi's hand in hers. "Lord Holmesfield's valet sought me out just a few minutes ago. His lordship is not faring well this morning. I know you're not close to your grandfather, but I thought you might want to see him."

Livi's mouth dropped open. Her grandfather had been sickly ever since she arrived in England, but he had a spine of steel. She couldn't really imagine him not faring well. "My grandfather?" she asked.

Sophie nodded. "I can't imagine he'll receive visitors other than you today."

"I can't imagine he'd want to see me." After all, he hadn't wanted to spend any time with her since she'd arrived.

But Sophie squeezed her hand. "You are his blood, Livi, no matter how much he blusters."

"All right," Livi agreed. If Sophie thought it was necessary, Livi clearly needed to visit with the earl.

❧

Gray dropped into a seat at the breakfast table and frowned. Where was his mother? She had made it quite clear she wanted a word with him, and he'd already searched all the main rooms of the house.

"Raw egg, sir?" a footman asked, biting back a smirk.

Gray glowered at the servant. "Just coffee. Thank you."

The footman nodded dutifully. "As you wish." He placed a cup and saucer in front of Gray before pouring a spot of coffee for him. "Cream? Sugar?"

"Black will do." Gray took a sip and then regarded the chatty servant. "Has Lady Radbourne come down for breakfast yet?"

The footman shook his head. "I have not seen her ladyship this morning, sir. In fact, you are the first to break your fast."

"Grayson!" boomed a voice from the doorway.

Gray almost swallowed his tongue in his haste to rise to his feet. "M-morning, Dash."

His half brother, Dashiel Thorpe, the Marquess of Eynsford, narrowed his golden eyes on Gray and heaved an indignant sigh. "What is to be done with you?"

"Spoke to Mother, I take it?"

Dash stepped into the breakfast room. "Violet stayed with us last night. It was too late for her to return after her visit."

"And she wanted to see the children," Gray added. "Lia and Lucien do adore her."

Gray snorted. "Between your children and Wes' marriage, she's about to come out of her skin wanting more of both. Hordes of grandchildren and married sons."

With a wicked gleam in his eye, Dash said, "One tends to beget the other." Then he shrugged. "Perhaps she's on to something. Madeline has been quite the calming influence on Wes, and I'm certain Cait had the same effect on me. If you were married and bouncing a bundle on your knee, I'm not certain you'd have time to create havoc."

Gray's mouth fell open. He couldn't believe Dash could even suggest such a thing. "So, should I just rush for the border with the next chit I see, like Wes did? Would that make you happy?"

His older brother cracked a smile, which was something of a rarity. "I suppose it depends on who the next chit you see is, and whether or not you've doused her with punch in front of all the *ton*."

A vision of Livi flashed in Gray's mind, but he shook the thought away. She wasn't for him. Her grandfather had great plans for her, and none of them included Gray. "That was an accident," he growled. "And it wasn't all of the *ton*."

Dash's golden brow rose with mild amusement. "You know better than to take that tone with me."

Gray dropped his gaze to the cooling coffee before him. "The punch was an accident," he repeated much more softly. Then he chanced a glance at his brother. "But I may have ruined her chances last night."

Dash turned his attention to the footman. "Leave us." As soon as the servant was gone, and it was truly just the two of them, Dash leaned forward in his seat. "Your mother told me a very interesting story last night."

More than just the fact that Gray had dumped a vat of punch on Livi at the Longboroughs'? "Oh?" he asked, afraid of the answer he'd hear.

"Your Miss Mayeux is half Lycan."

That was hardly news. She'd told him the very same thing almost within seconds of meeting her. "I wouldn't call her mine," he said.

Dash chuckled. "If you truly did ruin her chances, I think that's exactly what I'll call her. I won't have you ruin a young girl's chances and walk away, Grayson."

Gray shook his head. "I can't imagine Holmesfield would agree to any such alliance."

"Neither would Hythe, if he'd been given the choice," Dash replied. "So Wes took matters into his own hands."

"Are you saying I should abduct Livi and elope?"

Dash narrowed his eyes on Gray. "I'm saying we have to live by their rules most of the time, but we have our own we must adhere to, as well. That girl shares our lineage. She shares our mark, and I won't see her hurt at your hands."

So now Gray was the villain in all of this. "I have no intention of harming her," he growled, even though he'd already been warned against doing so.

"No," Dash agreed more amiably than was normal. "Cait seems to think your intentions are something else entirely."

Cait? What the devil did Cait have to do with any of this? "She's never even met Livi. How could she possibly know anything about the situation?"

Dash shrugged. "Call it women's intuition, if you'd like. And though her intuition is compromised due her present condition, I've never known my wife to be wrong. Which leads us back to you and your Miss Mayeux."

"She's not mine," Gray said again. "She doesn't even want to be here, Dash. If she could stow away on a vessel headed for America, she'd do it in a heartbeat."

"Then I suppose you'll have to change her mind."

Was he serious? "All of this so that I won't have time to create havoc for you? I'd think you'd want to meet the girl before deciding I should abduct and elope with her."

Dash only grinned. "Do try not to cause another scandal."

&

Livi waited until her grandfather called, "Enter," before she pushed open his door. She stepped inside his chambers as a series of coughs wracked his frame.

"Would you like water, Grandfather?"

The earl snorted. "So you can drown me?" He gestured toward a seat beside his bed. "Sit. I want to hear how the musicale turned out last night."

Bon Dieu! There wasn't a thing she could say about last night that he wouldn't get upset over. "There isn't much to tell," she hedged.

"Horrid affairs," he agreed. "But they are necessary if you're to fit in among society."

Livi cringed, remembering the events of the previous evening. When her grandfather learned what really happened, he'd be furious. Perhaps she could soften him up a little before the whole ugly truth hit his ears. "I can see that, though I didn't really get a chance to socialize last night."

The earl grunted. "What of Sophia Cole? Do you feel she is helping you?"

At that Livi nodded earnestly. "She is doing her best for me."

"The question is whether or not her best is good enough. Has she helped you meet important people?"

Livi wasn't certain who was important and who wasn't, but she figured her grandfather would approve of one name. "I met the Duchess of Hythe yesterday."

A series of coughs escaped the earl, but then his pallor looked a little better and he sat up straighter in bed. "Her Grace would be a good advocate for you." Then he rubbed his chin. "You should keep your distance from her grandsons, though," he warned. "Degenerates, both of them."

Livi nodded. "Lady Sophia said something similar."

"Good. Then her judgment is sound." Her grandfather sighed as he stared at her. "I am sorry Grace isn't here to lead you through this."

A twinge of pain squeezed Livi's heart at his words. "I've had to find my way through most things without *Maman*."

"Raised by wild men instead," the earl whispered. "Philippe should have sent you to me years ago, while your grandmother was still alive and would have known what to do for you."

He seemed so sincere that Livi couldn't help squeezing her grandfather's hand. "Papa did the best he could."

He agreed with a curt nod. "Your father and I have never agreed on anything, except for our love for Grace. We loved her in different ways, of course, but one is just as strong as the other. I'm sure he did the best for you that he was able to do. But I could have done more. I have more connections. Access to more influential men with full purses."

Papa's purse was plenty full with all of his enterprises, though Livi thought better than to say as much. And she was slightly taken aback by her grandfather's musings. The earl truly did seem to care for her interests, which surprised Livi more than a little. She swiped a tear from her cheek. "I'm here now, Grandfather, and I'll listen to everything Lady Sophia says."

"See that you do." He actually smiled at her. "If I'm feeling up to it, I'll go to the Assembly Room with you this evening."

And hear firsthand what had happened the night before? Livi almost blanched. She shook her head, more forcefully than was necessary. He might care for her interests, but he might think her best interests included a convent if he learned what she'd said at the Longboroughs'. "You should rest, Grandfather. I'm sure I'll be fine with Lady Sophia and Lady Radbourne."

"I might need a few days to get over this illness," he said with a nod as he lay back against his pillows. Then he raised his head and said, "You'll make me proud. I'm certain of it."

He had faith in her? Her heart felt like it was expanding to twice its size as tears pricked the backs of her lashes. "I'll make you proud," she whispered. But his eyes were closing and she wasn't even sure he heard her.

Livi would make him proud, even if she had to marry the most boring old peer who ever dared to enter an assembly room. And she would begin her search that night. After all, such a life had to be better than one spent behind convent walls. And hopefully, before her grandfather learned of her blunder at the Longboroughs', she could have a suitable suitor in the wings. If so, her grandfather wouldn't send her off to Ireland, would he? She hoped not.

Livi stepped out of his room and closed the door behind her. She could do this. She could. She was made of strong stuff. Now she just needed to prove it to everyone else. She searched the house until she found Lady Sophia in the yellow sitting room, where she sat embroidering. "I need you to make me perfect," she said.

Sophia finished her stitch and looked up, not even taken aback by Livi's statement.

"Can you make me graceful? And elegant?" Livi fiddled nervously with the sleeve of her dress.

"Has something happened that I'm not aware of, Livi?" Sophie asked. She set her embroidery to the side and regarded Livi with a most serious look.

"Not really," Livi prevaricated. She couldn't tell Sophie that she wanted to make her grandfather proud. "I just want to be the best I can be tonight. Teach me everything," she said as she sat down beside Sophie.

"Everything is a bit much for one day. We may need reinforcements."

Thirteen

"No," Sophie sighed. "I haven't seen Mr. Hadley this evening, either."

Was he avoiding Livi after the scene they'd caused the night before? Apparently, though Livi would have thought he'd have at least sought her out to make an apology, especially after paying her a visit in her private chambers the night before.

"Now, turn around," Sophie instructed.

Livi turned to look at herself in the mirror and gasped at the vision in green that met her eyes. Sophie had softened her hair by trimming some around the front and sides, and then Marie had swept the rest into an elegant mass of riotous curls held in place by silver combs that glimmered in the light of the candles placed about the room. One long curl draped over her bare shoulder.

She sucked in her stomach and turned to the side. "Are you certain it's supposed to fit this way?" Livi asked. She had a bit more bosom on display than she'd ever shown to anyone in her life.

"I'm positive," Sophie laughed. She stepped forward

and arranged that single curl so that it lay more perfectly over Livi's shoulder. "You look beautiful."

"No one will say I look like a whore?" Livi asked, grimacing at her reflection in the mirror.

"Ladies do not say the word you just used, Livi," Sophie scolded.

"Whore?" Livi repeated, certain she must look like a bumbling idiot.

"And she says it again," Sophie muttered to herself as she shook her head. "Don't use that word," her tutor ordered.

"What do you call them?" Livi asked.

Sophie appeared to mull it over. "I don't call them anything. Because a lady does not think of such things."

"You never think of wh—"

"Livi!" Sophie barked.

Livi rolled her eyes. "Strumpets. Tarts. Loose women."

"Strumpets, tarts, and loose women are none of your concern. Nor should they be part of your vocabulary," Sophie informed her. "Focus on the matter at hand, will you? Appearing delicate and refined tonight is your singular concern."

Livi snorted. "Delicate."

Sophie sighed heavily. "You said you're in this for the long haul, Livi. You said you are on a husband hunt, and I'm trying to help you. So stop saying words like that. Wipe them from your mind. Along with any other French curse words."

"Yes, Sophie." Livi would endeavor to forget all the words she'd heard every day of her life as she followed her brothers from place to place. Sophie had spent hours practicing dancing with her—playing the part of the man since neither Lord Radbourne nor Gray had turned up all day—until Livi could dance the waltz, the quadrille, and a few other dances she'd never heard of with relative ease. Sophie's feet were probably aching from all the dancing. Livi knew hers were. "Thank you for all of your help," Livi said softly.

"You're quite welcome." She smiled with a warmth that Livi was fast becoming accustomed to, where her new friend was concerned.

"You make me think I might actually pull this off."

"I have no doubt of it." Sophie pointed to Livi's reflection in the mirror. "Look at you. You're beautiful."

She looked for the beautiful girl Sophie saw and couldn't find her anywhere. She saw a girl playing dress-up in someone else's clothes. Sophie had been nice enough to let her have one of her own gowns and had even altered the bodice to fit Livi so she could be appropriately dressed. And it fit reasonably well, even if it did show more flesh than was necessary.

"You shimmer like an emerald in that color," Sophie assured her.

Livi thought she looked more like an artichoke. But perhaps it was the way the light hit the dress from a different angle. She'd take Sophie's word for it.

"I do have something for you," Sophie said quietly. "But if you get all weepy and make your eyes puffy, I won't be able to forgive you."

A present? For her? "You shouldn't have done anything special for me." Sophie had done enough as it was.

"I didn't," Sophie clipped out as she turned and retrieved a cask from the bedside. She held it out to

Livi. "Go ahead. It won't bite." Livi reached for it, and Sophie jerked it back at the last moment. "But mark my words—no crying."

"I promise," Livi said quickly as she took the cask and sat down beside the vanity. She opened it slowly. Inside was a folded piece of parchment and two small pouches. She opened the note and read the short salutation quickly aloud to herself. "I thought you might like these. They belonged to your mother…" Her voice trailed off as she got to the end. "It's from Grandfather."

"No weeping!" Sophie said, her own eyes brimming with tears.

Livi pushed the note to the side and shook the contents of one black velvet bag into her hands. A gleaming pair of earbobs landed in her palm. Livi couldn't breathe for a moment. They were beautiful. They were emeralds, almost the same color as her dress, fashioned with gold so that they would dangle from her ears. She opened the second bag and dumped the contents in her palm in much the same manner. A matching pendant on a gold chain necklace tumbled into her hand. She let the gold chain fall through her fingertips and regarded the pendant with awe. It was something of *Maman*'s. Her mother had worn this very necklace and earbobs. Livi swiped a tear from her cheek. "Will you put it on me?" she asked hesitantly.

Sophie hastened to her side. "Of course," she said as she took the delicate chain and stepped behind Livi to clasp it behind her neck. Then she helped her don the earbobs. Livi gave her head a little shake, and the jewels at her ears shimmered and danced in the light with her movement.

"So beautiful," Livi breathed.

Sophie squeezed her shoulder gently. "Yes, you are," she affirmed.

A knock sounded on the door. "Come in," Livi called absently as she bent to put on her slipper.

Lady Radbourne stepped over the threshold, and her dark eyes widened in surprise. "Oh, Liviana, you are as stunning as Grace ever was."

Livi sniffed back a tear at that comment.

"My lady," Sophie scolded, "I've been trying to keep her from crying."

Lady Radbourne smiled broadly. "Yes, of course." Then she pulled out a handkerchief from her reticule and offered it to Livi. "No puffy eyes, my dear. You want to be radiant when you walk through those doors tonight."

Livi took the linen gratefully and dabbed at the corner of her eyes with the cloth.

"I thought it would be best if we arrived with Lord and Lady Eynsford. They're awaiting us in the front parlor."

"Eynsford?" Livi frowned. She had heard that name before, hadn't she? It certainly sounded familiar.

Lady Radbourne nodded with enthusiasm, sending her dark curls bobbing about her shoulders. "Such a lovely couple. Lord Eynsford has taken a great interest in my sons' welfare. Taken them under his wing, so to speak."

The man Sophie was always threatening Lord Radbourne with. Livi knew the name sounded familiar. "Their older brother," she added, putting the pieces together.

But a moment later, she wished she could call the words back. Lady Radbourne turned a bit red, and even Sophie's eyes rounded in surprise. "Brother?" Sophie echoed. "You must be mistaken. There is no familial connection between the two families."

Livi shook her head. Why were the two women behaving so strangely? "But I thought Gray said—"

"You must have misunderstood him," Lady Radbourne hastened to explain. "And you mustn't repeat such a thing, Liviana. Not ever."

Somehow she'd made a mess out of things again, and she hadn't meant to. Did she have the wrong gentleman in mind? The one who employed Sophie to tutor the Hadley brothers? She didn't think so. "I'm sorry," she mumbled for nothing better to say.

Sophie smiled and linked her arm with Livi's. "No harm done. Let's not speak of it again, all right?"

Livi nodded as her friend directed her over the threshold and then down the steps.

"You will love Lady Eynsford," Sophie promised. "She told me she is most anxious to make your acquaintance."

A moment later, Sophie ushered Livi into the front parlor where a golden couple awaited them. Both Lady and Lord Eynsford were blond, and the latter possessed a set of golden eyes that were nearly identical to Lord Radbourne's. In fact, Lord Radbourne looked more like Lord Eynsford than he did Gray. The man before her was most certainly the one Gray had mentioned. He was their older brother, Livi had no doubt. So why had Sophie and Lady Radbourne tried to hide the fact?

Then the answer hit Livi like a great gust of wind.

Gray had actually referred to the blond Lycan as their half brother. Lord Eynsford had been born on the wrong side of the blanket. Thank heavens she hadn't mentioned his fraternal relationship with the brothers Hadley out in public. No wonder Sophie and Lady Radbourne had been so mortified. Gray should have warned her.

Lady Eynsford, a blond beauty with sparkling blue eyes, stepped forward and offered Livi her hand. "Miss Mayeux, I presume." Her Scottish brogue floated over Livi like a warm caress.

Livi nodded. "A pleasure to meet you."

"Oh," the lady gushed, "the pleasure is all mine. I am so glad ye'll be ridin' with us ta the Assembly Room."

"Radbourne and Mr. Hadley have gone ahead of us," the Lycan lord added. "We'll meet them there."

And when they did, Livi would have a few things to say to the elusive Grayson Hadley.

❧

Gray tugged at his cravat. He might as well be a caged wolf for all the freedom he possessed in the Assembly Room. Gentlemen glanced at him in mild amusement and ladies giggled behind their fans. "Why am I even here?" he grumbled.

Archer frowned. "Because Dash ordered us here, that's why."

That was the truth of it. "I should have left for London last night before he arrived."

His brother nodded in agreement. "Once again you should have listened to me. Now you are as stuck as I am. So try not to scowl at the ladies. After last night's performance, you would do well to seem polite and more than a little sober."

"Ah, Hadley!" A hand clapped Gray on the back. "I see you've washed the Avon from your person."

Gray glanced over his shoulder to find Henry Siddington smirking. Until yesterday, Gray would have never given the man a second thought. Now he would gladly throw Siddington into the Avon and not feel a bit of remorse. Behind Siddington, Lord Robert Hayburn and his brother, the Marquess of Lavendon, both nodded a greeting in Gray's direction.

"Washed the punch from his skin too," Lord Robert laughed. Then he stepped forward with a conspiratorial glint in his eye. "Did you mean to douse that awkward chit with your punch, Hadley? Or was it an accident?"

Awkward chit? Gray ground his teeth together, but before he could respond, Archer cleared his throat. "It's all Lavendon's fault."

The marquess scoffed good-naturedly. "I wasn't even there, Radbourne."

"No, but you made certain Grayson was more than deep in his cups before his arrival last night."

Lavendon shrugged. "And here I thought you Hadley men could hold your liquor."

"Liquor they can hold," Lord Robert chortled. "It's the punch they're incapable of hanging on to."

"I think I shall have to start attending musicales if they're to be so entertaining," Siddington chimed in. "Did Miss Mayeux actually say *nique ta mère* to you?"

Gray shook his head. "You are misinformed."

"By everyone in attendance?" Siddington smirked

again, and Gray had the overwhelming desire to smack the expression right from the jackass' face. "I haven't heard that phrase since I visited a Paris brothel some time ago. Where do you suppose she learned such a thing?"

Gray growled low in his throat, ready to pound Siddington right into the floorboards under his feet. But then the man's expression changed to one of appreciation.

"I say," Siddington murmured, "if she looks like that, she can say whatever she wants, just so long as she's straddling me when she says it."

Gray's head snapped in the direction of the main entrance to find Livi beside Dash, Cait, and Lady Sophia. His mouth went dry, and he blinked at her as though seeing her for the first time. Radiant would have been an understatement.

"Close your mouth," Archer muttered softly.

Siddington stood up straight and smoothed a hand down his waistcoat. "I did promise my cousin I would dance with her little friend." That damned smirk was back in place on the blackguard's face. "What trials I endure for family." Then he glanced back at Lord Robert and Lavendon. "Do excuse me."

Gray was about to block Siddington's path, but Archer hissed in his ear, "Do *not* make another scene."

"If he so much as thinks about Livi straddling any part of his person, I'll kill him," Gray growled. He watched closely as Siddington walked toward Livi, who was dressed in emerald green silk that shimmered under the lights of the chandelier like diamonds. He didn't realize he'd said the word "diamond" aloud until Lavendon spoke.

"A diamond of the first water," Lavendon murmured,

"is nothing more than a lump of coal to some." He sucked his front teeth in a most annoying manner.

"A duke's son is nothing more than a lump of body parts, once he's beaten to a pulp," Gray muttered back.

"Beg your pardon, Hadley?" Lavendon said, straightening his stance and adjusting his jacket. He looked a bit like a peacock spreading his feathers.

"You heard me, Lavendon," Gray snarled back, stepping toward the man. As he cocked his fist to punch the much-too-pretty man in the face, Archer grabbed his arm fiercely within his grip. Gray tried to jerk his elbow free, but Archer held it tightly. "Let me go, Arch," Gray growled.

"You making a scene will not help her," Archer said low enough for only Gray to hear. Gray and any other Lycan in the vicinity. He could already see Dash's ears perking up at the comment. He sent one dark amber look toward them, one so fierce Gray almost wanted to tuck his tail between his legs and slink into a corner.

"Thank you," Gray murmured to Archer as he lowered his arm and adjusted his own clothing. Then he leaned close to Lavendon and said clearly, "That lump of coal, as you so inaccurately described her, is mine. So stay away from her." Then he bumped Lavendon's shoulder hard with his and walked toward the lady in question. Lavendon stumbled under the assault but didn't say another word.

Livi was almost within his grasp when Siddington claimed her for the first dance. She looked at Siddington and smiled, then dropped into a curtsy. It was half a smile, one of uncertainty. Gray wanted fiercely to take her in his own arms and count to her as he led her into the dance. She was probably feeling nervous, and the very thought of her being fearful tugged at his heart. He followed her with his eyes as she walked across the room on the man's arm.

Dash coughed into his closed fist to draw his attention. "Eynsford," he muttered with a casual nod of his head.

"Hadley," Dash greeted him in response. "Behaving yourself?" he asked.

"Absolutely."

"See that you do."

That would be harder than one might think.

Fourteen

LIVI TRIED TO COUNT TO HERSELF AND LISTEN TO MR.
Siddington's questions at the same time. It was proving
to be more than difficult. She wished absently that he
would shut his mouth and just dance. But that didn't
seem to be in his plans.

"Do you think Her Grace will grow two heads
and sprout a tail tonight? Or just purple scales?"
Siddington asked.

Livi heard half of his question. "Purple scales?" she
questioned, finally looking up at him.

"It's easier if you don't look down at your feet,"
he whispered with what she assumed was a kind-
hearted smile.

"Easier for you," Livi said. Then she trod upon his
toe. He took it gracefully, with barely a wince. "I'm
so sorry," she whispered.

"It's quite all right. I had no need of that toe,"
he said with a smile. He could probably be quite
charming, if he tried. She looked up into his blue eyes
and couldn't help but compare the depth and feeling
she imagined within them to Gray's.

"Toes are highly overrated, Mr. Siddington. I hear they'll be out of fashion within the year."

He arched a brow at her. "Is that so?"

"Thank you for sacrificing yourself so that I'll have a dance partner," she said with a mental wince. He had done it at Sophie's request, she was well aware. Still, it was kind of him. "Sophie will owe you a favor."

"I'll ask her for something splendid. Do you have any requests? Suggestions, perhaps?"

"I'm sure you'll come up with something grand," Livi stalled.

"I'll save my favor for later. She's had a tough enough time of it since her father died." He turned her effortlessly about the floor. She wanted to question him about Sophie's life, but doing so would probably be socially unacceptable. Even more so than she already was.

The music slowed and Siddington drew her to a halt. He offered his arm. "Shall we stroll about the room? Or shall I return you to Sophie?"

"You have done your job for the night, I'm sure. You can return me to Sophie and wash your hands of me."

He grinned. There was a scoundrel lurking behind that exterior, she was certain. But he had done her a kindness, so she would attempt not to judge him.

"How many dances will you make Hadley wait before you grace him with your unwieldy feet? Three? Four?"

Livi hadn't planned to dance with him at all. "He barely knows I'm here. I'm certain he has no plans to ask me to dance." Hadn't he told her that very thing?

"Do you like a good wager, Miss Mayeux?" he asked.

"Much more than a bad wager," she tossed back with a laugh.

"Smart girl. If we were to wager on it, I'd bet he doesn't let more than one more man sweep you into his arms before he does so himself. He's nearly green with envy already. He's looking positively reptilian." He tilted his head toward the spot where Gray stood brooding alone in a corner. Gray's left foot tapped an impatient rhythm, and he looked a bit like a caged tiger she'd once seen in a circus. "By the way, you look positively radiant tonight." Then he shot her a wide grin, bowed in farewell, and left her standing beside Sophie.

"You did well," Sophie whispered at her.

"Did I?" Livi breathed back. "I stomped the poor man's toes so hard he'll probably have to have them amputated to ease the pain."

"It's not the first time a lady has stepped on Henry's toes, and I'm certain it won't be the last," Sophie assured her. "The next dance is a waltz and you'll need an appropriate partner." Sophie looked around the Assembly Room, mumbling to herself, "No, no, no, no, maybe... no, no," as her gaze moved from one man to the next. "Oh, brace yourself," Sophie whispered fiercely. "The Duchess of Hythe."

The portly old woman stopped in front of Livi and looked at her from the top of her head to the bottom of her feet. Then her eyes swept back up. Livi told herself not to fidget. She told herself not to worry. But she assumed that having the duchess' favor would give her entrance to almost any drawing room in Bath. So, she forced herself to curtsy.

"Oh, up with you, gel," the duchess said as she

took Livi's elbow and forced her to rise. The duchess tapped her fan against her arm for a moment, gnawing on her bottom lip. Then she said, "You're quite beautiful when you don't have punch down the front of your dress." She leaned closer. "And there's many a man I've wanted to tell to *nique ta mère*, and you can wager I will do so if one ever gets so busy looking down my dress that he dumps punch in my face."

Heat crept up Livi's cheeks. "It was a horrible thing to say, Your Grace. And I am woefully sorry for my blunder."

"Oh, stop the woeful comments. I think it's wonderful. You've knocked the *ton* on its ear, and it's about time someone did. Half the mothers in this room are trying to keep their sons from asking you to dance, and the other half are trying to talk them into it. You'll be this season's incomparable, my dear. Mark my words. With my help, you'll be able to take your pick of eligible men at the end of your visit to Bath. If not by the end of the night." She turned and snapped her fingers. Heads turned her way. "Miss Mayeux needs a partner for the waltz," she said.

Four handsome, well-attired men stepped in Livi's direction.

The duchess' eyes widened a bit as her gaze settled on one of the fellows. "Nathaniel, what a surprise." Then she turned her attention back to Livi. "My grandson, the Marquess of Lavendon," She gestured to the gentleman in question. "You'll find him quite an accomplished dance partner, my dear."

Livi curtsied before the handsome man. "A pleasure, my lord."

"Indeed," Lord Lavendon replied smoothly. Then

his gaze quickly flickered to Sophie before returning to Livi. "May I have this dance, Miss Mayeux?"

She didn't really have a choice, did she? Livi smiled at the marquess. "I would be honored."

Lord Lavendon offered Livi his arm and then swept her out into the middle of the ballroom. His green eyes sparkled with amusement. "You don't know how lucky you are, Miss Mayeux."

"*Non?*" she asked. With as much as her life had been turned upside down, she wouldn't have thought herself lucky.

The first chords of the waltz echoed throughout the room, and Lord Lavendon bowed low before Livi. When he rose to his full height, he towed her into his arms and said, "My grandmother likes very few people. She seems to like you. I would say you are very lucky indeed."

Well, that was fortunate. If the duchess could help Livi in society, perhaps Grandfather would never learn of the awful spectacle she'd caused the previous evening. "She seems delightful."

Lavendon tipped back his head and laughed. "She's a dragon." Then he grinned down at her. "I should know. I've lived with her most of my life."

What was Livi to say to that? Nothing if she wanted the duchess' support. "I met your brother yesterday in the Pump Room," she said instead of commenting about Her Grace.

The marquess winked at Livi. "My most heartfelt condolences in that case, Miss Mayeux."

Livi couldn't help but laugh. "What a horrible thing to say about one's brother, my lord."

"Do you have a brother?" he countered.

Livi nodded. "*Oui*, I have two brothers."

"And are they scurrilous reprobates?"

"*Non*." They were Lycans, which his lordship would probably find even worse.

"Well, then you see you are lucky. As I have but one brother and he most assuredly is a scurrilous reprobate."

Livi laughed again. He really was rather charming for all that he wasn't Gray.

"I understand Lady Sophia has taken an interest in you."

Livi nodded. "Do you know the lady?"

"Indeed," he replied and his eyes darted to where Sophie still stood with the duchess.

There was something in his gaze that caught Livi's notice. A longing, she was certain. But an arrogant one, she was equally certain. "And would you rather be waltzing with her, my lord?" she asked before she could stop herself.

Lavendon's green eyes focused on Livi and he frowned a tiny bit. "I would have asked her, had that been the case, Miss Mayeux. She is but a lady's companion. Do you think your company lacks in comparison to hers?"

That wasn't what Livi meant at all and she shook her head. "*Non*, my lord. It just seems as though your eyes can't help but find her."

"Beautiful and astute," Lavendon replied as he led her in a turn. "Alas, the lady in question has always been able to keep her eyes from finding me."

She had? Livi stared up at the marquess. Did he hold a *tendre* for Sophie? Might Lord Lavendon be Sophie's escape from the world of poverty and work?

"But if we're to talk about eyes," Lavendon continued, "I should warn you—Grayson Hadley is staring daggers at me this very moment with his. Why do his eyes seek me out while Lady Sophia's do not, I ask you?" He winked at Livi. "You see, I am not quite as lucky as you are this evening."

Livi's gaze flashed to where Gray still stood, apparently seething, in the corner. "Am I lucky to have Mr. Hadley's attention?" And why did she have it now, when he'd avoided her all day?

"I suppose only you know the answer to that," Lavendon remarked as he cocked his head to one side. "But I do feel I should warn you about Mr. Hadley's character, as I seem to be warning you about things this evening."

"His character?" Livi echoed. For all that she was annoyed with Gray, she hadn't questioned his character. In fact, he'd been quite kind to her since they met, if one discounted his tossing a glass of punch on her in the middle of a musicale.

Lord Lavendon nodded morosely. "You see, his twin absconded with my sister. As the two of them share not only the same blood but occupied the same womb at one time, I can only imagine Grayson Hadley capable of a similar despicable act. So do take a care with the man, my dear, lest you find yourself muttering vows over a blacksmith's anvil the way my sister did."

Livi only nodded, because what else could she say?

⚛

Gray was going to rip Lavendon's tongue from his head. The blackguard's words of warning had reached

Gray's ears, just as they had Archer's and Dash's. But Gray was the one being maligned, if for no other reason than that Weston was his twin. Hardly sporting of Lavendon, especially as the man wanted to be a part of the Hadley brothers' gaming venture and had come to ask Gray to support his suit. But that was neither here nor there. All that mattered was the way Livi had winced when she heard Lavendon's warning. For planting those unfortunate seeds in her head, Gray should do more than rip the marquess' tongue from his head. He should do much worse.

A fan touched Gray's arm and he looked down at his sister-in-law, Caitrin, Marchioness of Eynsford, standing beside him. Gray scowled at her. "You should take care, Cait. I'm not my most jovial self at the moment."

"Nay," she agreed. "Ye are a rabid wolf if yer expression is ta be believed."

He narrowed his eyes on his brother's wife. "You're not helping."

She sighed and stared out at the sea of dancers before them. "Is it help ye want?"

"I'd like to be left alone," he grumbled.

But Cait simply shook her head as though she had no plans to grant his wish. "Why dinna ye ask her ta dance yerself, Grayson?"

He scoffed. "Because she's here to meet important men, powerful men."

"Men like Nathaniel Hayburn?" Cait asked softly.

Gray could only growl low in his throat as he watched Lavendon lead Livi around the dance floor.

"Ye will be a powerful man yerself someday, Gray."

She always spoke in absolutes, as though the future was set in stone. Gray scoffed. "I will never be a marquess."

"Nay, ye willna be a marquess. Ye will be a wealthy self-made man with a sizable fortune at his disposal."

"From your mouth…"

Cait gazed up at him, her blue eyes earnest as she said, "Americans prize men who are self-made, ye ken? What ye think of as a hindrance might be an asset in someone else's eyes." Then she turned her own gaze back to the pair who had Gray's attention. "If ye willna ask her ta dance, then perhaps a turn about the room. I'd stay away from the refreshment table, if I were ye, however."

Even Cait thought to poke fun at him? Gray ground his teeth together. "Hardly amusing."

"I meant if ye're walkin' around the room, it'll be harder for anyone else ta overhear yer conversation, Gray."

Oh. Well, she was probably right about that. Still, Gray frowned again. "I haven't spoken to her since last night."

"Why no'?"

"I didn't know what to say. I still don't. I completely humiliated her at the musicale…" And then he'd been too dumbfounded to speak when he found himself in her bedchamber.

Just then the waltz ended and Lavendon bowed before Livi. He offered her his arm and then led her back to where Lady Sophia and the Duchess of Hythe still stood together.

"She seems ta have recovered rather well," Cait said. "Go over and ask her ta walk with ye, Gray."

Fifteen

LAVENDON DELIVERED LIVI BACK TO SOPHIE, WHERE the duchess still lingered. When the old woman raised her head to look for another dance partner, four more well-dressed gentlemen stepped in her direction. "The Earl of Honeywell is on your left," Sophie whispered.

He looked pleasant enough. Livi hadn't heard the earl's name or even a rumor associated with the man before now. He hadn't made any promises as far as she knew of in regards to seeking her out the way Mr. Siddington did or as the Marquess of Lavendon seemed obligated to do. "Is he poor?" Livi muttered under her breath.

Sophie smiled at her. "So cynical already?" Then she shook her head. "Fortunes are easily won and lost, Livi. But I haven't heard anything about Lord Honeywell in that regard."

Then the man had no need of her dowry. It couldn't be simply that he wanted to meet her, could it?

"The colonel, on the other hand," Sophie continued in sotto voce, "has buried two wives and has eight children for whom he needs to find a mother." That must be the rather tall man approaching on her right.

Livi pretended not to see him and turned her back. The Earl of Honeywell bowed before the duchess. "Would you be so kind, Your Grace, as to introduce me to the young lady?"

The Duchess of Hythe cleared her throat. "Honeywell, this is Miss Mayeux, Holmesfield's grand-daughter. Miss Mayeux, this is the Earl of Honeywell."

"A pleasure," Livi murmured.

"Indeed, it is mine." He smiled. "If this dance is not taken…" he began.

"It is," came a deep voice from behind her, and Livi spun around to find Grayson Hadley standing not a single pace from her.

"I'd prefer to hear it from the lady's lips," Honeywell clipped out. He regarded Livi with one raised brow and held out his open palm to her. She reached tentatively to take it. He had come to her, after all. And he had no ulterior motives, not that she knew of in any event.

"Honeysmell, if you want to keep that hand, I'd suggest you put it in your pocket," Gray growled.

Livi didn't miss the smear of the poor earl's name. In fact, he did smell a bit wretched now that Gray mentioned it. Unfortunately, not a bit like honey at all. She swiped at her nose. "I believe Mr. Hadley is correct," Livi said to break the heavy silence. "I nearly forgot. May I save a quadrille for you, my lord?"

The man gave one simple nod and glared at Gray, who glared back, a low growl emanating from his throat.

"You make me want to pop you on your nose," Livi

scolded as he took her hand and pulled it to rest in the crook of his arm. He led her around the edge of the room. "Where are we going?" she asked, as they skirted some potted palms and walked toward an open doorway.

"You need some air," Gray informed her.

She attempted to jerk her arm back from him. "I most certainly do not."

But he covered her hand with his and kept walking. "Do you want to cause a scene or do you want to come with me nicely?" he growled. "We can do it either way you like."

Another scene was certainly not what she needed in that moment. She feigned a smile and said between her gritted teeth, "You will pay dearly for this, Grayson Hadley." To all the world, she probably looked like she was flashing him a brilliant smile rather than threatening his life. The latter was much more accurate, however.

"Would you care for some punch?" Gray asked.

Certainly, he didn't intend to get her punch. After last night, that was the most absurd thing she'd ever heard. She'd be wearing it within moments. "I believe I'll pass. My dress is better green than red, I think. And it took forever to wash off that sticky punch." But that thought only served to make her remember his visit to her room when she was still in the bath. Heat crept up her cheeks.

"That's what I want to talk to you about," Gray said as he walked with her through the double doors and into the garden. They weren't the only ones in the garden, however. Other couples lingered in pairs, their heads pressed tightly together.

Livi took a step away from him, as she had no desire to make it appear as though they were intimates. But Gray didn't seem to notice. He kept walking, leading her farther down the garden path.

"Sophie will wonder where I've gone," Livi reminded him.

"She'll know where you've gone. What she'll wonder is how to decrease the damage it will do to your reputation." With that, Gray grabbed her fingertips in his strong grip and tugged her into an alcove in the garden. It was dark, with shadows dancing through the tall shrubbery. A moon, three quarters full, gleamed from between the branches.

"You plan to do more damage than you already have?" Livi couldn't believe the gall of him. She stomped her slipper-clad foot.

"The fault of last night's calamity rests solely at my feet. I was in a bit of a state when I arrived at the musicale…" He let the last trail off, simply shaking his head at himself.

"You were foxed." That was all she said, just *you were foxed.*

"Quite," he clipped out. "Then I tripped over that damn cane. And all was lost. Will you accept my apology?" He gave her a battered puppy expression. It had never worked on her with her brothers, and it would not work for him.

"If you offered an apology, I might find it in my heart to accept it."

He sighed heavily, blowing like the bellows the maids used to stoke the fire in the hearth of her bedchamber. "I just did," he said, quirking his brows at her.

"This is how an apology should go, Grayson." She shook a finger at him and hushed him when he began to sputter. "Repeat after me. 'I, Grayson Hadley…'" She stopped and waited for him.

"I, Grayson Hadley." He stopped and waited too, an amused look on his face.

"'Do solemnly swear that I am the biggest idiot that ever walked the face of the earth,'" Livi continued. She tried not to smile as she said it.

"I'm not saying that," he groused.

But she continued, "'And since Miss Mayeux is gracious enough to forgive my drunkenness that could have ruined her place in society and any chance for a decent marriage…'" She stopped and waited again.

"You don't want to marry," he tossed in with a snort.

"You, sir, are positively wretched at apologies." She rolled her eyes at him.

"Did I really ruin your chances?" he asked softly. A slow grin tipped the corners of his lips, and Livi felt it in her belly when it flipped. Oh, goodness. What was that?

She tipped her nose in the air in the same way she'd seen Sophie do it. "You may have."

"Well, in that case," he said, then one hand shot out and caught her arm. He tugged her to him in one swift move. She fell hard against the wall of man that he was and braced herself with her hands against his chest.

"What are you doing?" she asked.

"If your chances are already ruined, I'll have no choice but to marry you. And if I have to do that, I want to take full advantage of my position." He dropped his head toward hers. Livi was so startled that she didn't even try to move away from him. His lips touched hers, soft and harsh at the very same time. She'd been kissed before but never with such intent. His lips slid silky and smooth against hers as he caught her gasp in his mouth.

A little noise escaped her throat as his hands skimmed her waist and slid down over her bottom. Gray's tongue slid to tangle with hers in the most subtle of invasions, and Livi's knees buckled slightly. But his hand on her arse kept her tight against him. Tight against all of him. And she could feel every inch of him against her belly.

Finally, Gray raised his head and let her breathe, which was kind of him, considering the fact that she was about to swoon. Her heart pounded so loudly in her chest that she could outdo the clip of a team of runaway horses. She drew in a deep breath and his mouth skittered across her jaw, leaving a silky trail in his wake. He kissed the area beneath her ear and let his lips trail down the side of her neck.

He stopped at that spot where her neck met her shoulder and nipped it lightly with his teeth. "I want to make you mine." His voice rumbled right by her ear, making her quiver with… something. His tongue snaked out and licked across the spot he'd just abraded with his tongue. "Right here. Forever."

Just then, Grayson sprang several steps away from her. Livi realized a moment later that heavy footsteps crunched down the gravel path toward them. Thank heavens he had excellent hearing. Sophie and Radbourne rounded the corner and stepped closer to them. Sophie's hand was threaded through the crook of Radbourne's arm in a most intimate manner. And Grayson focused his gaze on their joining. "Did I miss the announcement that the two of you have decided to call a truce?" he asked.

Sophie stepped away from the viscount in one quick motion, her look scathing. "Hardly."

"And for a moment there, I thought you liked me," Archer said to Sophie with a wolfish grin.

Sophie absently picked at a thread on her sleeve. "One must keep up appearances. Even when one detests the other party."

"'Detests' is such a strong word."

"Yet not quite adequate," she sniped back. Then Sophie said loudly, "It is a bit stuffy in there. I'm so glad the four of us decided to take a walk in the garden."

"So am I," Radbourne agreed. "But I'm getting a bit chilled, and Miss Mayeux must be cold because her cheeks look all rosy." He shot Grayson a telling glance, and Livi wanted to hide her head in shame. "Perhaps we should find our way back to the Assembly Room."

"Of course," Sophie agreed and she motioned Livi forward. The two of them walked together, arm in arm, and the brothers walked just behind them. But all the while, Livi's mind was a muddled mess as she couldn't get Gray's kiss out of her thoughts. *Bon Dieu*! The way he felt pressed against her, the way his masculine sandalwood scent enveloped her senses, the way his dark eyes seemed to penetrate her defenses and see who she truly was. She'd never felt that way in her life. What would have happened if Sophie and Lord Radbourne hadn't stumbled upon them?

Just as Livi pondered that thought, she heard

Grayson yelp quickly, and a short scuffle ensued behind him and Lord Radbourne. She didn't think she could watch the scene, so she continued forward as though two grown Lycan men weren't pummeling each other in the garden. As soon as she entered the Assembly Room with Sophie, both of them were immediately swept away at the same time. Siddington collected Sophie. And the Earl of Honeywell led Livi onto the floor. It wasn't until he raised his arms during the quadrille that Livi remembered the nickname Gray had bestowed upon the earl. Honeysmell, indeed.

But all she could truly think about was Gray, who still hadn't returned to the ballroom.

❧

"You are a bloody idiot!" Archer hissed, shoving Gray's chest.

Gray stumbled backward over a bench, and his head landed among the sculpted branches of a potted topiary. He rose back to his feet and brushed the dirt from his clothes, but it was no matter. His attire was ruined for the evening. He could never walk back into the Assembly Room with dark smears across his cravat. But since he was already filthy...

Gray lunged at Archer, knocking his brother against the stone facade of the building. "Go to the devil!" he snarled.

Archer bounded off the building, amber fire darting from his eyes. "Have you lost your mind?" he demanded, grabbing Gray's jacket in his clutches. "Are you trying to ruin her? Did you not do a good enough job of that last night?"

"We were talking, Arch!" Gray growled. "No
need for you to don a suit of armor to defend the
lady's honor."

"Talking?" Archer scoffed. "And I'm Maria
Fitzherbert." Then he shoved his brother once more,
but this time Gray sidestepped the bench and remained
on his feet, and Archer stumbled forward.

Gray couldn't help but laugh. "Indeed? And does
the King know you're masquerading around Bath,
pretending to be my jackass brother, Mrs. Fitzherbert?"

Archer righted himself and narrowed his eyes on
Gray. "Don't be an imbecile. You weren't *talking* and
we both know it." He swiped at his nose with one
finger. "I have the same senses you do, don't forget,
brother mine."

Gray shoved his brother's shoulder. "And just what
is that supposed to mean?"

"It means I can hear things. I can smell things…"

"Indeed?" Gray shook his head, more irritated
than he could remember feeling in a very long time.
"I'm surprised you could hear or smell anything with
Sophia Cole hanging on your arm."

Archer took a step backward, his mouth falling open
in surprise. "We went in search of you, you dolt."

Perhaps, but goading his brother suddenly made
Gray feel so much better. "You seemed more chummy
than that," he taunted. "'Besotted,' I think, is the
word I'm looking for."

His brother's face turned an enraged red. "That is
the most ridiculous thing I've ever heard."

"Is it? Perhaps the gentleman doth protest too—"

Archer lunged for Gray, and both of them

tumbled to the ground, pounding each other without restraint. One of Archer's fists crashed into Gray's nose and blood trickled down his face. They rolled a few feet across the garden path, knocking over topiaries and growling at each other like a pair of dogs fighting for dominance.

Gray was so intent on pummeling the life out of Archer that he barely heard a feminine scream or the sounds of several people gasping. He forgot completely where they even were until a large hand yanked him off the ground and he found himself staring into Dash's furious amber eyes.

"Enough," the alpha growled. He may as well have yelled "Heel!"

Gray felt like whimpering, but he lowered his head in shame instead. "I'm—" he began.

"Don't say one word," Dash ordered.

Archer rose to his feet, brushing dirt and leaves from his trousers and jacket. He glared at Gray but took a step backward when Dash turned his attention on Archer instead.

It was then that Gray realized half of the Assembly Room had poured out into the garden. How long had they been standing there? Cait pressed her way to the front of the group, and Gray dropped his gaze back to the ground to avoid the expression of disappointment he'd caught in her eyes.

"Well, gentlemen," Dash said, loud enough for everyone in the assembled crowd to hear him without effort. "I think it would be in everyone's best interest if you two went on your way." Then he said so quietly that only Gray and Archer could possibly hear him, "Go straight to Brimsworth House and do *not* make me have to look for you."

Sixteen

LIVI SLID TO THE BACK OF THE CROWD AS GRAY AND
Lord Radbourne made a hasty exit from the Assembly
Room. What had gotten into the two of them? There
was no reason to create such a scene. She apparently
had misspoken when she'd called Grayson tame.

Sophie came up beside Livi, linking their arms
together. "Smile," her friend muttered softly.

Smiling was the last thing Livi felt like doing.
Crying felt more apt, for some reason.

Sophie jostled her arm. "Smile," she repeated. "It's
the only way to distance yourself from them. Act as
though you haven't a care in the world."

But Livi did have a care. An enormous care who
had just strode through the Assembly Room without
a glance back over his shoulder in her direction. Livi
feigned a smile.

Sophie laughed without mirth. "You look as
though you smelled something rotten. Can you not
smile better than that?"

Doing so seemed an impossible task. Livi shook
her head. How could she just pretend to smile when

Gray and Lord Radbourne had nearly torn the garden apart with their wolfish tempers? She'd borne witness to this sort of behavior most of her life, courtesy of her brothers; but Armand and Etienne had never done such a thing with so many people present. Never in front of society in such a blatant way. Though, in all honesty, her brothers kept more than a respectful distance from society for several reasons, not the least of which were their lack of desire to mingle with New Orleans' well-to-do and their lack of desire to capture a bride who had aspirations of joining the powerful yet disreputable Mayeux family.

Livi's musing was interrupted when the musicians began to play once more and the crowd began filtering back inside the Assembly Room, whispering about those unruly Hadley brothers. Soon the activity inside the Assembly Room returned to what it had been before the fight in the garden had distracted everyone.

"Thank heavens," Sophie whispered and tapped Livi's arm with her fan. "My cousin will be of great service. Dance with him, laugh gaily, and then we'll leave soon after."

"Why can't we leave now?"

"Because that will solidify an attachment between you and one of those uncivilized men in the *ton*'s minds. And we don't want that."

Livi nodded as though that made sense, but it didn't. Not completely. It wasn't as though Gray and Lord Radbourne had been fighting over her. But why were they fighting? What had happened to make them behave so horribly?

Sophie gestured Mr. Siddington toward them with

a flick of her fan and the nod of her head. A moment later, the gentleman bowed slightly before them. "You needed my assistance, cousin?"

"Henry," Sophie pleaded under her breath, "will you stand up with Miss Mayeux for this minuet?"

He smiled warmly. "It will be my honor." Then he offered his arm to Livi and led her to where other couples were lining up for the set. "Quite a dust-up outside, wouldn't you agree?" the gentleman asked.

Oh, Livi agreed. She just wished she understood it. "I can't imagine what provoked that exchange."

Siddington snorted. "Nothing. Everything. The Hadleys never need an excuse for causing a scene." He took her hand, raised it in the air, and began to lead her in a circle. "It's a wonder they're even allowed entry into these sorts of affairs. My poor cousin has been reduced to nothing more than a servant in their house. It's a disgrace."

At the moment, Livi agreed with his assessment. "Why is she a servant? Why hasn't her family taken her in?" Livi asked, though she probably should have held her tongue.

"She's prideful," Mr. Siddington replied. "My mother offered her shelter, but Sophie refuses to accept her charity." He shook his head in confusion. "But charity must be better than living with those beasts."

Livi simply nodded, for lack of anything to say. They were beasts, after all.

"And then there's Postwick, but I understand her not wanting to accept help from him."

Who the devil was Postwick? "I'm not familiar with the name."

Siddington's eyes widened a bit in surprise. "Indeed?" Then he leaned in conspiratorially. "The Earl of Postwick is a cousin of ours. He was Sophie's father's heir."

"Oh."

"Oh, indeed." He turned her again, and Livi wished she knew what Mr. Siddington meant by that cryptic comment.

❧

"I distinctly said, 'Do not cause another scandal,'" Dash roared as he stalked across his study.

Archer slid forward in his seat across from Dash's desk. "I was trying—" he began, but he stopped speaking when Dash sent him a withering glance.

"You're just as bad," their oldest brother complained. "I don't want to hear another word out of you! Not one single word!"

His voice cracked like a whip struck across Gray's back, and he bristled with the force of it. Dash in a temper made Gray want to tuck his tail and run. And they'd finally provoked him to the point where there was no return from it. Dash typically held his temper until he could explode with it, and now Gray feared it was time to watch the fireworks.

"What am I going to do with the two of you?" he growled as he dropped behind his desk with a weary sigh. Then he jumped to his feet again, as he obviously wasn't quite through with his set-down.

Gray braced himself.

"First, you ruin that girl's chances of a good marriage. I wasn't certain she had it in her to show her face in public again, after what you did at the

Longboroughs' last night. But she is made of stronger stuff, evidently." He shook his head. "Poor girl. She never saw the two of you coming. What was your mother thinking, involving either of you in that girl's entry into society?"

That girl had a name. Gray wished his brother would use it. "Miss Mayeux," he muttered.

Dash turned on Gray, piercing him with his furious golden eyes. "Did you say something?" he snarled.

Too late to back away now. Besides, Gray hated hearing Livi referred to in such a way. "I said her name is Miss Mayeux," he repeated with a little more force.

"You were calling her Livi in the garden." Archer snorted. "When you weren't too busy groping her to gather words."

Dash's blond brows rose in something akin to angry wonder. "I beg your pardon?"

"Muzzle it, Archer," Gray growled.

Dash rubbed at his forehead. If his headache matched Gray's, he was in serious pain. "Please tell me you didn't defile that girl," Dash said, his voice low and gravely. And dangerous.

"I didn't defile that girl," Gray quickly assured him. "I didn't defile Miss Mayeux."

"Then what, exactly, did you do in the garden this evening?"

"I got into fisticuffs with Archer." Gray stated the obvious, but he wanted to avoid any further discussion about Livi at all costs.

"Prior to that," Dash barked, gesturing with his hands for Gray to answer quickly. "What did you do with Miss Mayeux?"

Gray shrugged. "There's nothing to tell. I took her for a walk because she was overheated."

"She certainly was." Archer smirked.

Gray shot him a quelling look. But Archer just winked at him. Damn his eyes.

"And what exactly happened on this walk of yours?" Dash urged.

"Nothing. Archer and Lady Sophia stumbled upon us. I barely spent a moment alone with the girl. All I did was kiss her." He held up a hand. "I swear it, Dash."

Dash sank back down into his chair then, almost deflating a bit as he did so. "First it's nothing and now it's a kiss. I'm afraid of what else I'll learn the longer we discuss the situation."

So Livi was now a situation? She had been better off being "that girl." Gray shrugged. "It was nothing. How many girls did you kiss before you married Cait?"

"We are not discussing my past, Grayson."

"Precisely." Gray snorted. "But you *do* have a past, which includes more than kissing a girl in a garden, I'm sure."

Dash sucked in a breath of air and his face turned a bit on the reddish side. "No matter what I was involved in or with whom, I managed to keep my name and my father's name from being tarnished in public. There's a lesson in there for you."

Well, there was the matter of Dash's altercation with the Westfield pack, but with the color of his half brother's face, Gray thought the better of mentioning it. "I hardly think that kissing Livi is worthy of all this—"

"Now she's Livi?" Dash interrupted, and then he cast his eyes on Archer.

"I did tell you," Archer replied. "You weren't listening."

"And exactly how long has this been going on?" Dash asked, clearly listening now.

Archer shrugged. "I'm not his keeper. But I know he can describe the mark of the beast on the chit's thigh."

"Her thigh?" Dash roared.

Gray picked up a ledger from the desk and threw it at Archer's head, but his brother ducked just in time for it to sail past his ear. "What is wrong with you?" Damned Archer knew full well that Gray hadn't seen Livi's thigh.

Dash growled. He placed both hands on his desk and leaned forward, snarling like an enraged wolf. "You will go to Holmesfield at first light and beg for his granddaughter's hand."

The statement hung heavy in the air, like a storm cloud ready to burst.

"Marry Livi?" Gray asked, absolutely dumbfounded. Dash wouldn't expect such a thing if Archer hadn't opened his bloody mouth. It was one thing to think of marrying Livi when she was close enough for him to kiss, but something else entirely when the reality of his bachelorhood was actually threatened. "I haven't seen her thigh, Dash. She only told me about her mark's location. There's no reason for marriage."

His half brother snorted. "I hope you don't expect me to believe that nonsense. Tomorrow morning," he jabbed a finger in Gray's direction, "you'll go to Holmesfield, fall on your sword in front of the man, and beg for Miss Mayeux's hand. Is that clear?"

Gray's mouth fell open. "She doesn't want to marry me. Hardly a sporting thing for you to do to her."

Dash glared at Gray, irritation rolling off him in waves. "Who says she doesn't want to marry you? Have you asked her?"

Gray sat forward in his seat, hoping to make his brother see reason. "She doesn't want to marry anyone here. She wants to return to New Orleans."

"Does she now?" Dash's brow rose in question.

"Ever since I first met her," Gray assured his oldest brother.

"Then I suppose she shouldn't be showing you her thigh or kissing you in the garden, now should she?" Dash folded his arms across his chest. "You'll offer for her tomorrow."

"With all due respect," Archer interjected from his seat beside Gray, "Holmesfield will never accept any offer Gray would make. He'd never accept an offer from any Hadley man, for that matter."

Archer had a point, a good one. However the truth of his brother's words stung Gray a bit when he should have felt relieved.

"Cait and I discussed this at length on the way home from the Assembly Room. She's under the impression that Holmesfield can be reasoned with, and under the circumstances, I'm inclined to agree with her."

Cait? Had *she* talked Dash into this madness? "I hardly think Cait is in a position to know anything about this," Gray protested.

"And I disagree," Dash dismissed him. "She is also under the impression that the two of you could make a match of it, and after this discussion of kisses and thighs, I find I'm in complete agreement with her."

Damn it all. Where was Wes when Gray needed him? He could use his twin right now. But Wes was snuggled up all nice and warm with Lady Madeline in Kent at the moment. Blast him. "I've never seen her thigh," Gray stressed once more, though he would like to see it and touch it and... Those thoughts were better had when his brothers weren't present. Not that his protestations mattered in the least, as Dash didn't appear to pay Gray's words any attention at all.

Archer lit a cheroot. "Then how else would you know about it?"

"You know she told me." Gray glared at his brother. Why was Archer making this into something it wasn't?

"Oh?" Dash drawled. "She told you, did she? What self-respecting lady would tell you something about her thigh?"

"Nobody said she's a proper lady," Archer tossed in, crossing his ankle over his knee and looking supremely satisfied. "And she actually likes Grayson, so her judgment is in question."

Dash turned his glare on Archer. "Kindly close your mouth." Then glanced back at Gray. "You have insinuated yourself into this girl's life. Cait sees you married to her. And I don't want to hear anymore about this. Just make it happen." And with that final comment, he got up and left the room.

Archer whistled softly. "Well, I guess congratulations are in order."

Gray itched to toss his brother to the ground and

kick his ribs until he begged for mercy. "No thanks to you," he growled. "Why did you have to tell him about her mark? You know damn well I haven't seen it."

"So you say." Archer shrugged. "Anyway, I was just saving all the other marriageable gentlemen in England."

"That's hardly a complimentary thing to say about her. Livi is lovely and any man would be lucky to—"

"That's not what I meant at all, you dolt." His brother laughed without mirth. "I meant saving them from your wrath. You didn't see your expression tonight when she danced with Lavendon or the others."

He'd had an expression? Gray hadn't realized. He narrowed his eyes at his brother, wondering if Archer's judgment was sound or if he was being completely honest.

"You looked positively murderous," Archer continued. "I'd hate to see you sent to the gallows or shipped off to Australia for killing a peer." Then he shivered slightly for effect.

As though Gray couldn't control his own temper. "What a ridiculous thing to say."

"Is it?" Archer took a puff off his cheroot, and then he shrugged as if the conversation was of no consequence. "Anyway, you should be thanking me. At least now you can tumble the chit and get it over with. I know it will make it easier for me to be around you. All your pent-up lust and frustration is enough to drive a sane Lycan mad."

Tumble the chit? Gray's temper flared. "Don't talk about her that way," he growled.

But Archer only laughed in response. "And thank

you, little brother, for proving my point. All the marriageable gentlemen in England will be much safer after you've married your little French poodle."

Married to Livi. The suggestion both terrified him and made his stomach do little flips. He could hold her and kiss her whenever he wanted. He could, as his brother indelicately put it, tumble her every morning, noon, or night, if he wanted. But… "You know as well as I that Holmesfield will never agree to any such match."

Archer took another puff off his cheroot. "And yet Dash said to make it happen. So who are you more afraid of, Grayson? Holmesfield? Or Dash?"

Without a doubt he was more concerned about Dash. Still that didn't mean Gray had any idea of how to proceed with that curmudgeon Holmesfield.

Seventeen

A SCRATCH CAME AT LIVI'S DOOR, BUT SHE REFUSED TO acknowledge it. After the events of the previous evening, she didn't care if she saw anyone today or ever. Memories of Gray kissing her, holding her, and whispering words like *marriage* ran through her mind. Then the ridiculous fight Gray and Lord Radbourne had engaged in, rolling around the garden floor like two unruly beasts. She groaned, then rolled over in her bed, pulled the counterpane up over her shoulders, and closed her eyes to block out the sun that now spilled in through the drapes. Certainly she could plead a headache and stay abed all day, couldn't she?

The scratch came again, and this time it sounded a bit more impatient, if that was possible, like an angry mouse in a temper. Well, whoever it was could scratch all day until their nails were stubs for all Livi cared. She'd suffered day after day in English society. She'd tolerated balls and musicales and stuffy drawing rooms. She should be granted time to herself, if only for a little while.

"Miss Liviana!" Marie's voice came out in a hiss.

Livi groaned, hoping her maid would think she was still asleep and leave her in peace.

"Oh, for heaven's sake!" Sophie's voice filtered through the door. "She can't be sleeping with all the noise you're making." Then the door burst open, bringing both Sophie and Marie stumbling into Livi's sanctuary. "Livi!" her friend complained. "Out of bed. Quickly."

Quickly? Livi cracked an eye open. "Why?"

"I knew you were awake." Sophie crossed the floor and sat on the edge of Livi's bed. "Lord Honeywell is in your grandfather's parlor."

Livi pushed up on her elbows. "Why?"

Sophie snorted. "Is that the only thing you can say this morning?"

It was as good as anything else. Livi shrugged. "Why is he here?" she added a few extra words to appease her friend.

"To call on you, of course. Let Marie get you dressed and then hurry to the parlor."

But Livi didn't want to see Lord Honeywell. She didn't even want to see Sophie this morning. "I'm not feeling like receiving visitors today. Will you send him away, please?"

Sophie frowned at her and touched a hand to Livi's brow. "Are you ill?"

If she *was* ill, would everyone leave her alone? Livi nodded, not wanting to verbalize a fib.

"Hmm." Sophie's eyes narrowed. "That is a shame. You have quite a display of flowers lining tables in the parlor and music room."

"Flowers?"

"Despite Lord Radbourne and Mr. Hadley's best efforts, you seem to have caught some eyes last night."

That didn't make any sense.

"I doubt Lord Honeywell will be your only caller this morning—he's just the first to arrive. I do wish you were feeling better so you could greet them all. It wouldn't do for them to think you were putting them off."

"Have you seen Gray... er... Mr. Hadley this morning?" Livi blurted out before she thought the better of it. *Bon Dieu*, what was wrong with her? She certainly didn't want to see Gray this morning. Not after the spectacle he caused the night before.

"Is that what your sudden illness is about?" Sophie squeezed her hand. "Not to fret, Livi, Mr. Hadley did not return here last night. So you won't have to worry about seeing him or his disreputable brother this morning."

Well, that was even worse, wasn't it? "He didn't return?" Livi squeaked. "Is he all right? Do you know where he is?"

"Neither of them deigned to tell me their plans for the evening, but I'm sure they're both fine. They always are, no matter what sort of trouble they find themselves in. Hadley men seem impervious to any permanent damage."

Livi suddenly itched to leap from the bed. She didn't want to see Gray, she told herself, but she hated the idea of not knowing where he was or what had happened to him. When had the insufferable English Lycan gotten under her skin? When had she started to care about his well-being? And why could she still feel his kiss against her lips. "We've got to find him… I mean them."

Sophie laughed. "We will do no such thing. If they prefer to behave like dogs, then they can sleep outside for all I care. Besides, Livi, associating with them will only hurt your prospects. Now I know Lord Honeywell is not the most exciting of men, but he is here and you could use the practice of conversing with a proper gentleman."

At that moment a strangled scream from below stairs startled both Livi and Sophie. "*Bon Dieu*, what was that?"

Sophie leapt to her feet. "I think that was Lord Honeywell." She rushed to the door. "Excuse me, will you?" But she didn't wait for a reply before bolting from Livi's room with Marie quick on her heels.

Livi threw off her counterpane and followed the pair across the corridor and down the steps to the first floor, just in time to see Lord Honeywell dangling from Grayson Hadley's grasp. Livi, Sophie, and Marie all gasped in unison.

"And stay away from her," Gray growled before unceremoniously tossing Lord Honeywell out the front door into the street. Then he slammed the front door, which shook the foundation just the tiniest bit.

"Mr. Hadley!" Sophie scolded, rushing down the remaining steps. "Have you taken leave of your senses?"

But Gray didn't answer her. His dark eyes landed on Livi, still on the steps, and a roguish smile lit his lips. "What an interesting choice in attire this morning, my dear."

Livi glanced down at her nightrail to find it might as

well have been completely sheer for all the protection
it warranted her. *Bon Dieu*, she was an idiot. She had
been in such haste to find out what the commotion
was about that she hadn't even grabbed her wrapper
on the way out of her room. She took one last horrified look at Gray and then bolted back up the stairs
and flew into her chambers.

Gray couldn't help but grin as he watched Livi dash
up the stairs. If he'd ever seen a lady as beautiful, he
couldn't remember her. Seeing heat creep up her face
made him want to do all sorts of delicious things to see
if other parts of her colored just as prettily. The very
thought relieved a bit of the anxiety he'd been bottling
up since Dash's demands the night before. They could
make a match of it. A most delectable match if her
thumping heartbeat and rosy skin were any indication.

"Mr. Hadley!" Lady Sophia hissed once more,
breaking him from his reverie. "What has gotten
into you?"

He nodded his head once at his tutor in greeting.
Hmm, as soon as he married Livi, he would be free
of Lady Sophia's lessons just like Wes was. His smiled
widened. "Do excuse me, my lady. I have come to
have a word with Lord Holmesfield."

Lady Sophia smacked his arm when he started past
her toward the staircase where Livi had just been
standing. "You threw poor Lord Honeywell onto the
ground. You threw him to the ground!" Her horrified
expression would normally have given Gray pause, but
not today. "I have asked you and asked you to keep

your distance from Miss Mayeux, and this is what you do?" She gestured wildly toward the closed front door. "You tossed Lord Honeywell outside as though he were a pile of rubbish."

"I won't have other men calling on Livi. See that they don't." He brushed past her.

"And just who are you to say who can call on her and who can't?" Lady Sophia demanded.

Gray winked at her. "Her husband, just as soon as I can arrange it." Then he strode up the steps, grinning when he heard her indignant gasp.

He stopped outside the earl's quarters and took a deep breath. Men like Holmesfield respected power, and though Gray might not have political or financial power, he did have physical strength and a commanding presence. Hopefully, those two traits combined would be enough to gain the earl's favor. He lifted his hand to knock but stopped when he heard someone behind him.

"I was worried about you." Livi's summery scent washed over him.

Gray spun on his heel to face her, only to find her frowning at him. Even worse, she'd donned a wrapper, much to his chagrin. He much preferred her in that nearly sheer nightrail she was wearing when she'd first greeted him. Of course, he also preferred her smiling at him. "No need for that. I'm in one piece, as you can see."

"Can the same be said for Lord Honeywell, I wonder?"

Honeywell again? Gray scrubbed a hand across his face. "Don't tell me you'd like the odiferous fellow to call on you again."

Livi's eyes narrowed on Gray. "After the scene you and your brother caused last night, after the way *you* behaved at the Longboroughs' the evening before, I'm fortunate anyone called on me."

Gray winced at the censure in her tone. Still, her callers weren't something she would have to worry about much longer. "Forget Honeywell, Livi. I'll make everything right with your grandfather."

"*Bon Dieu*," she squeaked as though the suggestion horrified her. Then Livi stalked closer to him, shaking one finger in his direction. "Don't you dare wake him. He doesn't know about any of this, and I won't have you telling him."

"He doesn't know?" How was that possible? Holmesfield had seemed to take a vested interest in Livi's progress.

Livi heaved a sigh. "I've been fortunate thus far. So just leave, will you?"

Holmesfield's knowledge, or lack thereof, didn't change Gray's situation in the least. Dash knew, and Dash had ordered him to present himself to the earl and secure Livi's hand, one way or another. Surprisingly, Gray wasn't all that opposed to the idea now that he'd had several hours to get used to it. "I'm afraid I can't do that." He turned back to Holmesfield's door and would have knocked if she hadn't rushed forward and clutched his arm.

"Haven't you done enough? I won't go to a convent," she hissed. "Go away. You'll just make everything worse."

Blue fire flamed in her eyes and Gray couldn't help but smile at her. She was adorable in a temper.

Something he could look forward to the rest of his life. He reached his free hand out and tucked one of her dark curls behind her ear. Convents were not in her future; he was. "Were you truly worried about me?" He let his voice drop to a low rumble. "That is promising."

"Graaaaay," she complained, exasperation laced her tone. "You're being a pest."

"I think I like the idea of you worrying about me," he said, as though she hadn't spoken.

"If you don't tuck your tail and leave this instant, I will put you in a choke collar and drag you out myself."

"A collar, huh?" He bit back a grin. "What a naughty suggestion, Livi. Perhaps we can revisit that after we've married."

Her delectable mouth dropped open at that suggestion. "I beg your pardon?"

"Begging's not necessary, I assure you." Gray gestured toward her grandfather's door with a cock of his head. "After I finish with Holmesfield, we can discuss it more in depth."

Livi folded her arms across her chest. "Did you say 'married'?"

Gray nodded. "Just as soon as it can be arranged."

Her brow furrowed and she leaned closer toward him. "There's no need for that, Gray," she whispered. "You haven't ruined my chances. Just behave from here on out, or better yet…" Her frown deepened. "If you keep your distance all together, I should be fine. Sophie says Lord Honeywell won't be my only caller today. So all's forgiven. Just leave."

Leave her to the other men in Bath? The idea nearly

made Gray nauseous. Besides, Dash would never stand for it. "I'm afraid that's out of the question, my dear."

She stomped her foot. "Why?"

Because he didn't want to lose her to someone else. Because he adored her. Because he wanted to get a good look at the mark on her thigh, and had ever since he'd first met her. He might even want to taste it. He'd have to see it to determine. He adjusted his trousers at the very thought. But considering the frown on her face, he thought the better of saying as much. "Because Eynsford ordered it," he said instead. She would at least understand the hierarchy of a pack. She wouldn't question that.

Livi staggered backward, and Gray thought she would have fallen over if he hadn't caught her arm. "W-why would he do such a thing?"

Gray shrugged. "Holmesfield might not know what's gone on, Livi, but my brother most assuredly does. I'm to get your grandfather's blessing one way or another."

All the color in Livi's face drained away.

Eighteen

LIVI THOUGHT SHE MIGHT BE SICK. *LORD EYNSFORD* HAD ordered Gray to marry her? How utterly humiliating.

Bon Dieu! Her grandfather wouldn't be happy about the situation, nor would Papa, for that matter. Livi hadn't been sent all the way across the Atlantic only to wind up married to a Lycan who was barely accepted by society. If Papa had wanted that for her, he'd have let her stay in New Orleans.

Gray's dark eyes seemed to peer into Livi's soul, and the memory of his kiss flashed in her mind—the way his strong arms had encompassed her, the way his sandalwood scent had washed over her, the way tingles had raced across her skin.

Things would be different, she supposed, if he cared for her like Papa had cared for *Maman* before they'd left England. But he didn't. She thought Gray liked her well enough, but that was hardly the basis for a marriage. Livi shook her head. "Before you speak to my grandfather, don't you think you should ask me to marry you first?"

Gray smiled that charming smile of his and took

her hand. "Miss Liviana Mayeux, will you do me the honor of becoming my wife?"

Livi tipped her chin back, much the same way she'd seen Sophie do more than once. "*Non*, but thank you for your generous offer all the same."

"No?" he repeated as his eyes narrowed and incredulity dripped from his voice.

"*Non*," she said again. "So you may go back to whatever gutter you slept in last night. I don't need your pity nor Lord Eynsford's meddling. I'll inform Eynsford of that fact myself, if you need someone to explain it to him."

Gray heaved an indignant sigh. "I don't think you understand the gravity of our situation, Livi. Eynsford—"

"Is not my alpha and I don't have to answer to him."

Gray's eyes narrowed to slits. "Refusing me isn't an option. Holmesfield might not know at this moment what has gone on, but you won't be able to keep him in the dark forever. The sooner we're married, the better it is for you, for your reputation."

But not better for her heart. "I—" she began, but was interrupted when her grandfather's door opened suddenly.

The earl's valet stood on the threshold, glaring at the pair. "Lord Holmesfield would like to know what is going on in the corridor."

Gray tipped his head to Livi and said, "You'll thank me for this one day." Then he turned his gaze on the servant. "I've come seeking his lordship's audience."

"Is that Grayson Hadley?" her grandfather called from within his chambers.

Gray didn't wait to be announced, but brushed past

the valet and strode purposefully into the earl's room. "Good morning, sir. I thought it best if I presented myself to you before the gossip reached your ears. Please rest assured that I will provide for Livi and look forward to our future together."

Blast him! Did he really need to use the word "gossip"? Livi tightened her hand into a fist.

"What are you blathering about, Hadley?" her grandfather grumbled.

Livi pushed her way past the valet too. "Mr. Hadley is merely jesting, Grandfather," She turned her glare on Gray. "He hasn't been feeling well and is in no mood for your games, sir."

But Gray shook his head, all male arrogance, all wolfish male arrogance. "Your granddaughter is trying to preserve your good humor, Lord Holmesfield. But her attempt is in vain. Once you are out of your bed, you are sure to learn all the gossip involving Livi and myself. And you'll be sure to demand I marry her. But there is no need for demands, as I have come to ask for her hand of my own volition."

His own volition? Livi somehow managed not to snort. If it wasn't for Lord Eynsford, Gray would be sleeping off the effects of alcohol somewhere else this morning, not standing in her grandfather's chamber trying to ruin her life. "That is an exaggeration, Mr. Hadley, and now I'll ask you to leave my grandfather in peace. He's—"

"What is he talking about?" the earl asked again, struggling to sit up in his bed. "What's this about gossip?"

Gray stepped toward the bed. "Would you like some assistance, sir?"

Her grandfather glared at Gray. "I would like for you to tell me what you did to Liviana."

"I kissed her," Gray announced. "Last night at the Assembly Room. But even before that, all of Bath had linked the two of us together, and you can be certain that it's in Livi's best interest to marry me as soon as possible."

The earl scoffed. "I'd sooner see her shipped off to Newgate."

"I hardly think becoming a Hadley is worse than life in prison."

"I wouldn't be so sure," her grandfather growled. Then he speared Livi with his gaze. "Are people truly discussing the two of you?"

She couldn't really lie. Well, she could, but he'd find out soon enough and then where would she be? "It's not as bad as it sounds."

"Any attachment to him is as bad as it sounds. Worse, even." He pointed to the corridor. "Go to your room and put on some clothes, Liviana. When your fiancé," he spit the word, "and I are finished here, I'll send for you."

Fiancé? He'd capitulated just like that? And here Livi had thought her grandfather was made of sterner stuff. "But—" she began only to have the old man raise his hand and shoot her a withering glance.

"You are in your nightrail!" he bellowed. "Go get dressed for the day."

"I've got a wrapper," she protested, hoping to make him listen to reason before sending her away. "Grandfath—"

"You are in your night clothes! Go to your room this instant." And then a fit of coughs overtook him. "Now!"

Blast it! Livi didn't really have a choice. If she stayed, her grandfather would only get angrier, if his red face and coughing fit were any indication. What rotten luck. She sent one more scathing glare in Gray's direction before bolting from her grandfather's chambers to the safety of her own.

Perhaps she could still find her way to Bristol and hop a frigate back to New Orleans. Better yet, New York or maybe Boston. She didn't have to go home, after all. Not if Papa would only send her back to England to face Grayson Hadley. Gray who didn't really care about her. Gray who was only marrying her to appease his pack alpha. Well, Livi wouldn't have it.

⤜⤚

Gray couldn't help but watch Livi flee the room. It really was too bad she hadn't been more agreeable to the arrangement. Last night she'd seemed perfectly happy to be in his arms. Had she changed her mind in the light of day?

"You can take your eyes of my granddaughter's backside," Holmesfield growled. He truly did growl. All things considered, he would have made a perfectly good Lycan with his ferocious sound.

Gray smiled at the old man, hoping to appease him just a bit. "I am sorry, Lord Holmesfield. I meant no disrespect. I'm simply besotted."

The earl's eyes narrowed on him. "Tell me this is the first time you've seen her in her nightrail."

But he had seen her before in that exact set. The very first night they'd been in Bath. Gray couldn't really lie; the old man would see the truth on his face. So instead he took a step forward and offered up his hands in supplication. "I know I'm not the man you would have chosen for her, but I'll make her happy. I swear it. I'll see that she's always well cared for."

"I suppose you thought that diversion would distract me from my question, which is an answer in itself." Holmesfield pinched the bridge of his nose as though an ache pulsed in his brain. "But you are correct, Hadley. You are far from who I would have picked for my granddaughter. And I am far from pleased with the situation." He snorted in disgust. "I hope you have a houseful of daughters to plague you every day and night. It'll serve you right."

Hardly a complimentary thing to say about the fairer sex. Dash had a daughter whom he adored with all of his heart. Only time would tell if his forthcoming bundle would be another girl or not, but Dash seemed quite thrilled at the prospect. Gray simply frowned at the man, which made the earl laugh in response.

"Just you wait. Daughters run off in the middle of the night with scurrilous Frenchmen and flee the country. Granddaughters attach themselves to unruly blackguards while you're sick in bed." Then he shook his head. "I suppose I should be grateful *you* at least sought an audience with me. Philippe Mayeux just absconded with my Grace and I never saw her again."

The old man still seemed pained by the past. Gray sighed. "We'll be close at Hadley Hall. You'll be able to see Livi anytime you'd like."

"Don't try to appease me, Hadley." The earl's

frown deepened. "You'll leave for Lambeth Palace this morning, and—"

"My brother has already set out to acquire a special license on my behalf," Gray said. "I thought speed would be warranted under the circumstances." Or rather Dash had ordered Archer to ride like the wind for London, not that Gray could say as much. "I'd imagine he'll return sometime this evening."

Holmesfield gestured to the door. "Then be gone until tomorrow morning when you have the license in hand. I'd rather not have to look at you in the meantime."

There was really no need to torture the man with his presence, was there? Probably not. He'd just given his permission for Gray to marry his granddaughter, pretty much against his will. Why rub salt in the wound? Gray bowed slightly at him and backed out of the room and then down the steps.

But just as he reached the front door, a flurry of movement crashed into his arm and then clung to it. He looked down into Livi's furious face and forced himself to still, rather than clutch her to himself as he so desperately wanted to do.

"What do you think you're doing?" she hissed.

He forced his smile to retreat. "Right this moment, I'm trying to keep myself from kissing you." She looked so damned pretty when she was angry. He'd have to make her angry often. Somehow, he didn't think that would be difficult.

Livi released the clutch she'd had on his arm with a heavy sigh and stepped back from him. "You know that's not what I mean."

Gray let his eyes roam over her body. She'd quickly

changed out of her nightrail and had donned a blue walking dress, one that nearly matched her sky-blue eyes. But it held none of the fire her eyes did. He had to admit that he much preferred her in her nightrail. But he assumed he'd like her in nothing at all even more. He cleared his throat and picked a point on the wall to stare at for a moment. Just until he could gather his wits about him.

Livi began to pace in front of him, as she raised a hand to her mouth and worried her fingernail. "I can't believe you did that," she mumbled to herself. "What must he think of me now?"

Gray hitched his shoulder against the wall and watched her walk to and fro. "He thinks you're marrying below your station," Gray admitted. "But it cannot be avoided."

"It could be avoided if he would just send me home. No one need know of this little problem back in New Orleans."

The very thought of her being shipped back home was enough to make the hair stand up on the back of his neck. "I'm afraid that's not going to happen," Gray informed her. She may as well resign herself to it. She would be Liviana Hadley in fewer than twenty-four hours. He stepped closer to her and reached out a hand to grasp her elbow, stopping her pacing with a gentle tug to her arm. He clucked her under the chin with his crooked finger. "Accept our circumstances, Livi. We will be wed tomorrow morning."

"You don't want to marry me." Her eyes danced across his face.

He might not want to marry her exactly, but he did

want her. And it was unavoidable. He'd damaged her reputation, though he hadn't meant to. And now he must act. "How do you know what I want?"

She snorted. "When you tilt your head at me like that, you remind me of a hound we once had," she said.

He leaned close to her ear and whispered, "Does it make you want to scratch me behind the ears?"

She shivered lightly, just inches away from him. "That is the last thing on my mind," she said and she spun away from him.

It was then that Gray noticed the fastenings on the back of her gown were mismatched. "We'll have to replace your maid once we're married," he said as he reached for her shoulders. "She is woefully inadequate."

Livi glanced over her shoulder, a scowl upon her face. "Marie didn't dress me. I was in a hurry to get below stairs before you could do too much damage. These blasted English dresses are difficult to don by one's self." She reached one arm behind her back and then the other, wincing as she did so. "Not to mention all the underthings. Blast and damn," she muttered. Then she started for the stairs.

"Where are you going?" he called to her.

She stopped and looked over her shoulder at the sad state of her gown once more. "To dress. If I can find Marie this time."

Gray reached up to grab her waist and lowered her from the third stair where she was standing. She squealed lightly when he lifted her, and she clutched his shoulders until her feet hit the floor. Amid her protests, he dragged her by her fingertips down the corridor and into a small sitting room. Then he closed the door behind him. "I happen to make a fine lady's maid," he said, trying to keep from grinning.

"I'm certain you've undressed more than your share," she began. "But have you dressed them?"

He shushed her with a quick noise. He approached her and took her shoulders in his hands again, steadying her in front of him with her back facing him. He'd never wanted anything as much as he wanted to reveal Livi's naked back to his eyes. "You're not wearing a chemise?" he asked as he began to adjust her gown.

"I didn't have time. I was afraid of what you would say to Grandfather."

Gray inhaled deeply. The summery scent of her filled his nose again, and her heartbeat filled his ears. It beat nearly as loudly as his own. He reached out one tentative hand and slowly let the buttons slide free of their moorings until her back was completely exposed. Truth be told, he could have stopped at the third fastening, but he didn't want to. She kept trying to spin away from him, but he *had* undressed a lot of women, and he was fairly good at it. "Would you be still?" he groused.

She shivered again. He leaned down close to her ear and whispered, "I know I affect you."

Her voice quivered as she replied, "You do make my stomach turn on occasion."

Gray let the back of his curved fingers slide slowly up her back. Her breath hitched in her throat. "Admit it. You like me."

"I like stray dogs, but only after they've been bathed and prettied up."

"You can bathe me any time you wish," he said as he brushed the heavy mass of her hair over one shoulder. And lowered his lips to touch the other. "As long as I get to return the favor."

"You can fasten me back up now," she said. But he let his lips brush across her shoulder and up the side of her neck. "Stop that," she warned, swatting at him like he was a pesky fly.

He held tightly to her hips as she tried to move away. He fastened the lowest button. The one just above her bottom. "Are you wearing drawers?" he asked, letting his fingers skim the small of her back.

She sputtered.

He couldn't keep from chuckling. "I didn't think so. I like the thought of you naked beneath this gown." He liked it way too much, but they weren't married yet.

Just then, the door flew open and banged against the opposite wall. Gray spun with Livi in his arms, putting his back to the newcomer to keep whoever had just entered the room from seeing her state of undress. "Oh, no," Livi muttered. "Fasten me up. Quickly."

"Fasten what?" a male voice asked from the doorway. An American voice. Gray looked up to find a blond-haired man standing there, and another just behind him. They could be twins, except for the fact that one of them was obviously older by a few years.

"Fasten your lips together," Livi shot back at the newcomers.

"You know them?" Gray mumbled to her as he reached the top fastening. So much for kissing his way down her body.

"Yes, I know them," she remarked. "Better than I'd like some days."

The younger of the two men leaned casually against the doorjamb as the other stepped into the room. The woodsy scent of them reached Gray's nose, and he knew immediately who they were.

"Care to explain to me what we just walked in on, Livi?" the oldest of the two asked. "You can tell us before or after we rip his tail off. Or he can tell us after we're done with him, when he's begging our forgiveness for defiling our sister."

Livi stepped in front of Gray like he was a child that needed protecting. "You will do no such thing, Armand." She sniffed and raised her nose higher in the air. "He was simply fixing my gown."

"Fixing to take it off you seems more like it."

That was true.

"Now that you have your clothes on, you can introduce us to the man who was taking them off you," the younger of the two growled.

"Armand, Etienne." Livi sighed heavily. "This is Grayson Hadley. *My betrothed*." She emphasized the last. Both the brothers' eyes opened wider at her pronouncement.

The American Lycans looked at one another. "Then I suppose we don't have to kill him," the one she'd called Armand said.

The other one smirked. "But we *do* have to hurt him."

Gray shoved Livi to the side and ducked as the first fist flew. Then he collapsed atop a settee that broke into splinters beneath him as Livi's oldest brother tackled him.

"Armand!" Livi screamed. "Stop it this instant!"

"Stay out of this, Liv," Etienne warned as he jumped into the fray and sent his fist crashing into Gray's jaw.

Gray landed one solid punch to the younger brother's stomach as the older brother's fist connected with Gray's right eye.

"Good heavens!" Lady Sophia's voice came from the threshold. "What is going on in here?"

Through his good eye, Gray watched the Mayeux brothers jump to attention at Lady Sophia's entrance.

Nineteen

It was barely morning, and yet Livi couldn't remember a day ever starting off so poorly. She wasn't sure whether she should bark at her brothers, rush to Gray whose lip was bleeding and eye was purpling, or beg Sophie to forget the entire exchange. If only the floor would open up and swallow her whole, she could escape all of this madness. Though she knew Gray would heal shortly, he did look the worse for wear at the moment. She couldn't keep herself from crossing the floor and dropping to her knees beside the rubble that had once been her grandfather's settee.

"Are you all right?" she asked, wishing she had a handkerchief or something of use to offer her bleeding fiancé.

Fiancé? She still wasn't sure how that had even happened; but it wasn't in anyone's best interest to divulge that fact to her brothers.

A crooked grin settled on Gray's face. "Worried about me again?" he whispered, squeezing her hand in the process. "I'll be fine. You know I will."

From the doorway, Sophie huffed indignantly. "Mr. Hadley, what have you done now?"

Gray pushed up on his elbows and gestured to Armand and Etienne with a tilt of his head. "Perhaps you'll notice I'm the one bleeding, my lady."

"Probably well deserved," the tutor muttered under her breath, though everyone in the room heard her.

Armand dusted his hands on his trousers and winced under Sophie's scrutiny like a dog caught in the act of doing something he shouldn't have. "Please forgive me. Armand Mayeux at your service."

"Mayeux?" Sophie asked. "You're Livi's brothers?" She glanced at the pair and then at Livi as though seeking confirmation.

"I'm Etienne," her other brother said, reaching the threshold where Sophie stood before Armand could do so. "And you are…?" He leaned casually against the doorjamb. He might as well lick his lips to complete the lascivious look that reflected in his eyes. The reprobate.

"She's my friend," Livi announced as she scrambled back to her feet. "I do hope you'll treat her with more respect than you've shown my betrothed thus far."

Etienne's blue eyes flashed to Livi. "She's much prettier."

Livi scoffed. "So you only go around pummeling my friends who aren't attractive?"

Gray snorted at that, but Livi glared at him. This was all his fault anyway. If her brothers hadn't caught him practically undressing her, they wouldn't have taken it upon themselves to crash him into their grandfather's furniture.

"She is much more our type," Armand replied. Then he cast a scowl in Gray's direction. "Besides, *she* wasn't attempting to seduce our little sister."

Sophie gasped. "Well, I should hope not."

"But," Etienne bowed before her, "you may feel free to seduce me, Miss...?"

"Lady," Livi stressed. "Lady Sophia Cole and she's much too refined for either of you mutts, so leave her be." Sophie could barely manage Gray and Lord Radbourne as it was, depending on the day. She would be completely out of her element with Livi's wild brothers.

Sophie gestured to Gray on the ground and the smashed settee beneath him. "It looks as though a dockside brawl has transpired in here."

Etienne smiled roguishly. "Attended many dock-side brawls, my lady?" Then he winked at Livi and said, "Perhaps she's not as refined as you think, Liv."

Armand reached for Sophie's hand and then brought it to his lips. "Apologies, Lady Sophia. We were simply welcoming Mr... What did you say his name was?"

"Hadley," Sophie supplied with a frown as she extricated her hand from Armand's grasp.

"*Oui*, Mr. Hadley," Armand continued. "We were simply welcoming Mr. Hadley into our family. We Mayeuxes can be more impulsive than I'm sure you're accustomed to over here."

Impulsive? Livi snorted. Perhaps wild, barbaric, or ferocious were better words to describe her brothers.

"*Oui*," Etienne chimed in. "We've had our fair share of dockside brawls over the years. So if you like that sort of fellow..."

"Etienne!" Livi stomped her foot. "Leave my friend alone." Then she turned her gaze to her oldest brother. "Not that I'm not happy to see you. Well, mostly. But, Armand, why *are* you here?"

Armand shrugged slightly. "Father sent us to retrieve you."

"He did?" Livi's stomach flipped at the thought of going home, of leaving England and all its rules and social nonsense and… Gray. Her eyes flashed to her newly betrothed as he rose from the rubble on the floor. She'd never see him again if she left. But wasn't that what she wanted? A return to New Orleans' bayous and swamps? The smell of Cook's beignets in the morning and crawfish in the afternoon? The warmth that she'd missed ever since her arrival in England? Life with Papa and her brothers, day in and day out? For things to be the way they once were? "But I thought…"

"He realized his error in sending you away just after your ship sailed," Etienne continued. "He even told Father Antonio to bugger off and mind his own business where you're concerned."

Sophie gasped, which Livi could only attribute to her brother's crass language.

"Home just isn't the same without you, Liv," Armand added. "Like all the sunshine in New Orleans left when you did."

Her heart warmed at the sentiment. What a lovely thing to say. And her brothers weren't exactly known for their poetic words.

"Well," Gray began with a bit of a growl to his voice, "I'm sure we'll visit you on occasion." He tucked Livi's hand in the crook of his arm as though she was a possession he wished to keep.

She glared at him. Was he trying to incite her brothers to more violence?

"Or," Armand growled in response, "perhaps you can visit her on occasion after we bring her home."

"As she's to be my wife, I think I'll have a say about where she lives."

"Well, maybe she won't be your wife, then." Etienne added his growl to the mix. "There's no reason for her to marry some arrogant Englishman."

This was beyond the pale. Livi couldn't even think with all the growling and wolfish angling for dominance. "Out!" she ordered.

"You heard the lady," Gray added.

Livi yanked her arm from his grasp. "You too, Grayson."

Gray's dark eyes fell like those of a chastened pup. "Livi," he began softly.

But she stomped her foot and pointed to the corridor. "I can barely think with all of your grumbling and barking. Go away, all of you."

Etienne offered his arm to Sophie. "My lady?"

"And," Livi ground through her teeth, "leave Lady Sophia alone unless you'd like to lose every tooth you possess. I hardly think she'll find you attractive then."

Her brother dropped his arm. "I didn't miss your bossiness."

"And I didn't miss your idiocy."

Sophie glanced toward Gray. "Come along, Mr. Hadley. I should take a look at your eye and that lip of yours."

"I'll be there in a moment." Gray tipped Livi's chin

up so she had to meet his gaze. "I'm not through with you. I don't believe I ever will be."

The intensity of his stare made Livi's stomach drop to her toes. She didn't think she could ever forget him, even if she did return to Louisiana with her brothers.

It wouldn't be so bad, marrying him, would it? She could lose herself in his dark eyes and never wish to be found, but... Livi wished he hadn't been ordered to marry her, that he'd wanted to marry her of his own volition. "You should let Sophie look at your injuries," she said, turning away from him.

"I'll heal just fine," he protested.

But Livi didn't respond. She strode across the room, stepping over what had once been a settee to peer out the window.

❦

Gray slinked from the room, his eyes downcast, and his spirits even lower as he followed Lady Sophia and the Mayeux brothers into the corridor. He glanced back at Livi only to find her staring out the window as though she wanted to block out the rest of the world. He started back over the threshold, but Lady Sophia caught his arm.

"I'm not sure of all that happened in my absence, but I do think you should give her some time, Mr. Hadley." Then her gray eyes widened a bit in surprise. "Your eye looked so much worse in the parlor. It appears nearly healed in this light."

Gray shot his soon-to-be brothers-in-law a quelling glance. "Yes, well, we Hadleys heal quickly."

"I'd wager we Mayeuxes heal even faster," Etienne, the young brother, announced with his chest puffed up with pride.

"For heaven's sake!" Lady Sophia rolled her eyes. "It's hardly a competition." Then she sighed and returned her gaze to Gray. "Follow me into the kitchen, Mr. Hadley. Let me see what is to be done with the rest of your scrapes."

"Should we follow you as well?" Etienne asked.

"Absolutely not! Lord Holmesfield is recovering from an illness, and the last thing he needs is to have his rest disrupted by the three of you assaulting each other with pots and pans to determine which of you is the strongest male specimen."

"It wouldn't even be a contest," Etienne returned with a devilish twinkle in his eye, at the same moment that Armand said, "Our grandfather is ill?"

Lady Sophia nodded once toward the older brother. "When he's feeling better I'm sure he'll wish to meet both of his grandsons."

"Whether we want to meet him is another thing entirely," Etienne grumbled.

But Lady Sophia paid him no attention as she continued, "In the meantime, I'll send Flemming to see you both settled." Then she moved to walk down the corridor and they fell into step behind her, despite her previous instruction for them to wait.

Gray barked, "She didn't say 'heel.' She said 'wait.'" He rolled his eyes at them in what he hoped was a most annoying manner.

"Yet you seem to jump at her commands. Bit of a lapdog, aren't you?" the younger of the two teased.

Lady Sophia took Gray's shoulder in her hand and turned him toward the kitchen. "You go that way," she said with a ladylike shove. Well, as ladylike as a shove could be. Then she gestured to a sitting room not far away and said to Livi's brothers, "You two may wait here."

Armand started back toward the drawing room where Livi remained.

Lady Sophia heaved a sigh. "Leave her be for a moment," she warned, her voice soft but steely.

Just then, the butler rounded the corner and sucked in a breath.

"Oh, Flemming," Lady Sophia said, relief in her voice. "Do prepare rooms for Lord Holmesfield's grandsons." Flemming looked down his nose at the two of them. He would have an apoplectic fit when he saw the broken settee that littered the drawing room floor. "And there was a tiny accident with the settee," she tried to explain.

"Accident?" the butler said. Then he straightened his jacket. "I certainly hope no one was injured." Though the look on his face said the opposite. The old man would probably be overjoyed if someone was injured, especially if it was Gray.

"In fact," Lady Sophia chimed, "the Mayeux brothers might like to help you clean up that mess after they get settled in their chambers."

Amid their protests, Sophia turned away from the American pair and ushered Gray quickly down the corridor. "There, that might give Livi some peace for a few moments," she said, almost as though she spoke to herself.

"Should I return to her?" Gray asked, looking over his shoulder in the direction from whence they'd come.

"Definitely not," she scolded as they stepped into the kitchen. "I think you've done plenty this morning." She pointed to a chair beside a small table. "Sit."

"But—" he started to argue.

"I said sit, Mr. Hadley," she spoke over him.

Gray sat, but he wasn't happy about it. "If I could just talk to her…"

"You'd make things worse." She clucked her tongue at him as she spun away to retrieve a dampened cloth beside Cook's cutting board. "You need to give her a few moments to collect herself. As do her brothers," Sophia said as she crossed the floor and lifted the bit of cloth toward his eye. But then she stopped and tilted her head as though to peer at him from a different angle. "I could have sworn you were bleeding."

"Must have been the light in the drawing room," he murmured.

She leaned against the table and glared at him. "You Hadleys seem to be made of stronger stuff than I realized. What is it with the three of you?"

"I'm not certain to what you're referring," Gray prevaricated.

"The whole lot of you is impermeable to injury. Or you're really fast healers." She narrowed her eyes at him. "Is there some family secret of which I'm unaware?"

Gray nearly tripped over his own tongue. "Secret?" he repeated.

"Yes, there's something odd about all of you."

"I'll be sure to tell Mother you said so," a voice said from behind her. At that moment, Gray's twin, Weston Hadley, stepped fully into the kitchen. He was the mirror image of Grayson, aside from the scar on his face and the grin he'd sported since the day he'd married Madeline Hayburn.

"Weston!" she cried. Then she punched her hands to her hips. "Were you eavesdropping?" Gray nearly expected her to stomp her dainty little foot. But the glare she gave Wes was good enough.

Wes ambled slowly toward the table and plucked an apple from the bowl in the center. He took a bite and wiped his chin with the back of his hand.

"Do you have need of a napkin?" she scolded.

Gray chuckled behind closed lips.

"And what are you doing here?"

Wes shrugged. "I heard the family had rushed off to Bath, and Maddie was feeling lonesome…" He took another bite of his apple.

"Maddie!" Sophie shrieked. She rushed forward and grabbed his arm. "Maddie's here?"

"She's waiting in the parlor," he said from around a mouthful of apple.

"Do chew with your mouth closed, Weston," she admonished.

Gray piped in, "I believe Wes is impervious to your nagging, since he's already married."

Wes chuckled.

"If you're quite all right, I'll leave you to go and see Maddie," Lady Sophia said, crossing her arms and glaring at them both.

"Please do," Gray said with a shrug. "My injuries require no tending." It was mainly his pride that was injured, after all.

As soon as she quit the room, Gray rose from his seat and clapped Wes on the shoulder. "I have never been so happy to see anyone in my life."

"Do I smell Lycans about?" His twin sniffed at the air and turned up his nose.

"Two of them," Gray grumbled.

"And I heard a rumor that you were getting married. What the devil has gotten into you?"

"You seem well suited to it," Gray reminded him.

"Well, Maddie is the exception to the rule." Wes looked a bit uncomfortable. "Who's the chit?" He tossed his apple core into a nearby rubbish bin.

"She's not just some chit," Gray growled.

"Allow me to try again, then. Who is this love of your life?" Wes sweetened his voice into a much-too-honeyed sound.

Gray wouldn't really call her that, either. "Her name is Miss Liviana Mayeux."

"She's the chit with the Lycan bite on her inner thigh?"

"It's not a Lycan bite, you arse." Gray fought the smile that wanted to tug at his lips.

"Oh? Has someone other than you been nibbling on her thigh, then?" Wes grinned unrepentantly. "You sure you want to nibble on someone's leftovers?"

"No one has been nibbling her thigh," Gray insisted more forcefully.

But Wes had never let Gray cow him before, and he shrugged off the irritated sound in his brother's voice. "Not even you?"

"Not yet," Gray groused. "Who told you about her thigh?"

He shrugged. "Dash. We arrived this morning at Cait's invitation."

"You did?"

"Mmm. Missed you by about an hour and got the whole sordid story." Wes shivered dramatically. "Dash is making you come up to scratch, huh?"

Gray nodded. He wasn't really marrying her because Dash bade him to. Well, he was, but he was quite happy about the prospect. And Dash's order did make him feel better about doing it so quickly.

"Did those Lycans toss you into the settee?"

"They tried." Gray stiffened his shoulders.

"By the looks of the furniture, they succeeded," Wes laughed.

"There were two of them," Gray began to explain, but he quickly realized it wouldn't matter what he said. Wes knew Gray's heart almost as well as he did. They'd always been that way. Twins to the very soul.

"Tell me where things stand," Wes prompted.

Gray began to tell him the entire tale. When he was done, Wes nodded. "Thank God I've arrived," he said, adjusting his trousers and then flicking his nose in a very dramatic way. "Those American Lycans have nothing on us Hadleys."

"They want to take her home. And I want to marry her."

"We'll work it all out," Wes said, clapping Gray on the shoulder this time.

"I'm glad you're here."

"Me too, although I'm a little worried about there

being so many of us about with a full moon approaching. Do you think Bath can stand so many Lycans?"

"I suppose we'll find out."

Twenty

"LIVI?" SOPHIE SAID FROM THE THRESHOLD, MAKING Livi nearly jump from her skin.

Livi spun on her heel to find her friend standing just inside the drawing room with a pretty, petite blonde at her side; and Livi touched a hand to her pounding heart. "*Bon Dieu*, you took five years off my life."

"I had been calling your name." Sophie stepped farther into the room, an apologetic expression on her face. "I told everyone else to leave you alone, but Lady Madeline Hadley insisted on seeing you."

Lady Madeline? Livi frowned at the blonde. "You're—"

"Weston's wife," the lady confirmed. "And from all I've heard this morning, we might be sisters soon."

Sisters? Livi had never had a sister before. What a very strange thought. She supposed if she did go through with this madness, the blonde would be her sister. "Word travels fast."

Lady Madeline crossed the floor. "So do Hadley men." She offered her hand to Livi. "Considering the whirlwind you've endured, are you all right, Miss Mayeux?"

"Livi," Livi said. "If we are to be sisters, call me Livi."

"Maddie then." Lady Madeline smiled. "Are you all right, Livi?"

She wasn't sure. Not at all. "More than confused," she admitted.

"That makes two of us." Sophie dropped onto the room's still intact settee. "I'm not even sure what happened this morning. Between Lord Honeywell being tossed out in the street, Mr. Hadley's insistence that he's to marry you, and then your brothers appearing out of nowhere, I am nearly certain the world has been tossed on its side." She frowned as though the day's events had thoroughly taxed her, even though it was still morning.

"Life with Hadley men can be a bit unpredictable." Maddie tugged Livi toward the settee.

"Most definitely an understatement," Sophie replied.

"Perhaps." Maddie shrugged. "But well worth it when you have the right one." Then she gestured for Livi to take a seat beside Sophie as the lady assumed the chair across from them. "Is Grayson the right one for you?"

Livi choked on a laugh. That was the very question she'd been asking herself all morning. Though if she were being honest with herself, she'd wondered before today. But before she could say as much, Sophie slid forward on the settee.

"Maddie, it has been as though we have taken up residence in Bedlam. Not a single day goes by that makes any sense. If your Weston is truly like Lord Radbourne or Mr. Hadley, I don't know how you can stand it."

But Lady Madeline looked perfectly content, serene even. Despite the very poised lady she appeared on the outside, she must be a bit wild herself to live with a Lycan, to love a Lycan. Or did she know that her husband was a beast? Not every Lycan revealed his true nature to his mate. Livi leaned forward in her seat, hoping for a better glance at Maddie's neck. Had she been claimed? The lady seemed so refined, so elegant. Livi wouldn't be surprised if Lady Madeline had no idea who, or rather what, she was really married to.

"I love Weston with all my heart."

"Yes," Sophie agreed, "you announced that very thing to all the *ton* at your grandmother's birthday ball a few months ago. I'll never quite forget it."

"If given the chance, men… like Weston can be quite charming."

Men… like Weston? The way she said the words made Livi think the lady might very well know that her husband was a Lycan. Livi bit the inside of her cheek. She'd grown up with Lycans: her father, her brothers, her cousins… She'd never given any thought to marrying one herself. Until now. What would life as a Lycan's wife be like? How would she face the night of each full moon—with dread or with anticipation? She touched a hand to her neck. Her mother wasn't around for advice. And looking at the very refined Lady Madeline Hadley, Livi couldn't imagine asking such a question of her would-be sister-in-law. Besides, she'd just met the woman. Even Livi wasn't so bold.

She rose from her spot on the settee, nervous energy coursing through her, and returned to the window she had been peering through as though the great outdoors held all the answers to all of her questions. "I'm afraid I'm terrible company today." Livi leaned her head against the cool pane of glass.

"You needn't entertain us, Livi," Sophie said softly. "We only want to be of help."

But Livi wasn't certain that anyone could help, not if she didn't know what she wanted. "Papa has sent for me. He wants me to come home."

"And what do you want?" Sophie asked.

"That's just it. I don't have a clue. Since the moment I arrived in England I wanted to return home, but now…"

"Well, you don't have to sail with the tide," Maddie said. "Certainly your brothers can be coaxed into staying a bit longer in Bath. At least until you decide what you want."

"Speaking of brothers," Sophie cleared her throat, "both of yours are in town, Maddie."

"With Grandmamma, I know. They haven't been chasing your skirts, have they? I will flay Robert if he's made a nuisance of himself."

"I have managed the two of them all of these years, but my life would be much easier in helping Livi assimilate into society if the brothers Hayburn kept a more respectful distance."

"I'll talk to Grandmamma." Maddie nodded in agreement. "But in the meantime," she dropped her voice to a whisper, "we should figure out how to delay Livi's brothers from marching her across the Atlantic."

Sophie glanced around the room that was now empty, save for the three of them. "Why are you whispering?"

Maddie's eyes locked with Livi's, and in that

moment Livi knew without a doubt that Madeline Hadley was quite familiar with Lycans' abilities and their limitations. "My brothers," Livi whispered as well, "have excellent hearing. We probably should speak softly, so as not to be overheard."

Maddie's green eyes twinkled. "How might we distract your brothers, Livi?"

∽∾

"So," Armand Mayeux began as he leaned against the kitchen doorjamb, "with the full moon upon us, how do you English boys usually spend the moonful?"

Gray glared at his would-be brother-in-law. Blast the man for showing up in Bath at the exact wrong time. "By retreating into the forest, like any proper Lycan."

"You hide?" Armand chuckled as his brother joined him in the threshold.

"I don't think I've ever heard 'proper' and 'Lycan' used in the same sentence before," Etienne added.

"Oh? And where do you uncouth American boys spend your moonful?" Wes rested his hip against corner of the cook's preparation table, a threat in his voice if Gray had ever heard one.

"Wherever we feel like it." Armand shrugged. "Exploring the Vieux Carré on four legs is more fun than on two sometimes. Etienne," he gestured to his brother with a cock of his head, "enjoys paying the sisters of Ursuline a visit from time to time. But when we're particularly wild, there's nothing quite like playing with a few alligators."

Sisters of Ursuline? Nuns? They frightened nuns? Gray somehow managed to keep his mouth from falling open.

"Alligators?" Wes gaped openly.

"Do you mean to say," Gray began, "that you terrorize nuns?"

Etienne snorted. "Not in the least. You'd have to be in New Orleans to appreciate it."

Armand pushed away from the door and walked farther into the kitchen. "And if we were in New Orleans, we would take you out to the bayou and welcome you properly into our pack."

"I have a pack of my own, but thank you for the thought."

The younger American Lycan smirked from his spot just inside the doorway. "Still, tradition is tradition. You think you're worthy of Liviana. A little test of your mettle would be expected back home."

"Our father would never forgive us," Armand added, "if we just handed our sister over to you without knowing you're deserving of her."

Wes arched a brow at Gray, a devilish gleam in his eye. Then he pushed off the edge of the table, hung his arm around Gray's shoulder, and squeezed tightly. "I think we should take the brothers Mayeux out to tour the good city of Bath, don't you?"

That was the last thing they needed to do. The brothers Mayeux could probably scare up enough trouble of their own without any help from the Hadleys. "I believe I have plans today," Gray managed to grunt.

"What sort of plans?" Wes said with a laugh.

"I'm not certain yet. I'd have to check with Mother and Lady Sophia to see what they have in mind," Gray said, hating his own words even as they left his lips. They made him seem like the worst sort of pansy.

"Such a good little lad, tending to his mother," Etienne Mayeux teased, punching his brother in the shoulder in jest. Then they both laughed at Gray's expense.

Heat crept up beneath the collar of Gray's jacket, and Wes shot him a disappointed glare.

"Fine," Gray capitulated. "A tour of Bath. Where shall we begin?"

"The front door might be a good place to start." Livi's brothers moved into the corridor and started in that direction.

Gray and Wes followed, but from a distance. What the devil were they getting themselves into? As they approached the drawing room, Wes paused at the doorway for a moment. Then he stepped over the threshold and crossed to where Maddie sat in a high-back chair.

Wes leaned over the back of her seat and whispered into his wife's ear. Her face colored prettily as she looked at him with a scolding glance and swatted at his arm. Something tingled along Gray's spine. Envy? Perhaps. Lady Madeline touched Wes with such kindness and looked at him as though she considered him before all else.

Gray could only hope to have such a love affair with someone someday. He glanced over at Livi, who still stood facing the window. Lady Sophia made a noise in her throat and motioned for him to go to her. And then she turned and set about entertaining Armand and Etienne for a moment. Such a lovely lady she was.

"I believe that Wes and I are taking your brothers out to see a bit of the city," Gray said from a pace behind Livi.

"A bit of the city?" She snorted without even glancing at him over her shoulder. "You don't know my brothers quite as well as I do. If their outing doesn't involve liquor and wenches, I'll kiss your…" Her voice trailed off on the last.

"Kiss my?" Gray prompted, instantly intrigued about what she almost said. He wrapped a lock of her hair around his finger and gave it a gentle tug.

"Kiss your anything, if I'm wrong." She made a snuffling sound in her nose again. "I know my brothers much better than you do."

"I'll take you up on your bet," Gray teased.

"It wasn't a bet. It was a warning." She shot her brothers a dark glance. But they were totally absorbed in listening to Lady Sophia at the moment. "My brothers can outdrink you, out-whore you, and outtalk you."

"I like it when you use risqué words," he growled at her. "Can you do that after we're married? In the bedchamber?"

She bit back a smile. "I'm not one hundred percent certain there will be a marriage."

Oh, but she knew they would marry. Unless her brothers forced her to leave England. "My pack alpha and your grandfather said it would be so. I'm taking them at their word."

She rolled her eyes. "Don't look so overjoyed by the idea of our impending nuptials." She poked a finger into his chest. "I can still change my mind."

He grabbed her finger in a tight grip and held it to his chest. "But you won't," he said softly.

"Don't count on it."

"I count on one thing, Livi," he said, his voice almost so tender that it made him uncomfortable. "You want me. You're just afraid to admit it." He searched her face as he talked, but she didn't look at him. Her eyes drifted all around the room. She looked everywhere but at him.

Finally, she sighed heavily. "Just where are you taking my brothers. A club? A brothel? A gaming establishment? Tell me so I'll know where to send the coach to pick them up in the morning."

He tweaked the end of her nose. "I'll see them home safely tonight."

"A word of warning, Grayson," she started. Then she shook her head as though she didn't want to continue.

"Out with it, Livi," he said.

She looked over her shoulder toward her brothers once more. "They look innocent enough. But the things they have seen and done. It's enough to make me nervous. They are worse than they look."

"I think Wes and I can handle them."

Wes called from across the room, "It's too bad Archer's not here to accompany us."

"Such a pity," Lady Sophia mumbled.

Gray laughed. "Bath will be better with just the four of us."

"You will behave yourself, won't you, Weston?" Lady Madeline asked. She pouted up at Wes in a way that Gray found more than endearing. It was still a bit difficult to believe that Wes had captured the privileged duke's daughter and that the two of them were as happy as could be.

"He'll spend the entire night counting the minutes

until he can return to you," Gray informed her. The bad part was that it was the complete truth. Wes only had eyes for Lady Madeline. Always had and always would. He'd wanted her since he'd met her for the very first time. And now he had her. Gray looked again at Livi. Would she ever gaze at him with the unabashed want that was written on Lady Madeline's face when she looked at Wes? Probably not. There was always room for hope, though.

Perhaps he could take her brothers out and at least win them over to his side. For he feared that they could and would snatch Livi right out of his grasp, if they felt like he wasn't a fitting match for their sister. But what on earth would they consider fitting? They wouldn't hold it against him for being a Lycan, would they? Certainly not, when they were of the same breed.

"Whores or drinks?" Livi asked quietly from beside him. She didn't look at all pleased.

"Does it matter to you, Livi?"

She raised her nose into the air ever so slightly. "I'm still trying to determine my feelings on the matter." She sniffed. "Do whatever you feel led to do tonight. I'm certain my brothers will inform me of everything that takes place in the morning. If you're home by morning, that is." She avoided his gaze.

"Liviana Mayeux, if I didn't know you better, I might think that you were jealous."

She shot him a glance as she crossed her arms beneath her breasts. "You have been wrong before, I'm certain." Then she crossed the room and tugged her oldest brother to the side. She whispered vehemently in his ear. So vehemently that Gray couldn't make out a word of it. Damn her eyes. Armand looked up and grinned. "Why certainly, *bébé* sister," he crowed. "We'll take care of it for you."

Gray highly doubted that the Mayeux brothers would be doing much caretaking. But he would give his eyeteeth to know what Livi had just asked of Armand.

Twenty-One

As soon as Gray stepped inside the taproom, the tavern wench met his eyes and then giggled to herself. Bloody perfect. Wes would pick the very same taproom where Gray had numbed his senses earlier that week alongside Nathaniel Hayburn. And the woman did appear to recognize him. "Perhaps we should go to another tavern," Gray grumbled.

But it was too late to leave as the wench gestured the four Lycans farther into the establishment. "Mr. Hadley," she said in a singsong voice, "how nice to see you again."

"You know her?" Wes mumbled in Gray's ear.

"I had a few tankards this week," Gray replied. More than a few, but he thought the better of mentioning so at the moment.

"More ale, sir?" The girl crossed the room to greet the foursome.

"Thank you," Gray nodded. "A round for my brothers too. We'll try to stay out of your way."

"We're not your brothers yet." Etienne Mayeux

tossed over his shoulder as he sauntered toward a table on the far side of the room.

Armand's gaze trailed up and down the tavern wench's slender body, finally stopping at her bodice. "I don't suppose you have any rum, mademoiselle?"

"Rum?" She batted her eyelashes as she shook her head. "We've got gin, whiskey, and ale."

"Then a round of ale it is." The American tipped his head in thanks before heading toward the table his brother had already claimed.

"What do you think Miss Mayeux whispered to them before we left?" Wes muttered under his breath.

Gray would give his left arm to find out. "I haven't a clue." He glanced back across the taproom to find the brothers Mayeux with their heads tipped together as though they were Cassius and Brutus right before they turned Caesar into a sieve. "But I'm not happy about it, whatever it is."

"Well, I suppose we'll eventually find out, won't we?" Wes clapped a hand to Gray's back. "Come on, we'd best go take our seats before they conspire to bury your body somewhere along the River Avon."

"And here I thought they'd just converge on me in the senate with their daggers drawn."

Wes chuckled. "I would hardly think of you as Julius Caesar. That role is more befitting of Dash, don't you think?"

"Oh? Well, who am I, then?" Gray grumbled.

Wes frowned for a moment in thought. "Falstaff, perhaps."

Falstaff? That bumbling idiot? What a thing to say.

Gray glared at his brother. "I shall remind you that we're twins."

Wes' smile returned. "I am joking, of course." He gestured once again to the Mayeux brothers. "Should I have said Hamlet instead? As you are most certainly procrastinating against the inevitable."

At least the Danish prince was more regal than blasted Falstaff. Damn Wes straight to hell for needling him when he wasn't in the mood. Gray heaved a sigh. "I'm not procrastinating. I just don't know what to do. They're Livi's *brothers*, for God's sake."

Wes snorted. "Maddie has brothers too. And they'd been my friends before…"

Before Wes had abducted their sister and dashed for the border. "What should I say to them? How can I make them understand?"

Wes shrugged. "I'd probably have some clue if we had a sister."

Really, for being Gray's twin and best friend, Wes wasn't any help at all. "Why am I asking you anyway? You gave Madeline *back* to her brothers." Which was the exact opposite of what Gray wanted to do.

Wes' mouth fell open and his dark eyes narrowed. "I did what I thought was best for her at the time. You should ask yourself what's best for Liviana."

"I'm what's best for her," Gray said and stood taller as he did so.

"Then go over there and tell them that."

Gray would do that very thing. Armand and Etienne Mayeux were Livi's brothers, but he was going to be her husband… Unless they stole her away from him in the dead of night. Gray's hands became clammy and his breath hitched at the thought.

"I've never seen you so…"

"If you say like Falstaff, I will pummel you into the ground."

Wes chuckled and gestured to the Mayeuxes' table with a sweep of his arm. "Go on, Mark Antony, conquer your foes until they surrender at your feet. Is that better?"

"Somewhat," Gray growled. Then he tipped his head back and started for the table where his would-be brothers-in-law held court. "Sorry to keep you waiting," he said to the pair. "My brother and I haven't seen each other for quite some time."

"I am newly married," Wes announced as he dropped into a seat across from the Mayeuxes.

"And here we thought you might be plotting." Etienne grinned, though his eyes held no warmth.

"No reason for plotting." Gray took his own seat beside his brother and leaned back in his chair, hoping a casual air would put the Americans more at ease. "Just a bit of family business."

At that moment, the tavern wench arrived at their table with a tray heavy laden with tankards. "Here you are, gentlemen." But her foot caught the edge of Gray's chair and she stumbled forward, landing in his lap. Wes snatched the tray of four drinks from her hands just as they began to tip. A small amount tipped onto the floor before Wes righted the tray. Thank heavens his brother was there to support him. Or he would have gone home smelling like a brewery.

"Oh, Mr. Hadley!" She tried to scramble from his

lap, but the ale that had splashed to the floor sent her falling right back into Gray's arms.

"Here." Wes bolted to his feet. "Let me help you, miss." He lifted her from Gray's lap and placed her squarely in the middle of a dry patch of wooden floor. "There, now. No harm done."

"I say." Etienne leaned forward in his seat. "How well do you know the little serving maid?"

Gray gaped at Livi's brother. Surely he wasn't suggesting something improper. Gray was the one, after all, who'd caught her in his lap when there was nowhere else for her to go. Chivalry was dead, apparently. "I don't even know her name."

"But she seems to know yours." Etienne's eyes flashed back to the tavern wench. "Do you imbibe a lot, Mr. Hadley?"

"Do I imbibe…?" Gray echoed, barely believing his ears, "As much as any other man."

"But not just any other man is dead set to marry our sister," Armand added. "We need to be certain that Livi's future is safe with you."

Gray rose from his seat and began to tug at his clothing to set them to rights. "Livi will be perfectly safe with me. She'll never want for anything."

"Except maybe for her home and her family," Etienne put in. "No, Mr. Hadley. I'm afraid we'll need more than just your word that Livi will be safe with you and that she'll want for nothing. We'll need proof."

"Proof?" Gray growled. What sort of proof? What the devil did they want from him?

"Have you the income to support her, Mr. Hadley?" Armand asked as he handed Gray one of the drinks.

He took another and raised it to his lips, regarding Gray over the rim with a skeptical glare.

Gray couldn't tell them that he was the half brother of a powerful marquess, since he couldn't publicly claim Dash as a sibling, and he didn't have much else to recommend him, aside from the allowance Dash afforded him and the new business venture he, Wes, and Archer had just began. "I have enough," he grunted instead.

Etienne raised a hand to his cup his ear. "What did you say, Hadley?" he taunted. "Didn't quite hear you."

Gray leaned closer to him and mouthed plainly. "Your sister will never want for anything." He'd said it earlier, but they obviously hadn't heard him.

Wes interjected, "We actually have a thriving business we just embarked upon. It's doing quite well."

Or would be once they got the place up and running. Thank God Wes hadn't mentioned that last part.

Armand leaned forward, resting his chin on his elbow. "Pray tell," he said with a most irritating glitter in his eyes.

Before Gray could expound on their not-yet-established business venture, Etienne tilted his head toward Wes and touched a finger to his own cheek. "Associate with vampyres much?"

Wes lifted his hand to his scarred cheek. "An unfortunate encounter a few years ago."

Etienne shook his head. "Evil creatures. I wouldn't want Livi around something so dangerous."

"How often do you encounter vampyres?" Armand's brow furrowed.

Damn it to hell. Gray raked a hand through his

hair. He'd never had such intense scrutiny of his life or his brother's life. And how Wes received his scar was none of Armand or Etienne Mayeux's concern. "We don't associate with their kind. As Wes said, it was an unfortunate encounter. *One* encounter. I don't believe either of us has seen one since."

A cough over Gray's left shoulder drew his attention. He turned quickly to find the Marquess of Lavendon standing at his elbow, an eyebrow arched in Wes' direction. "Left my sister to carouse with this degenerate, did you?"

Gray sputtered. Damn Lavendon to the fieriest depths of Hell. That was the very last thing he needed Livi's brothers to overhear. Especially as they seemed to be doing their very best imitation of the Spanish Inquisition.

Then Lavendon's laugh boomed off the tavern walls. The marquess clapped Gray on his shoulder. "I jest, of course. So good to see you upright, Hadley." He leaned down and said in a conspiratorial manner that was more than a whisper, "That wench you had last week is asking about you." He nodded in the direction of the bar.

Gray hadn't had a wench last week. He glanced over in the direction of the marquess' nod. "I believe you mean the wench *you* had last week, don't you, Lavendon?"

The marquess shrugged. Then he grinned, a most irritating smile if Gray had ever seen one. "Had her last night too," he remarked. "Do you care if I join you?"

He didn't wait for an answer; he simply beckoned for an additional chair and lowered himself into it with a moan. "Lavendon, meet Miss Mayeux's brothers from America. How fortunate that Armand and Etienne have arrived in time for the wedding tomorrow," Gray said by way of introduction.

The brothers looked none too pleased, but they both greeted the man with a nod.

Lavendon's grin widened. "Got caught in the parson's mousetrap, did you?"

"Some men," Wes began, "quite enjoy matrimony. I'm sure Gray will be as happy with Miss Mayeux as I am with Maddie."

The marquess shrugged as though the topic suddenly bored him.

Etienne called for another tankard of ale. "Hadley was just telling us about his business venture," he said.

Gray hadn't been. But it would be rude to correct them.

"Oh, the gaming hell." Lavendon stopped to take a long draw of his ale, and the Mayeux brothers looked at one another with skeptical glances. "The jackanapes won't let me invest even though I'm family. Can you believe that?"

Armand pushed back from the table, gaping at Gray. "You plan to support our sister by operating a gaming hell?"

"It's not just any gaming hell. It's an upscale gaming hell."

Etienne held up one finger. "I've a good mind to drag Livi to the first ship headed west this evening."

Let him try.

Thank God, Weston was there. He pulled a shilling from his pocket and lined his glass up on the table. "I propose a little game, gentlemen," he said. He winked at Gray. Things never went well when Wes had that look in his eye. But whatever he had in mind couldn't be worse than Gray pummeling his brothers-in-law-to-be into the ground at the very thought of them absconding with his fiancée.

"Be careful with him." Lavendon gestured to Wes with a cock of his head. "No one ever beats Weston Hadley."

"Is that so?" Etienne asked as he narrowed his eyes on Gray and Wes collectively.

"We Mayeuxes are known for our luck as well." Armand leaned forward in his seat.

"I'd wager you won't beat Weston Hadley at his game. No one does. Learned that the hard way."

"We'll see about that," Armand replied quietly, a challenge most evident in his voice.

"Indeed. Tell us more about this game of yours," Etienne said as he dropped back into his chair. "I'd wager we Mayeuxes are more than a match for the pair of you."

Twenty-Two

Livi paced back and forth in front of the doorway as she nibbled a fingernail. She stopped to look out the window, searching the darkness for any sign of her brothers or Gray. They had been gone all day with no indication that they might ever return except for Gray's promise of "tonight." Tonight, apparently, was a relative term.

Sophie sighed heavily and sat her needlepoint to the side. "It's late. We should go to bed, Livi," she said. "At this point, when they do return home, they won't be fit for company."

"What if they're injured?" Livi glared at her friend. She couldn't help but think the worst. After all, she knew her brothers better than Gray did, and they hadn't been terribly happy with him when they'd left that morning. That morning! Good heavens, how many hours had it been?

"Your pacing at the window is not going to keep any of them from being injured," Sophie admonished.

"But what if they've done something to him?" Livi's fingernails would be a mess by the time her brothers and Gray finally came home.

"What on earth do you think they're going to do to him?" Sophie crossed her hands primly in her lap.

That was the question, wasn't it? But Livi didn't want to conjure up every last horrible thing her brothers might do. "How can you remain calm at a time like this?" Livi asked. Sophie sat there, so prim and proper, while Livi felt like her insides were being ripped out each moment that ticked by. "You don't know my brothers. They are wily beasts who have a penchant for trouble." Especially when they didn't like someone. And they didn't like Gray, not even a little.

"You don't know the Hadley brothers well, Livi. They are of the same ilk, those twins. When the two of them are together, they're a force to be reckoned with. I'm not afraid for them at all. But your brothers…" Her eyes narrowed at Livi. "Are you more worried about Grayson or your brothers?"

"Both," Livi muttered. She didn't know who to be more worried about. Her brothers could do a lot of damage when they set their minds to it. But Gray did have his twin with him.

Suddenly, the jingle of tack in the drive drew her attention. She raced to the window and peered out into the darkness. She saw two forms stumble from the carriage, but she couldn't tell if they were her brothers or Grayson and Weston Hadley. Then the two men reached into the carriage and hefted two lumps over their shoulders. "Oh, dear!" Livi cried.

"What is it?" Sophie asked, peering out into the dark street as well.

"They're home," was all Livi could croak.

"Good. Then you'll finally be able to get some

rest." Sophie reached her hand out to Livi. "Come along, dear. Let's go to bed before they see us hovering like old maids. Let's not give them that satisfaction."

Instead of complying, Livi rushed past Sophie into the corridor toward the front door and pulled it open. She stepped to the side as the men entered the house without slowing their gait. She couldn't see their faces, as it was still too dark to tell who was being carried and who was doing the carrying, but there were definitely full-grown men thrown over their shoulders.

The overwhelming scent of cheap perfume hit her before they even turned around. Rage crept up within Livi as she crossed her arms in front of her and gritted her teeth. They'd been out whoring, and now at least two of them were so foxed they couldn't walk, and the other two could barely do the same.

"Etienne? Armand?" Livi demanded.

One man turned, the feet belonging to the person thrown over his back knocking into her shoulder. She stumbled, and strong hands reached for her. "Beg your pardon, Livi," Grayson Hadley said. "Didn't mean to knock you over, love."

She tapped her foot on the hardwood floor. "Just what did you intend to do?" she asked.

He stood very still for a moment as though he had no idea what he was supposed to do next. He scratched his head with the hand that wasn't holding the back of Etienne's knees.

Weston Hadley nudged his shoulder hard enough to knock him off balance. "You were going to put the sack of lard to bed," he said with an intoxicated chuckle.

"Oh, that's right." Grayson laughed along with his

twin. It was a silly sound, and it made Livi want to roll her eyes at him.

"What did you do to my brothers?"

Armand's voice emanated from Weston's back. He tried to lift his head as he talked, but it must have been too difficult. "He dinna do nuffin', Liv," he slurred. "We played some cards. And we had a jolly good time." He patted Weston on the bottom. "He's a good sort, Liv."

"If you touch my arse one more time…" Weston warned.

Armand flushed. "*Bon Dieu*, was that your arse? I thought it was your shoulder."

"I'm certain you did," Gray intoned. He looked over his shoulder at Etienne, who now snored loudly. "At least mine's asleep and can't play with my arse."

"You had better put yours to bed," Wes muttered. He looked to be the most sober of the lot, but even he was foxed. "I have a lovely wife I need to see before I go to sleep."

"Right. To bed," Gray slurred. "G'night, Livi love." He bent to kiss her cheek, but she dodged out of his way. There was no way he would put his lips anywhere near her face when he reeked of whores and ale. When she dodged him, he stumbled past her and crashed into the wall.

Etienne woke with a grunt. "Where am I?" he complained.

"You're slung off Hadley's back like a sack of potatoes," Armand said with a hilarious giggle. "But don't touch his arse, 'cause evidently Hadley men really hate that."

"I had no plans to touch his arse, you idiot." Etienne patted the back of Grayson's thighs. "Put me down."

"If I do, will you be able to stand?" Grayson asked.

"Better than you," Etienne said.

Gray and Weston lowered both of Livi's brothers to their feet, and then it was like watching a game of lawn bowling, with all the pieces wobbling.

"*Bon Dieu*," Livi murmured. She motioned toward the stairs. "Sophie," she called.

Sophie appeared as though conjured out of thin air. Of course, she'd probably been waiting for the opportunity to step into the corridor and intrude.

"Which ones do you want, Sophie?" Livi asked.

"I'll take the Hadleys," Sophie replied with a disgusted shake of her head. "Come along, boys," she encouraged. When they didn't follow immediately, she snapped, "Now!"

"Yes, ma'am," they both said in unison, and they followed her into a nearby parlor like ducklings behind their mother. Foxed ducklings.

Livi had a feeling her brothers wouldn't be so easy to deal with. They weren't nearly as well trained. "Armand, Etienne, head for the stairs and I'll show you to your chambers."

Surprisingly, both Mayeux men started for the staircase, holding each other upright as they laughed at nothing in particular. They must have thoroughly enjoyed their evening with Gray, which did not speak well of her intended.

Livi followed the pair up the steps and then pushed her way in front of them to lead her brothers to their borrowed chambers. Before opening the first door, she spun around to face the duo. "Did you even do what I asked?" she whispered to keep the Lycans below stairs from overhearing her.

Both of her brothers stopped laughing and glanced at the other before shrugging their answer. Armand's eyes widened as though doing so would sober him up. "I can't remember what you asked, Liv."

"So glad you traveled all this way to be exactly no help at all to me." She pushed open the first door. "One of you can stay in here and the other across the hall."

"We're sorry, Liv," Etienne said as he braced the wall to keep from tipping over. "What did you want again?"

To find out how Gray really felt about her. She asked them to do one thing. Just one and instead they fell deep in their cups and were completely worthless. "Never mind." She shook her head. "Get some sleep and I'll see you in the morning."

Armand reached for her hand when she started down the corridor. "Livi."

She tipped her head back to glare at her oldest brother. "*Oui*, Armand?"

He frowned a bit and then tucked one of her stray curls behind her ear. "See you in the morning."

There certainly was no way around that, was there?

❧

Gray glanced back toward the corridor, hoping to catch another glimpse of Livi, but to no avail. Perhaps he'd just seek her out on his own. "I think I'll retire to my chambers, Lady Sophia. I find I am a bit tired. Thank y—"

His tutor heaved a sigh. "You no longer have chambers here, Mr. Hadley."

Gray couldn't have heard her correctly. "I beg your pardon?"

Lady Sophia narrowed her eyes on him. "Had you returned home at a respectable hour, you would already be aware of the circumstances, Grayson. There simply wasn't room for you *and* both of Liviana's brothers. And since your…" she paused as though searching for the right word, "…benefactor has a home outside Bath, your things have been sent on to Lord Eynsford's. I'm certain he's awaiting you even now."

Dash? Gray somehow managed to keep from groaning. The last thing he needed was another set-down from his oldest brother. "I won't take up much space here." In fact, he could sleep on one of the settees or the staircase. Better yet, he could keep Livi company in her own bed. That would be just the thing. They'd be married shortly anyway. Why shouldn't they start how he intended they go on? Because her grandfather would kill him. Or her brothers. Or all three of them teamed up. That's why. No matter how decadent the thought, Gray would have to put it to the side for at least one more night.

"I believe you have taken leave of your senses, Grayson. After the way you've behaved, I cannot—"

"Must you always be such a martinet?" Archer drawled from the threshold, drawing Gray's and Wes' attention.

Lady Sophia sucked in a breath as she placed a hand to her heart, clearly startled. "Good heavens, Lord Radbourne! What are you doing here?"

Archer's brow rose in amusement at her discompo-
sure. "Why? Did you miss me?"

"Like a hound misses a flea," she muttered, but
they all heard her, even Gray and Wes in their
inebriated states.

"Such honeyed words always drip from your tongue,"
Archer said smoothly. "I am touched, sweetheart."

Lady Sophia's teeth ground together. "What are
you doing here?" she repeated.

Archer strode into the parlor as he retrieved a bit
of foolscap from his jacket pocket. "I was playing
Grayson's errand boy, you might recall." Then he
thrust the little bundle into Gray's hands. "Your
special license all signed and ready, though why
you're stepping so calmly into the parson's noose is
beyond me."

Stepping calmly into the parson's noose? Archer was
the one who'd seen to Gray's rather hasty betrothal
with all of his talk of thighs and kisses. Traveling so
quickly to London and back must have dulled his
brother's memory. Gray glanced at the papers in his
hand, and sobriety started to sink in a bit. "My special
license." The papers that would bind him to Livi for
all time. A shiver skated down his spine.

Lady Sophia snorted. "After the way you behaved
today, Mr. Hadley, I'm not so certain it wouldn't be
in Livi's best interest to hop the next frigate across the
Atlantic with her brothers." Gray's mouth fell open,
but she clearly wasn't done as she gestured to his entire
person with a sweep of her hands. "Do you think she
deserves a man who spends his time getting foxed?
Getting her brothers foxed? The kind of man who

stays out until all hours of the night? Who thinks only of himself?"

"Now see here, we were simply—" Wes began, but she shot him a withering glare that made whatever he was going to say die on his tongue.

"Don't get me started on *you*, Mr. Hadley. Your expectant wife finally returned to Brimsworth House when she was too tired to remain here waiting for you to return. Is that any way for you to treat Maddie? You should be ashamed of yourselves, both of you."

Wes straightened and suddenly appeared much more sober. "Is Maddie all right? Is she angry with me?"

Lady Sophia scoffed. "Amazingly not. She didn't appear resentful at all of your time away from her. She said something about the moon and the fact that she didn't worry about you, because you would need her when it's at its fullest." She narrowed her eyes on Wes. "She didn't sound like the Madeline Hayburn I've known my entire life. I don't know what you've done to her—"

"That's because she's Madeline *Hadley* now," Archer tossed in. "Knows her place," he added, his voice dropping dangerously low. "Perhaps you could learn something from her, my lady."

Lady Sophia's face turned a rather enraged scarlet, the color only Archer ever seemed able to elicit from her. "There's not a lady I know whose place is beside any one of you. It's too late for Maddie but Livi—"

"Is mine," Gray growled, waving his new special license in the air. "Holmesfield agreed, my lady."

Lady Sophia shook her head and said softly, "I have no doubt you care for her in your own… unique way, but perhaps you should consider what is best for Livi. You know as well as I that she's wanted to return home ever since she arrived—"

"I didn't travel all the way to Lambeth Palace for no reason," Archer grumbled.

Their tutor folded her arms across her middle. "Heaven forbid you be inconvenienced, my lord."

And as a fresh round of bickering between Archer and Lady Sophia ensued, Gray exchanged a glance with Wes and then quickly escaped the room before his absence could be noted. In the corridor, he stopped in his tracks. Livi sat on the steps, her knees tucked up under her chin. She was, without a doubt, the most gorgeous sight he'd ever seen. He clucked his tongue at her playfully. "Lady Sophia would tell you that's not a very ladylike way to sit, Livi."

She heaved a sigh and wrapped her arms around her legs. "Then it's fitting, isn't it? I mean, I'm not a lady. Not really."

"Then you will fit in beautifully with the Hadleys, because none of us are truly gentlemen." He chuckled and dropped heavily onto a step beside her. He lost his balance at the last minute, as his ale-soaked brain refused to acknowledge his descent with any grace whatsoever. He grunted as he righted himself. "Hard to believe you'll be joining our ranks in the morning?"

"Foxed is not an attractive color on you, Mr. Hadley," she said, her chin still pressed to the tops of her knees, so much so that her voice was muffled. Thank God he was Lycan, or he wouldn't have heard her. She heaved a sigh. "And jasmine is most definitely not your scent. In fact, I find it to be the most noxious odor I have ever smelled and believe you should bathe with all due haste to prevent further offending me." She got to her feet in one quick movement, one that was much too fast for him to counter.

He reached for her, but she stepped away from him in a flurry of skirts. "Livi," he complained. "Come here."

She arched one delicate dark brow at him. "Come here?" She snorted. God, that was a pretty sound. "Should I call a coach bound for Bedlam? Because you are a fool if you think I'll allow you anywhere near my person after you've come home reeking of whores." Her voice cracked on the last, and she bit back a French oath. Then Livi raised her nose into the air and said, "It's unfortunate that Lord Radbourne wasted a trip to procure a special license. I don't think I'll be joining your ranks after all."

The words registered in his brain, but they took some time to do so. "I beg your pardon?" he croaked. "Don't tell me you're calling off the wedding because of a drunken night of carousing." He got to his feet and suddenly felt much more sober than he had before. Traumatic injury had a way of sobering one up. And he felt almost as though Livi had just plunged a knife into his chest.

She tapped the toe of her slipper against the floor. "Carousing? That's what you call it?"

He mulled it over for a moment. "When that's what it is, yes."

"Then let's call it what it really is. It's whoring. And I will not marry a man who cannot be faithful." She spun away from him to stare at a painting that hung in the corridor. "My desire for faithfulness is not one represented in most society marriages, I'm certain. But it's what my parents had and it is my desire to have it as well. I won't settle for less."

"I wasn't out whoring, Livi," he said. He reached for her again, but she stepped out of his grasp.

"Then why do you smell like a perfume-scented wench has crawled all over your person?" She pointed to her pert little nose. "You forget, Mr. Hadley, that I have senses very much like your own."

"Oh, that," he said with a heavy sigh. Damn the Mayeux brothers. They'd known exactly what they were doing at the time. Looking back on the evening, there was no doubt about it.

"Yes, *that*," she spat at him.

God, she was pretty when she was angry. Her eyes flashed furiously, and her cheeks grew ruddy. He wanted to see if she pinkened like that as much when she was aroused by lust as when she was angered. He shook the thoughts away. They would get him nowhere. Not on this night, he feared. He blamed the Mayeux brothers for that.

Gray heard his twin's footsteps in the corridor and looked up. His brother appeared around the corner, looking for all the world like he wanted to be anywhere but there at that moment. "Don't let me interrupt. I'm simply on my way home to my wife." He started past the both of them.

"You may want to bathe before you return home," Livi muttered. "To get the scent of whores off you. Although your wife may not notice, since her nose isn't overly sensitive." She shrugged. "Just a sugges-tion." She stared Wes down.

Wes' eyes narrowed. He was a scoundrel to be sure, but he was a faithful one. Lady Madeline had always been the one for him and always would be. The only one. "Ah, so her brothers won the hand this night, I see," Wes said to Gray with a heavy sigh. Then he clapped Gray on the shoulder and squeezed.

"It appears so," Gray muttered.

"What hand?" Livi asked.

"They thrust one wench after another into his lap all night, apparently well aware that you'd smell them and make a few deductions all on your own," Wes admitted. He gave Gray a sympathetic half smile. "Pity I didn't realize it at the time."

"Nor did I," Gray said. He nodded toward the door. "Go home to Maddie."

Wes nodded, bowed to Livi, and stalked toward the front door. His boot steps receded until he was gone. And it was then that Gray faced Livi. The uncertainty on her face nearly undid him. He reached for her, but she sidestepped him once again. He wasn't so inebriated now that he couldn't catch her, however. Losing the girl of one's dream had a way of sobering one up. What was worse was that she was hurt by it all. Dare she care for him a little? Perhaps she did.

Even amid her protests, he grabbed her to him. "Livi," he grunted when she kicked him in the shin. "Damn, you're the most annoying bundle I've ever wanted to marry," he muttered more to himself than to her.

She stilled, and he pulled her soft body closer to him with his arm around her waist. She was stiff as a board against him, and she sniped, "Perhaps you should find a more cooperative bundle, then. You seemed to have no problem doing so most of the night."

"I had no problem finding a bundle, Livi," he said softly, tipping her chin up so that her gaze had to meet his. "But the only bundle I want is you."

"Then why do you smell like a cheap whore?"

He couldn't keep from chuckling. "I love it when you use words dockworkers might say. Will you mumble them in my ear when we're in bed, Livi? Or do you just mean to shock me so I won't attempt to marry you?" He said it close to her ear as he drew her flush against himself.

She pressed her hands to his chest.

"You didn't answer my question."

She looked everywhere but into his eyes.

"I smell like a cheap whore, as you put it, because your brothers thrust them into my lap all night. My guess is that they were well aware that you would assume the worst, and then they could sabotage our relationship."

"Relationship?" She snorted again. "We don't have a relationship."

She could probably feel his aching length against her belly. If she couldn't, it was only because she didn't know what it was. But he was hard and ready and aching for a *relationship* with her. "I didn't take a whore, Livi," he said bluntly. How could he, when he couldn't get her off his mind? Livi with her tumbling hair and her foul mouth. Her wicked lower lip and her penchant for disaster.

He wanted her to be his disaster. Because he couldn't imagine life not knowing her. Not learning all of her nuances. What she liked for breakfast. What her breasts felt like filling his hands. What the mark on the inside of her thigh looked like. What kind of noises she would make when he slid inside her. He let his hand trail up her side to just below her breast. Her heartbeat sped up, but she didn't push him away.

"Let me go, Gray," she said, her voice heavy and heated.

"Never," he whispered, as he dipped his head and tasted the side of her neck. She tilted her pretty little head to the side, and her hands fisted in the lapels of his coat. His hand slid up to cup her breast, and her breath hitched in her throat.

"*Bon Dieu*," she whispered, her lips close to his cheek as he ran his thumb across her nipple.

"Believe me, Livi," he said close to her ear. He tugged her earlobe between his teeth and nibbled it gently. "You're the only woman I want. The only one I can think about. The only one I want in my bed." He lowered his voice even further and pulled her tightly against his bulging erection. "The only one I want to work my way inside of, slowly, taking every inch of you until you are mine."

She swayed in his arms. Did he weaken her knees? He could only hope so.

"You're only saying such scandalous things in order to shock me," she whispered, her voice unsteady.

"Did it work?" He chuckled, then let his teeth scrape the base of her throat. Dear God, he wanted to mark her as his for the whole world to see.

"It takes a lot to shock me, Grayson," she retorted.

He took that as a challenge. God, he shouldn't, but he did. He began to ruck her skirts up in his hands as he backed her toward the wall. When he had her back against the wall and his hand beneath her skirts, she stilled. "What are you doing?" she asked.

"Shocking you," he whispered just before his lips claimed hers.

His fingers trailed through her curls and pressed against her silky-smooth slit, and his tongue entered her mouth at the same time his finger dipped into her heat. She moaned against his lips. He drew his finger through her slickness, bringing some of her desire forward so he could circle that little nub in a way he knew would drive her wild. She wrapped her arms around his neck and pulled him closer when he found it, her tongue tangling with his until he began to circle that little pleasure point, his fingertips plying it, finding a gentle rhythm that made her lift her lips and pant into his neck. "Gray," she cried.

She didn't push his hands away. In fact, she spread her legs farther, and all he could think about was how much he wanted to dive beneath her skirts and get a look at that birthmark. She cried, clutching to him as her legs weakened. Her heartbeat thundered in his head, moving faster than a team of runaway horses. His manhood pressed insistently against her belly, and he was immediately afraid that he would disgrace himself with the sheer pleasure of watching her blue eyes blink closed, then open again. He wanted to sink into her. To take all of her.

She accepted all the pleasure he had to give her and clutched the back of his neck tightly as her desire slickened his way. "Gray," she cried again. "Goodness, shock me some more. Don't stop," she panted.

Her hips arched toward his questing fingers, and he increased the pressure. He increased the pleasure. He increased her need for him.

Her head fell back against the wall, and he was able to watch her face as he brought her over the top. She shuddered, clutching his coat tightly in her clenched fists. "God, you're beautiful," he breathed as he watched pleasure cross her face and she quaked in his arms. It took every bit of his control not to hike her skirts up and take her like a common whore. But she wasn't a whore. She was his Livi. She was everything. He slowed his fingers as her body began to stop its frantic pulse, and then he drew them from her heat.

"Did I shock you?" he whispered as he let her skirts fall back to her ankles.

Before she could answer, a whistle came from the corridor. A rather loud whistle to the tune of a crude song, one attributed to dockworkers. Archer. Damn his irritating hide.

"You have dreadful timing," Gray muttered as he stepped back from Livi, leaving her propped against the wall.

"If I had dreadful timing," Archer drawled, "I wouldn't have taken extraordinary measures to entertain Lady Sophia long enough for you to finish..." He glanced toward Livi. "...finish your talk, that is."

Livi flushed scarlet. God, she was pretty when she'd just been pleasured. He'd have to do it more often.

Archer touched the brim of his beaver hat and winked at Livi. "Welcome to the family, Miss Mayeux." Then he started for the front door. "Gray,

I'll meet you at Dash's after you're done saying whatever it is the two of you need to say to each other."

As soon as Archer made his exit, Livi poked Gray in the side with one very pointy finger. "You knew he was there?" she hissed.

What a ridiculous notion. "Believe it or not," Gray slid his arm around Livi's waist and drew her close to him, "my attention was focused elsewhere." Then he dipped his head and captured her mouth once again. His heart pounded and his erection throbbed just as heavily. It felt like he held her a lifetime before he gathered every bit of self-control he possessed to lift his head just a bit and take a tiny step back from her.

"Ah, Livi," he whispered across her lips. "Tomorrow." Tomorrow she would be his. Tomorrow he would finally have her in his bed. Tomorrow their lives would truly begin.

"Tomorrow," she echoed, with a soft little lilt to her voice.

Gray couldn't help but smile at his bride-to-be. Their future was indeed bright if they could go on like this the rest of their lives. "Dream of me tonight?"

An impish grin tugged at her lips. "I think I'll dream of a sober you, if you don't mind."

"A sober me?" he laughed.

"*Oui*. One who doesn't smell of ale houses and wenches."

Gray rolled his eyes, then tipped his head in her direction. "Until tomorrow, Miss Mayeux."

"Until tomorrow, Mr. Hadley."

Gray turned on his heel and strode through the front door into the cool night air. He inhaled deeply as he looked up at the nearly full moon in the heavens. For once, luck was shining down on him. Livi would be his and soon he would claim her, and soon—

From behind, a cool cylinder jabbed Gray in the back. "Make one sound," hissed a voice, "and I'll pull the trigger."

A moment later, Gray caught the familiar whiff of a familiar odiferous fellow. "Honeywell?" He started to turn around, but the gun pressed harder into his back.

"I will shoot you!" the man hissed. "Now walk down the steps and head toward the mews."

Gray was faster than Honeywell, but he wasn't faster than a bullet. And while he could heal from any injury, he couldn't heal from death. He started down the steps carefully.

Twenty-Three

IN THE CORNER OF HER CHAMBERS, LIVI EXAMINED HER reflection in the beveled mirror and winced. Brides were supposed to be beautiful and well rested, weren't they? Of course they were. They weren't supposed to be sleep deprived with dark circles under their eyes, of that she was quite certain. But there was nothing for it now. Besides she wasn't the typical bride, was she?

Still it was frustrating. She hadn't gotten one second of sleep the night before, though not for a lack of trying. Every time she'd closed her eyes, she saw Gray's face in her mind. The rakish twinkle in his eyes and the promising smile on his face when he'd lifted her skirts and completely shocked her. She couldn't get the glorious feel of his hands on her most private of places out of her mind, either. It was as though he had systematically found the best way to distract her from the insanity of their circumstances. By using tactics she had no knowledge of whatsoever, not until now.

"Miss Liviana!" Marie's impatient voice broke into Livi's thoughts.

"*Oui*?" Livi spun away from the mirror to meet her maid's eyes.

"I said," Marie stressed the word, "the earl is asking for you."

"The earl can wait," Armand said from the threshold.

Bon Dieu! Livi hadn't even heard her oldest brother approach. Not getting enough sleep had a way of dulling one's senses. "Armand?"

Her brother gestured to the corridor with a nod of his head. "Marie, out. And make whatever excuses you need to appease our grandfather."

"*Oui*, Monsieur Mayeux," the maid mumbled before escaping Livi's room in a rush of skirts.

"There was no reason to bark at her."

"She's used to it." Armand tugged on his jacket as though he was uncomfortable in his clothes.

"Just because she's used to it—" she began, but the growl emanating from her brother made the rest of Livi's words die on her tongue.

"Enough about your maid." He closed the door to her room and leaned his large frame against it as though he was barring the door from some villain. "I want to apologize, for Etienne and for me."

"Apologize?"

"We should have fought Father harder. We never should have let him send you away. We should have tossed Father Antonio into the swamps for even making the suggestion."

The image of that puffed-up priest dunked into Louisiana's murky waters made Livi giggle.

"And last night… last night we should've kept our heads, Liv. I'm sorry we didn't."

"You mean you shouldn't have gotten foxed," she said.

Her brother agreed with an incline of his head. "And we should have torn Hadley apart. Limb from limb."

"Armand!" she chastised.

But her brother clearly wasn't through. He stepped forward and grasped her hands in his. "You don't have to do this, Liv. No matter what that old man says. No matter what Hadley has talked you into. You don't have to conform to these idiotic English dictates. The Livi I know would never dream of doing so."

No, the Livi he knew wouldn't do so; there was no question about it. But Livi wasn't certain she was the same girl anymore. A lot had changed since she'd crossed the Atlantic on her own. Perhaps if she'd never met Grayson Hadley…

"The Livi I know would tip her chin up, tell the Earl of Holmesfield exactly where he could shove that special license of his, and bolt for the closest port city. Then she'd hop the first ship she found, start a mutiny within the crew, and captain the vessel herself all the way back to New Orleans."

"What a ridiculous thing to say."

"Then she'd make Father apologize for sending her off in the first place. And she might toss Father Antonio into a pit of alligators for good measure."

Livi grinned at her brother. "You make me sound like a hellion."

"You are a Mayeux."

"Only half."

Armand folded his arms across his chest. "The half

that counts. Don't tell me that pretty brunette has actually turned you into a proper English lady."

No, she was far from being a proper English anything, much less a lady. Livi doubted she ever would be. "Lady Sophia has tried her hardest with me."

"Come on, Liv. Let's leave this godforsaken place. Let's go home."

Leave Grayson? Livi's chest ached at the thought. Blast that English Lycan for somehow burrowing into her heart. Blast him for giving her a taste of pleasure, more than she'd ever experienced, more than she ever thought she *would* have the good fortune to experience. And blast him for making her fall in love with him. "I can't," she said, turning away from her brother and walking back toward her mirror.

"Of course you can."

Livi stared at her sleep-deprived reflection once more. She wasn't sure she recognized herself anymore, certainly not the girl Armand had just described, in any event. "I love him," she whispered.

Armand sighed heavily, then came up behind her and squeezed Livi's shoulder. "I was afraid that was the case. But I'm sure there's a fellow in Louisiana you'd like just as much."

Livi wasn't so sure and she shook her head. "And I should be quite angry with you this morning."

"Me?" Armand's voice raised an octave.

She spun back to face him. "You and Etienne. I can't believe the two of you thought to make me think Gray had spent the night whoring."

A corner of his mouth quirked up. "Figured that out, did you?"

At least he hadn't denied it. Livi shrugged. "It was fairly difficult to figure out the truth, actually."

"Meaning Hadley told you."

"I'm going to marry the man, Armand."

"He didn't strike me as such a lapdog."

Gray would not like to be referred to as such, Livi was certain. She poked her brother in the chest with a finger. "What was he supposed to do? Let me stay furious at him to keep the two of you in my good graces?"

Her brother frowned. "Actually, I hadn't even realized he'd figured out what we were about. More clever than I took him for."

She shook her head. "No, instead of doing what I asked—finding out how he feels about me—you got him foxed and tried to hurt me in the process."

"We weren't trying to hurt you," Armand protested. "We were…"

"Manipulating me, or giving it your best shot. How is that any better than what Papa did, Armand? Shouldn't I be allowed to make up my own mind about the situation?"

"But you're not making up your own mind," he growled. "You're marrying a man because our grandfather—who turned his back on our mother, I might remind you—ordered you to do so. You just said yourself that you're not even sure how Hadley feels about you."

And all of that was true. But, "I know how I feel about him."

Her brother's frown darkened. "So there's no talking any sense into you?"

"Papa gave up trying to do so."

Armand took her shoulders in his hands and held her back as though to see all of her. "All right, Liv. If this is what you want, then so be it. But I'm not leaving and neither is Etienne until we're satisfied you'll be happy here. That the English lapdog will treat you well. And if he doesn't, marriage or no marriage, I'll take you back home."

"Thank you." Livi threw her arms around his middle and held him tightly. How she'd missed her brothers. She'd always love both of their unruly hides.

"We love you, Liv. We only want the best for you." Then he chuckled. "And Etienne will be overjoyed to further his acquaintance with your Lady Sophia."

A knock sounded at the door. "Livi," Sophie's voice filtered into the room. "Are you in there?"

Armand shook his head, clearly bemused. "Were her ears burning?" he mumbled under his breath.

Livi gestured for him to hush, then called, "Come in, Sophie. I'm almost ready." Or as ready as she was going to be.

The door opened and Sophie stepped over the threshold, frowning a bit when her eyes landed on Armand. Then she refocused on Livi. "You haven't... That is, have you by chance seen Mr. Hadley this morning?"

Livi hadn't seen Gray since the night before, not even in her dreams, sober or otherwise. She shook her head. "He hasn't arrived?"

Sophie glanced again at Armand. "Would you mind giving us just a moment, Mr. Mayeux?"

Armand snorted. Loudly. "I mind very much. Why

don't you just spit out whatever it is you came here to say?"

Sophie winced and shifted her weight from one foot to the other as though she was incapable of being comfortable. "I'm sure there's nothing to worry about."

"You thought Hadley would be in my sister's chambers?" Armand growled. "Is that why you came here? Is he often found within these walls?"

Sophie heaved a sigh and met Livi's eyes. "No one has seen him since last night. Lord Radbourne said that when he left, Grayson was with you in the entryway."

A cold chill tingled at the base of Livi's neck, then trailed down her spine. "With me?" she echoed, while a slew of awful thoughts spilled into her mind. Had Gray decided she wasn't worth the trouble, after all? Had he been annoyed when she mentioned his sobriety, or lack thereof? Had he been angry about her accusations of womanizing? Did he think her a lightskirt after the way she'd let him have his way with her? Had he turned tail and fled far away?

"No one has seen Hadley since last night?" Armand barked. "Where the devil is he?"

Sophie finally met Armand's eyes and she squared her shoulders. "If I knew the answer to that, Mr. Mayeux, I wouldn't be worrying Livi right now. I'd hoped, perhaps, he'd said something when he left last night. Something that would give his brothers a clue of where to look for him."

A muscle beside Armand's right eye twitched. "Well, when you do find him, you can tell him that his ex-fiancée has returned to New Orleans with her family." Then he turned his glare on Livi. "Ring for Marie and have her pack your things."

"I'm sure that's not necessary, sir," Sophie protested. She reached her hand out for Livi. "Let's go see what your grandfather has to say."

Armand snorted, and Livi sent him a pleading glance. "What if Mr. Hadley is hurt somewhere?"

The expression on her brother's face made it clear he didn't think Gray was hurt anywhere, but he gestured to the corridor with a giant sweep of his arm. "Let's go see what the paragon our mother fled from has to say, by all means."

Livi ignored Armand's sarcasm and linked her arm with Sophie's. "His lordship is actually out of his chambers today," her friend said. "He, along with the vicar, Mr. Spann, are in the earl's study."

She tilted her head near her friend as they traversed the hall toward her grandfather's chambers. "Do you think Gray bolted?" she whispered.

Sophie slightly shook her head. "He seemed so adamant yesterday," she replied just as softly as Livi had spoken.

He had, but that was after his half brother had demanded he marry Livi, before he'd spent the day with her brothers, and before she'd proven herself a wanton.

Etienne stood sentry before their grandfather's study, his massive arms folded across his chest like an angry Zeus holding court on Olympus. His eyes briefly touched on Livi before looking past her to Armand. "Hadley is missing."

"I want Marie to pack Livi's things."

Etienne agreed with a nod. "Abandoning our sister…"

"He wouldn't do that!" growled Weston Hadley from inside the study, his voice so much like Gray's that Livi's heart lifted for a moment before plummeting once again.

"Please," Sophie begged. "Let's not rush to judgment. We should make sure nothing has happened to Mr. Hadley. None of you gentlemen were in the best condition last night," she reminded them as she directed Livi past Etienne and into the earl's study.

Crowded around the room stood Lord and Lady Eynsford, Mr. Hadley and his wife Lady Madeline, Lord Radbourne, Livi's grandfather, and a fellow she didn't recognize who had to be the vicar Sophie had mentioned.

"Did he say anything to you?" Lord Radbourne demanded as soon as he caught Livi's eye.

"Tomorrow." Livi echoed Gray's final words to her. "He said he would see me tomorrow. Today," she clarified. "No one has any idea where he would go?"

Weston Hadley glanced briefly at Lady Eynsford. "Nothing's occurred to you, has it?"

But the marchioness shook her head and touched a protective hand to her stomach. "I wish I knew where to look."

"What would Lady Eynsford know about the situation?" Livi's grandfather grumbled.

"My wife's… *intuition*," Lord Eynsford began, "is usually spot on. But in her present condition, she's not quite feeling herself." Then he shot a frown in Weston Hadley's direction.

Livi thought she must be missing something in the

exchange, but she was too preoccupied with Gray's disappearance to dedicate any time to wondering about the comment. "Perhaps he doesn't want to be found," she muttered. But with a room full of Lycans, nearly everyone assembled there heard her.

"This is an outrage," Armand growled. "I will not allow my sister to be treated so poorly. We'll leave with the tide for home. And the rest of you can all hang."

"You," their grandfather pointed one gnarled finger at Armand, "are just like your father."

Armand puffed out his chest with pride.

"That wasn't a compliment," Grandfather continued. "He swept in here with the manners of an oaf, stole my Grace, and left. You're not going anywhere with Liviana."

"Stole our mother?" Etienne echoed in outrage and at the same time Armand repeated, "Oaf!"

"Shut your mouths, both of you, so I can think," Grandfather ordered.

But such an order would never work with her brothers. Armand slowly closed the distance between his spot in the study and their grandfather's desk, his blue eyes cold enough to chill the entire room. He placed his hands on the edge, leaned toward to their grandfather, and said menacingly, "How dare you speak of my father like that, you delusional old man? Livi's too young to remember *Maman*, but I'm not. Our father is not an oaf. He loves his children. He would never shun us the way you shunned our mother. You should be ashamed of yourself."

Grandfather blanched but then said, "I wanted what was best for Grace, and I want what's best for Liviana."

"Good," Etienne chimed in. "We're in agreement then. The best thing for our sister is to leave this place and forget she ever met any of you."

"Armand, Etienne—" Livi began, but her words died on her tongue when Etienne directed her, rather roughly, truth be told, back over the threshold into the corridor.

"Now," Armand said, just a few feet behind them, "I want Marie to pack your things and I don't want to hear anything more about it." If one didn't know better, they would think Armand was a pack alpha. Then he surprised her by pulling her into his arms and holding her tight.

"I'm so sorry, Livi," he whispered. "I'm so sorry for what Hadley's done. Sorry you were sent to live with that old arse. Sorry I didn't stop Father when I should have." He tipped her chin up so she had to look him in the eyes. "I'll never shirk my duties again, and I don't care who I have to fight to keep you unharmed."

The sentiment in his voice brought tears to Livi's eyes. "None of this is your fault."

But Armand shook his head. "If I'd stood up to Father, none of this would have happened."

If Armand had stood up to Papa, she'd have never met Gray. Livi's heart ached at the thought. But perhaps Armand was right. If Gray had decided against marrying her, she certainly didn't want to stay in England. She didn't want to have to face him in society. It would hurt too much.

"Let's call for Marie," she said as she swiped at the tears now trailing down her cheeks.

Twenty-Four

How the devil had Honeywell trained his pistol on Gray all night long? One would have thought the man would get drowsy at the very least, but he hadn't. Honeywell looked as wide-eyed as any fellow who might have gotten a good night's sleep, even if he did appear a bit deranged. If only Gray knew what the devil the man wanted with him. But Honeywell had been very tight lipped about the whole affair, demanding silence and shifting the aim of his gun from Gray's chest to his head.

Sunlight began to spill through a crack in the window of the inn bedchamber in which Gray had been imprisoned the whole night. Daylight already? Damn it all, he couldn't spend all day staring down Honeywell's pistol. "When might you tell me what your plan is, old man?"

Honeywell narrowed his eyes on Gray. "I don't think I will." Then the odiferous man glanced at his pocket watch and smiled to himself. "Almost time."

"Time for?" Gray pressed.

"Time for me to step up and take your place, Hadley."

"My place?" If Gray didn't know better, he'd think his captor was foxed, but there wasn't a scent of spirits about the man. His usual unfortunate odor, yes. Spirits, no.

"Hmm." Honeywell rose from the chair in which he'd spent the night. "I've always thought you the worst sort of villain. Did you know that?"

Gray snorted. "And yet you are the one holding the pistol."

His captor shrugged off the comment. "The worst sort of villain. Your drinking, your gambling, your whoring. Your complete lack of social graces. And then you actually threw me out of Holmesfield's. I'm doing the rest of society a favor."

Perhaps he shouldn't have tossed the man out onto the street the day before. "I'm sorry I treated you so shabbily yesterday."

"A little late for that," Honeywell sneered. "But don't worry about Miss Mayeux. After her dowry pays my debts, I promise she'll be well taken care of." Then he pointed the gun at Gray's chest and pulled the trigger.

The blast hit him like a bullet in the shoulder, which was fitting because... well... It was a bullet in the shoulder. A burning sensation, as though he'd been stabbed with a hot poker, spread from his wound down his arm and across his back. Gray couldn't quite catch his breath, and he clutched at his shoulder and watched, unable to form a single word to stop Honeywell, as the man escaped out the inn window.

Dear God, he felt on fire and struggled for a normal breath. Would he die right here, right now? There was so much he'd left undone in his life. Did his mother know how much he loved her? Did Archer? Wes and Maddie? Dash and Cait? And Livi... Dear God! Would Livi ever know how much he loved her?

Sadly, the answer was no. She couldn't possibly know. He'd never told her. He hadn't even known until this very moment. But it was true. Her image flashed in his mind, her long, inky black hair spilling over her shoulders and her piercing blue eyes beckoning him to be a better man, her hand outstretched toward him.

"Livi," he breathed, and reached out to the image. The pain in his shoulder receded incrementally. Gray blinked in surprise and his next breath was slightly easier to take. Was his pain really receding? Or was he drifting to his death with Livi's image floating in his unconscious mind to ease his passage to the other side?

"What was that?" barked an unfamiliar voice not too far away.

"Sounded like a pistol," another voice answered.

Gray's unconscious mind wouldn't dream up two unfamiliar voices, would it? He didn't think so. And being in such a public place, clearly someone must have heard Honeywell's pistol and would be along momentarily to discover him in the rented room. Damn it all. His shoulder still burned, but the pain was in fact receding. If someone came to help him, they'd see his accelerated rate of healing and he'd be putting himself and everyone he loved in danger.

Gray lumbered to his feet with an oath and jerked a chair from beneath the table with his good arm. He shoved it beneath the door handle and sat down in it.

He'd have to keep everyone out, at least long enough for the wound to heal, which it seemed to be doing. He wasn't going to die. At least not like this. If anyone found out what he was, what his brothers were, they'd probably all hang from their necks at Newgate.

Heavy footsteps boomed down the corridor and Gray hung his head in his hand. Good God, couldn't they give him a few minutes to recover alone? A frantic knock sounded at the door. Gray tore at his shirt so he could look at the wound. If the warm substance dripping down his back was any indication, the bullet had gone straight through. So at least he didn't have to worry about anyone having to retrieve it. The pounding at the door continued.

"A moment!" Gray bellowed. What was he to do? Tell them to go after Honeywell? But they'd want to know why.

"Is everything all right, sir?" a man asked. The door handle jiggled and Gray planted his feet more firmly on the floor.

"A small misfire is all," Gray called back. "Everything is fine."

"Please open the door, sir, so we can confirm the circumstances."

"I'll open the bloody door when I'm damn good and ready," he called back. "Now go away."

The door handle stopped jiggling. Thank God. Gray looked down at his wound. It would be a good hour before he was fully healed. Then he would have to go to Dash's to change clothes before he could go to Livi. He couldn't marry her covered in blood. Well, he could; but he didn't want her to see him like this.

And he certainly didn't want her brothers to see him in such a state. Who knew what they'd think, and they already didn't approve of him.

Gray turned and opened the door, sticking his head out to look down the corridor. "Have someone ready a horse for hire. I'll be departing momentarily."

The innkeeper glared at him. "Did you do much damage?"

The damage he'd suffered was healing nicely. "No. I'm fine, thank you." Or would be soon enough.

"I don't give a donkey's arse about you. Did you do any damage to my room? You'll be paying for anything you've broken."

Paying for what was broken. Of course he would have to do that. Was anything broken? Gray didn't have as much as a shilling in his pocket. He'd spent all his funds the night before on Armand and Etienne Mayeux. The sole reason for leaving the gaming hell when they did last night was because Gray was out of funds. "I'll have to leave you my vowels," Gray offered. "For any damage you find. I'm good for them."

"The same way you're good for not shooting up the place."

"I never said I was good for not shooting up the place. But I'm guaranteeing that I'm good for any money I owe you." Truth be told, he didn't owe the man anything; if anyone did, it was Honeywell. Gray leaned heavily against the wall. Getting shot took a lot out of a man. More than he'd imagined. "Extraordinary circumstances," Gray said.

The innkeeper narrowed his eyes at him.

"If you want your money, you have no choice but to let me go and retrieve it."

"I'll send someone to accompany you."

"Of course, you will," Gray muttered. "I just need a few minutes, then I'll be ready to travel." He shut the door behind him and dropped back into the chair he'd occupied most of the night. He just needed a little time to recover his strength enough to ride. If he fell from a horse, there was no recovery from a broken neck.

⤜✦⤛

Livi bit back an oath as Armand accidentally dropped a satchel on her toe. Tears came to her eyes. Not because of the satchel, but because of the fact that she'd been left at the proverbial altar by a man she'd never wanted to begin with. But she wanted him now. And he'd turned tail and run.

"Bloody hell," she muttered to herself.

"Good God, Livi," Armand taunted. "Don't tell me you've picked up the way they talk too? Bloody this and bloody that. You'd think the whole place was a battlefield instead of high society. Although what I've seen of their society doesn't mark it very highly in my opinion." He gave her a gentle smile and ran his hand down her hair in the way that only an irritating brother can do. His voice dropped to a whisper. "Your destiny is in New Orleans, Livi. I can feel it. There's some decent fellow at home who will make you happy."

She nodded, biting her lower lip to keep from crying. Then she sighed heavily and gave him a watery smile. "We shall soon find out, won't we?" She nodded to the footman who was still loading her trunks and sank onto the settee in the front parlor. Even though she'd agreed to return home, she'd hoped the entire time she and Marie packed her bags that Gray would stumble into her grandfather's home and say he overslept or forgot the time, or something along those lines. Her hopes had bordered on the pathetic. She'd waited as long as her pride would allow her to wait. But the time had come to give up foolish hopes and try to pick up the pieces that were left of her heart.

The butler stepped into the room and held out a silver salver with a calling card. "You have a visitor, Miss Mayeux." He thrust the platter toward her.

"Whoever it is, tell them to go away, Flemming." She fluttered her hand toward the card. "And take that away." She brought her finger to her mouth to nibble her fingernail.

"He was quite insistent, miss," the servant declared. "Said he wouldn't go away unless you saw him. He's prepared to wait all night."

Who the devil could it be? It wasn't one of the Hadley men. They'd left as soon as Gray failed to show up for the wedding, as had their secret half brother, stating that they were going to find Gray and bring him back. Or so Sophie had told her. But Livi hadn't seen any of them in hours, nor their wives who had left along with them.

And after his heated exchange with Armand, their grandfather had stopped by her chambers to cast her a stern look, as though this was all her fault, before retiring to his own set of rooms. He hadn't even said a word. He'd just worn that accusatory expression he'd donned when she first arrived in England.

Was all of this her fault? Was it her fault Gray had run? Had she done something?

"Miss," the butler prompted. He tugged at his neckcloth.

She snatched the card from Flemming's hand and opened it. "Lord Honeywell?" she asked. "What does he want?"

A voice from the corridor reached her ears. "He wants to marry you," Lord Honeywell called as he walked into the parlor. "I heard Hadley was absent. So, that leaves a need for a groom." He straightened his jacket across his rounded belly. "I'm here to fill your need for a marriage. And any other needs you have, as well." He winked at Livi. His face was slightly sallow beneath his ruddy cheeks. And his collar was so high and starched that he didn't seem able to turn his head in either direction.

There was no way in hell she'd marry an ill-attired fop like Lord Honeywell. Much less bed him. She rubbed absently at her nose. What was that smell? Then Honeywell stepped toward her and she realized it was him. He breathed into her face when he next spoke. "You do look ravishing today, if I may say so," he said, and it nearly knocked her from her feet.

"Get out," Armand ordered.

A look of fear flashed in Honeywell's eyes. "I beg your pardon. Who are you?" He squinted as though he was quite perplexed.

"I'm Armand Mayeux, and my sister and I have had enough of perfidious Englishmen for a lifetime.

Get out." He gestured toward the corridor with a tilt of his head.

"B-b-but," Honeywell stammered. "I've come to rescue Miss Mayeux. Grayson Hadley is perfidious, I agree. But I have nothing but esteem for your sister. I don't care that her reputation is sullied. I want to give her the protection of my name."

The blood in Livi's veins turned to ice. How could the man say something like that? And to her brother of all people?

"What's this about a sullied reputation?" Etienne asked from the doorway.

Honeywell looked from Armand to Etienne and back. "There are two of you?"

"You didn't answer my brother's question," Armand barked.

"Q-question?"

"You said," Etienne growled as he stepped farther into the room, "something about our sister's reputation, I believe."

Livi wished the settee would swallow her whole. "It's nothing…"

"Everyone in Bath knows there's something going on with Miss Mayeux and Grayson Hadley. If one of them isn't muttering the vilest of curses or stumbling around foxed, then they're tussling outside assembly rooms or dousing each other with drinks. But I want to protect her from all of that. No one would say another bad word about your sister if she were to marry me."

"A regular Sir Galahad, are you?" Etienne snorted.

"Well, I think under the circumstances," Honeywell

shot Livi a look of desperation, "Miss Mayeux would be grateful for my willingness to overlook her indiscretions, make her a lady in name, and give her my protection."

He must think he truly was coming to her rescue. But even if her brothers hadn't come to England for her, she could never accept an offer from Lord Honeywell. Even if he was attractive, could turn his head in his foolish clothing, or didn't smell odd, she could never marry him. She could never love him. He wasn't Gray.

Gray, blast his abandoning soul! The faster she left England, the faster her heart could heal, or attempt to.

Livi rose from her seat and offered a conciliatory smile to her suitor. "Your offer is a kind one, my lord, but not necessary. I'll be returning to New Orleans with my brothers."

"What my sister means," Etienne grumbled, "is you can take your English arse and insulting offer and get the hell out."

Lord Honeywell blanched. "Insulting offer? I'm attempting to remedy your sister's circumstances. After the way she and Grayson Hadley carried on, no decent man would have her."

"You're not a decent man?" Armand asked smoothly, though there was a dangerous tone to his voice.

"Besides me," Honeywell clarified. "She won't receive any decent offers besides mine."

"And who is to say yours is decent?" Etienne barked. "Are you deaf, fop? Get. The. Hell. Out."

Honeywell sucked in a breath and scrambled toward the door. "Y-you're making a mistake."

"You're right," Armand called after him. "We

should tear you limb from limb for maligning our sister's name. I suggest you make haste before we change our minds."

As soon as Honeywell disappeared and the front door closed with a hurried slam, Etienne and Armand both turned their ferocious glares on Livi. "What was that about?" Etienne demanded.

"What is what about?" Livi squeaked.

Armand folded his arms across his chest, looking more imposing than Papa ever had. "Hadley has sullied your reputation?"

Livi gulped. "I didn't have much of a reputation to begin with," she hedged. "And what does it matter? We're going home, aren't we?"

Etienne snorted.

Armand's blue eyes narrowed. "Did he take your innocence?"

Livi's face flamed with heat. She wasn't as innocent as she'd once been, but she didn't think that was what her brother was asking. "No!" she declared. "I cannot believe…" she started, but stopped when her brothers exchanged a dangerous look she didn't quite understand.

"You take her to Bristol," Armand said to Etienne. "I'll stay here as long as it takes for Hadley to pull himself out of whatever ditch he's in. Then I'll kill him."

Etienne nodded in agreement.

Twenty-Five

GRAY CURSED THE POWERS THAT BE AS HE DISMOUNTED from his borrowed horse. He was officially *hours* late for his own wedding. Livi would be furious. She would be spitting mad. She would probably try to chop off his manhood with a dull knife if he so much as stepped near her. All hopes he had of consummating their marriage on their wedding night were dashed. She would probably make him sleep with the hounds instead of sharing her warm bed. And it was no more than he deserved. *He'd missed his own bloody wedding.* He tugged his watch from his pocket by the chain and glared down at it. Hours late. Too many hours.

Pebbles crunched beneath Gray's boots as he started up the walk to Dash's small manor, yet halted when the innkeeper swung from his horse and fell into step beside him. The man was like a dog with a bone. He wanted his money. All of it. Even though Gray didn't even owe him as much as a farthing. What an unfortunate turn of events. Damn it all to hell. He would kill Honeywell if the man so much as stepped into his path. And he would take great care to make it painful. But for now, Honeywell would have to wait. Gray needed to get cleaned up so he could go to Livi and beg for her forgiveness.

Gray brushed past the Eynsford butler and started for the cantilevered steps. But Wes' booming voice stopped him before he even reached the staircase. Gray hung his head and inhaled deeply through his nose. He would never make it to Livi if people kept stepping into his path. "Where the hell have you been?" his twin asked. His face was a mask of fury mixed with worry, which wasn't like him at all.

"Not now, Wes," Gray said as he put his foot on the first step. "Do pay the innkeeper at the door, would you?" he said over his shoulder. "I'm sure you owe me for something."

"Pay the bloody innkeeper yourself," Wes shot back, turning to walk back toward the parlor. Gray heard his twin mumble softly, "Disappear for most of the night and the next day, and expect to come as you please without explaining yourself."

He would have to explain himself, but not now. There wasn't time. Gray sighed. "I don't have any money, Wes," he said. "Take care of this for me and I'll owe you one."

"You already owe me. I've been out searching for your sorry hide all day."

The jingle of coins from Wes' pocket as he paid the innkeeper lightened Gray's heart a little, even though a vicious oath preceded the payment. He could count on his brother, if not anyone else. But then a door farther down the corridor opened, and Gray felt Dash's presence before he heard his half brother utter a word. Dash stalked down the hallway like an enraged beast. "He's back?" their oldest brother asked, his voice weary.

Wes jerked a thumb toward the staircase.

"I hope his body is in good shape, because the only way I'll accept what he did today is if he's dead. Otherwise, I'll have to kill him myself."

Oh, dear God. Dash in a temper was unlike anything Gray had ever experienced. And he'd hoped never to experience it again.

"Get down here," Dash snapped at Gray as he entered the nearest parlor.

As though his legs were not even his own, for one did not ignore the pack alpha, Gray went back the way he'd come. He swiped a hand down his face in frustration as he followed Dash into his parlor with Wes right behind him.

"Where have you been?" Dash barked as he dropped into a high-back chair. Then he sniffed the air. "And what did you do to make yourself bleed? Drunken brawl? Carriage flip? Deflower a virgin?"

Well, he'd planned to deflower a virgin, but there was little chance of that now. And less of one every second Dash delayed him. "Gunshot wound," he mumbled to answer his brother's question.

Wes sucked in a surprised breath.

Dash finally looked at him. His fierce golden brow softened for a moment in confusion. Then he heaved a sigh and said, "Of course you would get yourself shot."

"So nice of you to be concerned about my well-being," Gray said. He tugged his watch fob out again.

The day was quickly passing. If only his brother would hurry along this interview.

"Do you have somewhere to be?" Dash asked.

"I believe I'm late for my wedding," Gray said. *Very late for the wedding.*

"I'll say," Wes muttered under his breath.

"We've been looking for you all day," Dash said. "Who shot you?"

"Honeywell." Gray shook his head, still not quite believing it himself. "He caught me leaving Holmesfield's house last night. Evidently, he had a bit of a vendetta."

"*That's* what the smell was," Wes chimed in. "Every time I caught your scent, it was drowned out by the most obnoxious of odors."

"That's Honeywell." Gray hesitated for a moment and then blurted out, "If the two of you are through with me, I need to go to Livi."

Wes glanced at his toes and Dash almost looked sympathetic when he said, "I believe it's a little too late for that. Lady Sophia says Miss Mayeux is headed for Bristol."

"Probably there all ready," Wes added with a wince.

"Bristol?" Gray's heart clenched.

"To catch a ship bound for America."

"Why would she do that?" he sputtered.

"Some women detest being left standing at the altar. I'm not certain why." Dash rolled his eyes and growled low beneath his breath.

"You just let her go?" Gray growled.

A muscle twitched in Dash's jaw. "How was I to stop her or her brothers? They don't answer to me."

"She could at least have let me explain. Waited a few hours," Gray barked back. But when Dash raised one golden brow in warning, Gray softened his tone a bit. "Don't you think so?"

"She was quite hurt," Wes said softly.

"So, Honeywell had a nefarious plot, did he?" Dash asked.

"He planned to marry Livi himself to pay off his debts."

"I didn't know he had any," Wes chimed in.

Dash shook his head. "With the size of her dowry, she could pay off a hundred men's debts, I'm certain." He shot Gray a glance. "Caught *you*, didn't it?"

Gray's mouth fell open. "You know that's not the case." His blasted brother had ordered him to marry Livi, or had he conveniently forgotten that part?

"I know you made a fool out of yourself chasing after her skirts, causing tongues to wag all over Bath."

"Her skirts and her dowry are hardly the same thing."

Wes touched Gray's shoulder. "Everyone just assumed you got cold feet this morning. Including your Miss Mayeux." He winced again. "Poor thing had tears in her eyes."

He'd made Livi cry? Gray raked a hand through his hair. Damn it all to hell. She'd had tears in her eyes?

Dash pointed a finger at Gray. "Word of warning, you'd better stay clear of Cait and Madeline. They are ready to castrate you on sight."

"Sophia too," Wes added.

Bloody perfect. "I was held at gunpoint at an inn for hours, for God's sake," Gray bellowed. "I couldn't get away. Not until the idiot shot me and escaped out the window. And even then, I had to heal enough so I could travel and deal with the belligerent innkeeper." He scraped a hand down his face in frustration. "Dash, pray excuse me. I need to go get cleaned up and find Livi before it's too late." He waited a moment for his oldest brother's reaction.

Gray flinched when Dash rose from his chair and reached for him, but Dash just wrapped his arms around Gray in a quick, brotherly hug. "I'm glad you're all right." He pulled Gray's torn shirt apart and looked at the gunshot wound. "Looks like it's healing well."

"Still hurts like the devil."

"Explaining all of this to Miss Mayeux may hurt more." Dash winced. "If you can catch her, that is."

If he could catch her? He had to catch her. He couldn't let her leave for New Orleans without him. He couldn't let her go another day, another hour, another minute thinking he didn't want to marry her. Somewhere along the way, he'd become afflicted with the same insane malady that had overcome Wes with regard to Lady Madeline. Something like love. "Bristol is barely an hour away."

Dash agreed with a nod of his head.

"If I were you," Wes added softly, "I might not waste time getting cleaned up."

"She could already be aboard a vessel as it is," Dash added.

Blast and damn! He'd never forgive himself if he lost Liviana Mayeux for want of a bath and a clean set of clothes.

"Are you strong enough to ride?" Wes asked.

What choice did Gray have? He'd hurt like the devil all

the way to Bristol, but he'd lose Livi if he didn't. "I rode here," he said instead of answering his twin's question.

"I'll have my fastest hunter readied while you throw on a clean shirt and waistcoat." Dash rose from his seat and made his way to the bellpull.

Gray bolted for the corridor. "Thank you," he called over his shoulder before bounding up the steps two stairs at a time.

Gray could hear them talking from above stairs. "Do you think he'll catch her?" Wes asked.

Dash harrumphed. "Better question is what he'll do if he does." Dash was quiet for a moment. Then he said to Wes, "Accompany him to the docks, will you? Just to be sure he's all right?"

"I had planned to anyway."

"And give him this, if he needs it."

Gray ripped off his bloody shirt and replaced it with a clean one. There was no time to even contemplate what Dash was talking about. He didn't particularly care. He appraised his appearance quickly in the mirror. He wasn't as well put out as he could be. But it was certainly a start. Now to find Livi.

⁓

Until this very day, Livi had never wished that she'd been born an only child. Of course, until today, her blasted brothers had always listened to her. They might not have agreed with her, but they'd listened.

Bristol's sea air filled the carriage and she tore her gaze from the approaching port to Etienne, who hadn't moved as much as a muscle all the way from Bath. "What is Armand going to do to Mr. Hadley?"

"Nothing for you to worry about," her brother growled.

Well, he could growl at someone else. She'd been raised by Philippe Mayeux, and if Papa's growl hadn't ever terrified her, Etienne's poor imitation certainly wasn't about to do so. "I simply want to go home. There's no need injure the man."

"That's not for you to decide." Etienne's eyes narrowed on her.

"Oh, of course not," she goaded him. "I'm only the one whose heart has been ripped out of her chest. Heaven forbid I have a say in anything."

"We finally agree."

Livi sucked in a breath. "Arse."

Etienne cracked a smile. "So still not a lady, huh?"

"What's the point of pretending to be a lady when dealing with thickheaded brothers who won't listen to reason?"

"Reason?" Her brother snorted. "Retribution is what's important. More than anyone, you should want to see the wretch punished."

But Gray wasn't a wretch. He was… a coward? A libertine? A liar? Perhaps a combination of all three. Or maybe he just wasn't in love with her. "And yet I don't want to see him punished. That should have been enough for the two of you. But it wasn't, was it?" She kicked his shin.

"Ouch!" Etienne clutched his leg. "You kicked me."

"Quite observant of you."

"Are you going to be belligerent the entire voyage home?"

Livi sat her tallest and stared directly into her

brother's eyes. "That depends. Are you going to be a boorish lout the entire voyage home?"

Etienne released a heavy sigh. "What do you want, Liv?"

"I just want to go home. I don't want Mr. Hadley hurt."

Her brother shook his head. "Your kicking me or scratching me or whatever else you're considering won't change that fact."

Armand had remained in Bath and was currently lying in wait like a dog ready to pounce on a rabbit for Grayson to show his face. "If I'd known kicking you would open your ears and allow you to hear, I'd have done it when we were in Bath."

"If you hadn't given your virtue away to some English wolf who doesn't have the sense God gave a flea, we wouldn't have to seek retribution at all."

Livi's mouth fell open. They had been through this. More than once. "I did not give my virtue away." Her blasted brother still wasn't listening to her.

Etienne sat back against the squabs. "Armand and I both saw it. The little crinkle above your nose. So you can stop with the saintly act."

Saintly act? "Crinkle above my nose?" she echoed.

He touched his brow. "Your whole life, whenever you lie, there's a little crinkle above your nose, right here."

What a ridiculous thing to say. "I'm not lying."

He glared at her. "You had the crinkle."

"I don't have a bloody crinkle!" she ground out.

"Be glad we saw it and not Father. We can put our heads together on the voyage home and figure out what we're going to tell him. You can practice lying without crinkling."

Father? Why did he need to know anything? "I hardly—"

The coach jerked forward slightly before coming to a complete stop. Livi glanced out the window to see the Bristol Harbor a short distance away. "We're here," Etienne said as he opened the door and bounded out. Then he poked his head back inside the carriage. "Wait here. Let me see if I can find some sort of vessel headed west that'll be willing to take us as cargo."

Livi shook her head. "What about Armand?"

Etienne shrugged. "If he's back before we leave, he'll come with us. Otherwise, he'll have to secure his own passage." He narrowed his eyes on her. "Do not leave this spot, Liv." He touched his nose. "You know I'll find you if you leave, and I won't be very happy about it."

The coach door shut firmly and Livi leaned her face against the glass, looking out at the seaside town before her. People bustling about their chores, seagulls squawking in the distance, and dozens and dozens of ships.

How had it come to this? How had everything spun so much out of her control? Etienne strode purposefully toward the docks and hailed a man on the deck of a schooner. Livi sighed, certain without a doubt that her brother would secure their passage without delay. Then she would leave England never to return.

And what would happen to Gray?

Her breath hitched at the thought of what Armand

would do to Gray. She couldn't sit still, not while those awful thoughts filled her mind. Livi pushed open the coach door and stepped out into the wintry sunlight. The cold sea air whipped about her skirts, reminding her at once of the day she'd arrived at these very docks. All those weeks ago, she couldn't wait to stow away on the first vessel she happened past, to sail back across the Atlantic and give Papa and Father Antonio a piece of her mind. *Bon Dieu*, that seemed like a lifetime ago. So much had happened since then.

"Miss Mayeux," her grandfather's driver called to her. "Your brother said you were to wait here."

"My brother can go hang," Livi replied.

The driver sucked in a shocked breath. But he didn't try to stop her.

But then she saw Etienne rushing toward her. "There's a ship bound for home and I just booked passage. We'll need to board immediately." He took her elbow in his grip.

Livi jerked her arm free. "I want to stay," she said.

His face softened. "Livi," he started. Then he sighed heavily. "If he loved you, he would have been there for you." He gave her a most pitying glance, one that made her want to punch him between the eyes.

He was right, however. If Gray had wanted to marry her, nothing would have kept them apart. "All right," she muttered. "Let's go."

Twenty-Six

IT WASN'T DIFFICULT TO PICK OUT LIVI'S FAMILIAR scent as Gray walked closer and closer to the docks. "She's here. I'm certain of it." His heart filled with hope for the first time since the previous night.

Wes just nodded.

"Don't look so grim. I simply need to find her, explain everything, and she'll forgive me." He ventured a look at his twin. "I vaguely remember having to chase Madeline through the rain so you could get her back." He looked up at the clear sky above. "At least it's a nice day." He grinned unrepentantly.

"Just find her, will you?" Wes pushed Gray farther toward the docks.

But just then, a coach emblazoned with Holmesfield's crest passed them by. Holmesfield? Livi! "Wait!" Gray called to the passing coach.

The driver scowled and kept going.

"Oh, good God," Wes muttered as Gray started after the coach on foot.

"Driver, stop!" Gray yelled. When the coachman failed to heed, Gray bolted ahead of the carriage with his superior speed, stepped in front of the matched bays, and stood still as a statue. He tried not to wince when the team came to a stop mere inches from his nose. Steamy breath blew from the horses' nostrils into his face, and Gray had to step to the side to take a calming breath before streaking to the door of the carriage and throwing it open.

"It's empty," Gray said to himself when he surveyed the barren coach. His heart sank. Where was Livi? He looked up at the driver, who was holding his whip in his hand as though he planned to protect himself with it. Gray probably looked like a crazed idiot. "Where is she?" he asked the driver.

The man didn't need any clarification on who "she" was, apparently. He smirked and pointed out over the water. A brigantine stood against the horizon, already moving out to sea.

"She's on that ship?"

The driver nodded and looked fairly pleased about the entire situation. Damn his hide. Black-hearted coachman.

Gray looked back to the sea and his heart constricted. Livi was gone. She was actually gone. But he could still see the ship. She wasn't too far away. He could still reach the brigantine if he tried hard enough.

He ran back toward the docks, brushing past sailors and fishermen alike. He reached the edge of the farthest dock and began to tug off his boots. He'd swim all the way across the Atlantic if he had to. It wasn't too late, but it was damn close.

"Absolutely not," Wes barked as he caught up to Gray on the dock. "The water is freezing. You'll die of the cold. No."

"Don't tell me no, Wes," Gray said, almost ashamed of the pleading in his own voice. "I can't let her leave. I can still catch her."

Wes clapped a hand on Gray's shoulder. "Grayson." He squeezed his brother's shoulder in a rough, comforting grip. "Put your boots back on before someone thinks you're mad."

Gray ran a frustrated hand through his hair. "She's right there," he breathed, gesturing toward the brigantine, which was still within sight.

"There will be another ship."

Another ship. Gray glanced around the harbor. There were dozens of other ships. A shred of hope began to form. "I can follow her to New Orleans."

Wes nodded. "You could." He rubbed at the side of his nose as his lips began to quirk.

"Just what do you find amusing about this?"

Finally, a chuckle broke from Wes. "Aside from the fact that you're standing on the edge of the Bristol docks in your stockings?"

Gray glanced down at his feet and wiggled his toes. He supposed he did look fairly ridiculous, not that he cared what anyone else thought.

"Put your boots back on before someone steals them."

"Hadley!" a voice called from behind him.

Gray spun quickly, but not quickly enough. A blow hit his left cheek like a hammer across the side of his face. He fell to his arse. Gray leaned on his elbows and looked up at his assailant, working his jaw open and closed. It wasn't broken, but not through any fault of Armand Mayeux's pugilistic form.

The man glared down at him. "That's for ruining

my sister." He planted his booted foot on Gray's hip and gave it a hard shove. "And this is for making her cry." His boot shoved him toward the edge of the dock.

Wes shoved Armand back a few steps. Thank God, his twin was there or Gray might have found his way into the sea after all. But Armand advanced just as quickly as Gray lumbered back to his feet. Gray held up his hand as though that action alone could warn the man away.

Armand swung, but this time Gray was ready. He ducked and the American's fist flew over his head. Armand charged him like a bull and hit Gray in the side with his shoulder.

"Stop it!" Wes snapped. "People are staring." He pulled Armand off Gray and shoved the American back a step. Standing between the two of them, Wes held one hand on Gray's chest and one on Armand's. "Enough."

Even though he could have done without the punch to his jaw, Gray was never so happy to see anyone as he was to see Armand Mayeux. The earl's coachman must have been mistaken. Armand was still here, so Livi had to be as well. "Where's Livi?" he demanded. "I need to see her."

Armand spoke between heaving breaths. "If my brother did what I asked, she's far from here by now."

Gray glanced back at the brigantine, still edging its way out to the open waters. That didn't make any sense. Armand Mayeux was still in England. "But you're here."

"Stayed behind to kill you." Armand smiled menacingly.

"You wouldn't be the first to try it today," Wes grumbled under his breath. Then he shook his head and said louder, "No one is going to kill anyone."

Gray wasn't so sure about that. He might very well kill Honeywell for abducting him and shooting him, and then he might very well kill Armand Mayeux for sending Livi away before Gray could reach her.

Armand slowly grinned. "I wouldn't be so confident, were I you. After what he's done, I am well within my rights to rid the world of him."

Gray balled his right hand into a fist. How he would love to crash it into the damned American's nose.

Wes shot him a warning glance as though he knew precisely what Gray was thinking. "That will hardly help your cause," he muttered.

Armand snorted. "He has no cause." Then he glared at Gray. "I'm just glad she's gone. Away from you."

"There's nowhere she could go that I wouldn't follow," Gray said quietly.

"Follow her?" Armand charged at him again but Wes shoved them apart once more. "Is it not enough that everyone in England knows you took her innocence? Now you think you'll follow her home and spread the news there?" Armand shook his head viciously. "Not while there's breath in my lungs."

Took her innocence? The accusation made Gray's mouth drop open. "What's he talking about?" He glanced at his twin.

Wes shrugged.

"You are forever banned from seeing my sister." Armand tried to reach around Wes to grab Gray's jacket, but Wes pushed him back again. "Her virtue might not be intact, but let her have her pride."

"What the devil are you talking about? I didn't take her virtue." Gray snarled the last in the startled man's face. Not that he hadn't wanted to. Not that he hadn't dreamt about doing so. But he'd be married to her first.

Mayeux snorted.

Gray ignored him. His head spun as he tried to sort out a plan. But there was only one option. He had to find her, to make everything right. "I need to book passage to America."

"The hell you do." Mayeux lunged for Gray once more.

Gray had suffered enough. He sidestepped Wes and, with both hands, sent Armand Mayeux crashing to the docks on his arse. "See here! I don't know what you said to make her leave me. I don't know why the world has suddenly turned mad. But the one thing I am very certain of is Livi's innocence, and if you impugn her name one more time…"

"But she crinkled her nose." Armand glared up at Gray, though his eyes lost a bit of their hatred.

What the devil was that supposed to mean? The American made less sense the more he talked. Had the man been imbibing all day? "I beg your pardon?"

Armand shook his head as though to clear his mind. Then he pushed back to his feet.

"Keep your distance," Wes warned.

But Armand kept his eyes locked with Gray's. "Give me your word as a Lycan that my sister's virtue is intact."

Something Gray never thought he'd have to say to any man. He might not be the most refined gentleman in England, but he was honorable. Still, if he could somehow get Livi to forgive him, Armand Mayeux would be his brother by marriage. It would be better to have the man as an ally than an enemy. Gray swallowed his pride and said, "I give you my word, Livi is an innocent. I love her too much to ever see her sullied."

A strange smile settled on Armand's face as though he was still trying to make sense of the situation. "Damn it all, I actually believe you." He shook his head again.

"A lot of good it does either of us," Gray said as Livi's ship began to disappear against the horizon.

Wes heaved a sigh. "Let's find a vessel willing to take you to your lady."

Gray looked at his twin expectantly. Wes had to know he had pockets to let. What a sorry state he found himself in. No blunt. No clean clothes. No boots on his damned feet at the moment. But mostly, no Livi.

Wes reached into his coat pocket and pulled out a purse. He tossed it casually in Gray's direction. "From Dash," he said with a grin. "Said he thought you might need it." Then he clapped Gray on the shoulder and said, "What are you waiting for, brother?"

Armand raced to the closest frigate. "You," he called to someone on deck. "Where are you sailing to?"

"Glasgow!" the sailor called back.

Damn, damn, damn.

Gray scooped his boots off the dock and ran to

the next ship, a sloop of some sort. "Where are you sailing for?"

A rather tanned sailor looked over the side of the ship and said with a heavy Spanish accent, "Tomorrow we leave for Cadiz, señor."

Tomorrow, tomorrow. "What about today?" Gray stepped closer to the small ship and tossed Dash's purse in the air and caught it. "If you'll help me reach the brigantine that just left, you can have this whole thing."

The Spaniard shook his head. "Captain Alvarez is in town. You would have to talk to him."

Gray didn't have time to find some Spanish sea captain. He'd like to *borrow* the ship and sail it himself if he knew how. He shook his head and bolted toward a schooner not far away. A young boy leaned over the side, applying some sort of resin to the bow.

"Find your captain for me," Gray ordered, his heart pounding harder and harder, knowing that Livi got farther and farther away from him with each second that passed.

"*Excusez-moi!*" The boy dropped his bucket of resin into the water below.

Armand was at Gray's side in an instant. French flew off his tongue at a rate Gray could never have kept up with, though he did pick out the name Philippe Mayeux more than once. The startled boy spoke rapidly in return, and then he scampered off to parts unknown.

Armand heaved a sigh. "They'll take us."

But he'd only talked to a cabin boy. "They will?" Gray asked, not willing to let his hopes rise.

"I can't believe I didn't notice her to begin with, but my focus was elsewhere when I arrived." Armand gestured to the ship's name, *Madame Gracieuse*, emblazoned in gold letters on the side. "The Graceful Lady," he translated. "A play on my mother's name."

A play on Lady Grace Mayeux's name? Gray blinked at his would-be brother-in-law, who was now grinning ear to ear. "Your mother?"

"You didn't know my father runs a shipping empire?" Armand chuckled. "I suppose you don't love Livi for her money, then. What a relief."

At that moment, a salty old captain with a face full of scraggly white whiskers appeared on the bow. "Monsieur Mayeux?"

Again Armand spoke in rapid-fire French and gestured to Gray several times. The ship's captain ordered the gangway lowered, or at least Gray assumed he did, as the gangway was lowered after a bark from the old man. Without hesitation, Gray followed Armand up the gangway and onto the ship.

Armand chuckled. "Captain Lafleur actually spoke with Etienne earlier. Do you believe it?"

Gray wasn't sure he believed anything anymore. "We were very lucky."

"Luck?" Armand echoed. Then he shook his head. "Destiny. Providence. 'It is sometimes better to abandon one's self to destiny,'" he quoted.

Gray scoffed; he couldn't help it. "You are a brave man to quote Napoleon Bonaparte in England."

The American laughed harder. "Ah, but we are not in England, *mon frère*." He gestured to the deck at their feet. "We are aboard the *Madame Gracieuse*.

And if she cannot catch Livi, no one can. So abandon yourself to your destiny, Mr. Hadley, as you no longer have any control."

That was the damned truth of it. Gray couldn't make the schooner depart any faster than it was going to. Still, he couldn't help from pacing the deck as the French crew lifted the ship's anchor, echoed the captain's orders, and pulled ropes this direction or that, all very calmly and all very orderly. Their methodical nature made Gray want to rip out his own hair in frustration as he waited to depart Bristol to catch his destiny.

Twenty-Seven

Livi leaned against the starboard railing of the *Aspire*, staring at the dark water below but not really seeing it. She should have gotten married today. She should be in Bath at this very moment, surrounded by her brothers and her new family. She should have had Grayson by her side for now and always. She certainly shouldn't be on her way to blasted Boston with Etienne!

"My child," someone behind her mumbled, breaking Livi out of her reverie.

She turned around to find a Catholic priest standing just a few feet away with a greenish tint to his plump face. Father Antonio's visage flashed in her mind and Livi scowled. If she never saw another Catholic priest in all her days, it would be too soon. "Father," she mumbled in both greeting and farewell before walking to the other side of the ship.

Before she could settle against the railing on the port side, she spotted Etienne headed in her direction. "Boston?" she grumbled. "You couldn't have found some place closer to home?"

Her brother shrugged. "Captain Lafleur said this was our best option if we needed to leave quickly. Which we did. We'll only have to be in Boston a day or two."

"It's freezing there," Livi complained. She knew she was being difficult, but she couldn't help it. Nothing had turned out right, and it seemed nearly impossible for her to be pleasant.

Etienne looked over her shoulder and smiled. "Ah, Father Patrick, is the sea air not helping you?"

Father Patrick? Her brother was already acquainted with the man of the cloth? Perfect. She'd have to suffer meals with the priest all the way to blasted Boston. Or she could hole up in the cramped quarters Etienne had managed to secure for her. That option was probably safer for everyone.

"I think I just need ta get my sea legs, Mr. Mayeux," the priest replied, his Irish accent soft and lilting against the breeze.

"And a bit of ginger," Etienne suggested. "You might want to ask about some in the galley. It can work wonders."

"Thank ye. I think I'd be lost without yer assistance, my child."

Etienne returned his gaze to Livi and smiled. "Nice fellow, but not built for sea travel."

Livi heaved a sigh. "I am going to my quarters. I'll reemerge in godforsaken Boston." But before she could move another step, the sound of a cannon in the distance caught her attention.

Father Patrick's face turned from green to white and back. "Ye doona think there are pirates?"

Etienne laughed. "Not in the Bristol Channel, Father." He left Livi, returned to the starboard side, and shook his head as though he couldn't quite believe what he saw.

"What is it?" Livi asked, crossing the deck to stand beside her brother.

"I think," Etienne began, "it's *Madame Gracieuse*."

"The *Madame Gracieuse*?"

Etienne didn't answer her, though. He rushed past her, yelling to the seamen, "Lower the sails! Lower the sails!"

Livi rushed up beside him and tugged on Etienne's sleeve. "What's happening?" she asked.

He looked down at her for no more than a moment as he stared at the quickly approaching ship. "It appears as though we're being hailed."

"Hailed by whom?"

"Armand, would be my guess," Etienne said. "Perhaps he dispensed with Hadley's body much quicker than any of us expected." He grinned down at her until she punched him in the side. He winced and rubbed the area. "What was that for?"

"For wishing Gray dead."

"Oh, I more than wish it," he said, much too chipper for her own happiness. He rubbed his hands together expectantly and his eyes twinkled. "I can't wait to hear how Armand did it."

Livi lifted a hand to shield the sun from her eyes and tried to pick Armand out from the others on the deck of the ship. But then she saw *him*, the last man she'd ever expected to see again, standing there on the bow of the ship, his pose mimicking hers. Gray lowered his hand from atop his eyes and crossed his arms over his chest. His stance was wide, his legs parted to help him keep his balance. His coat billowed behind him, caught by the fierce wind. Gray spoke over his shoulder to Armand, who stood at his side, pointing toward the *Aspire*.

Livi's heart skipped a beat when Gray raised his hand and waved at her. She lifted her fingers to her lips despite their quivering.

Etienne's arm dropped around her shoulders. "What's wrong, Liv?" he asked. "I told you that it's just Armand. No need to worry that we're being besieged by pirates." He gave her a reassuring squeeze just as a tear fell down her cheek and a miniscule amount of hope bloomed in her heart.

Livi lifted her hand to wave back. When she did, Gray stepped toward the rail and leaned both hands up on it. He moved his mouth as though he was speaking to her, but she couldn't make out the words. They were snatched away by the wind as quickly as he spoke them. But his schooner was rapidly approaching.

Livi stepped forward, placing her hands on the railing to keep from falling to the deck in a giant heap of muddled thoughts. Gray was coming after her.

"Who's that with Armand?" Etienne asked, scrunching his face up as he regarded the other ship, which was coming closer and closer every second. The *Aspire*'s sails had dropped, allowing the *Madame Gracieuse* to overtake them. "Is that Hadley?" Etienne groaned. He looked down at Livi, taking in what must have been a shocked expression.

It was. It was him. He was coming for her. Grayson Hadley did want her after all.

Gray's schooner pulled alongside, and Livi watched as Gray and Armand looked at one another, a challenge in both their eyes if she'd ever seen one. Then they launched themselves over the railing, to the wild cheers and hollers of *Madame Gracieuse*'s crew.

Livi's gaze was trained on Gray as his foot found purchase on the top of the schooner's rail. Then he and Armand jumped from schooner to brigantine at the same time. Of course Armand jumped a little farther, having done this sort of thing before, landing hard on the deck behind her. Armand had grown up at the shipyards, and his footing was surer than most. But Gray faltered as he swung his arms and barely caught the *Aspire*'s rail. Livi screamed and closed her eyes, unable to watch him sink into the blue depths of the sea below.

"Pull me up, Mayeux," Gray's voice called, and Livi's eyes flew open. That was when she saw fingers clutching the outside rail of the ship. She rushed forward and looked over the edge. Gray's eyes twinkled up at her. "Afternoon, Livi," he said, as though he was meeting her over tea. A grin tugged at his lips, although he still struggled to pull himself aboard. He hung there like a giant fish on a hook.

She motioned for Etienne to come and help him. "You certainly know how to make an entrance, Mr. Hadley," she said as casually as he had.

His knuckles were white, but he still smiled, looking more handsome than she'd ever seen him, despite the fact that he dangled over the ocean. "We Hadleys never do things the easy way."

"Pull him up," she ordered.

Both her brothers stood there looking at her like she'd lost her mind, until she tugged her slipper from her foot and advanced toward them, fully prepared to beat them both about their heads until they pulled Gray from above the murky depths. They fended her off with a snort and finally went to pull one very uncomfortable Lycan onto the ship.

"Thanks for letting me hang there," Gray said to Armand, his voice dry and emotionless. "I thought you were on my side."

"You should have shoved him over, Armand," Etienne grunted. "Were you hoping for a sea burial so we could hide the body?" he asked.

But Gray didn't appear to pay any attention to her brothers' bickering. He strode directly toward Livi, and her belly flipped upside down. Her heart did a little dance that matched her belly's ferocity. Gray didn't wait for her to acknowledge him. He swept her into his embrace and pulled her to him, her body flush against the corded length of his. Gray's lips lowered, taking hers as though he owned them. His kiss was fierce, his lips pressing hard against hers. But after a moment, a growl rose up from his throat and his lips softened, sliding gently over hers.

Livi could barely draw a breath as his hands slid down her sides to cup her bottom, drawing her even closer to him. The slipper she still held in her hand dropped to the deck as she wound her arms around his neck and kissed him back.

Gray's tongue entered her mouth, invading her in the most simplistic of ways.

"Hadley!" Armand called. Somewhere in the back of Livi's mind, she heard her brother, but she didn't want to acknowledge him. But Gray lifted his head and looked down at her, that twinkle in his eye now heated and charged with passion.

"Hello, Livi," he said, his voice gravelly and deep.

Livi pulled herself together enough to look around the deck and take in all the onlookers, the crewmen and that Irish priest. *Bon Dieu*, they were making spectacles of themselves. "I'd appreciate it if you'd let me go," she whispered.

"Never," he growled.

Etienne growled low in his throat, and Livi realized Armand was holding their brother back. "Let me go so I can kill him. He certainly doesn't expect us to sit here while he mauls our sister in front of everyone."

"Stop it," Armand ordered softly. He would make a fine alpha one day.

"We need to talk," Gray said quietly, paying her brothers no mind at all.

"Let me go, Armand. The coward left her at the altar." Etienne still struggled to get loose. "And now he thinks he can lay claim to her in such a manner?"

"Heel," Armand barked.

The events of that morning hit Livi like a wave, as cold as the sea water Gray had almost fallen into. "Talk?" she asked, still breathless from their passionate kiss.

"Talk," he repeated with an enthusiastic nod.

But the memories stung. Livi raised her hand to slap him across the cheek, but he caught her arm in a gentle grip. "I promise to let you beat me to within an inch of my life, Livi, if you'll give me a chance to explain everything to you first."

What could he possibly say that would make everything all right? Livi dropped her gaze from his, turned on her heel, and stalked across the deck toward her cabin, wearing only one slipper.

"Livi!" he called after her. "Liviana Mayeux, don't walk away from me!"

Livi heaved a sigh and slowed her gait. Not because he called her name, never that. No, no. Walking a deck with only one slipper was simply difficult.

"I was abducted, shot, and left for dead." His voice finally halted her completely.

Left for dead? Livi spun around to face him. "I've never heard such rubbish in all my days."

"It's true." Gray closed the space between them in only three steps, while her brothers, the crew, and Father Patrick still watched.

Bon Dieu! Didn't they have anything better to do than to stand around gawking at her? Livi cast her brothers a scathing glare until the two of them turned their gaze away. "Who would abduct you? You have nothing," she whispered, just loud enough for him to hear, standing as close to her as he was.

"I had *you*." Gray tipped her chin up so she had to look into his eyes. "Honeywell wanted you and thought if I was out of the way, nothing could stop him from swooping in and playing your hero."

Honeywell? Livi's legs nearly buckled beneath her weight, even though she'd been on more ships than she could count in her days. "I beg your pardon?"

Gray reached for her hand and placed it on his

chest, right below his shoulder. "If his aim had been better, I would be a rotting corpse inside a rather nasty inn."

Livi's mouth went dry. Had he truly been shot? She was at a complete loss for words and simply gaped at Gray.

He squeezed her fingers. "Luckily, we Hadleys heal quickly, but as it was, it took longer than I would have liked."

"He shot you?" Livi breathed out. "He really shot you?" What if Gray hadn't been a Lycan? What if he wasn't able to heal himself? What if Honeywell's bullet had hit Gray's heart?

"I know what you must have thought. Wes told me everything." He frowned. "I'm so sorry I wasn't there, Livi." The sincerity in his gaze brought tears to her eyes. "Don't cry, love. After everything today, I don't think I can take seeing you cry."

But she couldn't help it. Livi threw her arms around his neck and held on tightly. "What if he'd killed you?"

"He didn't," Gray whispered in her ear, smoothing his hands across her back in comforting circles. "You won't get rid of me so easily."

Only he could joke about such a thing. Livi released her hold on Gray and took a slight step backward. She couldn't stop looking at his handsome face. What if she'd never seen it again? "And then you jumped from one sailing ship to another. Are you mad? Did Lord Eynsford order you to chase after me?"

Gray winced, confirming her worst fears.

"You don't owe me anything," she said at the exact

moment he replied, "I would chase you to the ends of the world, Liviana Mayeux."

Because his pack alpha demanded it? Livi couldn't bear to ask the question, but he must have seen it in her eyes because Gray shook his head.

"Don't ever think that," he growled.

"But you said…"

"I'm a fool, Livi. I only told you what I did so you wouldn't back out. You understand pack rule," he explained. "Dash *did* order me to marry you, but I was elated about the prospect." A roguish grin settled on his face. "I'd never been so happy."

He seemed so sincere. But Livi didn't think her heart could take being hurt again. Grayson Hadley was not the sort of man she'd ever envisioned herself with. He was far from perfect, and he could tear her heart to shreds faster than any man on Earth.

"Livi!" Armand called. "Do you want me toss him overboard? Or are you going to keep him?"

Gray's eyes never left Livi's, but his voice rang out as he called, "I thought you were going to help me, Mayeux."

"I got you this far, but you're on your own now, Hadley," Armand returned. "Just because I believe you doesn't mean Livi will forgive you, and she's my sister. I have to abide by her wishes."

Armand believed Gray? The same Armand who was going to stay behind in England to kill Gray when he reemerged in Bath?

Gray lowered his voice once more. "Well, what's it to be, Livi? Do you want your brothers to toss me back? Or do you want me to love you for the rest of our days together?"

Livi bit her lip as she studied the man she should have married that morning. There was only one way to tell if he meant what he said. If given the chance, would he stand proudly beside her and say his vows, or would he flee? "You truly want to marry me?" she asked.

He smiled again, and she felt it all the way to her toes. "More than anything."

"Father Patrick!" Livi called, though she kept her eyes trained on Gray, prepared to detect the slightest bit of hesitation on his part. "Would you mind marrying Mr. Hadley and me?" The priest ought to be good for something, oughtn't he?

"I-I…" the Irishman stammered. "That is, this is highly irregular, Miss Mayeux."

But Livi's life was irregular, so why should her marriage be any different? "Are you incapable of performing the ceremony?"

"I-I…Well, I suppose I could."

Twenty-Eight

GRAY STARED INTO LIVI'S PRETTY BLUE EYES, TRYING to sort out what she was up to. Oh, he'd marry her. He'd happily marry her, but there was some nefarious plot spinning in her mind. He could see it in her eyes. Just as soon as he had her all to himself, he'd find out what it was. He glanced over at the portly priest. "I have a license, if you need it."

The man tugged at his collar. "Do ye mean ta do this right here? Right now?"

"We should have married this morning," Gray said. "But I was unavoidably delayed, so right now would be just the thing, Father." He claimed Livi's hand and turned her so they were both facing the priest.

"Liv!" Etienne Mayeux hissed. "Have you lost your mind?"

If the American Lycan didn't shut his muzzle, Gray was going to send him crashing over the side of the brigantine. But before he could even growl, Livi said loud enough for all of the assembled onlookers to hear, "I lost my heart. Be happy for me." Then she cast a look at the priest that could only be described as half smile, half grimace. "I don't want any 'obey your husband' nonsense tossed in. We just want to say our vows, and you can save your condemnation for my brothers."

Armand choked on a laugh. "Just because he's wearing robes doesn't mean he's like Father Antonio."

"Better safe than sorry," Livi muttered.

The priest's gaze flashed to Gray as though asking permission or perhaps assistance. Gray shrugged and said as loudly as Livi had, "Do what she says. I'm just happy she'll have me."

"But love, cherish, obey…" The man let his words die off.

Gray smirked; he couldn't help it. "You don't know her like I do. I'll be the one doing the obeying, Father."

"Can we get on with it?" Armand complained.

The priest glanced from one Mayeux brother to the other and apparently satisfied himself that neither was going to object to Livi's demands. "Very well." He pulled a small leather-bound bible from inside his robes. "I wasn't plannin' on performin' a ceremony today. I need just a moment."

"For the love of God," Armand grumbled. "Just pronounce them man and wife and be done with it before someone shoots him again."

"I'm tryin' ta find my place." Father Patrick scrubbed a hand across his jaw as he looked at the book in his hands. "What are yer names?"

Exasperated, Armand groaned aloud. "She's Liviana Caresse Mayeux and he's…" He glared at Gray. "Tell the man your name."

"Grayson Francis Hadley."

The priest smiled tightly. "Very well. Mr. Hadley, repeat after me. I, Grayson Francis Hadley, take thee, Liviana Caresse Mayeux, ta be my lawful wedded wife. Ta have and ta hold from this day forward, for better, for worse, for richer, for poorer, in sickness and in health, ta love and ta cherish till death us do part, accordin' ta God's holy ordinance; and thereto I plight thee my troth."

Gray sucked in a breath. After the night and day he'd had, Livi was just moments away from being his forever. He squeezed her hands in his and repeated his vows, staring into her beautiful blue eyes.

Father Patrick then turned his attention to Livi. "Yer turn, miss. I, Liviana Caresse Mayeux, take thee, Grayson Francis Hadley, ta be my lawful wedded husband, ta have and ta hold from this day forward. For better, for worse, for richer, for poorer, in sickness and in health, ta love, cherish, and ta ob—" He glanced up nervously at her. "—honor, till death us do part, accordin' ta God's holy ordinance; and thereto I give thee my troth."

A look of victory flashed in Livi's eyes. Then she repeated, "I, Liviana Caresse Mayeux, take thee, Grayson Francis Hadley, to be my lawful wedded husband. To have and to hold from this day forward, for better, for worse, for richer, for poorer, in sickness and in health, to love, cherish, and honor till death us do part, according to God's holy ordinance; and thereto I give thee my troth."

The priest glanced back at Gray. "I doona suppose ye brought a ring with ye, Mr. Hadley?"

But Gray did have a ring. His mother hadn't a

multitude of possessions, but she did have an heirloom from her grandmother. A sapphire that was smaller than Gray would like, but it sparkled nearly as brightly as Livi's eyes. Nearly. He reached into his jacket pocket and felt... nothing.

Panic surged through him. He'd lost his mother's ring? Dear God. One of the few trinkets his mother had of any worth.

"You haven't changed your mind?" Livi asked, anxiety lacing her words.

Gray shook his head fiercely. Heaven help him if she thought that. "No, no," he tried to assure her. "I just seem to have lost the ring."

"Jumping from the *Madame Gracieuse*?" Livi suggested with a frown.

Etienne bent where he stood and then rose back to his full height, his palm outstretched. "Looking for this?" he asked. "Must have fallen out after I helped you up."

Gray heaved a sigh of relief as he retrieved his mother's heirloom from Livi's brother. "Thank you," he muttered. And he meant it. Clearly, Etienne hadn't been in support of the marriage, so that simple gesture did go a long way. Gray turned back to Livi and couldn't help the boyish grin that must be spread across his face. He lifted the ring up for her inspection. "I hope it fits."

Livi heaved a sigh herself as she stretched her hand out to him. "One way to find out."

Gray slid the sapphire on her finger, and though it was a tiny bit loose, the fit was nearly perfect.

"It's beautiful," she said, gazing down at the glistening blue gem.

"Yes, yes," Armand grumbled. "Let's finish this, shall we? Father?"

"Oh, aye. Of course." The priest cleared his throat. "All right, Mr. Hadley. Ye may kiss yer bride," he said, his eyes still as wary as they had been when he'd began the ceremony.

"Oh, I fully intend to," Gray said, and then he swept Livi into his arms and asked, "Where are your chambers?"

She pointed toward the stairs and he strode off in that direction.

Gray stomped down the corridor and then the wooden steps with Livi in his arms. He wasn't at all certain what was proper for a newly married couple, but as they *were* newly married, he didn't give a damn about propriety.

"Gray," she protested, as he strode purposefully toward her lodgings. "What about my brothers?"

He quirked a brow at her. "I have absolutely no interest in inviting your brothers to join us." A grin tugged at his lips at her bewildered expression.

"Join us?" She punched him in the shoulder. "What are you doing?"

He shrugged as well as he could with her in his arms. "Before we leave this ship, you'll be my wife in every way. I won't take the chance that anyone will find some loophole or some way to take you from me."

Gray stopped at the last door in the corridor. She hadn't halted him at any of the others, so this must be the one. He shoved the door open with one hand and tilted to take her through the narrow opening without putting her down.

Marie stood at the wardrobe unpacking some of Livi's dresses. She turned and dropped the gowns she held to the floor in surprise.

"Out!" Gray barked.

Marie's eyebrows drew together. "I beg your pardon?"

"Beg all you want," Gray said. "But you must do so as you leave."

Marie punched her hands to her hips but didn't take a step toward the door.

"Fine," Gray muttered as he began to slowly lower Livi to her feet, letting her slide down his body until her feet touched the floor. "But I plan to kiss my bride. Among other things." He said the last against her lips, her gasp reaching out to tickle his nose and other parts of him that were certain to have her maid escaping the room in a trice.

❧

Gray's hands threaded into Livi's hair as she looked up at him. His lips lowered to touch hers, softly at first. A moan rose up her throat, and she reached for the back of his neck as she stepped onto her tiptoes to get closer to him.

"Bride?" Marie squeaked.

"Do you think she's aware of how close you are to being disrobed?" Gray asked of Livi, an unrepentant grin making him look boyish. Or as boyish as he could while he looked like he could, and would, ravish her at any moment.

"You plan to disrobe me?" Livi teased. "In broad daylight?"

"You can wager upon it." He spun her away from

him and began to work the fastenings at the back of her gown.

"You may want to go, Marie," Livi said, holding her hair to the side.

"Well," the maid started.

"Out!" Livi and Gray both snapped at the same time.

The maid bustled past them both and out the door. Gray kicked it shut with his booted foot. When Livi's fastenings were undone, he leaned down to whisper in her ear, "I cannot wait another moment to see the birthmark on the inside of your thigh."

Livi's heart skipped a beat as he spun her back around and began to pull the few pins that secured her hair, letting them fall to the floor with delicate little clinks. He stepped back for a moment and shrugged out of his coat, unbuttoning his waistcoat as he sat down on the edge of the small bed. When he was free of his cravat, he jerked his boots from his feet and tossed them to the floor with heavy *thunks*.

He was handsome in his shirtsleeves, but he was even more handsome when he tugged his shirt over his head. Livi's breath stopped and she raised a trembling hand to her lips.

Gray had a fine dusting of hair across his chest, and she reached out to touch it as he stepped closer. Her hand played in the springy curls until her fingertip brushed across his nipple and he sucked in a breath.

"You are wearing too many clothes," he warned as he gripped her gown by the sleeves and began to pull it from her shoulders. With very little finesse, he shoved it over her hips and picked her up. Then he laid her gently on the small bed wearing nothing but her chemise, her stockings, and her single slipper. She giggled to herself when she remembered what had happened to the other one.

Gray looked down at her, his gaze skeptical as he asked, "And just what part of this do you find amusing?"

She lifted one foot, pointed to her slipper, and said, "My slippers, if you must know."

Gray jerked her remaining slipper from her foot and tossed it over his shoulder. Then he shoved her chemise up a bit and began to roll her stocking down her leg. He let his hand slide along the sensitive skin of her thigh. "Where is it?" he asked, his voice gravelly all of a sudden.

"You just threw it over your shoulder," she said, pointing to some unknown spot behind him.

"Not the slipper," he said, his hand sweeping higher, so high that the backs of his fingers brushed her curls.

She sucked in a breath. "I don't believe you need any help finding *that*," she said, her face flooding with heat. A nervous chuckle, warbling because of her uncertainty, escaped her lips.

"Where's the birthmark?" he asked as he tugged the stocking over her foot and tossed it in the direction her slipper had gone.

"The other thigh," she whispered, her belly suddenly flooding with heat as he rucked her gown up toward her waist and bared her thighs. With a wicked smile curving his lips, he pressed her legs apart and pulled her remaining stocking down and off.

His eyes narrowed as he surveyed the intimate flesh of her inner thigh. His thumb drew little circles that stole her breath even more. "Gray," she protested.

"Livi," he countered. He suddenly froze. His thumb stopped circling, and he stared down at the uppermost portion of her inner thigh. She tried to close her legs, but he would have none of that. He tsked at her as he kept her legs open. He could see all of her in that position if he raised his eyes but a scant inch. Gray lowered his head toward her thigh, and Livi squealed, pulling away from him.

But he simply held her tighter. He growled playfully as he touched his lips to that birthmark. His touch was tender until she felt his playful little teeth nibbling the sensitive skin of her inner thigh. Her belly clenched, but she didn't push him away. He was much too intent upon his task to be thwarted now. Instead, she simply lay back against the bed and closed her eyes.

The man was positively wicked, and she jumped when his hot breath blew against her nether curls.

"Shhh," he said, as though he worked to gentle a stubborn mare. "I simply want a taste."

A taste? What on earth was he referring to? Then his tongue touched her and she no longer wanted to push him away. He licked up her slit, letting his tongue press hard at that little nub that pounded so fiercely. Livi spread her legs a little further to give him access. There was no way she would push him away. Instead, she threaded her fingers into his hair. His tongue played about her flesh, around and around that little nub, until her hips could no longer remain still. Livi arched to meet his questing tongue as a wave of sensation, very much like what he'd provoked in that dark corridor the day before, built up within her.

"Gray!" she cried as the pleasure threatened to

cleave her in two. But his ministrations stopped. He stilled and stood up, shucking his remaining clothes. He'd left her unfulfilled, her blood pumping within her veins so hard he could probably hear it. A sheen of sweat began to form on her body. She should have turned her head as he disrobed, but she wasn't able to tear her eyes away. There was no way she could keep from looking at his narrow hips, his broad chest, and his manhood jutting from within a small nest of dark curls. "Come back," she beckoned.

Gray tugged her fingers gently until she sat up just long enough for him to pull her chemise over her head. He stilled and took her in, like she was a pretty painting he wanted to study.

With a low moan, he laid her back and looked down at her nipple, its rosy tip so close to his mouth. "Dear God, you're beautiful," he breathed before he took her nipple into his mouth.

"Gray," she pleaded, the breathless sound of her voice foreign to her own ears.

Gray settled himself between her thighs, rocking against her core as he came up to kiss her.

She ran her fingers into his hair and tugged gently. "Please?" she whispered. She had no idea what she needed, but she felt certain he had the answers to her questions.

He chuckled as his manhood probed her center gently. He rocked his hips, settling closer and closer. "I promise to fix it for you," he said.

"When?" she breathed, arching to meet his thrusts.

"Now," he said quietly as he thrust inside her. He stilled when she stiffened. "Are you all right?" he asked, his breath heavy and filled with longing.

Livi lay very still, not certain how to feel about the way he filled her. The ache of his possession began to dissipate and she nodded against his shoulder. He slid ever so slowly, sheathing himself fully inside her. Small noises escaped his throat beside her ear, and she'd never felt so wanted, so desired. To have a man as strong as Grayson Hadley murmuring helplessly in her ear was a heady feeling.

One of his hands slipped down between them as he raised himself up on the other and looked down at her. As he began to move within her depths, he stroked across that little nub of pleasure and she couldn't tell which was more fulfilling, the breathtaking slide of his manhood inside her or his fingers strumming her higher and higher.

Livi clutched his arms as the pleasure built within her. His lips lowered to hover over hers. "I love you, Livi," he breathed against her lips.

The waves crashed over her like water over the falls. It stole her wits, her breath, and her very being. Gray stilled while his fingers continued their play, and she quaked around his length. She clutched at him until he milked all the pleasure from her.

"*Bon Dieu*," she cried when it was over. Her body was languid and soft, her muscles like water. But Gray took her hands in his and raised them above her head, pressing them firmly into the mattress as his hips began to move again.

"Mine," he grunted as his jaw tensed. Yes, she was his. There was no doubt. He moved inside her, faster and faster. "Put your legs around me," he urged.

When she wrapped her calves around his back, he

slid even deeper inside her, touching some place that sent her once again over that waterfall, and this time he joined her. Gray shuddered above her, his hands still pressing hers to the mattress as he spent himself inside her. The jolt of his completion made her sheath clench again and he cried out her name, his hips moving until he'd taken everything she had to give him and given her all of himself in return.

Gray collapsed onto her chest, then rolled to the side, taking her into the crook of his arm just as surely as she'd taken him into her heart.

Livi sighed as she burrowed closer to Gray, and he trailed lazy circles across her back. "For a while there," he yawned, "I thought I might never see you again."

She'd had the very same thought, the very same fear. Livi rose up on her elbow to look at him, her husband, so handsome, so strong. "But you found me."

"I don't plan on ever losing you again." A roguish grin settled on his face. "Lie here beside me for a minute, and then we'll cross back to the *Madame Gracieuse*. I just want to enjoy a few moments of bliss in your arms."

How could Livi possibly refuse such an offer? She lay back down and snuggled against her very warm husband.

Twenty-Nine

GRAY AWOKE TO THE CREAKING OF WOOD AND THE swaying of the ocean beneath him. He blinked his eyes wide. "We're moving?" he asked, tasting the salty sea air on his tongue.

In his arms, Livi stirred. "Mmm?" she groaned, more asleep than awake.

Dear God. They'd fallen asleep. And where the devil were they? "Livi," he said, trying to hide the panic in his voice. "My love, I think we're moving."

Livi rubbed at her eyes, then slowly pushed up on her elbow. "Uh-huh." She smothered a yawn with her hand. "It feels like we're sailing."

But they couldn't be sailing. Gray scrambled from the small bed. "I have to get home. *We* have to get home." What would Dash say? What about Archer and Wes?

Livi lifted the counterpane to her chest and yawned once more. "If we're out to sea, Gray, there's nothing we can do about it."

But there had to be something. They couldn't be stuck on a ship. That was madness. The full moon was a night away. He couldn't be a bloody wolf on board a blasted ship. "They're going to have to turn around." He found his trousers in a heap on the floor and quickly pulled them on. "We have to go back," he said. "There's a full moon tomorrow, Livi."

"Well, then I'll have to keep you here all to myself and out of sight, won't I?" She giggled.

"I hardly find that amusing," he grumbled as he tossed his shirt over his head. "Stay here. I'll sort it out."

"You wouldn't be the first Lycan to spend the moonful onboard a ship," she called as he slipped from the cabin into the darkened passageway in his bare feet.

Moonful on a ship. That sounded like the worst sort of nightmare. Something had to be done. Gray quickly found the ship's steps and climbed back to the main deck. The nearly full moon glowed in the heavens and stars twinkled above, mocking him. He and Livi must have been asleep for quite some time for it to be so dark.

"So the married man finally emerges, does he?" came a now all-too-familiar voice just a few feet away.

Gray turned his head toward his new brother-in-law. Armand leaned casually against the railing. He cast a smirk in Gray's direction, then turned his attention back to the darkened horizon before them.

"Where are we?"

Armand chuckled. "Do you not recall jumping aboard the *Aspire*? Hopefully, you remember you took a wife this afternoon."

Gray was certain Armand Mayeux thrived on needling him. "I remember all of that perfectly well.

What I don't understand is why we are at sea when we should be in England."

Armand pushed away from the rail and shrugged. "Well, you absconded with Livi before any real plans could be decided. Captain Payne needed to continue on his course, and I didn't think it would be wise to seek your counsel at the time. There are certain things I don't want to ever witness."

Gray's mouth fell open. "I'm just supposed to stay on this ship?"

"I suppose Livi could always toss you overboard." Armand grinned as though he'd be happy to oblige his sister, should it come to that.

"But I have to get home. I have to get back to my family—"

"Not to worry, my new brother. Etienne will explain everything to them. Once he dispenses with that Honeywell fellow of yours anyway."

Etienne? Honeywell? "Your brother left the ship?"

Armand nodded. "Someone had to. And I like you better than he does."

None of this made any sense. "But why?" Why would Etienne return to England, while Gray found himself bound for America?

"That lord who shot you. He thought he could take advantage of Livi. Etienne will see that he doesn't take advantage of anyone else." His grin widened. "And I think he has aspirations of stealing Lady Sophia away from your brother, not that he'd admit as much."

Gray must still be sleeping. All of this was a dream. Not one thing Armand Mayeux said made any sense at all. "He wouldn't have to steal Lady Sophia from

Archer. In fact, my brother would pay Honeywell to take her, I'm certain."

Armand snorted. "That's not the impression that I got."

What the devil? "What gave you any impression at all? The two of them despise each other." Lady Sophia was a cold fish if Gray had ever met one. Not Archer's type in any way. His brother tended toward busty blondes with hips a man could grab hold of. And probably ride all night. Gray's thoughts returned to Livi, who was warm beneath the counterpane in their bed. He suddenly wanted nothing more than to get back to her. He turned in that direction. But then his original purpose for coming above deck sneaked into his path. "So, we're on the way to New Orleans?"

"By way of Boston."

"We'll be trapped on a ship the night of the moonful."

Armand nodded, continuing his appraisal of the nearly full moon in the sky.

"Doesn't that concern you at all?"

His new brother-in-law finally turned to face Gray. "Does it concern you?" His eyes opened wide, somewhat mocking. "You're not afraid you'll lose control with my sister, are you? If so, tell me now."

Gray wasn't afraid of that at all. Only of someone stumbling upon him in wolf form. There weren't that many places to hide on a ship. "I'd never hurt her," he said instead.

"Livi would lop your stones off with a dull knife from the galley if you ever did anything to hurt her." He clapped Gray on the shoulder with a chuckle. "If she could get to you before I did, anyway."

This conversation had been far from reassuring and less than helpful in so many ways. "What do you plan to do during the moonful?" Gray and his brothers usually retreated to the forest to seek solace within the surrounding nature. They didn't stay in close proximity with regular people. And they certainly didn't set sail aboard ships.

"Same as always. What are your plans?"

To toss his blasted brother-in-law into the Atlantic. Gray narrowed his eyes on the other man. "You've done this before? Spent a moonful in the middle of the ocean?"

Armand nodded. "More than once. There's nothing to it, Hadley. And as there are no ladies on board, aside from my sister, the population is safe from my lusty wolfish nature."

Gray heaved a sigh and swiped a hand down his face in frustration. "Do you stalk the deck and howl at the moon?"

The American chuckled. "Livi will lock me in my chambers. And much to my dismay, she'll lock you in yours along with her."

Heat crept up Gray's cheeks. He would be locked in with Livi on the night of the moonful. He'd claim her as his own in a ritual more basic than any marriage ceremony. His manhood twitched at the thought of it. He'd bite the sensitive skin where her neck met her shoulder and leave his mark upon her, like he'd wanted to do ever since their very first kiss.

"I'm not certain your hasty marriage onboard a ship by an Irish priest will please my father." He must have seen how confused that statement made Gray feel because he continued. "Under other circumstances, he might very well try to nullify your marriage." He sent Gray a sly look. "But if she wears your mark…" He shrugged. "Not even Philippe Mayeux would disregard the significance of a bite mark."

"Thank you for the suggestion," Gray muttered. He must be making headway, at least with Armand, if the man was willing to give Gray information about how to win against their father. "Do you think he'll hate me on sight?"

"I think he'll absolutely loathe you and call you a money-grabbing whoremonger, and he'll give Livi a hell of a time about it all."

That was hardly reassuring. "Didn't he send her off to be married?"

"He sent her off to be married to a man of wealth and prestige." He snorted again. It was a most annoying sound.

"I may not be a man of wealth or prestige, but I love her."

"And that is the only reason you're alive today, Hadley," Armand said with a haughty smirk as he strolled away toward a dark corner of the ship.

Gray stood at the rail for a while, looking at the clear sky and the nearly full moon whose light bounced off the sea. He'd once given Wes a hard time for falling so deeply and so completely in love with Madeline. But now Gray completely understood how his brother felt. His heart was so full that it was near to bursting. Livi was his, and tomorrow he would claim her for an eternity.

Usually, when the moon was this full, a feral wildness rested just beneath his skin and he wanted a woman like nothing else. But a certain peace had settled within his heart on this fine night, sailing the ocean. He certainly wanted a woman, but not just any woman. He wanted his and only his. He wanted her fiercely, desperately, and completely.

The crescent-moon mark on her thigh crept back into his thoughts, and his heartbeat quickened at the thought of tasting it again. But then he remembered her father who was waiting at the other end of the journey. The man wouldn't be able to deny the way Gray felt about Livi. But was he worthy of her? He would be some day. Livi was worth a bloody fortune, but that didn't even signify for Gray. He didn't want a single piece of it. He just wanted to meet her father, show him he could be a good man, a good provider, a father for his grandchildren, and to gain his trust. He could do that, couldn't he?

The thought of being a father to Livi's children made a little part of his heart ache with sweetness. He couldn't wait to run his hands over her burgeoning belly, to feel a life they created growing within her. He wanted to see her chase a child across the courtyard at Hadley Hall and kiss the bottoms of tiny baby feet. He wanted it all.

But what would her father see when he met Gray? A wastrel from a poor family who was part owner of a gaming hell? Or would he just see a man who loved his daughter?

"You look like you're a million miles away," a soft voice said from beside his shoulder. He turned and looked down into Livi's eyes, which were almost black in the moonlight. "What are you thinking about?"

"Nothing important," he murmured as he put his arm around her and drew her into his side.

"You're not worried about the moonful, are you? Armand and Etienne have sailed under a full moon more times than I can count."

He shrugged. He wasn't as worried about that as he once had been. Now he was much more worried about proving himself to her father. To being a man she could respect and love. "I'm not worried about anything."

She burrowed more closely into his side, her summery scent teasing his nose. He wanted to draw her into himself, as close as she could go.

Livi placed a hand over his heart. "I won't leave your side. Everything will work out. Just wait and see," she murmured, her breath tickling his chin.

"I know," he replied. Though he wasn't certain he agreed.

❧

Livi tiptoed out of the small cabin, careful not to wake Gray. After the day he'd had yesterday, he could use as much sleep as he could get. After the night they'd shared, he might sleep all the way to Boston.

She nodded in greeting to some of the *Aspire*'s crew and finally made her way to the front of the brigantine. She leaned against the ship's railing and closed her eyes, content to let the sea breeze wash over her skin. What a truly wonderful adventure she was on. Life with Gray would never be boring.

A familiar hand landed on her back and Livi smiled, knowing who stood behind her without even needing to look. "Thank you, Armand," she said softly. "For everything."

He heaved a heavy sigh and then leaned his large frame against the railing at her side. "You're sure this is what you want? You're sure he is who you want?"

"*Oui*, I'm sure." Livi opened her eyes and tilted her head to see her brother, who looked troubled. She slid her arm around his and leaned her head against his shoulder. "In time you'll accept him."

Armand shook his head. "It's not me you need to worry about, Liv. I'm concerned about what will happen when we finally set foot in New Orleans. You know Father won't be happy with this turn of events." He slid his arm around her and hugged her to him. "The man has nothing to recommend him, nothing that will mean anything to Father."

Indeed, very few men would be deemed worthy by the powerful Philippe Mayeux, but Gray didn't have to live up to her father's expectations. He only had to live up to hers. She rested her head against her brother's heart and smiled against his chest. How comforting she'd always found Armand's embrace.

No matter how strong and rigid he appeared to the world, when it came to her, he'd always been the most tender of men. How like him it was to worry about Father on her behalf. But it was pointless to predict Papa's reaction to anything. "He has my heart. Papa will see I'm happy. That should be enough for him."

Armand tipped her chin up so she had to look him in the eyes. "I told your husband he should claim you tonight. Father won't try to break that bond, but…"

He frowned. "Well, make sure that's what you want, Liv. There's no going back after you've been marked."

Livi touched a hand to her shoulder. "I know that."

"You have the day to decide whether you want to wear Hadley's mark or not. You can always lock him in your cabin and stay on deck through the night if you choose otherwise."

And destroy Gray in the process? Livi gaped at her brother. "You think I should run out on him?" She couldn't imagine ever doing any such thing, especially after everything they'd been through.

Armand shook his head. "I can't make that decision for you, Liv. You're on your own path. I just want you to be sure of what you're choosing. There are some things that can't be reversed."

And some things she would never want to reverse. She wasn't certain why or even how she'd fallen for Gray, but she had. Her heart had been in shambles yesterday when she thought he'd run out on her, but when she'd spotted him on the *Madame Gracieuse*, when he'd jumped from the schooner to her brigantine, when he hadn't hesitated in the least at her suggestion they marry that very moment—she'd known he loved her too. "Thank you for worrying about me." Livi smiled up at her brother.

Armand heaved a sigh. "Made your decision already, hmm?" He dropped a kiss to her brow. "Do at least one thing for me?"

After all he'd done to help Gray get to her? "Anything," she vowed.

"Rummage through Etienne's trunks. Your husband is going to need more than the clothes on his back during this voyage. I think he's worn the same trousers two days in a row."

Despite his protestations or dire warnings, Armand liked Gray. Livi could see it in his eyes, and that warmed her heart more than a little. She nodded her head in agreement. "*Oui*. That sounds like a brilliant plan."

Gray had never experienced a moonful in closed quarters. Not with others who could learn his secret if he exposed it unwittingly. A little help might be in order, perhaps. She called to Armand's retreating back. "Do you know where I can get some whiskey?" she asked.

He turned back, one eye squinting as he appraised her, his gaze incredulous. "You insult me, Livi," he said with a smirk. "Do *I* know where to get whiskey?" He scoffed.

She rolled her eyes at him.

He winked. "I'll take care of it."

She would never repeat it in public, but she was grateful for having at least one ne'er-do-well brother on board right that very moment. She might have need of that whiskey. Or Gray might, at least. She couldn't have him howling at the moon through the portal in their room. That simply would not do.

Thirty

THIS WAS FOR THE BEST, LIVI HAD NO DOUBT. AS THE day progressed, she'd watched Gray pace the deck of the *Aspire* as though it were a cage. When she'd asked about his anxiety, he'd laughed off her questions and mumbled something about stretching his legs. No, as the day went on, she had no doubt about what she needed to do. He'd thank her in the morning. At least she hoped he would.

As the moon sank low over the ocean, Livi and Gray made their way to Armand's quarters. She knocked softly on the door.

"C'm in," her brother called from inside.

Goodness. Livi knew that slurry voice. Armand was already foxed. Hopefully, he'd left enough for Gray.

After shooting her an amused look, Gray pushed open the door, then preceded her into the room. He chuckled when he took in Armand's relaxed pose where he lay sprawled across the bed. "Tipping it a bit early, aren't you?" he teased.

Armand pointed to the portal, where the sky was darkening. "A lame attempt at escaping the pull of the moon." He held a bottle out to Gray. "One for you?" He tipped the bottle with one of his fingertips and, if not for Gray's quick reflexes, it would have been a puddle on the floor.

Gray caught it in his strong grip and held it out to Armand. "Thank you, but I need to keep my wits about me tonight."

Armand narrowed his gaze. "On a night such as this, the last thing you need to keep about you is your wits." He nodded toward the bottle that Gray kept, trying to foist upon him. "That's for Livi, not for you," he finally said, giving Livi a dramatic wink. "Just as you requested, m'dear."

A puzzled expression settled on Gray's face.

"I'll explain it later," Livi promised. If Armand's current state was any indication, her brother would be asleep within moments. "We should get to our quarters before the moon rises much higher," she warned. The last thing any of them needed was for her husband to sprout a tail and pointy ears in the corridor of the ship. She took the still-outstretched bottle of whiskey from his hands.

"Do we need that?" Gray asked, as they stepped from Armand's cabin to the outside.

Livi locked her brother's door, then pocketed the key. "We might," she hedged. "Better safe than sorry." Then she started toward her quarters, knowing Gray would follow right along.

"Livi, the last thing I want to do is lose my inhibitions with you."

But losing a bit of his control was exactly what he needed; it was best for everyone. Livi stopped in her tracks, then reached up to cup his face. "You're not worried you'll harm me, are you?" She snorted, hoping to lighten his anxiety just a bit. "You're worse than an innocent on her wedding night," she teased.

"Very amusing." He slapped her bottom. As she scurried toward their cabin, he called after her, "I'll get you for that."

"Promises, promises," she sang.

He growled and ran after her, a low rumble in his chest as he followed her through their doorway and into their cabin. She locked the door behind them and said, "Turn around."

The apprehension on Gray's face returned tenfold. "Why?"

"Because I don't want to hold the key in my hands all night. I imagine I'll have better things to do with them." Heat crept up her face as his gaze darkened with lust.

"Why didn't you say so?" He spun away from her and counted to ten.

Livi kicked up the corner of the rug and tucked the key beneath it. Then she pulled the stopper from the whiskey decanter and poured a glass. She held it out to him as he turned back around. "Drink," she instructed.

Gray shook his head. "No. I told you, I want to have my wits about me." He sat down on the edge of the bed and began to tug his boots from his feet. He followed with his coat and waistcoat, and then his cravat. He tugged his shirt over his head and let it land like a fluttery bird on the floor.

"You'll find this easier if you have a few drinks," she said.

"Find it easier to bed my wife? I sincerely doubt that."

❧

Find it easier? Livi had lost her bloody mind if she thought he'd flummox this up. The day he claimed his wife would be a day to remember. Not a day that he was so foxed he couldn't string two thoughts together, much less a memory. Absolutely not.

She sat down on the only chair in the cabin and crossed her pretty little hands in her lap. "That's too bad. I thought we might be able to play a little game."

A game? His ears almost twitched. "What sort of game?"

She looked everywhere but at him, and the area above her nose wrinkled as she scrunched it. "I'm a little nervous," she said, as though confessing to a priest. She began to wring her hands together. "I thought a few drinks might make you a bit more pliable. Less… scary."

"I scare you, Liv?" He got to his feet and approached her. "I'd never harm you. I don't have to claim you at all tonight, if you don't want. It's not too late for you to lock me in like you did Armand."

"I want to be with you, but I'm worried." She nibbled her bottom lip. "Humor me?" she asked. "Play my game?"

Gray sighed heavily. "Tell me the rules."

"Sit," she said as she pushed him down into the chair.

Then she ran her soft little hands across his naked chest, and his manhood immediately responded.

"Liv," he growled in warning when her fingertip slid across his nipple. "Take some of those blasted clothes off, will you?" he asked as nicely as he could under the circumstances. He put his stocking feet up on the table and crossed them. "I'll watch."

Gray didn't know what he'd expected, but the pull of the rising moon was nothing compared to the pull of Liviana Hadley.

She held a full glass out to him. "For every item I remove from my body, you'll have to take a drink."

He could play her game without getting foxed, couldn't he? Of course, he could. He'd been drinking ever since he was old enough to tip back a bottle. Gray tossed back the contents of his glass. "What's coming off first?" he asked, a grin tugging at his lips.

❧

Livi took a deep breath and kicked off a slipper.

Gray arched a dark brow at her. "That's all I get. A slipper?"

She refilled his glass. He lifted it to his lips and talked around it. "I suppose this will get me another slipper." But he drank it anyway.

She kicked off the other slipper, and it sailed across the small cabin to thump against the wall.

"Shh," Gray warned. "I believe that Irish priest is on the other side of that wall."

"He might want to find other accommodations, then," Livi said. "Because I have a feeling things might get a little loud in here."

Indeed, the sound of growling had a way of permeating the walls.

"Only if I do it correctly," Gray said. Then he drank the next glass she poured for him. He leaned back in his chair, studying her with those dark eyes of his. "What will she take off next, I wonder?"

She tugged a pin from her hair and let it clatter to the floor.

"Oh, no," he said, lowering his feet. "That's not nearly worth the price I'm paying. All of them," he directed.

Livi's heart lurched within her breast. But she tugged all the pins from her hair until the heavy mass tumbled about her shoulders. She poured another glass for him. She had his full attention, his gaze both intense and appreciative.

"So pretty," he said.

His trousers were tented by the length of him, and she had a nearly insatiable urge to strip his trousers off and to feel the swell of him within her grip. She licked her lips at the thought. He needed to drink enough so he'd sleep through the night, sleep through the transformation, and not wake until morning.

Oh, she wanted him to claim her, wanted him to make love to her all night, but he wasn't accustomed to sea travel, not during a full moon. She couldn't risk him changing into his wolf form and alerting everyone to his presence on the ship. That would be a disaster. For both of them. "Drink," she said.

Gray tipped the glass back and drained it dry. "What's next?" he asked with a smirk almost as big as the twinkle in his eye.

Livi spun around and presented her back to him. He quickly worked the fastenings of her gown until she was able to slide it down her arms and over her hips. Then she stepped out of it.

"I do love the green garters," he said slowly, licking his lips. "Can they be next?"

She pointed to the glass. He refilled it himself and downed the whiskey in one quick swallow. She untied one garter and rolled her stocking down her leg. When he drank another glass without her urging, she bit back a grin. How nice to know she affected him so. She'd have to remember that on nights that weren't ruled by the moon.

Honestly, this game of hers was affecting her as much as it was him. Her belly clenched each time his eyes landed on her body. And her drawers were wet with wanting him.

"Are you foxed yet?" she asked as she tugged her last stocking off. He drank three glasses in quick succession, stopping only momentarily to wince on the last one.

"Not hardly," he grunted. But he rested his head in his upturned palm.

Perhaps her plan was finally working. The last three glasses had her tugging her chemise over her head and shoving her drawers down to her ankles.

He looked supremely satisfied as he noted, "You still owe me for that last drink."

"I have nothing left to take off, Mr. Hadley," she informed him.

"I can see that, Mrs. Hadley," he teased. His gaze roamed her body hotter than any caress could have been. "Hold your breasts in your hands," he ordered.

She couldn't possibly do that, could she?

"You owe me, Livi," he said, nodding toward the glass as he refilled it. "Just pick them up in your hands. Let me watch."

"You're a pig," she said.

"Wolf," he corrected.

She did want to keep him drinking, didn't she? To avoid the pull of the moon. So she did as he requested. Heat built deep in her belly as she lifted her breasts in her hands. Her thumb slipped across one dark peak and her breath hitched in her throat.

"That feels nice, doesn't it?" he asked. He tossed back another swallow. "Sit down on the bed."

"Why?" If they stopped now, he would never pass out. He would become a beast and everyone would find out. He wasn't like her brothers. He hadn't done this before.

"Because you owe me." He took another swallow.

The bed was no more than a foot from where he sat so casually, his elbows on his knees while he regarded her. He reached for her hand and took it in his, tugging it down toward her nether curls. "Gray," she protested.

"Here," he whispered, his words raking across her skin hotter than any caress. He dragged her fingertip toward that nub that was pounding so loudly in her ears. "Touch here," he said and he pulled his hand back. He pressed her legs open wide and sat back. He took another drink. "Do it for me, Livi," he asked. She couldn't refuse him, not with her blood singing in her veins and her finger playing about the damp folds of her heat.

"Gray," she protested, but she found that little nub

and began to circle it. He praised her quietly, urging her on. Her protests quickly became pants, leaving her mouth unheeded. She didn't care about the noises she made. She only cared about the way he made her feel.

He licked his lips as he opened the placket of his trousers and shoved them down his hips.

Livi let her fingers circle faster and faster. "You have me so hot, Livi," he ground out.

Not nearly as hot as she was. Goodness, she would burst into flames any moment. Then she felt it, that buildup that she still didn't understand, even though he'd provoked it so many times. "Gray," she cried. And when she did, he reached for her, pulling her up with one strong hand around her back, and brought her to straddle his lap.

"Livi," he growled as he centered her over his manhood and held tightly to her hips, sliding inside her as far as he could go. He stilled and screwed into her, holding her tightly. He brushed her hair back from her face with tender fingers. "God, Livi," he growled. His thumb took over where her fingers had been and his lips played along the side of her neck. He nibbled her gently while he coaxed her higher and higher than she'd taken herself, with his length filling so fully.

She rose and fell on him, holding tightly to his shoulders. And just when she felt like she would break, she was flung headfirst over that precipice, the feeling of falling washing over her like warm rain. And just as she came apart, he bit into the side of her neck, his sharp little teeth piercing the tender skin where her neck met her shoulder, marking her as his. He joined her in release, calling out her name as he pulled her tightly down onto his shaft, fitting them together deeper than they had ever been before.

Gray's chest rumbled with a poorly concealed chuckle. "Don't ever try to play me again, Livi," he warned. "I will always win when it comes to whiskey."

She could barely catch her breath. "I think I won that round, Mr. Hadley."

He stirred within her. "Then I think we should have another round, Mrs. Hadley."

Another round? "The whiskey didn't affect you at all?"

He chuckled again. "Were you honestly trying to get me foxed?"

Figured everything out, had he? Livi shrugged. "I thought it would help with the moonful. It helps my father, my brothers when they're aboard a ship."

"You're the only thing I need to soothe my savage beast, Livi." Then he rolled her to her back and hovered right above her. "And now, my dear, you are stuck with me for the rest of your days."

She couldn't think of anything more lovely. "You only want me to soothe your savage beast, Gray?"

He shook his head. "I want you because I love you, because you have driven me mad with want ever since that first day at Holmesfield Court." He lowered his head and captured her mouth in a kiss before continuing to their next round and the one after that.

Thirty-One

After reaching Boston, Gray had a good mind to hop the next ship bound for England instead of finding one headed for New Orleans. But Livi was so excited about seeing her home, seeing her father again, that he'd abandoned the idea almost at once. And now that they'd nearly reached their final destination, anxiety settled in his belly, much to Armand's ever-growing amusement.

The air had grown thicker the last few days, making breathing a more laborious chore than it had ever been before. Gray had never even thought about the process of breathing until the last leg of this voyage, but the farther south they traveled, the more difficult the act had become.

The clothes he'd borrowed from Etienne Mayeux's trunk clung to his skin, damp with dew that never seemed to dissipate. How the devil did people live in such a climate?

At least Boston had been reasonable. Cold, to be sure; but one could breathe there. Still, anything was bearable as long as Livi was at his side. In all his years, he'd never felt as connected to another person as he did to his wife. And being a twin, that particular reality had been more than a little surprising. But ever since that fateful night in the North Atlantic when they'd come together and he'd claimed her as his for all time, he'd felt completely at one with Livi.

As he finished a letter to send home once they reached port, reassuring his mother that all would be well and that he and Livi would return to England just as soon as they could, the frigate they'd boarded in Boston suddenly slowed to a halt. Had the crew dropped the sails? Had they lost their wind? Certainly they couldn't be there already.

"Gray!" Livi's voice rang down the corridor outside their cabin door. "Gray! We're here!"

Blast it all! A fresh wave of trepidation washed over Gray as he folded his letter and tucked it into his pocket. He opened the cabin door and quickly ascended the wooden steps leading to the main deck. Livi stood at the top, an impish grin spread across her pretty face.

"Isn't it wonderful?" she gushed. "Come quick." She reached out a hand to him, which he instantly took.

Livi towed him to the railing and gestured to the land just within view. Honestly, it looked like any shipyard he'd ever seen, with a number of storage buildings set off from the docks, scores of ships floating in the harbor, and preoccupied sailors bustling about the yard on one assignment or another; but Livi was so exuberant that Gray nodded in agreement.

"Wonderful," he echoed.

She wrapped her arm around his middle and squeezed

tight. "Liar. But don't worry about Papa," she said softly. "He'll love you. I know it."

Gray wasn't certain about that. After all, he'd had more than one discussion with Armand during this journey, and his brother-in-law hadn't painted the most welcoming picture of Philippe Mayeux. Gray would be lucky to leave America with his tail intact.

As though summoned by his thoughts, Armand appeared on deck and clapped a hand on Gray's back. "If he tosses you into the bayou, I'll fish you out."

"Much obliged," Gray grumbled.

"Eventually," his brother-in-law chuckled.

"Armand!" Livi complained. "Don't frighten him anymore than you've already done. Papa will love him. I know he will."

From the corner of Gray's eye, he saw Armand smirk. "Love turning him into 'gator bait perhaps."

Before Livi could make any sort of retort, the frigate's gangplank was lowered. Armand tipped his head at the pair and then disembarked as though he hadn't a care in the world. He probably didn't. No one was threatening to turn him into 'gator bait, after all.

"Come on." Livi tugged Gray toward the gangplank as well. "Papa is probably in his offices at the port."

Bloody wonderful. Gray wouldn't even get the opportunity to get used to breathing the heavy air of New Orleans before he'd have to lay eyes on his intimidating father-in-law. But the time had come, apparently, for him to face his destiny, and perhaps his maker.

The trio navigated the docks and meandered along a path littered with warehouses. Livi seemed to bounce with more glee each step she took, and Armand waxed poetic about the familiar scents of home and humid air. Gray couldn't even find the words to reply because his stomach was so twisted in knots.

"Here we are!" Livi nearly sang as she gestured to a warehouse emblazoned with the letters *PRM* above the main doorway.

Armand draped his arm around Gray's shoulders. "I'm sure he'll make it a quick death. You won't even know what hit you."

"You're too kind," Gray muttered as he moved away from his brother-in-law, which only left Armand grinning wider.

"Behave!" Livi ordered her brother. Then she walked toward Gray, smiling at him with her enchanting smile that always left Gray a little breathless. "You'll be fine," she whispered, sliding her arm through his.

Armand pushed open the hearty oak door and then led the way up a flight of stairs at the far end of the cavernous room lined with boxes, crates, and shelves. "Father!" he called. "Are you here? You'll never guess who I found."

"Armand?" came a heavy French accent from a room at the top of the stairs.

Armand barreled through the door, while Gray and Livi followed at a slower pace. An enormous man with wavy black hair rose from a seat behind a well-used desk.

Philippe Mayeux, Gray had no doubt. He looked like Armand but broader, more intimidating than Gray had imagined.

The man gaped at the trio for only a moment. Then

his face transformed to a broad smile as Livi dropped Gray's arm, bounded across the office, and threw her arms around her father's waist.

"Papa!" she gushed, holding him tight.

Philippe Mayeux squeezed her in return, then smothered her face with kisses. "*Mon bébé* girl finally comes home. Can you forgive me, *mon trésor*?" He took a step back as though to see all of her and make sure she was unharmed.

Gray knew the moment the Frenchman spotted the bite mark on Livi's neck. The man's face stiffened in anger, and then his gaze shot across the office to land on Gray. His mouth fell open, but no words came out as though surprise had turned him mute.

"You might want to run," Armand muttered. "I've never seen him speechless before."

Gray had the same thought, but he wasn't a coward. He wouldn't abandon Livi simply to avoid whatever punishment her father had in store for him. Whatever it was, he would endure it. He had to. Because at the end of all that, Livi would still love him, and she'd still be his wife, no matter what Philippe Mayeux did to him. "Sir…" Gray began.

"Radbourne?" Mr. Mayeux finally said, staring at Gray with such intensity that a shiver of apprehension crept up his spine.

Still, Gray managed to shake his head. "Radbourne is my brother."

A ghost of a smile settled on Mr. Mayeux's face. "Of course he is." He nodded slowly. "Of course. Edward would have been my age now. I was sorry to hear about your father."

Gray hadn't expected those words to come from Mr. Mayeux's mouth. He hadn't even realized the man had known his father. Had his mother mentioned something to that effect? Gray couldn't remember. "I—uh—thank you," he said slowly. "It was so long ago that I don't really remember him."

"It *was* a long time ago," Philippe Mayeux agreed. "You look like him. Did you know?"

"I've heard there's a resemblance between all my brothers and our father."

"Indeed." The man nodded once more, then his face hardened anew. "Are you... What is your name, Mr. Hadley?"

"Gray—Grayson."

"Well, Grayson, am I to assume you are the one responsible for the blemish on my daughter's flesh?"

Gray gulped, but he nodded. "She is my wife, sir."

"Wife? *Bon Dieu*." Philippe Mayeux rubbed his brow as he shook his head as though trying to sort out the problem. Then he glanced at his son. "Where's Etienne?"

"Left him in England," Armand muttered. "He had some business that needed attending."

"Can't wait to hear about that," Mr. Mayeux grumbled. "All right, then. Take Liviana home. Grayson and I will meet you there in a while."

"*Non*, Papa!" Livi rushed forward. "You mustn't hurt him. I couldn't stand it if you did."

At that, Mr. Mayeux actually chuckled, a deep rumbling sound that echoed off the office walls. "I have no intention of hurting the man, Livi. Now, do as you're told."

But she shook her head stubbornly. "You mustn't kill him, either. I know how you think, Papa, always looking for loopholes."

Philippe Mayeux heaved a sigh as though he suffered the trials of Job. "Nor do I have plans to kill the young man, Livi. Go home with your brother. When next you see your husband, you can look him over for wounds, if you so choose."

Livi's gaze shot to Gray, and he nodded. "I'm sure I'll be fine, love," he said, though he wasn't quite sure that was the truth.

"Come on, Liv." Armand draped an arm around her. "After all the tasteless fare we've suffered through these past weeks, I am dying for some of Cook's beignets."

"Not one scratch?" Livi asked, her eyes still focused on her father.

Mr. Mayeux shook his head. "You have my word, Liviana."

Finally appeased, Livi allowed her brother to escort her from the office. She did look over her shoulder before the door shut behind them, and she mouthed the words, "I love you."

As soon as the door closed, Philippe Mayeux advanced toward Gray. "A damned Hadley," he sighed. "I don't suppose Edward came into a large fortune before his untimely death?"

So even in America the Hadleys' penniless state was well known. The truth of that was a bit lowering. "I wish he had, sir." Life would have been very different, had that been the case.

"Wishful thinking on both our parts, then." The

Frenchman gestured to a chair before his desk. "Go on, have a seat. We have much to discuss."

Gray dropped into the chair, just as Livi's father sank back into his.

"Before we begin, I want you to know that I owe your father a debt. If not for him, I would have never met my Grace, and I wouldn't be the man you see today."

Gray breathed a little easier at these words. Perhaps Philippe Mayeux wouldn't kill him after all.

"But regardless of that debt, I will not see my daughter live in rags."

Gray shook his head. "Of course not, sir. I—"

But Mr. Mayeux held up his hand, silencing Gray's words. "I suppose if you were Radbourne, she'd at least have a title and that is worth something."

"Sir—" Gray started again, only to once more be halted by the Frenchman's upward palm.

"Let me finish." He sat a little taller in his seat and leaned his elbows on his desk. "I know you English look down on those of us who spend our days working for a living, but it is an honest way to provide for one's family. Livi is accustomed to being provided for"—he pushed out of his chair and began to pace, as though sitting still was an impossible chore—"and therefore, I will not harm you. I will not kill you. Not even a scratch will mark you as long as you do what I ask. And 'gators have an aversion to the English, I hear. They leave them floating instead of gobbling them whole." Not even a grin tugged at his lips.

Gray sat forward in his seat. "What is it you want from me, sir?"

Mr. Mayeux shrugged. "I want you to work for me."

The air rushed out of Gray's lungs. He certainly didn't expect Philippe Mayeux to offer him a job. Never in a million years would that thought have crossed his mind. "Work for you?"

"I have several enterprises. Find a business that appeals to you and run it for me."

Gray wasn't certain what to say. On one hand, he was relieved the man didn't intend to turn him into 'gator bait, but on the other, his pride stung from Philippe Mayeux's lack of faith in his abilities to care for Livi. "I am already running a business, sir."

The Frenchman's eyes narrowed on Gray, disbelief etched across his brow.

Gray cleared his throat and said more clearly, "That is, my brothers and I are opening a gaming establishment. We embarked on this venture together, and it would not be right of me to abandon them."

A twinkle lit Philippe Mayeux's blue eyes. "Gambling?" At Gray's nod, the man guffawed. "And here I was concerned you would think yourself too good to put in an honest day's work."

No one had ever thought a Hadley too good for anything before. What an odd thing to hear. "Well, that is not the case, sir."

"I see it's not." The man dropped back into his chair and his blue eyes scrutinized Gray intently. "You're *opening* this establishment? It's not already open?"

"Not quite yet." Honestly, they'd be a lot closer to the opening if Gray had gone to London instead of Bath, but then he would have never caught Livi, and that would have been a travesty. "But I'm certain it will be a success."

"I wish I shared your certainty, Grayson. But, as it turns out, I am older and I've seen many men fail at various endeavors. I won't take that risk with Livi's future. *Non.*" He shook his head. "Since you're not afraid of work, and since you feel a loyalty to your brothers, you'll simply have to do both. I'll set you up in Bristol as the head of my European division of PRM Shipping. And you can still work with your brothers on your gaming establishment. If the time comes that the brothers Hadley are wildly successful, I'll accept your resignation from PRM. But until then, you'll do both."

He wasn't really asking, was he? And honestly, his reception could have been much worse. Death, dismemberment, 'gator bait. "I wouldn't feel right displacing someone from their job."

The Frenchman shook his head as though Gray was a dolt. "I am extending my shipping empire by opening an office in England. You're not displacing anyone."

He was creating a position and an entire office so he could make sure Livi was well cared for. All things considered, it was generous of her father. And Gray did want the best for Livi, as well. How was this situation any different than men marrying for large dowries or young lordlings living off their fathers' allowances? But it was different. Different because Gray would make the England office of PRM more successful than his father-in-law could possibly imagine. And he'd do it with Livi by his side.

After a moment, Gray nodded in agreement. "In that case, thank you, sir. I know very little about shipping, but I'm certain I can learn."

Apparently satisfied with the outcome, Philippe Mayeux grinned like a schoolboy who'd gotten his way. "Livi can teach you all you need to know. She sat here at my knee when she should have been engaging dancing instructors or learning the art of polite conversation."

If not, she wouldn't have been the Livi he loved with all his heart. Gray shook his head. "I wouldn't want her any other way."

The twinkle reappeared in his father-in-law's eyes. "I suppose I didn't blunder too badly by sending her to England then, did I?"

"I am eternally grateful that you did."

Philippe Mayeux scratched his head. "Are you wearing Etienne's clothes?"

Gray shrugged. "That's a bit of a long story, sir."

"Well, then you can tell it to me on the way home. If I know Livi, she'll wear a hole in my rug if I don't take you there soon."

❧

Livi paced her father's drawing room. What was taking them so long? She lifted a nail to her mouth to chew the tip.

"Will you stop?" Armand complained as he popped a fresh beignet into his mouth. "You're making me seasick and I'm trying to eat."

"We're not on a ship," she grumbled.

"No, but my cabin on the ship didn't spin around as much as you're making this room spin. Sit down, will you?"

Livi frowned, but she did sit on the settee beside

her brother. "You don't think Papa will really kill him, do you?"

Armand shoved another beignet into his mouth. Unable to speak legibly, he shrugged.

"Maybe I should have told Papa I'm expecting. He wouldn't kill the father to his grandchild, would he?"

Armand choked on his snack. Eyes watering, he coughed into his fist until he cleared his throat. "You're expecting?"

Livi didn't think so. She supposed it was possible, but she'd just suffered through her courses last week. "No, but should I have said so?"

With an expression of relief, Armand shook his head. "I don't think it's ever wise to lie to Father."

Just that moment, the large front door slammed shut. Livi bolted back to her feet.

"It's them, Liv. Sit down and whatever you do, don't lie."

"Lie?" her father bellowed as he crossed the threshold into the drawing room, a smiling Gray behind him in one piece. "Who's lying?"

"Lying in wait," Livi said before her brother could speak. "I asked Armand if he would lie in wait for you at the offices, just to make sure Gray was all right."

Her father narrowed his dark blue eyes on her. "Did you know when you lie, there's a crinkle right above your nose, Liviana?"

Armand looked vindicated. "Warned you."

"Oh, never mind all that." Livi crossed the room and slid her hand into Gray's. "I take it all went well?"

Papa nodded. "Chose a man who loved you. Your mother would have been proud." Then he leaned forward and kissed her brow. "Don't think, *mon chaton*, that just because you've married some Englishman you can escape me. You'll visit me once a year. Or I'll visit you."

He'd accepted Gray. Livi's heart nearly burst from her chest. "Of course."

"And," Papa said, his voice full of emotion, "I'll expect timely reports about how PRM is doing in England."

"PRM?" Her father didn't have any offices in England.

Papa smiled and she thought she saw a tear in his eye. "I'll let your husband explain everything to you." Then he stood his tallest. "Armand, a word with you in my study, if you don't mind."

A moment later, Livi and Gray found themselves alone in the drawing room. He pulled her into his embrace and held her tight. "That wasn't nearly as bad as I expected."

Livi grinned against his chest. "I told you he'd love you."

Gray shook his head. "No. He loves you and just wants your happiness."

"Then he has nothing to ever worry about."

REGENCY ENGLAND HAS GONE TO THE WOLVES!

The Wolf Who Loved Me

Castle Hythe, Kent
Four months later…

MADDIE HAD ALWAYS SUSPECTED THAT MEN WERE THE most perfidious of creatures. Now she was certain of the fact. It didn't seem to matter whether the man in question was one's own derelict brother, a detestable fortune hunter, a disreputable gambler, or even the King of England. Not one bit. Men *were* perfidious creatures. All of them. Well, at least all of them that Maddie knew.

She leaned across the expanse of her bed and squeezed her dear friend Lady Sophia Cole's hand. Poor Sophie was the last person Maddie would have ever imagined as a victim of men's perfidious natures. Yet it had happened nevertheless, and there wasn't a blasted thing either of them could do about it. Perfidious men, after all, ruled the world. However, one particularly powerful lady might be up to the challenge of that ambitious endeavor, if anyone was.

"I'm certain we'll think of something, Soph," she said soothingly.

Sophie shook her head as though she knew Maddie had no real hope of solving her dilemma. "Something? Shall we dress as highwaymen and rob Lord Radbourne with pistols as he returns to Kent from that farce of a trial?"

Well, that wouldn't be the *first* plan to pop into Maddie's mind on how to reclaim Sophie's pilfered fortune. Still, the idea made her smile. "And don trousers? Grandmamma would be scandalized."

Despite her new status as an impoverished gentlewoman, Sophie giggled. "Heaven forbid we scandalize the Duchess of Hythe."

Maddie rolled her eyes. Sophie had never been a particular favorite of Maddie's grandmother, but if ever there was a time to try and appease the duchess it was now. "Do *try* to stay on Grandmamma's good side."

"Does she have one?"

"Indeed she does," Maddie declared. "And Lady Eynsford happens to live on it. So if we play our cards right—"

"What a terrible thing to say." Sophie groaned and flopped backward across Maddie's feather mattress and stared at the canopy above them.

Considering that Sophie's recently deceased father had played his cards *wrong*, Maddie could see her friend's point. "Poor turn of phrase on my part. I apologize. But you're not listening, Soph. Lady Eynsford is the key to getting your fortune returned. Or as much of it as possible, whatever that blackguard hasn't spent."

Sophie pushed up on her elbows, her grey eyes intent enough to make Maddie wince inwardly. "I'm listening now."

Maddie took a deep breath, and words just poured from her mouth. "I don't know why, but Lord Radbourne and those brutish brothers of his follow Lord Eynsford around like a pack of puppy dogs."

"Puppy dogs?"

"Like he's their master or something. It is very strange. But what is more important is that I've never seen a man so besotted with his wife as Lord Eynsford is."

"You're right. That is strange."

"Do be serious." Maddie folded her arms across her chest. "If we are able to whisper the circumstances of your predicament to the marchioness, she could have her husband order Radbourne to return his ill-gotten gains."

Sophie dropped back onto the bed and laughed which, considering the fact that Maddie had just suggested the best plan for restoring her friend's place in society, was the tiniest bit irritating.

THE TAMING OF THE WOLF

Westfield Hall, Hampshire
January 1817

CAITRIN MACLEOD VOWED NEVER TO STEP FOOT IN England again—or at the very least, to keep her distance from Lycans in the future.

It was safer for everyone that way.

The visions had started days ago, wild visions where she saw wolves and their mates together under the light of the moon. There were several of them, all part of a family of Lycans. Most days, they were simply the Westfield family. But one night each month, the male members walked on four feet instead of two under the light of the full moon.

Those visions weren't troublesome; she was quite used to them. But lingering around the edges of her visions was a wild wolf, an outsider. A danger.

She'd begun to see visions of a golden wolf, the wild one, earlier that very day. But she couldn't tell the others what she'd seen, or she'd risk affecting the future. And she didn't want to be the one.

Caitrin closed her eyes tightly and tried to will the vision of the Westfield wolves into her mind. She sighed with contentment when she realized all was well. None of them would return until the sun rose in the sky. The estate was empty except for her and any servant who happened to be still awake. No one would know if she donned her silk wrapper to sneak downstairs and retrieve her book while everyone was away. Maybe then she could try to get a few hours of sleep.

She crossed to the chamber door and opened it quietly. On bare feet, she padded along the corridor and down the main staircase.

Cait turned the corner into the darkened study and stopped short. Standing behind the duke's desk was a tall man, one she'd yet to meet. Most of him was hidden in shadow, but his face was lit by the moonlight that filtered through the drapes. He was a blond Adonis, tall and lean. A vague memory of him, maybe from one of her visions, created unease within her.

"I'm sorry. I dinna ken anyone was up at this hour." She turned to leave.

"Don't go," he said. Then he closed his eyes tightly and took a deep breath. "You needed something in Blackmoor's study?"

"Aye, I left a book in here yesterday when I came ta find Her Grace."

"Having trouble sleeping?" he asked, his tone amazingly familiar. As though he'd known her for a lifetime.

"Aye. At times, I canna get thoughts out of my head." Why had she told him that? He probably didn't care to hear how her visions played in her mind at all hours of the day and night, preventing her rest.

He walked around the desk and perched a hip on it. His hips were narrow, his shoulders broad. *Stop ogling the man's body, Cait.* His eyes narrowed at her, as though he knew she had a secret. She closed her eyes and tried to get a vision of him, something to tell her who he was. But her mind was blank, which was more than disconcerting. *Her mind was blank?* That had never happened before.

"I canna tell yer future," she muttered under her breath.

"Pardon?" He raised an eyebrow at her.

"Ah, there's my book," she said, smiling at him, hoping he'd believe she hadn't a care in the world.

Before she could turn around, he reached out and grabbed her by the waist. She couldn't even utter a gasp as he drew her body flush against his.

"What are ye—" she began, but he covered her mouth with his, his lips hard and urgent.

She shouldn't let a man she'd never met before take such liberties. But he smelled so good. Felt so good. Tasted so good.

Her tongue rose to meet his as a whimper of pleasure left her throat. Her heart beat wildly as he tilted his head and deepened the kiss.

Cait had been kissed before, but never like this. Never so thoroughly that she couldn't think straight. Never so expertly that her legs threatened to buckle. Never with enough passion that she could drown in it.

FROM

THE WOLF NEXT DOOR

Langley Downs, Hampshire
December 1816

PRISCA HAWTHORNE WAS FAIRLY CERTAIN BEDLAM WAS in her future. Still, she couldn't help herself. She had to leave, to see if her wolf had returned. It was a foolish thing to do, Prisca well knew. How many nights had she gone in search of him, only to return home tired and disappointed? Still, something in her soul told her she'd be successful tonight. And she never questioned that feeling; it had always been correct in the past.

She slipped into her long, wool coat as she padded across the cold marble floor. After all, it would be simply foolish to traipse around her property in the middle of night in only her flimsy nightrail. More foolish than searching for an elusive wolf.

Prisca pushed open the double glass doors that led to the veranda. The frosty winter wind swirled around her, lifting the edge of her coat and making her shiver. This was surely madness.

She quietly closed the doors behind her and rushed across the veranda, down the stone steps, and out toward her garden. The moon was full tonight, lighting her way, which made her smile. He only came to her when the moon was full. She sped up her pace.

The garden was not in bloom this time of year, but the hedgerows and topiaries still kept their form. Prisca pressed forward down the path, first around one hedge and then around another.

She spotted him and stopped in her tracks.

He *had* come.

Standing in a shaft of moonlight, the wolf seemed to be waiting for her. Prisca's heart pounded out a familiar beat, and anticipation coursed through her veins. He was still the most magnificent creature she'd ever seen, with his regal black coat, icy blue eyes, and proud stature.

If anyone else had seen her approach the dangerous creature, her conveyance to Bedlam would have been summoned immediately. But she knew from their past encounters that he was, if not tame, of no risk to her.

She was the only one who'd ever seen the wolf. At times, she doubted he was real. In fact, it seemed like a lifetime since she'd seem him last.

Prisca smiled at the beast and stepped forward. "There you are. I didn't know if I'd see you again."

She sat on a stone bench and patted the space beside her.

The wolf appeared to heave a sigh, though that seemed an odd thing for him to do. Then he slowly walked toward her. He stopped before her feet, peered up at her with his cool blue eyes, and rested his head in her lap.

Prisca stroked his coarse black fur and closed her eyes, reveling in the feel of him. There was something so familiar, so comforting in the animal. Which was why she could never tell anyone about him; they'd all think she had lost her mind.

The wolf pressed closer to her, and Prisca laughed. "I missed you, too. You should visit me more often. You could even stay here," she suggested. Wouldn't all of Hampshire faint if they discovered she kept a wolf for a pet? "I'd take good care of you."

The wolf closed his eyes, and Prisca scratched behind his ears. She told him all about her brothers and the goings-on around their village, just like she always had whenever he visited her. All the while, the wolf enjoyed her ministrations and seemed content to stay there forever.

Suddenly, he lifted his head with a jolt, looked her straight in the eyes, and ran out of the garden and into a copse of trees at the edge of the property as though he'd been summoned by some invisible force. It happened so fast that Prisca couldn't even call out for him to wait.

She sighed in defeat, wondering how long it would be until she saw him again.

TALL,
DARK AND
WOLFISH

Arthur's Seat, Edinburgh
July 1816

IF ELSPETH CAMPBELL REVEALED HOW MUCH SHE wanted to leave the cold, damp cave, her coven sisters would surely think she was mad. Her plaid slipped from her shoulders, and she fought the shiver that threatened, trying to close her eyes and mind to the chilly Scottish air. She couldn't pull the plaid back into place until the ceremony was over.

They were meeting earlier than scheduled, as Caitrin foresaw trouble on the horizon for the *Còig*, though she hadn't revealed her fears to them yet. Truthfully, Elspeth didn't think Caitrin was certain what threatened them. They all knew the visions were clearest for their seer when the five of them were together.

To her right, Rhiannon tightened her grasp on Elspeth's hand while Sorcha and Blaire closed the space between them, which tightened the ring of four around Caitrin. In the middle of their circle, the seer's eyes were closed, her hands stretched toward the heavens.

Caitrin hummed an ancient melody, passed from one generation of *Còig* witches to the next. Then she stopped and all was quiet in the cave—so quiet that Elspeth could only hear the drumming of her own heart and Sorcha's rapid breathing to her left.

"I see a handsome man," Caitrin began softly. Her lilting voice echoed off the dark cavern walls.

"I'd like ta see one of those," Sorcha giggled.

The murderous look Rhiannon shot the youngest witch prevented any further levity from entering their circle.

"He bears the mark of the beast," Caitrin continued as though she'd never been interrupted.

Chills shot down Elspeth's spine, which had nothing to do with the loss of her plaid or the cool air in the cave. *The mark of the beast.* She'd heard those words her entire life.

"He will disrupt us. He will try ta take Elspeth from our circle."

Suddenly Elspeth had three sets of eyes on her. It would have been four, but Caitrin's were still closed as the vision played out in her mind.

"The beast canna be allowed ta break our coven. Disaster will fall if he succeeds." Caitrin's haunting blue eyes opened and she focused them on Elspeth.

Sucking in a surprised breath, Elspeth tried to snatch her hands back from Rhiannon and Sorcha, but their hold tightened. Her heart pounded faster and she felt certain she would faint.

Caitrin stepped forward and touched her fingers to Elspeth's brow. "Do ye ken the man I speak of, El?"

A nervous laugh escaped Elspeth's throat and she